Thin White Lines

John P. Sutton

TRAFFORD

Canada • UK • Ireland • USA • Spain

© Copyright 2004 John P. Sutton.
All rights reserved. No part of this publication may be reproduced, stored in a retrieval system, or transmitted, in any form or by any means, electronic, mechanical, photocopying, recording, or otherwise, without the written prior permission of the author.

Cover design by Charles Richardson

Note for Librarians: a cataloguing record for this book that includes Dewey Decimal Classification and US Library of Congress numbers is available from the Library and Archives of Canada. The complete cataloguing record can be obtained from their online database at:
www.collectionscanada.ca/amicus/index-e.html
ISBN 1-4120-2540-0
Printed in Victoria, BC, Canada

TRAFFORD

Offices in Canada, USA, Ireland, UK and Spain

This book was published *on-demand* in cooperation with Trafford Publishing. On-demand publishing is a unique process and service of making a book available for retail sale to the public taking advantage of on-demand manufacturing and Internet marketing. On-demand publishing includes promotions, retail sales, manufacturing, order fulfilment, accounting and collecting royalties on behalf of the author.

Book sales for North America and international:
Trafford Publishing, 6E–2333 Government St.,
Victoria, BC v8t 4p4 CANADA
phone 250 383 6864 (toll-free 1 888 232 4444)
fax 250 383 6804; email to orders@trafford.com

Book sales in Europe:
Trafford Publishing (UK) Ltd., Enterprise House, Wistaston Road Business Centre, Wistaston Road, Crewe, Cheshire cw2 7rp UNITED KINGDOM
phone 01270 251 396 (local rate 0845 230 9601)
facsimile 01270 254 983; orders.uk@trafford.com

Order online at:
www.trafford.com/robots/04-0368.html

10 9 8 7 6 5 4 3 2

DEDICATION

To my mother Arbunyan who is in heaven;
my daughters Ila, Tinessa and Heather;
my grandchildren Tre, Caila and Caleb;
and Cheryl Newton.

FORWARD

The events in this book occurred as depicted based on my review of notes, daily reports, weekly reports, investigative reports and recollection. Most of the names have been changed to ensure the privacy of those involved, especially those criminals who have been rehabilitated and have established a new life. There is no intent to defame, slander, smear or embarrass any person living or dead.

Many drug investigations involve an undercover agent interacting with drug traffickers and purchasing drugs from them for subsequent prosecution. In this subculture, there is a communication vernacular that is widely utilized in drug trafficking deals. In order to work safely and proficiently in drug investigations, an undercover agent must be articulate in this vernacular and develop a persona that depicts a drug trafficker that is adaptable to different drug trafficking communities; must talk the talk and walk the walk. Drug undercover investigation is analogous to an aerialist performing without a safety net where a slip often results in injury or death.

The Detroit airport parking lot incident in chapter 8 is as surreal today as then. The stench often surfaces and lingers for long periods. Sharing them offers some relief.

Profanity, drug vernacular and idiomatic expressions are utilized to provide a vivid description of the events and the characters involved.

A special tribute is given to the following agents mentioned in this book who have fallen asleep in the arms of Jesus: Special agents George L. Heard, Enrique "Kiki" Camarena (killed by drug traffickers in Mexico), Sim Willis, Jack Enoch, Sam Ozment, Harry Sumega, Robert Moffett. A Special tribute is further given to Special Agent Kenneth Adams (from our days in Detroit-was killed by drug traffickers while working undercover).

A special tribute is also given to those agents, officers and cooperating individuals not mentioned who gave the maximum they could in the fight against drug trafficking.

CHAPTER 1

I GRADUATED from California State University at Los Angeles, but never dreamed or imagined that my life would ever be or end up like this. I guess a good starting point would be my dealings with RAUL.

I telephoned Raul and ordered 12 "boys" and 8 "girls" (12 ounces of heroin and 8 ounces of cocaine). Raul asked if Billy would be riding shotgun (coming with me). Billy had initially introduced me as Beenum to Raul for our first drug deal. That time I also met Raul's henchman "Florencio." I told Raul that I would be riding solo (coming alone); that I could not find Billy, that Billy was just another expense and always wanted a "pinch" from the packages. Raul agreed to meet with me for the deal at a prearranged location in an alley in the Alisio village area of East Los Angeles.

About two hours later, I drove over to the alley, parked on the surface street, got out of the car, lit a Kool Filter King cigarette and walked gingerly eastbound in the alleyway. As in-

Thin White Lines

structed, I crossed over two crossing streets and continued walking slowly east in the alley. A few minutes later, Raul and his henchman, Florencio, entered the alleyway a block and a half ahead. They walked rapidly toward me. Florencio, wearing a dark dress coat and khaki pants, was carrying a small shopping bag in his left hand. Every few steps he readjusted his open coat displaying for me to see the two .45 caliber automatic pistols he was carrying; one under each armpit. During my first meeting with Florencio in the little broken English that he spoke, he related that he was "un assasinado," a word I took to mean a killer.

He tried to intimidate me in every way he could, bluffing and playing the role of a bad henchman that wanted to be feared. If it were not for the dope deal, I would have acted a fool with him. Certainly I would not let him talk to me in a bullying manner. I was a few inches taller, in better physical condition and I did not have an upper bicuspid tooth missing like he did. I did not like him trying to talk to me in a threatening manner and patting me down for weapons like he was some kind of Tijuana policeman. On that occasion Florencio showed me one of his .45's as he pointed the other at my stomach. They were the big 1911 models, each emblazoned with three different colored gold grips and two clear carat size stones on the outer side of the grip that Florencio called "diamantes." I had never feared another man before, but there was something about Florencio that made me more aware of his presence. He deserved close watching.

While walking toward me, Raul raised his hand and gestured for me to stay where I was. I walked over to the right side of the alley stopped and waited. After exchanging pleasantries, Florencio again displayed his two .45 pistols and took a position to my left side as I faced Raul. At one point, Florencio walked toward my rear. I immediately backed up to the fence and put Raul to my right and Florencio to my left. For some reason, I could not keep my eyes off Florencio as he paced menacingly to my left, sporadically to my front and on one occasion between

Raul and me. When Florencio spoke something in Spanish, Raul then advised that Florencio wanted to search me. I told Raul that I had the money that we should just do the exchange and get the deal over. As an alternate, Raul suggested that I give him the money; he would count it then give me the drugs. I disagreed and insisted on a fair exchange. I then recommended that Raul give me the drugs, let me inspect it and that I would pay him.

"There is no need to search me Raul, I am not packing. I'm in your territory and I am alone." I said.

Raul replied, "Yeah, but I have only met you one time and now you are doubling up on your order and you come down here without my man Billy Ese, that's how the police do business amigo. I've been down once amigo and I ain't going back again."

At that time Raul raised the hem of his polo shirt revealing that he was also carrying a three-colored golden grip .45 in his waistband. He was a mobile arsenal. As Florencio moved toward me, I backed up to the wall relating that I was concerned that they were the police for they were the only ones with guns. I then shifted the focus on the deal to the next week drug deal relating that I had a partner in with me and if this deal went without complications, my partner would want a kilo and a half of boy (heroin) and a kilo of girl (cocaine) and that I would want at least a pound of each if the prices were good and the dope was good. Raul related that he did not want to meet anybody and remained focused on the pending deal, relating that he would only deliver large quantities of cocaine and heroin on the other side of the border somewhere in Tijuana. According to Raul, I had to be searched this time and if all went well all other deals would go smoother and we would be regular businessmen. Raul added that after doing business for about three or four months and after he got to know where I lived, that he would drop drugs off to me on consignment.

Thin White Lines

Raul said "Come on Beenum, let Flo (Florencio) search you. He got the drugs, we can do the deal and be on our way."

"Okay, go ahead if you must, I got a Roscoe, I'll give it to you."

As I reached into my right waistband, Florencio stuck the muzzle of one of his .45's in my ear and pulled the hammer back and screamed, what I believed to be, profanity in Spanish at me. I reached into my waistband and pulled out a .32 caliber Iver Johnson pistol, broke it down in front, unloaded it and handed it to Florencio. Florencio unwillingly removed the .45 from my ear and held it in the left hand with the shopping bag. He examined the pistol and spoke something in Spanish that caused Raul to chuckle. Raul related that Florencio thought I was carrying a sissy gun "un pistola de cabrone."

Raul related that Florencio still wanted to search me. I consented. Florencio patted me down around the armpits, waist, lower back, upper leg, lower leg and ankle and stated "el is limpio." He must have thought I was overly endowed, for he by-passed the bulging five shot aluminum weight .38 Colt Cobra holstered between my left leg and left testicle and a small 6.25 caliber 8 shot automatic pistol holstered on the opposite side.

The haggling continued back and forth about the deal and Florencio became more menacing. At one point I was riled to the point that I started to physically attack Florencio to let him know that he was not as bad and mean as he was trying to portray himself to be. Florencio withdrew one of the .45s and pushed me with it hard in the solar plexus. It must have been my shortness of breath from the blow that stopped me from attacking him.

At that point I just wanted to do the dope deal, get it over with and go on my way. Raul stated. "Beenum why don't you just pay me? Do you have the money?"

I assured him that I had the money and flashed $24,000 that

I had secreted in two brown paper bags in the small of my back that Florencio had failed to find. When I removed the two bags, Raul looked at Florencio briefly with a disgusting stare. Florencio became more menacing as though he wanted to jab me again with the pistol. I had prepared myself to knock Florencio out and break his arms.

Florencio again moved toward me in a threatening and menacing manner but was restrained by Raul. Raul remarked, "Hey, cool it, we are here to do business, not fight."

Florencio relaxed and moved back staring menacingly. Little did he know, that despite carrying three guns, he had just escaped an "ass whipping," perhaps one that would have been more severe than he had ever experienced. I could not help thinking that I would have to one day get physical with Florencio for what he had done to me. I was in deep thought when Raul stated, "Hey Beenum, let's do the deal. Your package costs $20,000 — 12 for the boys and 8 for the girls. Just pay me now. Flo will give you the package and we can be on our way. Both packages are better than the ones you got from me the other day," he assured.

I agreed, fast counted $19,800 all in 100s, and handed it to Raul as $20,000. Raul told Flo to give me the package. Instead of complying, Florencio extended the package outward to me. When I reached for it, he snatched it back quickly referring to me as "cabrone."

Raul shouted, "Cut the bullshit Flo. Give him the package."

Florencio again extended the package to me and as I reached for it he quickly snatched it back.

Raul shouted, "Come on Flo cut the shit."

Florencio relented and handed me the package and immediately walked away mumbling in Spanish and broken English. There was no doubt that he was referring to me as a motherf____r.

Raul, apparently sensing that I was very angry, told me to join him for a Mexican snack. I angrily walked back to my car and drove up to the main street and started following Raul in his red Corvette. I was relaxed that Raul was alone; that the bad Florencio had gone his way. While following Raul, I remembered that I had not inspected the dope. I opened the bag and noted that it contained three, 3" long rubber contraceptives that contained a brown rocky, dirty-like substance, secured together with masking tape. There were two 4" long rubber contraceptives, each containing a white powdery substance. As I followed Raul eastbound on Olympic near Soto, I remembered that there was something odd, something missing. I guess weighed the 3" contraceptives in my right hand and they appeared to be approximately 12 ounces, the two 4" contraceptives appeared to weigh 10 ounces. It was then I realized that there was no acid like smell coming from the heroin package. I continued to follow Raul on Olympic Boulevard and at the first red light we caught, I took my finger nail and bust one of the contraceptives and noted the brown dirt-like substance was unlikely heroin. There was no acid smell and it looked more like dirt as I examined it closer. I started to panic, reached into the glove compartment and got a marquis reagent. I cracked the vial, placed a pinch of the substance into the reagent, shook it and nothing happened.

While gazing at the vial, a horn honked behind me. I looked up the light had changed to green. Raul's red Corvette was nowhere in sight. I pulled over to the curb, parked and removed a cobalt thiocyanate reagent from the glove box and mixed a portion of the white powdery substance with the solution in the glassine envelope and shook it. Nothing happened. I then drove nervously eastbound on Olympic for about a mile until I saw Raul's Corvette parked at the curb. As I pulled up parallel, Raul shouted, "What the hell happened to you back there, you must have dozed off at the light, you are no f_____g junkie are you?"

"No man, I'll tell you about it later."

I followed Raul to a little corner Mexican (cafe) restaurant, where we parked on the lot rear of the restaurant. I immediately exited the car and told Raul that I had been "burned." Raul assured me that I had not been burned, that as long as I was with the "dope man," I had not been burned.

I followed Raul over to the outside counter of the cafe where we each ordered a beef burrito. I began to show concern about the dope when Raul removed his sunglasses, stared at me and rubbed his right hand from front to back of his head three times and put his sunglasses back on.

About a minute later a neatly dressed Mexican male walked up to the stool next to me and ordered a cup of coffee, he drank part of it and quickly walked away. As he was walking away, I noticed that he had left a brown shopping bag on the stool next to me. I called out, "Hey mister, you left something." He did not respond and continued walking away. I grabbed the bag and started to walk toward the man.

Raul gabbed my arm and asked "Hey Ese don't you want your dope?"

"Yeah, when can I get it?" Raul laughed and stated, you got it in your hands now Ese, you have it in your hands."

I opened the bag and noted it contained five rubber contraceptives similar to the ones in the other bag. Raul related, "You will find the heroin and cocaine a little stronger," that he had not cut it but had it delivered to me just like he had obtained it. I felt relaxed, examined the heroin, noting the acid like smell. I pinched a hole in one of the cocaine packages, took a pinch between my fingers and felt them immediately go numb. I secured the dope in the trunk of my car and joined Raul back at the counter. I asked Raul, if he had counted his money. He advised that he had not. That it appeared to be twenty thousand. I removed my money stash from the small of my back, removed four 50s and handed it to Raul. I then told Raul that I had purposely shorted him $200. He took the $200, patted me on the shoulder, chuckled and stated, "I like you Ese. I like you a lot. You and I are going to be business partners just like the May Company and the Broadway."

"Yeah, I look forward to doing business with you again. But I don't want to have to jump through hoops with Florencio. That guy is crazier than you realize he is," I remarked.

"You know Beenum, I never did business with a brother before, you know brothers draw a lot of heat. The police just seem to enjoy stopping you guys. I wanted you to ride with me but you know, when the police see a brother and a Chicano riding together, they figure that they are up to no good, so they stop and search them. Many times they bust them on a humbug."

After relaxing more, I told Raul that I was very angry with Florencio and that I did not like to be treated that way.

Raul stated, "Beenum, Ese, let me explain something to you. Firstly, I played you off with the fake dope package for insurance see! I wanted to see if the jump out boys would jump out to bust me. Flo, as crazy as he is, he seems to think that you are the police or something like that. It is like driving a car; you have to have insurance. In case you happened to be the police or happened to be working for the police, you know like snitching for the police. I've been down twice. I did CYA (California Youth Authority) time and a ten-year federal stretch at Lompoc and McNeil Island. I am not going back to jail, never again. I will flee to Mexico before I go back to jail Ese. Jail is no country club or Barrio Ese, it is a most motherf___r. Have you ever been to jail'?"

"No, not for more than 45 days," I answered.

"All jails are full of people like you and me Beenum, humps like us who try to make a decent living but can't for whatever reasons. If I could make this kind of money on the legit side, I wouldn't sell dope, neither would you huh?"

According to Raul, he had now taken a liking to me for even when I was missing my dope, that I had shown concern for a total stranger that I thought was leaving something behind. Raul related that he would have checked the bag out. If it was full of money or something of value, he would have kept it; that without determining what was in the bag I was letting a stranger know that he was leaving something behind. According to Raul, that showed "character, not stupidity."

Raul went on a big diatribe about how he had gotten into the dope business, how much money he had made, how many women he has, excluding his wife and two ex-wives. Raul advised me that he could sense that I had not been in the dope business very long and that I was not the police or working for the police. I told Raul that because of Florencio, I was close to walking out on the deal. I related that I was about an inch away from beating Florencio up for the way he was treating me. Raul stated that I could make more money working for him if I could beat Floremcio. Florencio was described as a hired killer, a henchman, a very necessary part of the dope business because of the number of enemies on the street. Raul described his enemies as followers, Los Angeles Sheriffs Department, the international Los Angeles Police Department, the California Bureau of Narcotic Enforcement, the Federal Bureau of Investigation, the Federal Bureau of Narcotics, the U.S. Customs Service, the Internal Revenue, dope addicts, dope dealers, snitches and good citizens who want to rid neighborhoods of dope dealers.

I was very impressed for I never fathomed a dope dealer could have so many enemies. Raul continued relating that he could deal effectively with the foregoing enemies but there was one type of enemy out there that wreaks havoc on all illegal business "the Jackers."

According to Raul the "Jackers" are groups of bandits who hijack those engaged in illegal activity by robbing them of money, drugs, contraband and the illegal things. The Jackers had ventured into robbing after-hours clubs, illegal gambling houses, dope dealers, dope houses, stash pads, number runners, number banks, bookies and off-track betting houses, prostitutes and trick pads, chop shops, and all illegal businesses. They were causing mass confusion because none of the victims could afford to call the police.

Raul related an incident where "the Jackers" had robbed a dope dealer, tied the dealer and his wife up and raped their 15-year old daughter. Out of anger, the dealer reported the rape, drug and money theft to the police; three weeks later the dealer caught a federal case.

After talking with Raul for several hours, he agreed to sell me kilogram quantities of heroin and cocaine at a later date. Raul related that because of "the Jackers" henchmen like Florencio were being gainfully employed, that Florencio or another henchman would always be around when he did business. I made arrangements to meet with Raul two weeks later for the multiple kilogram heroin/cocaine transaction.

Two weeks later, I telephoned Raul and ordered three kilograms of heroin and two kilograms of cocaine. Raul agreed to sell me the five kilograms for a discount price of $100,000 south of the border, in Tijuana, Baja, California, Mexico. Prior to the delivery Raul wanted to meet, see the money a day before the deal; initially he wanted me to pay him up front and he would deliver the drugs to me on the U.S. side of the border, somewhere in the Logan Heights area of San Diego or in a drop car somewhere in San Ysidro, California. I disagreed with those arrangements and agreed to meet with Raul at 2:00 p.m. on the Sears parking lot at Olympic and Soto that day. I could not hesitate to ask Raul, "Will Florencio be with you?"

"Yeah Beenum, always. You don't have a problem with that do you?"

"Naw Raul, I don't. I really don't want to have to go through all of that physical thing with him again. That's kind of crazy you...."

"No Beenum, I'll hold him at bay, just come alone with plenty of the green, all 100s, maybe a few 50s."

"Okay. Please hold Florencio down, for I was very close to letting him know that he cannot punch and treat me like I am some kid, some little boy, I am a man just like he is and I really don't appreciate that."

"Beenum, It'll be alright, you'll see, I'll have him under control, after I see you got the money and mean business. I'll go down right away to put things together for your arrival, you come alone okay!"

"Okay, I'll see you at 2:00"

I drove over to the Sears parking lot and as I turned south off of Olympic blvd onto Soto Street, I saw Florencio get out of a blue Chevrolet occupied by three male Mexicans, and walk south on Soto toward the parking lot. He was wearing khaki pants and a Pendleton shirt, with bulges on both sides. I drove passed Florencio and checked him out in the rear view mirror. As soon as I glanced at him, he opened his shirt sporadically displaying his armor. I pulled over to southwest end of the parking lot next to Raul's red Corvette. Raul got out of his car and joined me in mine.

"Hey Ese, I am beginning to like you, I like a man who has a sense of time. Some guys make you wait for them for 20 or 30 minutes, I don't like to wait."

"I don't either Raul. I like to go ahead and do the business and leave. I don't like hanging around. I saw your boy Florencio when I pulled in."

"Yeah, there he is now," Raul related.

Florencio walked over to the driver's side of my car and again displayed his armor.

"How you doing Flo?" I asked and immediately Florencio pulled out a .45 pistol, stuck the muzzle in my ear and mumbled something in Spanish. I was not scared until he pulled back the hammer, mumbled something in Spanish.

Raul, screamed at him in Spanish twice before he placed the pistol back into his waistband.

"Raul, you see how nervous I am? That's why I don't like being around this motherf___r," I stated.

"Beenum, only I can call Florencio Flo, when anybody else calls him Flo he thinks they are referring to him as a Bitch. You know man, it is a macho thing."

"I didn't know. That's was the first time I called him that. He put a gun in my ear before remember. He jabbed me a few times. I don't know how much of this shit I can take from this guy," I advised.

"Beenum, relax. It's going to be okay." Raul said something to Florencio two cars ahead and stared back at me in a menacing manner.

"You got the money?" Raul asked.

"Yeah, it's in the trunk. If I get out to get it, Florencio won't act a fool will he?" I asked.

"No, I'll talk to him." Raul exited the car, and joined Florencio for a few minutes and came back advising that everything would be okay. I went to the trunk removed my leather attaché case and got in the back seat of my car, opened the attaché case and removed a bundle of $100s and handed it to Raul to count.

Raul counted the bundle and asked, "How many do you have?"

"You count them. There are 10 bundles, ten thousand to the bundle, you can count every one of them if you want to" I responded.

"No, I know the money is there Beenum. Why don't you give me the money and let me deliver the goods to you in San Diego, National City or San Ysidro. That way you won't have to cross the border, and you will be getting across the border prices and good quality material, material uncut, straight from the factory" he assured.

"No, I can't let this kind of money go without having my hands on the materials." I stated

"Why not?"

"Would you?"

"Yeah I would. See Beenum in this business, there has to be a lot of trust. I trust you but Flo doesn't. He still thinks you are the man. I know better because the man does not spend the kind of money you spend and let it ride. That deal with the gun and the dummy package was a test. You passed that one. Flo has another test for you. Wait here a few minutes."

When Raul got out of the car, I secured the $100,000 in the trunk underneath the spare tire.

Raul exited the car, met with Florencio and joined me back in the car. After a few moments I saw Florencio dart in between the cars. Then I heard sounds like gunshots — POW, POW, POW, POW, POW, and POW. Flo ducked down between the cars and faced me with both hands on the pistols in his waistband. I saw three male Mexicans exit Florencio's car and walk separately in the parking lot and form a semicircle facing in our direction. I heard a burst of three pow, pow, pow sounds and saw a fourth male Mexican run through the parking lot carrying a brown paper bag, a bag similar to the one containing the dope from Raul two weeks prior. The fourth male Mexican entered a gray low rider type Chevrolet, peeled rubber and sped southbound on Soto. The first thought that came to mind was that I was about to be robbed.

"Man, what in the hell is all of this?" I asked.

"It is part of the test Beenum, part of the test. We will just wait five minutes and I will see if you passed." We waited, not knowing what to expect, I spoke calmly disguising how nervous I had become. I took ten deep breaths – inhaled deeply ten times, held it momentarily and exhaled convincing myself that all was okay. I asked Raul if he was satisfied and assured him that I was ready to do business. He advised that he was ready then asked me for a $100 bill. Raul tore the $100 dollar bill in half, gave me half and told me to meet him the following day at the "El Gato Verde Bar" on 5th and Constitution Avenue in Tijuana, Mexico between 3:00 p.m. and 4:00 p.m. He insisted that I come alone.

"ESE, I don't want to meet nobody, comprende? I mean nobody but you, not even Billy. This deal is between you and me and nobody else," he strongly advised.

"I'll be alone, I don't want to be involved in anything physical with Florencio," I warned.

"Don't worry about Flo, he's on his job. Sometimes he over does his job but I pay him good wages ESE, good wages. He wants to earn his keep, you know man, and he likes to impress me."

"Raul, there is no need for this guy to toy with me, tease me, taunt me and piss me off like he does. One day, I will let him know that he is not the only bad motherf___r around here," I warned.

Raul smiled, looked around the parking lot and advised that the coast was clear. We exchanged greetings and he and Florencio departed the area.

I drove slowly out of the parking lot northbound on Soto toward Olympic. I ran the amber/red light at Olympic, checking the rearview mirror to see if I was being followed. I sped two blocks north of Olympic, made an immediate u-turn and parked behind a broken down truck on the west side of Soto facing south. I waited a few minutes then drove southbound on Soto three blocks and took surface streets westbound to avoid being followed.

I could not keep my mind off of Florencio. I guess he had made me much angrier than I had realized. I thought of numerous ways to get revenge. I could not let him talk to me and treat me that way and walk away like it was nothing. I kept thinking of ways to get even with him. Each diabolical thought was insufficient punishment for what he deserved. I made arrangements to meet with Raul in Tijuana the next day.

The drive down from Los Angeles was very soothing and relaxing. It was one of those days when there were very few clouds in the sky. The temperature was about 75 degrees with a slight breeze coming inbound off the Pacific Ocean. When I passed the San Juan Capistrano Missions, I thought of the swallows, how they always arrived back around the first days of spring and how methodically they departed in the fall. I could never understand why our fine-feathered little friends could leave such a lovely place.

At San Clemente, I stopped for a slight repast and gasoline and drove on. Just north of San Diego, I saw the U.S. Border Patrol checkpoint checking for aliens in northbound traffic. While driving south I almost ran over three male Mexicans who dashed across the freeway in front of me about one mile south of the check point. They had apparently jumped the border heading north for work. I could not help but think of how much dope was entering California by border jumpers called "mules." The "Coyotes" who for large sums of money smuggle illegal aliens packed in car trunks, fuel tanks, under all kinds of dry goods, in the most inhumane fashion, all trying to make a livelihood, to earn money to care for themselves and family. I thought about how many migrant workers from Mexico came north to work, some called "Braceros" and how many had returned home penniless with deflated testicles and a beer gut; how addicted or irresistible many of them were to blond, blue-eyed prostitutes and beer.

I never recall a businessman referring to them as lazy. They were all touted as having the best work ethics and their labor was cheap and they expected no job related benefits.

I crossed the border into Tijuana at the San Ysidro Port of Entry/Exit at about 2:00 p.m. and drove down a dirty road below the elevated overpass leading into the downtown section.

Thin White Lines

Under the elevated road were shanties, some constructed of cardboard, cardboard/tin, and abandoned pieces of wood and car and truck parts. Little children barefoot in dirty, ragged, torn clothing played about the shanties; some ventured upon the dirt roadway. I stopped to the right side of the dirt road and took a good look at human existence at its worst. Smoke from the makeshift chimneys flowed upward and into the sky from some of the shanties. At the west edge of the shanties, several operated little snack stands where they cooked on the ground, in small pans and other containers that would hold charcoal.

Each east or westbound car stirred up clouds of dust that filled the air and fell upon the shanties. Inside the dusk filled shanty village you could see several people puffing on cigarettes. The dust was too thick to determine if they were male or female. Horns blew, hordes of people moved on and below the elevated road. In the distance, the loud sounds of music came and faded from the downtown and peripheral area of the city. Big trucks passed in both directions, creating large clouds of dust in their sway. While sitting in the car several little children approached trying to sell cigarettes, candy, gum, or white powder they called Spanish fly. A little ragged boy, less than ten years old tried to sell me a 3/4" rubber band stitched with sewn tassels of dangling thread that he called a French tickler; even one handed me a piece of black discarded paper and stated "un peso, un peso por me." A crippled man ambled up to the car, tried to speak English apparently trying to ask if I wanted a woman. When I told him no, fearing that I did not understand, he gesticulated sexual intercourse sliding his thumb between his index and third fingers and shouted "se vende senoritas por ocho Dolores." Despite telling him no, he insisted and described the senoritas as " muy joven, Bonita Y dulce, todas para ocho dolores." A young female came over and asked, "You want to fuckee, fuckee, me, yes?"

"No, I am just resting. I don't want anything."

The young female raised her dirty dress, revealing no panties. She played in her pubic area and asked if I wanted to have sex with her. I declined. She continued, "I am 15. Suckee fuckee, suckee fuckee, fuckee por siete dolores."

I declined and she persisted and reduced the price down to three dollars. Despite telling her no, she remained persistent and would not go away. I had to get rid of her. I gave her about a dollar in change and told her no. When she tried to get in the car, I pushed her back and drove away. I parked two doors up from the "El Gato Verde Bar" and as I started to enter the bar a man dressed in steel gray colored pants and matching shirt with a badge stopped me. His badge looked like the ones you get out of a crackerjack box, a kid's toy and he had no pistol on his side. In broken English, he told me that I had violated a parking law and had to pay a $20 fine. I argued with him that I was not, that there were other cars parked in the same area. He was persistent and when I did not concede, he blew his whistle several times. I gave in and handed him a five-dollar bill and walked into the bar about ten minutes before three.

As I entered the bar, a tall neatly dressed male brushed up against me and either tried to lift my wallet or give me a quick pat down for weapons or both. Immediately upon his contact with me, I extended the leather saddlebag I was carrying away from both of us. I felt him quickly pat down both of my rear pants pockets contemporaneously apologizing. The quick frisk was symptomatic of an old professional pickpocket. He was way off his cue this time. I felt the money clip in my left front pocket and relaxed. Before I could walk up to the round bar in the center of the floor, a Barfly eased up to me and asked me to buy her a Tequila. I consented and immediately the barfly ordered two Tequila. Immediately upon arrival of the waitress with the drinks, slices of lime and salt shaker, the barfly downed one Tequila, poured salt on the dorsal side of her left hand, licked the salt, sucked the lime and ordered another round, naturally at my expense. I immediately paid for the four tequilas and gave the waitress a dollar tip.

I was fully cognizant that the barfly was drinking water and I was being served diluted tequilas. When the waitress arrived with the third round of drinks, I distracted the barfly and switched drinks. The barfly grabbed the switched drink, down it quickly and gagged before she could order another round. While gasping for breath, she slowly but loudly uttered "Aqua, aqua por favor." The waitress rushed back to the counter and ran back with a glass of water. The barfly drank the water cautiously, staring at the waitress and bartender. After I pulled the drink switch two more times the barfly departed to the farthest corner away from the bartender and me. I occasionally glanced at her and noticed that the three diluted Tequilas she had consumed had affected her. Maybe it was the shock of tasting the Tequila as opposed to the customary water. After each order of drinks the waitress handed both of us a cash register printed tab. I paid mine each time along with a tip. The barfly secured hers in her bosom.

I gazed around the circular bar, that surrounded an elevated stage and noted there was a huge man sitting alone at 11 o'clock of my position and a smaller man sitting at 2 o'clock of my position, both starring at me continuously. I got up and went into the bathroom at the far end of the bar and upon my return, I noted the two men appeared to have met briefly and the larger one waked back to his seat. I was sure that neither Raul nor Florencio had arrived.

I felt uncomfortable with my back toward the front door and when the first seat between the two starers became available I rushed over and took it. I gazed at my watch, it was 3:30 p.m. Raul and Florencio had not arrived. I began to feel uneasy but was relaxed when the emcee 7 walked upon the stage and announced that the "Show is about to begin Damas y Caballeros, Ladies and Gentlemen," he spoke in both Spanish and English and after each pause a four-piece band in the far left corner of the room played loud music and paused. The M/C announced that Miss Beautiful (La Senorita Bonita) would be dancing for our pleasure. After he stopped, the lights went out like a power shortage, a few seconds later the spotlight flashed on the stage, highlighting one of the most beautiful women, at least I had ever seen, fully clad in a black see-through dress. She tossed her head back and turned 360 degrees displaying a copper colored beautiful face with dimples in each cheek and a dimple in her chin. As the band played loud and fast she danced in a circle on the stage. She was beautiful, sexy, and classy and projected an aura that she was all woman, well built, with large, not too large grapefruit size breast, a small waist, beautiful shapely athletic legs accentuated with perfect buttock that protruded outward and nicely. Momentarily I lost sight of my real purpose of being there. After two dances, the dancer removed all outer garments, except a G-string and small tassels on her breast. The M/C joined Miss Beautiful on the stage and advised that she would now dance personally for those customers who placed money on the stage. Immediately in front of me four customers placed a dollar on the stage. Ms. Beautiful danced a minute for each. All I could see was her back. The muscles in her back, arm shoulder and ventral side of legs were beautiful. Again, I lost sight of my purpose of being there. The three diluted Tequilas that I had consumed made me forget that I had over $100,000 in a leather saddlebag that I had brought into the bar. I placed the saddlebag on my left shoulder and double belted it down with two straps. I had approximately $600 personal cash in my left front pants pocket.

Two more men placed dollars on the stage and Miss Beautiful danced for them. I checked the money in my pocket and noted that the smallest bill I had was a five. I did not want to portray a big spender. I decided against putting money on the stage. The big guy to my right placed a dollar on the stage. Miss

Beautiful came over and danced for him reeling back with her hands on the stage. At one point she pulled back the G-string and parted her labia major with her hand. I stared <u>wantonly</u> at her. She danced to the Latin music, moving her body in rhythm to the beat and continued to display her vaginal orifice. I looked in her beautiful face and thought I was hallucinating. I thought she winked at me. I stared at her face. She winked again. Again, I thought the wink was just an entertaining gesture. When the song ended, Miss Beautiful stopped, walked over to a fan at the outer side of the stage and toweled her body and face. She stared in my direction again and winked. The band started up again. Miss Beautiful walked directly over to me and started dancing for me. She reeled back on her hands with her knees bent forward and gyrated in a very inviting way to me, simultaneously moistening her full red lips with her tongue, on occasion running her tongue out of her mouth past the bottom of her chin and occasionally fluttering her eyelashes and winking seductively. Again, I thought I was hallucinating and momentarily lost track of my reason for being there. While dancing in front of me, I thought I heard Miss Beautiful say she had something for me. I believe she had said it four times but I was not certain.

A man sitting next to me nudged me and stated, "If you don't want what she said she has for you I'll take it. Tell her to give it to me."

She apparently overheard the man and remarked, "No, it is for Beenum" and winked again at me.

I was certain that I had not told anyone in the bar that my name Beenum. Either I was more affected by the diluted Tequila or Miss Beautiful was clairvoyant. I sat and watched her dance two more dances, checked my watch and noted that it was now 4:00 p.m. Neither Raul nor Florencio had arrived.

Miss Beautiful's finale was a five-minute nude dance that terminated with her squatting down picking up an egg with her vagina. Pandemonium broke out, the strobe lights flashed and flickered, the band played extremely loud, men jeered, whistled, screamed and someone in the back of the room screamed in a loud baritone, near bass voice ha ha ha ha ha ha ha ha, huey huey huey, W-a-a-a-a-p a a, W-a-a-a-a pa and the El Gato Verde was a mad house.

After the noises subsided, the lights came on, Miss Beautiful now fully dressed walked off the stage, came up to me and stated "Wait right there, I'll be back."

"Okay, I'll be here," I assured her.

Another dancer took the stage. She was half as pretty as and less agile than Miss Beautiful. A few minutes later Miss Beautiful, carrying a small piece of luggage, joined me at the bar and suggested that we go to the cafeteria up the street.

We exited the "El Gato Verde bar" and walked south of Constitution Avenue three blocks to a cafeteria. Before I could be seated, a shoeshine man walked up and started shining my shoes advising that it cost "un dollar." I told him no several times, but he was insistent having already splotched both shoes with brown polish. Miss Beautiful stated "He is harmless, he doesn't take no for an answer from Gringos, plus he has already washed you car."

"You wouldn't bet would you?"

"Yeah," I shouted, "I bet you don't know my car."

"How much do you want to bet that I can't describe your car or point it out to you?"

"I'll bet you $20"

"Why not make it $50 or $100, make it worth my while."

"Okay, I'll bet you $50. Here is my $50 let me see yours!"

"You don't need to see mine for I am sure I will win."

"Okay, let's shake on it." We shook hands and Miss Beautiful asked me if I would pay her if I lost. I assured her that I would. Miss Beautiful described the two-tone light brown Cadillac Eldorado I was driving and told me that my license plate number was California license number RON112. She further related that I had parked two doors up the street from the "El Gato Verde bar."

We sat down. I ordered Carne Asada, coffee and orange juice and soft corn tortillas. Miss Beautiful ordered a Denver omelet. Sometimes when consuming alcoholic beverages and seeing women in dim lit bars, they are by one's imagination very beautiful and when seen on well-lighted streets or during daylight hours in a non-alcoholic beverage consuming environment, they are often twice and sometimes three times less attractive. Miss Beautiful was prettier than I could imagine. She was prettier than I ever imagined a woman could be. For some reason, I had the strong feeling that she would at some point become ugly. She was a physically gorgeous female specimen, one who deserved to be given the $100,000 that I was then carrying in the saddlebag.

"You know, I have followed you here and you seem to know my name but I don't know yours Miss Beautiful."

"You do. You just called me by my name. My name is Miss Beautiful."

"No that is your stage name, what is your real name?"

She commented, "I am sure Beenum is not your real name. What is your real name?"

"My name is Willie Lee Henderson. Isn't that a silly name?"

"No, it isn't silly. I don't believe a man like you has a name like that. That is not your true name."

"I'll prove it to you if you will prove to me your name is Miss Beautiful."

I then reached into my left sock, removed my undercover driver's license and handed it to Miss Beautiful.

She mumbled, "Hmmm, your name really is Willie Lee Henderson. You live in Pomona. That's not far from where I live."

"Where do you live?" I asked.

"Montebello, just down the road from you. I used to live in West Covina. I was born in La Puente."

"What is your name? I have shown you who I am, why don't you show me who you are. How did you know my name is Beenum?" I asked.

"I just know Beenum. I just know. You will find out soon enough. You know Beenum, when I saw you, I started wondering what is a guy like you doing down here. I am sure you are thinking the same thing about me."

"No I'm not, I don't judge people. You are one of the most beautiful women I have ever seen," I added.

"That's what a lot of men tell me, then they try to get intimate with me. You probably thought I am some green carder, some poor dumb Mexican whore, a whore who would go to bed with any man in Tijuana for $5, $10 or $20. You know Beenum, you can buy three or four whores here for $20 or less. I am a fifth generation Spaniard. I was not born in Mexico neither was any of my relatives.

I could tell that Miss Beautiful was becoming emotional. I tried to calm her by relating that being beautiful is complimentary, something that she should be proud of, especially since none of us could ever change from what we are. Miss Beautiful became more emotional and related an incident that made her sadden. Miss Beautiful related that one of the saddest moments of her life had occurred in the "El Gato Verde bar." While dancing nude one night, after the finale, the manager passed on a request that a customer had requested that she dance one more time. Halfway into the dance, the customer placed ten $100 bills on the stage and requested that she allow him to perform oral sex on her on the stage for the $1,000. When she refused, the manager became angry, cursed her and tried to get physical with her. All during his ranting, the manager was trying to explain that she would earn $500 with the balance going to him for supervising the deal. When she cried and ran into her dressing

Thin White Lines

room, a strange man followed her to the dressing room and begged and pleaded to her to let him in her dressing room, apologizing for the behavior of the customer. When she opened the door, she saw a very neatly dressed man of Latin extraction, not from Tijuana. He calmed her and identified himself as the real owner of the "El Gato Verde." The man gave her $1,000 as a token of his guilt for such an incident having occurred in his establishment and especially for the harm that it had caused her.

According to Miss Beautiful, the same man had described me to her and had given her something to give to me. Miss Beautiful reached inside of her bosom and handed me Raul's matching half of the torn $100 bill. According to Miss Beautiful, she now works for the owner of the "El Gato Verde" in other capacities. She bragged about being Florencio's woman. Almost immediately all of the beauty I had seen in Miss Beautiful diminished, faded like the wind, although she was undoubtedly beautiful, alluring, exotic, tantalizing, and caused many men to lust for her to the maximum. For some reason, I envisioned her as a pig, a whore, a harlot, and a toothless, unwashed diseased woman. A woman, not a lady, but a gutter slut that should be avoided like a leper. It was difficult restraining me. I had to compose myself and ask her twice to let me see her driver's license. When she handed me her license smiling, her upper center bicuspid teeth appeared to be missing, they were to me no longer shining, but appeared black, missing with the matching bottom teeth broken and heavily stained. Miss Beautiful's true name, according to her driver's license, was Guadalupe Sanchez, California driver's license number N552616Z. She told me to call her Lupe. I guess out of prejudice, I had always seen the dope business as a man thing; seeing women involved was utterly disgusting in all ways, maybe it was more a personal thing, a situation wherein I introspected that this, somewhere in the future, could be my daughter—a young woman lost to the legit world, flirting on the periphery of a business where danger, death, mayhem, arson, kidnapping and drive-by shooting, ambushing from behind parked cars, trash cans or distant windows were all part of doing business in a contra culture that has emerged upon us and is here to stay for a long time. Perhaps the strongest thing is that she is so talented and beautiful. Just as the customer wanted to give her $1,000 to perform a lewd act, many legitimate men would jump at the chance of domesticating someone who appeared as wonderful as Lupe. I noticed that all while she danced, although it was considered lewd, her beauty mesmerized all of the patrons.

Surprisingly, Lupe in the daylight was prettier than imagined. She was articulate and had the aura about her that many executives desired to have beautifying their office. I could not help but see her involvement with Raul and Florencio as something ugly and distasteful, devoid of any class or respect. I must have lost conscious for we had sat for approximately five minutes without uttering a word until she spoke.

"What's wrong Beenum, why are you so silent? Is everything okay with you? Man you look like you are about to faint." Lupe took a paper napkin and swabbed perspiration from my brow.

"No I'm okay, I was just in deep thought."

"What were you thinking about? What ever it is you don't have to perspire like that. Maybe it is from the barfly. You know they sometimes play intimately with customers to get them to buy watered down drinks. They get half of the money from the drinks they entice you to buy and a percentage of the waitress' tips", she explained.

"No, nothing is bothering me, I'm okay" I responded.

I started thinking of giving Lupe the benefit of the doubt. Maybe she was unaware of Raul and Florencio's business; maybe she was duped by both of them. I found it difficult to believe that she could be unaware of Florencio's business for I am certain the .45s he wore in the streets that he slept with them at night. For some reason I could not imagine a puke like Florencio having a lady like Lupe. Florencio in my mind was the walking epitome of a walking rectum with a hemorrhoid condition. Up close he smelled like one, even his breath was foul, and his mouth, when he talked, resembled an overloaded outhouse. I had never been taught to hate, but there was something about Florencio that made me hate his existence.

"Lupe, how long have you been seeing Florencio?"

"For almost a year now. He is not an attractive man but he is real kind to me. I was told that he had attacked the man who offered me the $1,000 in the bar and broke his arm and leg. The word got out and nobody has ever approached me like that again. The first dozen of flowers I ever got from a man was from Flo. All the other men asked me out or tried to date me only gave me 1,2,3 flowers, one surprised me with a half dozen. Shortly after the incident with the man, Flo sent me two- dozen roses on five occasions before I saw him again. Even then he never came on to me strong like other men. It was six months before he even asked me out. We went out six times and on each occasion he treated me like a sister, very courteous. He opened the door for me; pulled back my chair. He did all of the nice things that sometimes a woman realizes that she has never experienced. It grows on you Beenum. It pulls you strongly toward that person." She explained.

"How is that Lupe" What do you mean it pulls you closer? Do you find him attractive? I would have thought that you would be more attracted to Raul than Flo. I believe Flo is less attractive than Raul." I related.

I wanted to tell her that in my opinion, Flo was a huge mobile cesspool, a urinal that had never been cleaned, a sleaze ball, a pile of feces deposited by the mighty condor, vomituse, a pile of maggots— a person whose behavior instilled fear and intimidation, a bully, a henchman whose occupation dictated an ephemeral life.

Lupe explained that Flo was not attractive physically, but that there were things that he had done for her that made him special, made him very handsome to her. She added, "Beenum, you know regardless how bad a person is outside, on the streets or in the eyesight's of others, there are always many good qualities about that person that even good and bad perceivers can never understand."

She went on to add that although she was not a mother, she could never imagine a parent not seeing something good in his or her child.

I knew from her conversation that Lupe was blinder to life than I had first imagined she could be. Perhaps she was fully incognizant that Raul and Flo were involved in drug trafficking. Maybe her love, care and concern for Flo had blocked out her mental ability to discern what their true occupation were in life.

"You have dozed off on me again Beenum. You are in deep thoughts, what seems to

be bothering you? You are in good hands here. Everything is going to be okay. You will see," she assured me.

"I am not worried. I was in deep thoughts, that's all, just deep thought."

"A peso for your thoughts," she offered.

"They are not important Lupe. Tell me how did you get this half 100 dollar bill?"

"Flo gave it to me. He also gave me specific instructions to give to you that he got from Raul."

"Do you know why I am down here Lupe?"

"Yeah, to buy some dope, what else would you be down here for, dealing with Flo and Raul" she asked.

"If you know that then what is your role in this?"

"Raul wanted me to check to see if you had the money, to see if someone is following you and to help you get your package across the border safely."

"How do you propose to do that? Why didn't Raul show up? Where is Florencio?"

"They are all here. The packages are here. Rather Raul got a big one in today straight from Culiacan. There are other customers here other than you, you know. Let's get the money check thing completed, then we can go from there Beenum."

We walked back and entered my car and drove around Tijuana then proceeded south up a gravel road to a gravel scraped crude parking lot that abutted a frame unoccupied house. I opened both sides of the saddlebag containing the $100,000 and showed it to Lupe. I sat and smoked two cigarettes watching Lupe fast count each bill marking each $10,000 on a small sheet of paper. She counted each bill, added up the figures.

She then stated, "Okay Beenum, I am supposed to take this (the $100,000) to Raul, pick up your package and deliver it to you between 8 and 9 p.m. in front of the "El Gato Verde bar."

I snatched the saddlebag from Lupe and advised, "Hey there is no way I am going to separate myself from my money. The deal is to make an on the spot exchange, just like in a store, I pick up an item go to the counter and pay for it. It is not how Raul told me it would be, I am not doing a deal like that, especially not down here."

"Hey Beenum, cool down, don't have a stroke on me. We are going to work this out to your satisfaction," Lupe assured.

Upon realizing her involvement, despite her physical beauty she became less attractive to me. Immediately I started imagining Lupe as being Florencio's fraternal twin. To me, she had the same rotten disposition; rotten personality as Florencio but appeared to be devoid of being as violent.

"Lupe, how are you supposed to help me get the dope across the border?"

Lupe opened her cosmetic bag, pulled out a maternity girdle and waived it in my face, stating, "With this. It works every tune. It is against the law for customs agents to search a pregnant lady," she laughed loudly and further remarked, "What if I went into delivery during the search" and laughed louder.

"Lupe, have you done this before and how many times?"

"At least 50 times Beenum and I have never even pulled into secondary."

The use of word secondary was alarming to me. I suspected that she could be a cooperating individual, (CI), source of information (SI) or snitch for U.S. Customs. I talked in generalities and threw in a few hints to bait Lupe into utilizing other phrases and words to determine if she really was affiliated with a law enforcement agency, to no avail.

"Lupe, let's get the deal over with. I want to be northbound on Interstate 5 at least 100 miles north of here by 8 p.m. I have customers waiting. I can't make money down here; all I can do here is spend money."

"Okay, drive back to the "El Gato Verde" and I will meet with Raul and Flo to see what other arrangements can be made."

We drove back to the "El Gato Verde" where Lupe got out and advised me to wait inside. I would be contacted later. I fought off eight barflies while nursing a beer and watching the floorshow. While at the bar several little boys came into the bar sporadically peddling shoe shines, Spanish fly, marijuana cigarettes, French ticklers, Chiclets gum, candy, popcorn and pussy from their little sister, cousin, aunt or mother. Older men sauntered in pimping/pandering women that they apparently did not own or know. An older moderately dressed, half drunk man came over from the other end of the bar and told me to beware of Tijuana "trick pads" that he described as a house of prostitution where you pay a moderate price for conventional sex and while in the act, a thief hiding in the closet picks your pockets, socks and shoes for money and valuable items.

After waiting anxiously about an hour, the bartender approached and called me to the telephone. It was Lupe.

"Beenum, we are ready to do the deal. Raul did not show up

there for fear that something big is suspected to be going down. Some of the people he pays bribes to gave the bribes back to him; some took off unexpectedly for Chihuahua for vacation. There is a rumor that there are some Mexican Federal Judicial Police (MFJP) folks from Mexico City in town. Raul has had his feelers and runners out and have not been able to confirm it."

"Lupe if there is heat down here, we can put this caper off for a cooler day. I can't take another pop (arrest)."

"Have you been cracked (arrested) before?" Lupe asked.

"Only for traffic tickets. I really can't stand to be locked down, you know Lupe. I like to be free to move around. Have you ever been cracked Lupe?" I asked

"No, never and I don't ever intend to. Listen Beenum we are ready to do the thing now. Raul is with a state policeman now and he is ready to roll"

"With a state policeman! Lupe, what the hell is he doing with a pig?"

"Don't be alarmed Beenum, the policeman works for Raul. He is cool. He makes five times more money working for Raul than he makes on his real job."

"Lupe, I guess it is okay if you say so. I could not work with the police, they scare the shit out of me."

"Don't worry Beenum. It's cool. We have back up plans. Even if something goes wrong, we can buy out of it. You can buy any and everything you want here. Everything is for sale."

"That is good to know Lupe. I am ready." I advised.

"Okay Beenum, the bartender has an envelope with instructions. Follow them to the tee. You wait at the designated spot until the delivery is made, you understand me? The movement of your package will be made when the time is right, but it is very important for you to stay in place. In case there is a problem a car will approach you from the rear and flash hi-beam lights three times, then pass you from the rear and flash from low to high beams two minutes later. If that happens walk back to your car, drive back to Anthony's on the pier in San Diego and stand by for two hours, okay? Do you want me to repeat it?"

"No, I got it Lupe. I got it to the bone." I assured her.

"This is going to go like clockwork Beenum. I will be behind you in a yellow mustang. When you cop, get into your car and follow me and we will do the cross over okay?"

"Okay."

"Just follow all the instructions Beenum and you are going to be impressed. I'll see you later. Let's roll."

"I'm rolling."

I got the envelope from the bartender, entered my car, made twelve immediately right turns and parked on Constitution Avenue about six doors north of the "El Gato Verde," turned the lights off and waited five minutes. I then drove over to the Arena and proceeded to the meet location.

CHAPTER 2

AS INSTRUCTED, at 8:00 p.m. I got out of my car and walked into the dark alley south of Leon's Bodega, somewhere in the hippodrome section of Tijuana. I walked slowly over to the third telephone pole on the south of the alley east of the main street. I leaned against the pole and felt it sway. The ragged lamp at top flickered off and on. Somewhere ahead of me in the distance, the shouts of Ole' grew loud and faded. On occasion the jubilators appeared close and then far away. I heard the sounds of cats in various areas of the alley, crying out like in pain or in conversation with one another. I had no real sense of where I was and did not know the nearest location of a telephone nor did I have coins to operate one. I became more alarmed realizing that even if I found a telephone, would I be able to communicate with the operator. I felt my heart beat faster, my lips turn dry and perspiration bead up on my brow. My heart beat faster, further realizing the persons known and some unknown to me were aware that I was in possession of $100,000 (Official Government Advanced Funds –OAF) in $100 bills in a leather saddle bag and about $600 personal funds in my pockets. The smell of dried urine filled the air and on occasion a breeze swept through the alley filling it with the smell of burnt onion, garlic and burning wet newspaper. The sound of music, from Congo drums, bongos, timbales rang in the air from several cantinas in the area. Numerous cars passed on the main street behind me—many of them backfired. Contemporaneous gunshots rang out, some loud like that of a small pistol, others like shotgun blasts and often as they quelled the sound of a rapid firing fully automatic rifle sounded and subsided. On one occasion the shots were so frequent, it seemed as though the shooters were playing a song. I grew more tense and frightened. Sweat, not perspiration beaded up under my arms and trickled down to my elbows. I felt the sweat in my groin roll heavily down my legs like urine. I waited, waited, waited, checking my watch every few seconds, with the passing time appearing to be at a stand still.

During those few sporadic moments when it was quiet, I could hear my heart beat rapidly and loudly in my chest; the quiet moment often ended with the loud sound of cars backfiring, simultaneously with the sound of gunshots ringing in the air in the distance and close by. The loud noise of people exiting bars, laughing, talking made it even scarier. I had never in all the wildest dreams or nightmares ever found myself in such a situation. Never did I dream or imagine ever being in such a place, at such a time, alone, and so far away from home, so far away from friends, in an environment where the language was different, spoken faster than English and with many different words and phrases that are not often known by those outside. It was even more complicated because most adjectives followed the nouns. The parts of speech, nouns, adjectives, were light years away from my mind. My safety was of the utmost concern.

It was more frightening realizing that Florencio was in the area or would likely come to where I was. In the distance I thought

I saw the movement of someone on the roof of a building on the south and what appeared to be two people on the roof of the building directly across the alley. I nervously paced around inside of a 6-foot circle and glanced at the building immediately behind me. I thought I saw the head of a man immediately duck down on the roof of the building to my rear, the second building off the main street on the south side. I know that during periods of fear one's imagination has a tendency to be highly active and seemingly in one's favor.

I felt perspiration flow from under my arms like a faucet; and my pants were wet in the seat as though from a number one accident. I felt as though I was an aerialist, a tight ropewalker, yes as though I was walking a tight rope 100 feet above the ground with a strong, gust of wind blowing and no safety net underneath. Gunshots rang out sporadically but unendingly. The only thought I could think was that the imaginary people on the roofs were death angels. Death angels standing by until the word was given, and then they would come after me.

To add to my woes, I was in a divorce process with an embittered wife. It was only a few days prior that unexpectedly she had telephoned and related that she had had a dream the night before that she felt a moral obligation to share with me. In the dream I was "shot down like a mad dog in a dark alley." Almost contemporaneously I heard the bark of excited dogs in the distance ahead of me and a chorus of terrified dogs barking close by. I stared up into the sky nervously; gazing until I spotted the moon, noted that it was full, with tiny dark clouds flitting slowly by. I became more alarmed realizing that it was also Friday and the 13th of the month. I had never been superstitious before, but now there appeared to be something meaningful to all of this. My mind could not venture from the thought that there was death in the air, death in the area. The cats cried and meowed louder. I could not think that they were any other color that black. If only I could relax. I then tried to relax by inhaling deeply, holding my breath for a few minutes and exhaling slowly, repeating to myself that I was inhaling relaxation and exhaling tension. I completed the exercise twice and just as I began to feel relaxed, gunshots rang out in the alley about forty yards ahead of me. A man ran across the alleys and scaled a six-foot wooden fence. Three men ran after him shooting and hollering. My heart beat faster and I felt my legs become weak and felt a bit of uneasiness in my head. If I could only smoke a cigarette, I knew that would relax me, but I could not for it was not the proper time.

I checked my watch. Although it seemed as though hours had passed, I had only been in the alley twenty minutes—perhaps the longest twenty minutes of my life. I paced around nervously in my six-foot circle. I thought I saw two heads quickly duck down from the roof of the first building of the main street on the south side of the alley. I backed up to the telephone pole and then realized that almost the entire south side of the alley, from the third building off the street as far as I could see up the bill was lined with a seven-foot concrete fence.

I gazed nervously up the alley and thought I saw a transformer move on a distant telephone pole. I started to think that in my fear I had begun to hallucinate or maybe someone had laced my Tequila; maybe it was just one of the idiosyncrasies of being terrified. I waited, waited, waited, waited, paced and waited. I looked at my watch thinking that at least two hours had passed, to my dismay I had been in the alley only 25 minutes. From the beginning, I had decided to give this caper only an hour and then I would put it down. While staring east into the alley, nervously thinking of death, I was startled by the sound of quiet footsteps on broken glass, approaching me from the rear. I slowly slid my right hand into my front pocket down the bottom hole and retrieved my aluminum weight 5-shot .38 colt Cobra revolver and brought it up into my left armpit. I readjusted the saddlebag. As the footsteps came closer, I pulled the hammer back, placed it in a position under my left armpit and prepared

Thin White Lines

to shoot high grain soft lead jacketed hollow point rounds into the thorax area of 2-3 males 5'6" to 6' tall. As I nervously but cautiously turned around I simultaneously placed my index finger on the trigger in readiness to shoot. I was startled by a small ragged Mexican boy, approximately ten years old holding the hand of a ragged bare-foot approximately nine year old girl. I relaxed re-holstered my gun and said "Hi."

The little boy stated nervously, "Senor Quere chichar mi Hermana Por Diez Dolores, Diez dolores, no peso Dolores)'

"No I don't understand, no speakee Spanish," I advised.

The little boy then blurted out in English, "You want to fuckee, fuckee my sister for $10, fuckee, suckee for three hours for $10. Ella is muy joven tiene nueve anos."

"I don't understand no Spanish," I tried to warn. The little boy would not relent and yelled in English, "You want to fuckee, suckee, she fuckee, she suckee for three hours for $10. I stay, I watch okay?"

"No, no, I don't want your sister," I shouted.

Tears flooded my eyes, I felt sad enough to cry. The expression of the little girl was most pitiful. Her ragged dress and dirty face were worse than the kids I had seen earlier in the squatter's area. She gazed around as though unaware of what was transpiring and she had a look, an aura about her that indicated that she had been the victim of pedophiles on numerous occasions.

For a moment, I lost consciousness of my purpose for being there. The thoughts of adopting both of these little children without court procedures danced in my mind. It was apparent that nobody really cared for them, for if they did certainly they would not be subjected to such a violent way of life. I pondered that I could easily ask them to go with me, put them in the trunk of my car like the "coyotes" and drive them up to Los Angeles where I could provide a good life for them. In the past I had been in places where children were dressed as poor and used by parents and other adults to panhandle. I could not vision these poor children as being anything else but what they were, victims of a poor society where everything was fair for monetary gain; that such young human flesh could be subjected to such peril.

The little boy pulled on my left pants leg, shouting, begging me to pay $10 for his sister. Again, I thought I was hallucinating. I had never heard people describe such a bizarre thing, could not believe it existed and certainly that it would ever happen to me. The little girl apparently sensed the refusal and appeared sad. I handed the little boy $10 and told him to keep his sister; that I did not want his sister. He argued for a few minutes, thanked me numerous times, then walked east in the alley. I watched them stop momentarily at the rear of three cantinas on the north side of the alley. A few minutes later they slowly walked down the alley into the darkness out of sight. For some reason, I could only believe that this little panderer had something to do with Florencio.

A few minutes passed. I looked at my watch and time seemed slowly passing at a slower than snail pace. A ragged man pushing a broken down grocery cart ambled down the alley, mumbling something in Spanish that appeared to be merely a mixture of words. One leg appeared shorter than the other and caused him to rock from side to side and flap his left leg as though it was painful at the knee. As he came closer to my position, his face appeared dirty, hair stringy and dirty and he smelled of freshly spilled whiskey. He pushed the cart to the edge of the alley way and started spreading rags and items on the ground as though setting up camp.

My thoughts wandered again and I became angry with myself for allowing to be put in such a position. My ex-wife's purported dream of my death danced in my head. Gunshots rang out intermittently, some closer, others in the distance. Dogs barked, cats cried, a mixture of Latin music of various drums, including timbales vibrated the air. From an upstairs apartment on my right front, amidst the various sounds, someone was playing music loudly. I recognized the voice of the singer as being that of Yma Sumac, a singer my former music appreciation professor had touted as having one of the best voices in the world. Even then, not knowing the meaning of the words in her song, for some reason I always had a belief that they were about death, suffering, sin and sadness. Her singing made me sad. Minutes passed, seemed like hours, and the voice of Afro-American singer Celia Cruz bellowed out of the apartment. Almost like being hypnotized I felt my heart beat slower and my whole body relax. I could really relax if I could only smoke a cigarette, but the time had not arrived. I gazed at my watch. I had been in the alley 35 minutes. I began to think that this deal was humming right along; about that time I thought I heard a noise somewhere close by of someone humming. Again my imagination was running wild.

A few minutes passed and ahead of me up the hill in the alley, two figures emerged, walked together in the center of the alley for a little while then separated, one to the south end and the other to the north end of the alley and they walked slowly in my direction. As they came closer, I adjusted the saddlebag, secured the belts under my arms, placed my right hand on my gun and prepared to shoot. They walked within ten yards of me. Both stopped lit a cigarette, stared occasionally in my direction and talked to each other across the alley. After they talked for a while, I felt relaxed. They seemed to be Raul's advance party.

I looked up the alley and saw two men walking toward me. The one on the left was carrying a small piece of luggage in his left hand and a shining object in his right hand. When they walked under two dim lighted lamps, the item in the man's right hand appeared to be a revolver and he resembled Florencio. As they came closer, they spoke briefly with the advance party, and then joined me. I noticed the ragged homeless man appeared to be part of the group for he had moved his makeshift house up the alley on the south side about ten yards east of the advance party.

I extended my right hand to Raul and stated, "Hey I am glad you made it. When those two guys came down the alley I thought I had had it. That I had bought the farm."

"No, Beenum, they work for me, the man on the other side is a Baja State Policeman. He works for me. I pay him more money."

Before Raul could finish, Florencio approached me from the left and stuck the muzzle of his pistol in my ear and shouted a volley of profanity in Spanish and broken English. I reached up and slowly removed the gun out of my ear only for Florencio to place it back.

"Look Raul, this is hardly the way to treat a business person. Tell this man to stop or we can forget the deal."

Raul spoke rapidly in Spanish to Florencio. Florencio slowly backed away and stood closely by. Raul advised that Florencio would never accept me for anything other than an enemy. According to Raul, Florencio flashes on me because I resemble an inmate that had raped him when he was doing time at the California's men s Colony at Chino.

"I never did time in Chino. The most time I ever did was two months, rather 45 days and that was at Wayside Honor Ranch. Talk to this man, let him know that is the last time I'll take that kind of shit from him." I warned.

"I will. You ready?" he asked.

"I am as ready as can be. Can I see the merchandise?"

"Sure."

Raul snapped his fingers and Florencio handed him the small piece of luggage. Raul opened the luggage, flashed it toward me and stated, "It's all there Beenum. Check it out if you want to."

I retrieved one of the packages and noted the acid smell of heroin coming from the glassine hermetically sealed packages. I shook one in my hand and noted that it appeared to weigh more than two pounds. I handed the package back to Raul, quickly reached into my shirt removed a pack of cigarettes and asked him if he had a light and if he wanted to count the money. Before Raul could reply, I lit the cigarette and inhaled the smoke in two long draws. Almost immediately, I heard a loud chorus of shouts, "POLICIA! Levante Sus Manos Cabrones Pronto or Se Murio!" Two flares were fired, that rendered the alley as bright as day. Simultaneously a burst of automatic gunshots with tracer rounds filled the alley. A "jump out crew" (hidden law enforcement officials) emerged from everywhere, immediately subduing Raul and the two lookouts (advance men). I broke and ran as fast as I could east in the alley, noting the sound of automatic gunfire and tracer rounds bouncing off the concrete wall on my right. While running as fast as I could, about half way up the hill, I noticed Florencio running almost keeping abreast of me. I ran faster for a distance and turned around quickly and struck Florencio with my fist just above his nose as hard as I could. Florencio's legs went forward and he fell backwards and went limp.

I ran to the next street turned left, ran northbound two streets, turned left and then walked slowly west bound. I walked west in the alley past three cross streets until I came upon a very busy street. I turned right and walked north on the outer edge of the makeshift sidewalk. A few minutes later a car pulled up beside me and stopped. Two young neatly dressed Mexican Federal Judicial Police officers (MFJP) got out and instructed me to get in the car. The young driver spoke in English, "Are you okay Beenum? You didn't get hit in all of that fancy fireworks did you?" He asked.

"No, I thought you guys were shooting at me. I was afraid for a while."

"No, we had you covered like a blanket. We could hardly wait for you to light the cigarette."

"Did you get everybody?"

"We got everybody in the alley, three people at the stash, two or three people at Raul's house. I don't know if we got the girl, the dancer yet. We will get her. We have the Port of Entry covered." he assured.

The front passenger remarked. "That Flo was one fast running crook for a person with legs half as long as yours, he was out running you. He probably would have escaped if you had not stopped him. What did you hit him with, your pistol?"

"No, he ran into my fist, that was traveling at a faster rate of speed in the opposite direction," I responded.

The driver chuckled and remarked, "We should also charge him with low flying without a pilot's license. Ha, ha, ha. You Feds in the states really know how to make a case," he commented.

"We do our best. Without your cooperation, we could not have made this case.

You know there is reportedly a lot of local cops down here on the take." I related.

"Yeah, there is always corruption all over the place. One of the bad guys in the alley, with Raul, was state policeman. Another policeman was arrested at the stash pad. We will get to the bottom of this," the driver assured.

"You are not alone; we also have corruption in the States." I advised.

We drove over to the Army barracks where the prisoners were being interviewed. The driver insisted that I remain in one of the motor homes that had been driven down for the operation. I asked if I could join them in an adjoining room during the interview. I was advised that there was some prohibition about U.S. Agents being present during their interview. It was a restriction the U.S. had started, however, as far as they were concerned nobody could tell them what to do in their investigations, especially no foreigner could tell them. The driver told me to stay in the mobile home for a few minutes, about ten minutes, and then join them in the rear of the military police building. He would leave the door open. I was advised to watch the interview from behind the two-way mirror in Room 3. The other U.S. Agents were with other MFJP searching several other locations.

I stayed in the mobile home for about ten minutes, and then went to Room 3 to watch the interview. From Room 3, I could see Raul, Florencio and another male in one room, three other males in the adjoining room. There were four MFJP in each room. Raul and Florencio, handcuffed in the rear, were seated in front of a metal gray desk occupied by a large MFJP clad in khaki pants, a plaid Pendleton type shirt and an olive drab green military fatigue jacket.

Two young neatly dressed MFJP agents flanked their side about five yards to the left and rear of the seated MFJP. An MFJP agent stood quietly with an Uzi. To his rear the head of a male appeared and disappeared momentarily from the window of a holding tank in the rear.

The interviewer spoke softly in Spanish. Each time he paused Florencio went into an angry tirade, screaming and moving his head from left to right and at one time he stood up. The MFJP to his left gently pushed him down. The interviewer continued, Florencio repeatedly fussing, cursing and shouting and stood up four more time. Raul remained calm.

After a few minutes, Raul was taken out of the room. The interview of Florencio continued. The interviewer paused readjusting the tape recorder and occasionally stopped to write. On two subsequent occasions Florencio went into his outburst but was a bit milder than when Raul was in the room. The interview of Florencio continued for about 20 minutes. At that time an MFJP joined them and spoke madly at Florencio in Spanish. The interviewer then stood up, took out his .45 automatic and struck Florencio twice across the face. He fell back and shouted profanity in Spanish and English.

One of the younger MFJPs joined me in Room 3 and related that Raul had been interviewed and that he had spilled his guts. Raul related that Florencio had been a fugitive from Mexico

City where he had killed an MFJP about six years ago. According to the young MFJP, Florencio was about to receive an interview that he would never forget. The MFJP added that Raul had ratted out the Black agent, a guy named Beenum that escaped, the one that ran in the alley; the MFJP chuckled and mocked Raul, "Man that guy is one of the biggest heroin, cocaine dealers in the Los Angeles area. He's got a house bigger than the President's house and lots of cars." Raul had claimed that Beenum had $250,000 in $100 in the saddlebag he was carrying. He was willing to point out Beenum's house for additional consideration. Raul identified a Tijuana resident named Pablo Uvalles as the biggest marijuana trafficker in Baja, California. According to Raul, Pablo would not sell less than ton quantities.

The interview of Florencio continued. He took both blows to the head as though he was immune to pain and continued struggling with the MFJP on his sides. I had begun to think that Florencio was getting the best of the interview, that his captors did not intimidate him. Florencio stood up leaned over and spat in the interviewer's face. A silence fell upon the room. The interviewer wiped his face and left the room followed by two MFJP agents. The other MFJP agent pointed the Uzi toward Florencio and yelled in Spanish. Florencio yelled back at the top of his voice as though he was in full control. The MFJP agent kept a position in front of Florencio and to his left about 15 feet.

In a short while, the other two MFJP agents returned, accompanied by a short middle-aged agent and a tall neatly dressed, suave, well-polished agent. At the sight of the smaller agent, Florencio's expression immediately changed to fear. The smaller agent sat behind the desk and spoke quietly. All of Florencio's responses were followed by "Senor, si Senor, no Senor, es possible Senor, no, no Senor." Even when responding to questions, Florencio appeared extremely anxious to please his interrogator and on occasions used Senor three, sometimes four times before giving a response.

Thin White Lines

I looked at the MFJP in the room with me and asked, "What is going on here? Is the interrogator using hypnosis?"

"No, that's Ramon E. Herrera. He is like the head of the MFJP—like the head of the FBI in the States. Florencio knows that he is about to get one of the toughest interrogations that he has ever had. Are you sure you want to watch this Beenum?"

"Yeah, maybe I can learn something," I said.

After a short while a White American-looking man wearing Levi's, a blue waist length windbreaker and dark glasses walked into the interview room and took a seat in the far south corner somewhat out of my view. I mirrored him from the glass on the opposite wall. There was no doubt he was an American. He sat and observed the interrogation without displaying any emotion. When Raul and Florencio were questioned about firearms and explosives, he wrote something in a little pad he had in his windbreaker pocket. There was something very strange about him.

"I am sure you can, but I doubt if you will ever be able to use it in the States," the MFJP advised and left the room. Two men brought a tripod into the room, set it up in the corner and left. They returned in a short while, one carrying a small tub of water, the other one carrying what appeared to be a cattle prod. The water was placed at the base of the tripod and the cattle prod was placed on Ramon's desk. Florencio looked at the cattle prod and became hysterical. he started spouting out words rapidly, never forgetting Senor. He continued talking, even when not questioned.

Ramon stood up walked around the desk and placed his hand on Florencio's shoulder in what appeared to be a show of affection, compassion and concern. He paused and asked Florencio what appeared to be a repeated question. On each occasion, Florencio said calmly, "No Senor, no Senor, no Senor." This went on for about five minutes as Ramon paced back and forth behind Florencio, making him stretch his neck from side to side trying to keep his interrogator in sight. I felt a sigh of relief seeing this bad ass Florencio afraid of such a small man. Florencio's answers were all "no Senor," which did not bode well with Ramon. At one point, Ramon walked over in front of the two-way mirror, smiled and winked. He went back behind the desk and shouted at Florencio.

Florencio made a fatal mistake—he stood up and spat on Ramon. Florencio appeared shocked at what he had just done. The two young MFJP snatched Florencio up from the chair, dragged him over to the tripod and ripped off all of his clothing. They stretched his arms and handcuffed them to the top of the tripod. Ramon removed two washbasins from the cabinet, and spread Florencio's legs wide and made him stand wide legged with a foot in each basin. The basins were filled with water. The cattle prod was plugged into a wall socket.

Ramon walked up to the naked Florencio and struck him several times about the face with a yawara stick (a 5" long stick with a steel ball bearing on each end). Florencio stared at him without showing dislike for the pain. Ramon activated the cattle prod and prodded Florencio on his testicles. Florencio screamed and squalled at the peak of his voice, "Por Favor, Jesus Cristo, no mas, no mas, no mas Senor." Ramon prodded him again, letting the prod rest longer on Florencio's privates. Florencio screamed, yelled, squirmed and squalled, "Por Favor, Lo siento, Lo Siento, no mas Señor, no mas Señor." Ramon relaxed a few minutes, resumed striking and prodding Florencio for another ten minutes. Florencio's voice changed from a deep baritone/bass to a feminine whimper. He buckled up and went limp. He had been given a beating that I never thought happened in law enforcement. I began to sympathize with Florencio for I had always been taught that regardless how outrageous and bizarre the crime, once in custody, the perpetrator had a right and expectation not to be harmed. I was cognizant that for some rea-

Thin White Lines

son, even today in this Century, there will be law enforcement officers inflicting physical injuries upon prisoners.

While feeling sympathetic for Florencio, a short time later, he was taken out of the room on a stretcher and one of the arrested Baja State Policemen was brought in shackled and tortured just as badly. They took him out on a litter. After a third prisoner was hooked up to the tripod, the MFJP rejoined me in the observation room and asked, "Have you seen enough or do you want to watch more?"

"No, I have seen enough. I think I will go out to the mobile home and relax." I advised.

The MFJP recommended that I be handcuffed and paraded in front of Ramon, Florencio and the other defendants. A medic came in and wrapped my head with an elastic bandage. Bandaged my left arm and placed in it a sling. I was then dragged into Florencio's interview room and pushed into a chair in the far corner. A few minutes later two other MFJPs came in, dragged me into the interview room containing Raul, pushed me onto the floor, screaming obscenities in Spanish. With a sad expression on my face and faked tears in my eyes, I slowly stared at Raul. Raul winked a couple of times and stated in Spanish, "Lo Siento Beenum, and Lo Siento." In my mind I thought no I am the one who is sorry.

A few minutes later the two MFJPs came in and dragged me out of the interview room. After a short while two other MFJPs joined me laughing. They related that Raul had identified me as one of the biggest heroin/cocaine dealers in the Los Angeles Metropolitan area. Raul then added that I had $500,000 in the saddlebag.

I inquired about the identity of the Gringo in the interview room and was told that he was from the American Embassy in Mexico City and that he worked with the Department of Agriculture involving some reforestation program with Mexico—a spook. He had all the markings of a spook.

"Okay, we are going to be here for a while. You are staying overnight aren't you?" He asked.

"Yeah, I'll stay as long as needed. Have you seen any of the other agents?"

"No, but I heard two en route with three prisoners. Stick around Beenum, Our Jefe, el Senor Ramon wants to congratulate you. You helped us solve a murder including one of our own. I think El Jefe wants to show you his appreciation."

"Okay, I won't go back until the other agents go back. I'll stand by. What is the total bad guy count?" I asked.

"Fifteen so far. We are sending a fresh crew over to the Imperial Hotel. Raul has four different customers over there," I was advised.

I got in the mobile home and dozed off. I was awaken the next day about 9:00 a.m. Raids had taken place in ten locations during the night and thirty-five suspects were arrested, a large sum of money, large amount of heroin and cocaine had been seized. The most important emphasis was being placed on the arrest of Florencio for murder of an MFJP.

We shut down about noon and went back to the hotel with a date to have dinner with the MFJP. That night, when Ramon came down to the lobby, I was only able to recognize him by the four young bodyguards that surrounded him. He was clad in a long sleeve, tailored, white Guayabera, with fancy embroidered epaulets with embroidery and lace covering the two upper breast pockets. He wore a Rolex, President model wristwatch on his left hand, a large yellow gold large diamond ring on his left hand and a 1?" wide yellow gold bracelet on his right hand, with a medium size yellow gold diamond ring on his left little finger. His Guayabera had a wide-open collar that displayed a thick yellow gold medallion and chain around his neck. Ramon's black pants appeared to be silk and his black leather Cuban heeled shoes shone like patent leathers. Ramon's hair was long and neatly combed back. Except when he donned Ray-Ban sunglasses, he had the appearance and aura of a wealthy Spanish Aristocrat.

When we met for dinner, Ramon insisted that another agent and I ride with him. The other agent and I sat in the back. Ramon sat in the right front. The driver, a neatly dressed MFJP, was also one of Ramon's bodyguards. We were followed by three cars containing MFJPs and five U.S. drug agents.

Ramon asked, "What did you think of the interrogation?"

Not wanting to be uncivil I remarked, "1 guess it went well sir. It was different than we are able to do. We have to be concerned about the rights of every person we arrest." Ramon interrupted and related, "When we arrest a person down here, he has no rights, he has only the rights I am grateful enough to provide. Beenum you guys up in the States are going crazy. The bad guys have more rights than the good ones. What is law enforcement coming to?"

Ramon was from the old school, rather a different school. According to him, all law enforcement officers should have the right to protect good citizens with all of the resources available to them. Ramon expressed sentiment that good physical punishment of defendants was appropriate, it provided something that the penal systems did not-physical pain and humiliation. In Mexico, there were fewer repeaters, fewer drug addicts, fewer homosexuals, fewer child molesters, and fewer bank robbers. All this he attributed to the physical punishment that is often levied on an arrestee during interrogation. Ramon was of the opinion that if a man committed a crime, when caught he should come forward and confess and beg the court for mercy. Mercy should only be granted if the defendant was remorseful and vowed not to break the law again. Ramon added that a lot of Americans get arrested in Mexico and start screaming about their rights being violated when subjected to physical pain. It was confusing to him why Americans could expect different treatment than Mexican citizens. He believed that since they were foreigners, punishment/ penalty should be more severe.

Ramon ranted on about the U.S. criminal justice system being corrupted by flamboyant fast talking attorneys. Then he asked, "Beenum before you started this caper, do you remember that I told you that if you had to, if it got too dangerous to shoot the bad guys that I would take the responsibility for killing them?"

"Yes I remember and I was curious if you were serious. I thought you told me that merely to relax and ease my mind."

"No Beenum, I have the authority to do that. You are carrying a gun here in Mexico on my verbal authority. I have given all of your agents authority to operate down here that you could never give to me in the States."

"I was unaware of that," I replied. I could tell that Ramon was not too pleased with the reciprocal arrangements and I tried to switch the conversation over to the beautiful .45 automatics he carried. Ramon continued on relating that he was more powerful than the FBI, judges, coroners and medical examiners in the states. According to Ramon, he had the authority to take a human life devoid of any subsequent inquiries. The only explanation that he was required to give was that the deceased had disrespected the Mexican flag. Immediately, I started thinking about the dissidents who burned, defecated, urinated, tore, and mutilated the American flag with impunity. I could not help but wish that they would have travel to Mexico and disrespected the Mexican flag in Ramon's presence.

We were driven to a huge hotel restaurant about twenty miles outside of Tijuana called "Papagayos." There were many cars parked in the parking lot and the sound of music from two different bands filled the air. Upon arrival, the owner met Ramon at the door and escorted us to a private room. He was very respectful, courteous and overly trying to please him. We were the most poorly dressed in the restaurant, but were subjected to the best service.

Ramon told us to order whatever we wanted, that it would be on the Mexican government. There were fifteen of us at one table, six of Ramon's bodyguards roamed around with Uzis in plain view. Several remained outside in the parking lot on foot, in a mobile home and driving around the area in cars.

Most of us ordered steak and lobster and Tequila sunrises. I had a funny feeling that our tab would far exceed $2,000 and neither Ramon nor the Mexican government would be required to pay one dime.

Ramon sat at the head of the table and demanded that I sit up front close to him. During the meal he continued expressing his gratitude for the arrest of Florencio and related that I would receive an award from the Office of the Attorney General of Mexico. He related that the meal and later festivities were his personal treat for a job well done.

After finishing dinner, waitresses hurried into our room and removed all of the dishes and placed our drinks on the edge of the table in front of us. Ramon nudged me with his foot and winked his eye. The two double doors opened, a band, Congo, bongo timbales players, trumpeters came into the room playing a fast Latin song very loudly, followed by two beautiful nude female dancers. The owner rushed up to Ramon's left side and placed a small step-type stool next to the table. The dancer danced up to Ramon, walked upon the stage, one to the opposite end and the other one at Ramon's end of the table. They danced several sexy dances, shaking and writhing their bodies in sync with the music. Shortly fifteen very attractive females, all dressed in thin almost see through type evening dresses of various alluring colors, pink, light blue, beige, white, gray, mauve, teal, turquoise, red, yellow and green. The best-dressed and most attractive females gravitated to Ramon. The nude dancers continued dancing. After a while a very beautiful young female came over and sat on the edge of my chair. Ramon, seeing the female comes over to my chair, shouted, "Ustedes estan en paraiso."

He could have spoken no truer words, we were in paradise. We drank, danced, and played with the women until about 1:00 an. I began to think what a hell of a job this is. The next thought was that we were possibly being video taped for future insurance or compromise. My thoughts drifted back to the fun I was having. I noticed one by one couples were gradually leaving the table and walking to rooms on the second and third floor levels.

I suspected that Ramon was treating me royally for a future favor or request. I was on target after returning to the table from the rest room, Ramon asked if I would come down to Tijuana three weeks later and assist them with developing a good case against Pablo Uvalles, the major marijuana trafficker. According to Ramon, Raul would have been in jail longer enough to be more willing to introduce an agent to Pablo Uvalles for a large marijuana transaction. By then Raul would be convinced that I was not just another defendant in his case. I agreed.

Ramon advised that he was about to retire with his lady and asked me if my lady was cooperating. I told him I was not certain. He then spoke rapidly in Spanish to my date. She jumped up and shouted, "no, no", which angered Ramon and he responded with a choleric tone. He then related that my date did not want to spend the night with me. Ramon snapped his fingers and the owner ran over to the table and squatted next to Ramon. Ramon spoke in English and loudly, "This young lady does not want to go with my friend." The owner pleaded, "Momentito El Jefe, momentito por favor." He walked over and started talking Spanish to my date. She continued saying, no, no and shook her head. The owner then begged and pleaded with her in English that she apparently did not understand any Spanish. She would not relent her answer was, "No no, no, no puedo." The owner pleaded and pleaded and she consistently stated, "No, no, no, no puedo." She then stood up, shook her head and started to cry. I felt very embarrassed and sorry for her. I did not really want to become intimate with her realizing that she was in fact a prostitute. I had strong fear of a new social disease that was making its debut, called Herpes Simplex II.

Ramon became irate and displayed a rancorous attitude toward the owner and female, lost his temper and forgot about the beautiful young lady sitting on his lap. He stood up. The young lady fell to the floor. Ramon then commenced lambasting the owner relating that he had been mistreated, that his friend had been mistreated and embarrassed in his presence. Ramon ranted loudly, boisterously in Spanish and English, intermittently throwing a few English profanities. His outburst became so loud the veins swelled in his neck; droplets of saliva exited his mouth as though he was having a Gran Mal Epileptic seizure. The owner pleaded and pleaded with Ramon trying to reconcile the loss by offering a much prettier and younger girl for me. Ramon insisted that the hurt was done and that he had been made to feel less than a man in front of his friends. The owner continued to plead trying to right the situation by offering to provide two beautiful young ladies for me for the night. All alternative offers were unacceptable to Ramon. Ramon poured Mescal Tequila in a glass of ice, mixed it with grenadine, stirred it then drank it down and slammed the glass on the table. Ramon then drew his two .45s, walked out into the atrium area and fired both guns until they were empty. He walked back into the dining area and yelled "This place is closed forever" in English and "Este negocis is cerrado para siempie." The owner dropped to his knees and pleaded and begged Ramon not to close his business. His pleas fell on deaf ears.

I felt very sorry for the owner. He had left his family and friends at a function at his house, personally came down to provide a grand feast and women for Ramon and his entourage all free, at a financial loss and the only reward was the permanent closing of his business based on the failure of a prostitute to cooperate, to cooperate at a time that was so crucial to him.

Ramon reminded me of the old adage about the fox and the

sour grapes. When departing the premises, he nudged me on the arm and related that it was likely that both women had a venereal disease. Ramon related that in one of his past arrest escapades that he had consorted with a very beautiful and young prostitute, who supposedly had just arrived in Mexico City from a small town in the State of Oaxaca. According to Ramon, she must have put something in his food that was stronger than "Spanish fly." Ramon boasted that he had reached coitus five times with the "Jovencita" and was contemplating making her his little wife, "Mi esposita." Three days after the encounter, he had one of the worst sexual diseases that he had ever experienced. Ramon related that when he urinated that the pain felt as though he was pissing fire and Jalapenos simultaneously with additional throbbing and intense pain in the small of his back. He further added that he shot up the jukeboxes, shot out the windows, fans, closed the business forever and jailed the owner.

According to Ramon, almost all of the "whores" at Papagayos had been duped into whoring by fast talking slicksters from big and small towns in Mexico. They were country girls that had been lured to the cities for good paying jobs, jobs that started in whorehouses all across Mexico. Some of the young girls were actually purchased from poor farmers. Some had been raped by relatives or friends, once impregnated they were looked upon as outcast in their own rural communities. Ramon added that Mexico, and most of all Central and South America were paradises for men; women were second class or third class citizens, those men at the beginning of time and forever will always be in charge. He went on explaining that most of Mexico was Catholic; did not believe in contraceptives or abortions but practically all of them would readily commit an adulterous act, if impregnated and the opportunity arose, they would not hesitate to relent to an abortion. They would thereafter pray to God for forgiveness.

It was strange hearing Ramon sentiments, how little he

seemed concerned about moral crimes. He related that he was married to a very beautiful woman, had four daughters at home and two sons by his "esposita." Ramon described an "esposita" as a minor wife and related that minor wives existed before Christ; that in most Hispanic countries, it was customary for the wife to know and expect her husband to have a minor wife.

Ramon asked several times if I would come back in a few weeks and work undercover on Pablo Uvalles. He promised that I would be given an award from the Office of the Attorney General of Mexico. I assured Ramon, that if there were no complications and the clearance was given that I would return to assist the MFJP in another Quinn-Martin production under one condition, that during the arrest that the shooting would not be aimed so close to me. He agreed.

When driving back to Los Angeles two days later, I thought of my newly established friend Ramon, my friend who closed down a three story hotel restaurant/bar resort solely on the refusal of a whore to have sexual consent with his newly found friend. When I pulled the big Cadillac up to the U.S. Port of Entry at San Ysidro, a young immigration officer ran my car license plate number in the computer and then asked, "Do you have anything to declare?"

"No, I do not."

"Why were you in Mexico, for business or pleasure?"

"Both." I responded.

"What are you bringing back to the States?"

"One liter of Mescal Tequila, one liter of Grenadine, one can of Coco Lopez and one can of Corona beer."

The immigration officer exited the booth and asked me to open the trunk. I complied. He searched the trunk, looked under the front seat, opened the glove compartment and then told me to pull over to secondary. I wondered why he never checked my saddlebag, which was on the floor in front of the glove compartment.

After I pulled into secondary, the inspector requested my identification and immediately searched my saddlebag. I handed them my badge and credentials identifying that I was a federal narcotic agent. The supervisor placed a telephone call to my office in Los Angeles to verify my identity. I was then released. I learned then to cross the border going and coming in tandem with other agents. It was difficult trying to explain the $100,000 flash roll. I pondered how I managed to get involved in federal drug law enforcement or how I had even gone into the law enforcement profession.

CHAPTER 3

A FEW WEEKS later, I went back to Tijuana, accompanied by other Federal Bureau of Narcotic agents (BNDD agents), U.S. Customs (USC) agents and the MFJP. We met with Ramon at the Mexican Army Base south of Tijuana and formulated plans to immobilize major marijuana trafficker Pablo Uvalles. While discussing preliminary plans, I started a conversation with Ramon. I asked if Papagayos was still closed. Ramon looked at me as though I had insulted him and stated, "Come take a ride with me Beenum. We'll see if it's still closed."

"1 didn't mean to doubt you, El Jefe. I was just making conversation," I tried to assure him.

We entered a chauffeur driven car with three bodyguards. One was the driver; one occupied the front seat. Ramon and I sat in the rear. Ramon spoke in Spanish and we proceeded north toward downtown Tijuana. Ramon advised, "Beenum, we're going to take a little trip to Boys town. Thereafter we will go out to see if Papagayos is still closed, okay?"

"Sure, El Jefe. I am with you. You are in charge." I responded. Ramon spoke in Spanish and the bodyguards laughed. Two turned around and smiled at me.

Ramon advised that he had related that he told the bodyguards I had said that I was going along with him for he was in charge. He added that as we would say in the states "You are fucking a right."

I chuckled.

En route, Ramon told a broad history of Mexico from his view, explaining that there were approximately 60,000,000 people in Mexico, approximately ninety-nine percent Roman Catholic, one-third of the population is available for work. Approximately 36,000,000 are a mixture of Mestizo Indians and Spanish. The Mestizos occupied Mexico up until the Spaniards came. According to Ramon, like most civilizations, the Mestizos and other Indians of Central and South America believed in the second coming of a supreme being.

Cortez sailed from Spain to the New World and landed in South America. When he disembarked wearing armor breastplate, and was surrounded by other Spaniards, the Indians thought he was the Second Coming and they bowed and started praying. Cortez and his men placed all the Indians in captivity, colonizing almost all of South and Central America.

Ramon was a student of history, and apparently a well-learned man. He related that Mexico was rich in natural resources; oil, timber, silver, gold, copper, zinc, natural gas, lead and a few highly secret metals that are precursors for nuclear weapons.

Ramon further related that the geographical location of Mexico provided a Mediterranean climate of long hot summers, mild wet short winters with many valleys and plains with extremely rich soil that produces corn, cotton, wheat, coffee, sugarcane, various fruits and vegetables and spices. Additionally, Mexico produced the best marijuana and opium poppy.

Ramon did all of the talking. He was a very proud man — a man who enjoyed his work, the power and authority he wielded in his position.

In other prior conversations, I got the impression that Ramon enjoyed closing businesses or stopping certain activity or actions. He seemed to marvel at having bodyguards, drivers, commensurate with the authority to go anywhere in Mexico he desired. Perhaps most thrilling to him was the authority to take a human life with little to no justification; that his verbal authority overruled any Grand Jury or coroner's inquiry; that he even had the authority to verbally authorize a non-Mexican citizen to take the life of a Mexican citizen while engaged in an enforcement activity.

After a long diatribe, we arrived in Boys town. My initial naiveté led me to believe that Boys town was an orphanage. I quickly learned it was a long street filled with small one-room frame houses, small "shotgun houses." Houses you could look in the front door and out the back; Houses that were less than 20 feet long and less that 12 feet wide, whorehouses that lined the streets like soldiers in gray, white, beige, blue, pink, green, brown in color, all trimmed in white. The street was a brown dirt unpaved narrow road with wooden boardwalks on each side. Thick clouds of dust rose and fell behind each passing car.

"Here we are," Ramon related. I began to wonder what was our purpose there. My initial thought was that I was not about to consort with any female there, not even if I was utilizing someone else's penis.

We got out of the car. I followed Ramon to a small pink and white whorehouse. Ramon spoke Spanish to the whore inside. She, a pleasing plump, young, over made up whore, seemed to instantly recognize Ramon's authority. The room had a twin bed, no nightstand, a make shift closet on the left, a large mirror on the west wall and a large mirror above the bed. Left of the headboard area was a washbasin. A toilet and small shower were recessed behind the washbasin. In front of the makeshift closet, candles were burning around a statue of the Madonna and Christ child. After speaking Spanish to the whore for a few minutes we left. We entered six whorehouses on the north side of the street and four on the south side. Each whorehouse had a statue of the Madonna and Christ child surrounded by burning candles.

We got back into the car and drove toward Papagayos. Ramon related that all of the whorehouses he had ever entered had a statue of the "Madonna and Christ child" surrounded by burning candles. He added that it was puzzling to him how a prostitute could have such an item in a whorehouse. According to Ramon, despite their plight in life, they were all bound for hell.

Ramon related that the 16-year-old daughter of an influential friend of his in Mexico City had runaway with a "Gringo" her dad would not allow her to date. The father, for some unknown reason, suspected that his daughter had been turned into a prostitute and was working the Boys town section of Tijuana. Ramon promised his friend that he-would personally check for his daughter. He could now advise that he had checked.

We arrived at Papagayos and found the once beautiful building was boarded up. Some of the windows on the second and third floors that were not boarded were broken. Most of the beautiful flowers, except the rugged bougainvillea, had died. Ramon remarked, "You see Beenum, I don't want you to have any doubts about this business being closed, closed forever. I won't even allow it to even be sold—it is closed," he further remarked and inhaled deeply pulling air through his partially opened mouth and teeth.

We proceeded back to the Army base and continued plans to immobilize Pablo Uvalles. I placed a taped telephone call to Pablo. A female answered, "Hello."

"Hello, may I speak to El Senor Pablo please?"

"Uno memento por favor", she shouted.

"Hello, Quien Es", Pablo asked.

"This is Beenum Pablo, Raul's friend from Los Angeles."

"Oh yes, how are you doing Beenum?"

"I am fine. I tried to call you four times yesterday, two times the day before to let you know I was coming down. Did Raul call you about me?"

"Yeah, Beenum, he did. Are you in town now?"

"Yeah; I am holed up at one of Raul's houses. I don't know the telephone number here and Raul stepped out for a few minutes."

"Well, are you in to do the business now? Raul told me about you. We can do business today or tomorrow. It depends on how much you want."

"My partner and I are discussing two or three tons, depending on the price and whether we will have it put on the other side or take delivery here, it depends."

"It does not matter. I got 20 tons standing by for sale and another 20 tons coming up in a few days. I can put as much as five tons across in one shipment," Pablo assured.

I terminated the conversation with the understanding that my partner Cesar and I would meet with Pablo in two hours at his residence. Pablo gave detailed directions to his house.

After terminating the conversation, Ramon became excited relating that Mexico City would never believe that a Tijuana drug trafficker was capable of a 20-ton marijuana cache. Ramon contemplated setting up surveillance, delaying the deal until Pablo got his other shipment in. He could see a 40-ton marijuana arrest/seizure as being the biggest in Mexico. After an hour of discussion, he relented to completing the "Little Quinn-Martin Production" as soon as possible.

After putting on a Kel transmitter, Cesar (a U.S. Customs agent) and I entered an undercover vehicle and drove over to Pablo's house.

Pablo's house from the outside resembled an ordinary Southern California Stucco home but it was unpainted and surrounded by a cheap partially damaged chain-link fence. It appeared extremely large for the neighborhood and the rear extended all the way back to the next street. When approaching from the front, the rear appeared surrounded by an approximate 6-foot stucco wall and half of the rear appeared to be three giant steps rising to the third floor. Facing the house across the street made the rear look like a three-story building on the back street. The lower level windows and front door were covered with rejas a kind of security gate that made this firetrap resemble a Tijuana jail. The lawn was neatly manicured, with flowers bordering the entire yard. Two weeping mulberry trees flanked the walk mid-distance between the sidewalk and entrance door.

A Mexican male who identified himself as "Hector," admitted Cesar and me into the residence. We were taken into the back of the first floor to a huge family room where Pablo was sitting at a large bar. The ceiling of the room was covered with smoke stained mirrors; the center of the room was tiled in shiny wooden parquet, bordered on each side by a six foot steps of thick burgundy shag carpet that also covered the wall about 18 inches from the floor all around the room. A huge black refrigerator was on the east wall beyond Pablo. A bartender paced up and down the long bar cleaning. Two beautiful, scantly clad women walked about cleaning tables as Pablo sat at the right corner drinking black coffee and Irish cream on the side. Hector spoke Spanish and left the room.

"Come on in Amigos and join me", he stated. He looked at me and remarked, "You must be Beenum."

Yes, I am Beenum." I shook his hand and related, "This is my partner Cesar."

After exchanging pleasantries and flattering Pablo about his beautiful home, Pablo wanted to take us on a tour, but we declined. Pablo walked over to the large black refrigerator, placed a glass in the receptacle and ice fell into the glass. He then placed it in the next receptacle and water filled the glass. Pablo related that the refrigerator was now going on the market. He related that there were no other ones like it in Mexico or the United States. Pablo snapped his fingers and two beautiful young waitresses appeared. They left and returned in a short while with trays of food, diced lobster tail with tooth picks, large shrimp, dips, chips and crystal glasses, tea, coffee, grenadine in small shot glasses, sesame seed cookies, smoked salmon and a dish of rubbery tasty meat, Pablo referred to as "tripas."

Pablo bragged about his riches, how much money he had made, how much dope he had sold, how much bribery he pays, how frequently he traveled, how bad his henchmen were, how many children he had with his wife, how many children he had outside of his house and how much pussy he gets. He ranted on and on and Cesar and I listened. Pablo related how influential he was, how many people he had killed in Mexico and in California and Texas. At one point, I thought we had lost focus, that we were having a social meeting with Pablo, that all of his boasting was merely "the false bravado of a contracultrist" as we had discussed many years prior in college. I immediately discharged that notion for Pablo, as he was describing, was good for all of the things he was mentioning. Prior intelligence linked him to Victor Bono and Florencio Mationg, two defendants convicted for the brutal murder of two U.S. Border Patrolmen in California. Bono and Mationg reportedly were long time customers of Pablo.

Pablo was a talker. He ranted on, and on about his exploits and gradually came back to how much pussy he was getting. He made our undercover role easy. That is, we did not have to ask questions, or use veiled hints to elicit intelligence. We let Pablo talk. I was praying that my Kel was working properly for it was going to be very difficult if I had to write this report accurately.

Hector came back into the room and related, "Pablo there are two suspicious cars parked outside, one up the street about four houses and one down the street. There are two Gringos in the car up the street. When I walked by the car down the street, I could not tell if it was a Gringo or not, he ducked like he was trying to conceal himself when I walked past him. When I sneaked back past him, he ducked again. I saw a little red light under the dash like he might have a police radio," Hector reported.

Hector left the room momentarily, returned with a .45 automatic pistol and a long barrel revolver. He related that he was going out and would make the suspicious persons identify themselves, placed the pistol in his waist and left the residence. I immediately asked Pablo if I could use his bathroom. I went into the bathroom, pulled the Kel mike close to my mouth and spoke into it facing four directions advising that a man was coming out of the house with two guns to I.D. the occupants on the far north and south points. I flushed the toilet and rejoined Pablo and Cesar at the bar. I waited to hear possible gunshots, but they never came. It was too late for the north surveillant unit to move or for the south unit to pull off. I felt relaxed for I was confident that the MFJP would deal with Hector appropriately.

A short time later, Hector came back into the residence advising that the suspicious persons were Gringos and suggested that Pablo telephone his police contacts. Hector looked at Cesar and winked. He then looked at me and winked. "Are those guys with you guys," Pablo asked in a calm voice.

"No I don't know what you are talking about. We came alone. We came in the blue Caddie out front," I assured.

"Well, that's no problem, this is my town, I own this motherf____r. I'll have the police tow them away," Pablo advised. Pablo made a telephone call; spoke in Spanish and English advising to tow them away. After hanging up, Pablo took us up to the balcony of the second floor and remarked, "Let's watch this show."

A few minutes later two trucks, each followed by a police car arrived. One went north immediately hooked up the two USC surveillant agents vehicle and pulled away with them shouting inside. The other two trucks towed the other surveillant unit away. The two police units then drove up to Pablo's house. Pablo went down and met with them for a few minutes. After returning Pablo related that he had expected only two policemen; that it had cost him more for each officer had brought along a partner.

At no time did Pablo indicate any suspicion of us. At one point I had to restrain myself from laughing for I knew that the policemen and Pablo were in store for a rude awakening unlike any thing they had experienced before.

I told Pablo that we wanted to buy three tons of prime marijuana to be delivered to us in San Ysidro, National City or San Diego. Pablo quoted a total price of $75,000 and indicated that he had the best marijuana in all Mexico and had the best prices.

"Pablo we would like to see the marijuana before we actually pay for it. We would like to pay for it upon delivery on the other side," I advised.

"No problemo, you can see it today or tomorrow morning, it does not matter with me. I usually want to be paid before I put it on the other side. Since you and Raul have done a lot of business and he has vouched for you, I'll ship it to you on the other side, when you inspect it, then you can pay me how's that?" he asked.

"That's fine Pablo," Cesar advised.

"We have been burned before so we like to do business on a cash and carry basis, you know just like when you go into a store, you pick up the item you want, then you pay for it." Cesar added.

Pablo asked, "What do you mean you been burned before?"

"Well it was like this Pablo. On many trips we saw good grade marijuana, paid for it and when it was delivered we had a bunch of marijuana with a lot of stems and big pieces of wood in it. Our customers complained a lot and we had to drop the prices in order to move it," I related.

Pablo got indignant stood up and paced around in front of us, slammed his fist down in the counter several times and stated, "You guys don't understand what I said, I said I have the best marijuana in all Mexico. If you don't want to do business with me go somewhere else. There are signs all over Tijuana offering marijuana for sale…"

"No Pablo, we did not mean that you would do us like that. We were just making conversation." I tried to assure him.

Pablo then advised that we could see the marijuana now, then asked loudly, "Do you guys have the money to do the deal now or do you have to come back. You look like you are bare ass to me. Do you have the money?"

"Yeah, we have the money. Cesar get the money and bring it back." I asked. Hector, who had remained docile in the background, advised he would go with Cesar to get the money. When they left the residence, I asked Pablo why he did not have henchmen like Raul at his house. I was alarmed at his response. "You know Beenum," he stated, paused, and shook his head from side to side then continued, "That's a good question. I never thought about it. Maybe it is because I am the baddest motherf____r in all Mexico. Nobody fucks with me, not even the cops, not even that bad ass MFJP called Ramon from Mexico City. Even he knows not to fuck with me. I understand he was up here a few weeks ago kicking asses and taking names. I heard he busted one of the policemen that did some work for me, but that motherf_____r never came my way. I didn't leave town like a lot of the other narcotrafficantes, I stayed right here and dared that motherf___r to come my way. I had a posse bigger than his and they were better armed." Pablo remarked. His face seemed to swell; his speech became slurred and started breathing rapidly and mixing Spanish and English trying to accentuate a point.

Pablo asked, "Excuse, Pardoname uno momento por favor, one minute" and ran up the stairs. Shortly Cesar and Hector came back into the residence. Pablo came struggling down the stairs with a wooden crate. The bartender ran up to assist. Pablo refused, warbled up to the bar and set the box down in front of me, reached inside, removed four fragment grenades, handed two to me and asked, "Do you know what these are?"

"Yeah, they look like grenades," I responded.

Cesar's eyes went wide and his mouth flew open.

Pablo shouted, "Grenades, Grenades! Man these are frag grenades; these pinos will cut you four to five new assholes. These are bad hombres."

Pablo, apparently believing that he was not convincing enough ran back upstairs, returned in a short while with what I initially believed to be some sort of musical instrument in a white/green leather carrying case. He unzipped the case and handed me a light antitank weapon (LAW) and the rocket and asked, "Do you know what this is?" I played dumb and replied, "Yes, it looks like some kind of sky rocket. It is real?"

"Real. Let's go outside and let me shoot it at you. If it doesn't work then I will give you five tons of marijuana, come on, come on let's go outside," he pleaded.

I begged out of it relating that it was probably real. Not satisfied, Pablo went back upstairs and struggled back down and handed me two canisters that he stated were something like Lucite that burned underwater at 3,000 degrees and 5,000 degrees above water. According to Pablo, "This shit burns ten times hotter than the fires of hell."

I examined the canister and handed them back to Pablo. He then handed me a heavy, olive colored ammo can. I opened the can and noted a brown canvass cover with markings "C-4 plastic." I told Pablo that I knew what the C-4 plastic was.

Pablo apparently not convinced that I believed he was a very bad person, a person to be feared, asked us to come upstairs. Cesar, Hector and I followed him upstairs to the second level to a huge room. On the south wall of the room, he opened a thick metal door displaying a huge vault and told us to step in. I waited until Pablo entered the vault and followed. There were large crates of ammo on the floor, a u-shaped gun rack that almost covered the vault, canisters, boxes, all kinds of rifles, AK-47s, Infield 303s, M-14's, M-l's, Winchesters, Shotguns, LAWS grenades in crates, and two mortar launchers, boxes/crates marked mortars. Pablo seethed, sucked air through his teeth, ranted and raved about how bad he was; that he is not afraid of the little MFJP "Pinche cabrone Ramon." I was praying that the Kel set was working properly, further praying that Pablo's outburst did not anger Ramon to the point of affecting his arrest while Cesar and I were undercover.

I began to think of how crazy Pablo was for he had digressed from reviewing $75,000 and finalizing the sale to how treacherous he is. I told Pablo that they had more arms and ammo than the U.S. or Mexico army and went downstairs. Pablo was still angry and wanted us to take a trip with him to one of his ranches. Pablo assured that we could inspect the marijuana at that time. Cesar and I disagreed with the trip. Pablo would not relent.

"Pablo why don't we just show you the money and come back and do the deal tomorrow," I suggested. I then got the black attaché case from Cesar, opened it, and handed the attaché case to Pablo to inspect, telling him there was $120,000 in the attaché case. Pablo thumbed through the eight rolls, counted one, closed it up and attempted to walk upstairs. I grabbed Pablo by the right arm and removed the attaché case, stating, "Not so fast Pablo, let us see the marijuana first."

Much to our dismay, Pablo wanted to show us the marijuana that night, relating that it was at a ranch about an hour or so away. I knew it would be very difficult for surveillance to follow us in the rural area, especially since we did not have an airplane or helicopter—they would not be available until the following day. Pablo insisted that he show us the marijuana that night and remarked, "What kind of dope dealers are you guys? You don't want to do the deal. You guys are like some of those gringo cunts in California, they tease you until you are ready to make love, and then they walk away. It is either now or never."

During the preplanning phase, Cesar and I had agreed not to travel that night, not to do the deal during the night and not to let the bad guy(s) separate us and for both of us to be with the flash roll ($80,000 intended only to be shown not expended). I decided to break a cardinal undercover rule and agreed to travel with Pablo to the stash and leave my partner (Cesar) at Pablo's house. Over Cesar's objection, I decided to travel with Pablo. I joined Pablo and a tall muscular, young Mexican male that seemed to appear from nowhere. He got in the rear. The bulges around his waist were .45 automatics, not love handles. I joined Pablo, the driver in the front seat, in a blue four-door Ford LTD and we drove away. I asked Pablo where we were going, thinking that he would tell me knowing that I would not really know. All Pablo would say was "to one of my ranches just a few miles out of town." Pablo circled the block of his residence, twice then pulled upon a main street headed south, drove for a block and a half and stopped. After watching a few minutes he headed south for about a mile, pulled over to the side of the road, parked and turned the lights off. A few minutes later we drove away. Pablo then turned on the radio and increased the volume so high that I had to repeat myself and asked him to repeat himself. Despite telling, Pablo the loud music gave me a headache, he would not turn it down. I engaged him in general conversation and asked him about things I thought he would not understand to distract him so I could turn down the volume.

I stated, "Pablo I heard it is snowing Palisades stones in Mexico City."

"Yeah, that's true," he responded.

I turned the volume down. A minute later Pablo turned the volume back up. We drove on. As we passed certain lighted buildings, I asked Pablo about them, secretly giving my direction to surveillant units. We drove for twenty minutes. No cars passed.

No headlights appeared in the rear. Pablo bragged that he had 20 henchmen at one ranch and 15 at the other and did not hesitate to state that they were heavily armed and would not hesitate to shoot. Pablo related that he had been stopped, detained and beaten once by the MFJP from Mexico City. While driving, he raised the right part of his sweater displaying a .45 pistol and Keloids from the beating. Pablo sucked wind between his teeth, shook his head from side to side stating, "I will never be beaten again. I will kill or be killed before I take another beating again."

There was no doubt in my mind about his statements. I was hoping that the Kel set was working properly and was advising Ramon of Pablo's conversation.

We drove on to a remote area and turned left down a dirt road. We continued on past trees, a broken down building, and a small lake on the right, a mile later a park on the left, around curves, and over numerous holes in the dirt road. Dust rose and drifted down slowly as we passed.

About 30 minutes later we came upon a beautiful valley. The outline in the distance appeared to be plush green foliage. We drove on for a few minutes and came upon an opening on the right. Pablo turned right onto a gravel/grass road, stopped and flashed his lights off and on three times. In the distance to our right about 1500 yards headlights came on flashed high beam/ low beam three times and went dark. A few seconds later headlights came on about 1500 yards to our left, flashed high beam/ low beam three times and went dark.

We drove down the road underneath a gate, past trees in spots, over a wooden bridge, turned right and proceeded up a meandering road, then down into another valley. We pulled up to a large white barn-like building with a huge paved parking lot. As we pulled up six well-armed men approached and exchanged greetings with Pablo. Pablo spoke loudly in Spanish and about eight other men appeared quickly, all armed with M-14s, AK-47s and two or three with Uzi's assault weapons. Several also wore side-holstered revolvers. The one that appeared to be in charge wore two long pistols like Roy Rogers and carried a shouldered Uzi that flopped about when he walked.

Pablo talked to the headman for a few minutes. Then they all left the immediate area. We went into the barn like building where I saw more 20-pound bales of marijuana than I could count.

"Pablo, you must have 100,000 pounds of marijuana in here…," I remarked.

"No, I only have 20 tons. I'll have close to that amount when my next shipment comes in." Pablo said. I inspected numerous bales, noting that they were neatly, tightly wrapped in burlap and further wrapped in thick plastic. Pablo stated that they wrapped it in plastic to control the field rats from eating it.

After a short while, Pablo took me outside to the rear of the building where five semi-tractors and five tanker trailers were parked. They were not new, but well maintained with chrome rims. I joined Pablo on top of one tanker where we inspected the inside false bottom. Pablo stuck a stick down to the bottom and diagonally inside of the tank, removed it displaying a tarry substance. According to Pablo, the front and rear sections were hollow, each capable of carrying 2 1/2 tons of marijuana. This is how Pablo smuggled marijuana into the United States. His drivers also unloaded it upon delivery.

When we went back into the building, I noticed that the north upstairs area had sleeping quarters and there was an upstairs locked room facing outside in four different directions. Pablo took me in the rear of the office where he had a cache of weapons, grenades, AK-47 assault rifles, British Infield 303 rifles with scopes, and 50 caliber tripod machine guns, 6-LAWS. Pablo picked up one of the LAWS, pointed it outside and simulated firing it. He put it back in a crate and related that the rocket had a speed of 4000 feet per second, heat seeking or laser target finding capability, a range of 1500 yards and would penetrate 12" of case harden steel. Pablo again sucked air rapidly through his teeth, shook his head from side to side and stated, "This is one bad motherfucker, a most bad motherfucker." Pablo related that he had just as many weapons at his other ranch. I tried to convince Pablo to take me to his other ranch but he refused. I was thoroughly convinced that Pablo was as bad and demented as he purported to be, that he would kill at the drop of a hat, had killed people before, had people killed and that he would not hesitate to do it again. The keloid type welts on his back were more convincing that he did not want to ever again be arrested, that he would fight to the bitter end.

Although he was only about 5'6" tall, 170 pounds, Pablo had a complex that made him appear 9' tall. He gave me a 20-pound bale of marijuana as a sample to show my partner Cesar and we left. While driving back to Tijuana, he repeatedly nudged me, sucked air through his mouth, shook his head from side to side and repeatedly asked, "Am I a most bad motherf____r Beenum, Am I a most bad mother_____?" I assured him on each occasion that he was and further attempted to get him to take me to his other ranch to no avail.

When we got back to Pablo's house, I was glad to see Cesar and to know that he was okay. Cesar seemed relieved that I was okay, but disappointed that I had tripped with Pablo, splitting up the surveillant units. We made arrangements to complete the deal with Pablo the next day between noon and 1:00 p.m. Cesar and I exchanged handshakes on the deal and left the residence. Hector walked us out to the undercover car and reminded Cesar to tell me that he was on our side and wanted to leave with us. We declined his offer.

Cesar and I secured the 20 pounds of marijuana in the trunk of the undercover car and drove from the area.

"What's with Hector, Cesar? He seemed to be so friendly." I asked. "He was Ramonized. When he went outside to make the guys in the cars identify themselves, it seems at though Ramon grabbed him and Ramonized him." Cesar related.

"What do you mean by that?"

"Ramon gabbed him, spanked, threatened and intimidated him, threatened to arrest his wife, little wife, and children; then threatened to kill Hector and burn his house down if he did not fully cooperate. Naturally Hector agreed. According to Hector when he found out the main MFJP was Ramon; he had no other thoughts other than to fully cooperate. While you guys were gone, Hector took me outside and pleaded with me to really explain the extent of his cooperation to Ramon. He is petrified of Ramon. Hector cooked me a lobster and a steak and tried to serve me all kinds of drinks trying to be cooperative," Cesar related.

We drove over to a prearranged location car and joined Ramon, other MFJPs and U.S. Drug Agents inside a Winnebago motor home. Ramon was screaming, hollering and apparently using profanity in Spanish. The part of Ramon's conversation that I could discern, he was very angry that "Pablo was riding high" as he explained and had state and local policemen on his payroll. The two U.S. Customs surveillant agents had actually been arrested when towed from the area of Pablo's house. Despite role playing and disavowing being involved with any law enforcement agency, it cost $1,000 bail per agent to get them released from custody unharmed. I became concerned that he was angry because I had digressed from the original plan. MFJP and agents begged and pleaded with him in English and Spanish, but he did not relent his anger. I thought it was best that I offered an apology for digressing from the plan and spoke, "Licenciado Ramon, I am sorry for not sticking to the plan. I know I must have confused surveillance when I tripped." I pleaded.

Ramon seemed more irate, "Sorry. Why in the hell are you sorry Beenum? You guys did a good piece of work. We had the eyeball all the time. We had a bird in the air and we have had a bird dog on Pablo's LTD and Chevy truck for two weeks. We are glad you tripped," Ramon assured. He then walked over put his arm around me and reiterated, "Good job, Beenum. Good job." Ramon then turned to several MFJP agents and stated, "El Beenum tene cajones mas grande que un toro." They all chuckled.

After Ramon finally relaxed it became evident that he wanted to arrest Pablo as soon as possible. In listening to the Kel transmission it appeared as though Pablo had referred to Ramon as a Maricon. According to Ramon nobody had ever called him a Maricon and walked away without a "good ass whipping."

We drove back to the military base and formulated plans for the "take down" the next day. Cesar and I emphatically stressed the potential danger at Pablo's house, one ranch and related that we did not know the location of the second ranch.

Ramon became indignant and indicated that we were down playing the strength and power of his organization. He indicated that he could mobilize the whole army base if deemed necessary, additionally military troops and MFJP could be flown in as soon as possible. Ramon rekindled his anger and insisted on taking Pablo then. It took a half-hour calming him down to agreeing to make the "take down" the next day. I was very glad he relented for I was tired. It was midnight. Prior to leaving the base, we had to again convince Ramon not to do a pre-dawn raid. He relented, relating that he wanted all Tijuana to see him in operation, to let the people know that all policemen are not corrupt, that Pablo had lost his license to deal dope. That Pablo would, despite relating that he would not go back to jail, in fact would be jailed the following day. Ramon bragged that he would go back to his hotel room devise a plan to arrest Pablo and seize his heavily armed and fortified ranch and residence without firing a single shot.

I went back to my hotel room wondering how Ramon could execute such a "take down" without firing a single gunshot. Unlike in the United States, Ramon and his subservient MFJP agents were walking, search warrants. There was no need to prepare a lengthy detailed affidavit, have it perused and edited and amended by a prosecutor, then delivered far away to the residence of a judge for his signature. Ramon was the shortcut. He could also give us commensurate authority to search a residence in Mexico, authority to shoot and kill if necessary. Thereafter Ramon would be the Coroner's Inquest and would rule the shooting "Justifiable Homicide." Ramon could delegate authority to foreign agents that could and would not be reciprocated in the United States. I was a bit perplexed with Ramon's power and authority, seeing him extremely incensed about Pablo and indicating that we would take Pablo down the next day without firing a single shot.

Yes today was Pablo's day—a day I somewhat hated to see arrive, for I had for some unforeseen reason gotten to like Pablo, admire how he strutted, personified his Napoleonic complex with the false bravado of how bad he was; how he strutted around like an American entrepreneur giving orders and jubilating inside when seeing his orders carried out. There was something strange about fellowshipping, even in an undercover capacity, drinking the best of liquor, eating the best of food and riding around in nice cars all at the expense of the to-be-arrested defendant and the United States Government. It was also thrilling walking' the tight rope of death in an undercover capacity with contracultralists that engaged in murder and mayhem as part of an everyday business enterprise. It is terrifying realizing while walking the-tight rope; one can make the slightest mistake that could cause your instant demise in a violent way. It seemed as though every narcotrafficante had a point to prove, that violent death, assaults, kidnapping, drive by shootings and human torture were expected of the trade and the .45 automatic pistols with grips emblazoned with three different colored gold and precious stones were a status symbol of how treacherous the carrier was or wanted to be.

Perhaps what I regretted mostly about Pablo's day was the beating I knew he would be subjected to, a post arrest beating that would change his baritone voice to that of a soprano and thereafter during the interrogation most of his responses would be "Si Senor, Si Senor, Por favor no mas, no mas, no mas."

Yeah Pablo deserved all that he had coming. He would once again be Ramonized causing the word "Maricon" to flee from his vocabulary forever.

We met at the military base at 9:30 a.m. and were briefed. Ramon indicated that he would give the bust signal. I joined one MFJP and a U.S. Customs pilot in a "sky master" aircraft, Flint 954. It was a weird plane with two propellers, one in the front and-one in the rear of the fuselage. We went airborne at 10:15 a.m. over Pablo's house and circled. There were other small aircraft in the proximate area. The Tijuana airport was east of our location. Commercial airplanes took off every ten minutes, came west in our direction, banked left or right and flew north or south-bound out of sight.

As we hovered over Pablo's house, I noticed a military helicopter hovering off the coast west of our location and a small helicopter flew south. A short distance east of the smaller helicopter a group of Mexican soldiers in tracks and jeeps had massed up in a makeshift parking lot.

Ramon came on the air in Spanish, thereafter 25-30 units responded. The MFJP related we were set to go. A few minutes later a large black smokestack bellowed upward on Pablo's street a block and a half south. A few minutes later two fire engines, with emergency lights, siren and horns in operation sped down the street past Pablo's house. The military helicopter moved closer to our location. The sirens sounded louder, horns blew and people rushed out of houses and adjacent buildings and rushed toward the fire. Two people came out of Pablo's house. A few minutes later all ten people from Pablo's house were in the prone position. A voice came over the radio in Spanish, then related in English "Bad guy 1 in custody," "Bad guy 2 in custody," "Bad guy 3 in custody," "Bad guy 4 in custody," "Bad guy 5 in custody," "Bad guy 6 in custody," "Bad guy 7 in custody," "Bad guy 8 in custody," "Bad guy 9 in custody," "Bad guy 9 in custody."

Ramon's voice came over "Diez-Cuatro." Ramon instructed the MFJP to bring Pablo to his location. A few minutes later, ten MFJP walked up to the side of Pablo's house. A short time later five additional male Mexicans exited Pablo's house and were immediately taken into custody. Ramon had seized Pablo's residence, arrested Pablo and fourteen henchmen without firing a single shot. Pablo was driven over to Ramon.

A short time later, we landed and I joined Ramon with Pablo at a prearranged location and stayed in the background. I could see Ramon handcuffed to the rear and shackled at the ankles. He stood semi-erect on his knees facing Ramon where he was seated in a metal folding chair in front of him. Ramon had a bottle of club soda in his left hand and a sweiger stick in his right hand. He shook the bottle of club soda until it foamed. Ramon then squirted a portion of the club soda down Pablo's left nostril and shouted, "Quien es el hombre mál que todos los hombes de la mundo?"

Pablo jerked his head back into the hands of an MFJP standing to the rear, struggled and laboriously uttered, "Usted Senor, usted senor, usted." This went on for ten minutes with Pablo struggling and screaming, "Usted senor, por favor senor, usted senor, por favor senor no mas, no mas."

Ramon punished Pablo almost to the point of death with the club soda, cattle prod, his fist and swinger stick. His face was black and blue, darker under the eyes and heavily swollen. Pablo had been Ramonized and was now coughing up every bit of valuable enforcement information he could recount. Ramon was convinced that he had (twisted Pablo) converted Pablo, that Pablo would be his cooperating individual (CI), that he would never again traffic in drugs, that Pablo would never again be the bad ass "narcotrafficante" that he had touted himself to be.

While standing in the distant background seeing Pablo being physically punished, I wondered why the Mexican utilized such an archaic technique, according to American standards. Whether they ever thought that physical punishment could make even the most innocent confess to a crime to alleviate being further punished.

I remembered a mistake another agent once made regarding physical punishment. I remember an incident a little while ago where Ramon and his crew had arrested a very handsome white couple for possession of three kilograms of brown Mexican heroin. Ramon interviewed them inside of their hotel room. Seeing Americans with Ramon, the couple became feisty and spouted profanity at Ramon, calling him a short sleazy Mexican motherf____r" and shouted something about having rights. Ramon remained calm for several minutes trying to elicit information regarding how and from whom the couple had obtained the heroin. They were very uncooperative and continued to call Ramon abusive names. Ramon summoned the cattle prod and placed the male in the bathtub and prodded him about the groin until he fell weak. He slapped the female very hard on the same cheek. A young U.S. agent gabbed Ramon and yelled, "That's a fucking enough. Ramon that's enough." Immediately Ramon's bodyguards grabbed the agent and restrained him.

Ramon gave all of us the admonition that he was in charge in Mexico; that nobody, especially no American, could or should ever tell him how to enforce laws in Mexico. Ramon became angrier than I ever thought he could be and related that we as American agents should be most pleased with his cooperation, especially being allowed to carry guns in Mexico, being allowed to shoot to kill if necessary without any subsequent problem; for even being allowed to physically arrest a Mexican citizen in Mexico. Ramon let us know that he and his government, in the spirit of cooperating, were providing cooperation that could never and would never be extended to him in the U.S. I remember how Ramon had ranted on about Americans traveling like "Marco Polo" but wanting to change everything everywhere they (Americans) went. According to Ramon, America was the greatest country in the world, greater than his own country. He went on and related that not like the Mexican peso, the U.S. dollar is spendable all over the world. Ramon had the funny idea that eventually there would be one world currency, the U.S. dollar.

After fully interrogating Pablo, Ramon decided to raid his ranches. I felt sorry for Pablo for he looked like he was near death and was so naive to the point that he sounded like a stuck or broken record; the only words he uttered were "Si senor." He uttered "Si senor?" to everything and provided directions to his second ranch. Before he was beaten into submission Ramon stuck his .45 in Pablo's ear and made him telephone both ranches for safe passage. We then proceeded in Pablo's truck and MFJP truck and a Winnebago motor home in tandem to the first ranch. I stayed in the motor home and had a long discourse with Ramon en route. Despite his propensity for beating arrestees, I found him to be a very duty oriented man devoid of the corruption that often plagues many in his organization. Ramon related that the most frequent type of corruption involved an official being paid not to perform a function or not to see a particular activity and that sometimes the pay off was the unexplained deposits of money in one's account followed by a subsequent request. According to Ramon, his only corruption involved free sex every now and then. Money was of little or no consequence for he seemed to have more than his share.

We arrived at the first ranch at about 5:00 p.m. The sun was low in the sky and it had cooled down. We expected a smooth arrest. As we entered the gateway 100 yards from the main building, gunshots rang out, automatic weapons, shotguns and repeater rifles. The awful stench of gunfire filled the air, a cloud of bluish gray smoke filled the air. The projectiles sounded like Howitzer rounds passing. Approximately 300 rounds had been fired before we could gain our composure and respond to being caught in an ambush. Rapid fire of a 50-caliber tripod machine gun filled the air spraying the MFJP truck like target practice. Pablo's truck in front had been allowed to pass through the entrance way about 50 yards before the shooting started. I peeked out the upper front window and saw two MFJPs fall to the ground from both front sides. Neither raised his gun, but moved slowly groaning and moaning in pain, agony and fear. Twelve MFJPs in the rear of the truck jumped out and immediately obtained prone positions in a fan like semicircle around the truck. Gunshots plowed the ground in front and around them. A large MFJP stood up momentarily in an attempt to enter the cab of the truck and I saw a bullet exit his back with viscera and clothing about the size of an orange. He fell to the ground immediately with no rise or fall in his chest.

I became frightened as bullets ripped the front and parts of the motor home. Ramon, six MFJPs and I fell to the floor. All I could hear was the continuous sound of gunshots commensurate with Ramon's cursing and yelling. Gunshots ripped across the windshield and doors of the motor home. I peaked through the window and saw the MFJP driver had been shot several times in the chest area. He moved and wheezed in deep pain coupled with a few words of profanity. His body then went rigid. His shotgun rider on the right front crouched his big body in the little space between the seats and firewall with an Uzi held tight with both arms. The shooting continued for what seemed like hours. We hugged the floor of the motor home and prayed for dear life.

All of a sudden the shooting stopped and voices in Spanish could be heard yelling in the distance. Ramon and the MFJP immediately jumped up. The passenger in front pushed the dead driver out on the ground, started the motor home and drove it

Thin White Lines

slowly up toward the main house and stopped. Ramon loaded an M-16 with scope and handed it to me relating the shooters had run out of ammo and were sending runners to the house. The 50-caliber machine gun had jammed.

Ramon removed the LAW confiscated from Pablo's house, from under the left seat, jumped out the rear of the mobile home and quickly fired it into the second floor of the main building. The center of the second floor lit up instantaneously like a fireball and immediately the fire went out and black smoke bellowed into the air. He told me to shoot the suspects on the hill on the right. I pointed the M-16 toward the hill on the right, but could see no irregularity of outline. I scanned the hill and again could not see the shooters. I brought the scope back to the crest of the hill and noted a shiny object reflecting from the sun, Ramon, screamed, "Shoot, shoot, shoot those cocks___rs Beenum, shoot." I laid a base of fire in the area of the shining object. Almost instantly three men fell to the ground tearing down a camouflage blind, revealing two other shooters with their rifles pointed directly toward our position. I placed the cross hairs of the scope of my rifle on the shooter on the left, steadied it on the bridge of his nose, stopped breathing momentarily and squeezed the trigger gently with a burst of 3-4 rounds. I saw his head jerk back quickly and violently. I then focused on the other shooter, placed the cross hairs of the scope on his left shoulder pectoral area and squeezed a short burst and watched his body jerk back violently, indicating that there were no live shooters on the north front hill. Contemporaneously the other MFJPs obtained positions under the left side of the mobile home and laid a continuous base of fire in the direction of the shooters on the left bank. Ramon loaded the LAW three times and fired three antitank weapons into the main building. A few minutes later three runners came out of the building. Two ran toward the right hill carrying ammo. The other ran to my left. I placed the cross hairs of the scope 6" in front of the first runner and fired a quick burst at his chest and watched him fall quickly to the ground. I repeated the same on the second runner and watched his body jerk violently backwardly and collapse. We fired on the small shacks on the right and left of the main building until nearly exhausting our ammo. The whole valley was filled with smoke from burning buildings and gunshots.

When it was all over, three MFJPs were dead, 17 bad guys were dead, and 40,000 pounds of marijuana, a huge cache of arms were seized. Only two people knew who had killed seven of the bad guys. According to Ramon, he killed all of them. I thought Pablo would again be physically punished by Ramon and had begun to feel somewhat sorry for him.

Ramon asked if he could see one of my guns. I reached into my crouch area removed my 5-shot aluminum weight .38 caliber "Colt Cobra" loaded with 150 grain soft lead jacketed rounds. Ramon cursed and spoke angrily and violently to Pablo and occasionally struck him about the head and chest with my weapon. Pablo did not plea nor did he answer the questions posed to him. Ramon took Pablo to the back of the building between two tanker trucks, made him take off his pants, underwear and placed him in a bending position. He then called me over to ensure that Pablo's chest was almost parallel to the ground. He then came around to the front and ordered Pablo to lower his head. Ramon told me to stay up front and keep my eyes on Pablo's forehead. He then took my service revolver, placed in the area of Pablo's rectum and fired two rounds. Both bullets exited Pablo's head. He fell to the ground dead.

Pablo had committed the "death wish" according to Ramon. He had given the impression that he was cooperating but ultimately gave the order for the ambush. He had deceived the law, especially after being arrested. According to Ramon, Pablo had killed before and killing him was more than justified. Justified for we are now certain that Pablo would never kill again. Ramon advised that he had sentenced Pablo to death for leading us into an ambush.

En route back to the base, I fell somewhere between deep sleep and a blue funk. I could vaguely hear Ramon talking to Cesar in the cab of the motor home. I then started recalling that I had just killed seven bad guys and then had a daytime nightmare. To make matters even worse, the spook I had seen on the first bust was waiting for us at the Army base. He merely spoke briefly to me and moved amongst the MFJP and soldiers as though he was one of them.

There is eeriness from killing a man that is almost indescribable. There is always the thought that you have taken a human life, irregardless of the circumstances, coupled with a strong feeling of guilt, a feeling, rather a sense that despite how treacherous, how dangerous, how killing that person alleviated you and other law enforcement officers from being killed, that your taking of a human life, irregardless how legally justified, that doing so is wrong. There are always subsequent nightmares of the deceased having some good about him and being loved by his family and others. Those dreams came to me twice en route with the killing bullet always leaving the barrel of the gun in slow motion, taking forever to reach the target. The dying starred at me innocently in the eyes begging me not to kill them that they did not deserve to die. The dying always atoned for all wrong doings and even asked God for forgiveness. They told me that I did not have to kill them, that I could have shot the gun out of their hands or shot them in the arm or leg. Whether shot in the head, heart or leg, all the dying always had a sucking chest wounds with part of their abdominal visceral exposed to me. It seemed as though they lived forever breathing laboriously, with painful rales and ronchi. Even you begin to forget the terrifying sounds of their bullets passing Close to your body at 4500 feet per second. You, before the kill, start pondering alternative actions you could have taken. Maybe you could call the bullet back, pull it back abort it from reaching its target.

On this day, en route back to the army base, is when I had this daytime nightmare twice. I had killed seven men in one day. Perhaps it would not have been so sad had others fired at the group. I was the only shooter. Almost immediately after my first shots three men had fallen from behind the blind and at a distance of about 100 yards I could hear their death rattle. The sounds echoed in my ear.

Upon arrival at the army base, plans were formulated to utilize the military in taking down the second ranch. Ramon asked, "Beenum are you going to saddle up and ride with the posse or have you had enough for the day?"

"I think I will sit this one out Ramon, you know the kind of paperwork we have to complete in these cases", I replied.

"Yeah, you guys have to write a what do you call it, a Sears catalogue in all of your cases. Our reports will be completed today. You will have all the information you need." Ramon assured. I watched Ramon and his men depart the base in a cloud of dust followed by two trucks of Mexican soldiers.

CHAPTER 4

DURING THE EARLY 60s, the CIA and other governmental agencies trained expatriated Cubans, Puerto Ricans, Dominicans, Mexicans and other South Americans for insertion into Cuba for a proposed Coupe d'Etat against Fidel Castro. These Soldiers of Fortune (SOF), were trained in hand-to-hand combat, guerilla warfare, special forces tactics, intelligence acquiring human, signal, imagery and last but not least alternative income acquiring tactics from legal and illegal sources.

"The Company" which had grossly underestimated Castro's strength and intelligence capabilities inserted the SOFs into Cuba. They were quickly beaten, many slain and thousands were held as prisoners of war; some were killed for their disloyalty to Cuba.

Others were punished unmercifully, maimed, crippled and released. Castro used most of the captured SOF as bargaining chips, which he later traded for tractors. The CIA delivered or caused to be delivered large numbers of tractors to Cuba for the release of about 60,000 SOF who had no monetary reward forthcoming or job guaranty. Like many survivalists, about 70% of those released re-entered into the American society with little difficulties, 10,000 to 15,000 opted the easy out, the alternative income acquiring method with many robbing dopers, dope houses, stealing shipments of dope and selling it on the street. This went on for several years until the traffickers got smart, hired bodyguards, henchmen, killers, full and part -time and fought back. The SOF then went full time into drug trafficking, initially starting with cocaine and venturing into heroin, marijuana and dangerous drugs.

The BNDD launched "Operation Eagle" to immobilize these well-trained SOF. Every Cooperating Individual (CI) available was questioned regarding Cuban/Puerto Rican and Hispanic former Bay of Pigs invaders being involved in drug trafficking. A major effort was undertaken to dismantle the CIA trained drug trafficking groups that had set up camp in most major cities in the U.S. with a pipeline for heroin, cocaine and marijuana funneled through Mexico.

A CI from Compton, California cut Special Agent (SA) Joe Gordon into the LA based group. Intelligence collated indicated that there were about 35 significant Cuban/Puerto Rican CIA trained drug traffickers in the Los Angeles area. Joe and I formulated a plan to knock off at least 25 of these major traffickers.

We assumed an undercover role of Big John and Joe; two major Black Los Angeles based dope dealers. Through the CI, we met and negotiated with a go-between for the proposed purchase of a four piece (4 ounce) heroin sample as a prelude to subsequent multiple kilogram heroin purchases. We knew that BNDD, operating on a shoestring budget, would not allow multiple kilogram heroin purchases to walk. Consequently, we had to negotiate up the ladder to the highest trafficker in the organization before spending a significant amount of money.

Joe and I negotiated up to the main L. A. based dealer, Jimmy Raville, a Black Cuban who lived in a swank house in Carson,

Thin White Lines

California. We ordered a kilogram of heroin, advising that we would come back the next day to buy 10 kilos. A white Cuban was scheduled to deliver the heroin to us in the Silverlake district of Los Angeles. We picked up foot, stationary and mobile counter-surveillance before the delivery. The deliveryman drove by us twice in a white Chevrolet, circled the block, drove gingerly past us to the corner, parked, exited his car and started walking toward the undercover car. Joe and I exited the U/C car. I grabbed the $12,000 official government funds and we walked toward him. As we came near, we could see he was carrying a brown paper bag in his left hand with his right hand resting on a .45 pistol in his waistband. The deliveryman appeared frightened but businesslike. There was no doubt in either of our minds he was a killer; he would not hesitate to kill. Perhaps he was frightened of our sizes, which aggravated the situation. Joe and I walked toward him. As we came near, he readied the .45 automatic and we heard the hammer as it was pulled back. The first thought in my mind was a possible hit for the $12,000. I immediately started thinking taking this crook "10-7" (out of service—kill him). Upon meeting, Joe extended his right hand and simultaneously shook the crook's hand and stating,

"Hey man I'm Joe; this is my partner Big John. How are you doing?"

The delivery man removed his hand from the gun and exchanged handshakes with us and

We all relaxed. About that time a car containing two white surveillant agents passed. The deliveryman stated,

"There seems to be a lot of heat in the area. Our people (counter-surveillance) had picked up several cars with two guys each riding around in the area. Let's get this one over and talk later you got the money?" He asked.

"Yeah, let us see the package," I responded. The deliveryman then handed me the brown bag. I examined it and noted a brown rock substance weighing approximately one kilogram with a strong acid smell similar to heroin. I handed the $12,000 to Joe and kept the heroin. Joe handed the $12,000 to the deliveryman. We exchanged farewells and left the area. While departing the area, I performed a presumptive field test on the heroin and noted a positive reaction for heroin. We drove back to the office, met with surveillant agents, processed the evidence, forwarded to the laboratory and prepared preliminary reports. Joe and I negotiated several subsequent times with the Cubans for the purpose of delivery of ten kilograms of heroin.

Prior to the proposed delivery date, orders came down to do the nationwide roundup of all the suspects in "Operation Eagle." The 10-kilogram heroin seizure was aborted. Like good obeying soldiers, we rounded up the Los Angeles-based Cubans. We arrested less than 21 in the Loss Angeles area and less than 1,000 nationwide. I don't recall any subsequent intensive enforcement efforts directed toward these superbly trained alternative income-acquiring soldiers of fortune.

Although it will never be acknowledged, they were trained at the request of an U.S. Government Agency. During that training process, the focus was so intensely directed toward obtaining a desired result—removal of Castro from office—that a clandestinely created monster, a monster that today preys heavily on the weak and strong communities of America continues to thrive and eat at its core like a cancer.

The dope thing grew strong all over America. Many soldiers returning to the States after a tour in Vietnam were addicted to heroin, had strong marijuana abuse habits; non-veterans were following the lead of the soldiers; they too were doing a thing called "chasing the dragon," smoking number 3 Southeast Asian heroin on aluminum. Thai sticks hit the streets and became fashionable in all communities. White heroin number 4 from the Golden Triangle, Laos-Burma and Thailand, started showing up on the west coast, then made its way east. I did a three day undercover caper up in Bakersfield, California for a kilo and a half of heroin for $35,000. The crooks told me they had to travel back to North Carolina but would return as soon as possible. I flashed the $35,000 to three Black crooks, then checked into a hotel to await delivery. I provided them with a telephone number to the hotel and my room number where I could be reached.

I needed the three-day rest for I had had two wisdom teeth extracted that day, drove from Los Angeles to Bakersfield, met with the crooks, negotiated and flashed $35,000. My mouth was swollen and the painkiller the dentist prescribed did not ease the pain. On the third day, during the early morning hours, the crooks delivered approximately 3 pounds of white heroin to me in my hotel room and were arrested in lieu of payment by surveillant agents. Initially we thought it was a burn but it immediately responded presumptive positive to the field test. Since this was one of the first and largest white heroin seizures, the heroin was hand delivered to the laboratory in San Francisco. About three days later, I received a telephone call from the analyzing chemist advising that the heroin was 100% pure.

Further investigation revealed the heroin source was Leslie Atkinson, a former black U.S. Army Sergeant heavily involved in heroin trafficking as a soldier. His partner was identified as Herman Jackson, another Black former U.S. Army Sergeant.

I learned, or rather experienced, my first disparate treatment on the part of the BNDD. Almost all of the agents involved, some had minor involvement were given monetary incentive awards for the case, from the agent that wrote the surveillant reports to those in suck ass positions with management. I did not even receive a letter of commendation or award.

During the same period I was assigned Duty Agent for a week. The BNDD office had relocated to a two story federal building on West 6th Street, diagonally across the street from Central Receiving Hospital. About the second day, I was called to the reception area to handle a duty call. At the desk, I was introduced as the Duty Agent to a neatly dressed middle aged Caucasian male that looked very much like former President Harry Truman. He wore a gray plaid suit, beautiful matching necktie, a narrow brim Stetson felt hat, highly polished shoes, and bifocal glasses and his fingernails were neatly manicured. His hair was neatly cut and he spoke like a college professor, initially using numerous polysyllabic words. Shortly into the conversation he changed to using words he apparently thought I would have less difficulty understanding. The man related that drugs were an awful cancer that was eating at the core of the American cardiovascular system, that certainly more efforts should be deployed to eradicate this great evil from our society. The tone of his voice and the aura about him indicated that he was a gentleman with money; that he was one of those Americans who were fortunate to have been born with mountains of riches; that he had never experienced hunger or the want of any material thing.

We sat in the interview room and chatted for about 15 minutes. He related that he lived in a mansion in Beverly Hills on Doheny. I guessed his age between 60-65 years old. He was a patriotic man that expressed an appreciation for America, Americans, the American flag, soldiers, the police, and certainly he had nothing but high admiration for all crime fighters, especially drug agents. He related how dangerous he believed drug law enforcement was and related that he took his hat off to all drug law enforcement officers.

After about twenty minutes of this heart warming and enlightening conversation, I finally decided to ask this man what BNDD could do for him or what was his purpose for contacting us. The man turned directly toward me, looked me straight in the eyes and stated, "I am glad you asked. I hope you will believe what I am about to tell you for it is as true as I am sitting in this room."

Immediately I began to think that I was about to be introduced to the biggest case of my career. I adjusted my seat, pulled out my pen and prepared to write and asked, "Sir please tell me. I will believe you." I assured him.

He stated, "Adolph Hitler, is alive, in good health and is living in Beverly Hills. He has dyed his hair blond and has several close friends that are Jewish."

The man looked me sternly in the eyes for a few seconds. I did not know whether he had told a joke and somewhere I had missed the punch line until he asked seriously, "You don't believe me do you?"

I was speechless for several seconds. The only reply I could make was to ask, "Have you seen him? Have you seen Hitler in Beverly Hills? Do you know his address?"

The man looked at me very seriously and answered, "Yes, I have seen him several times. The last time I saw him was a week ago at the Chalet Gourmet house on Sunset Boulevard. I do not know the number of his house or the street name but I can point it out to you today, right now."

"Okay sir, that is very interesting. I will see what we can do with this valuable information. I cannot go with you right now. Can we do it tomorrow?" I asked.

"Sure we can do it today or tomorrow, I have plenty of time," he assured.

I left the room a few minutes and returned with another agent. The man added, "Another thing I think you should know. The Russians are causing 35% of the babies in America to be aborted. They use a laser beam that is directed at women in their first trimester. The laser sometimes burns these women and causes them to have ugly varicose veins on their legs," he related.

"Sir that is very interesting, do you have any information about drugs or dope?" I asked.

"No just about Hitler and the Russians aborting 1/3 of our babies. You know the Russians have the most powerful laser in the world. It is strong enough to dry up the Pacific Ocean", he related.

"Sir, before we moved here, the FBI was in this building. All of the information you have related falls under the jurisdiction of the FBI. We are the Bureau of Narcotics and Dangerous Drugs, not the FBI," I advised him.

"Well, the people over at the hospital told me you were the FBI", he related.

"No sir, they moved to West Wilshire, to 11000 West Wilshire Boulevard." I advised.

"Well I guess I'll have to go over there. You are such a pleasant person to talk to and I was thinking that I would be working with you on this information."

I faked calling the FBI and pointed the man in the direction of their office, approximately ten miles away. I watched him leave the building, walk over to Central Receiving Hospital where he entered a chauffeur driven Lincoln and departed the area west bound on Sixth Street.

The next day I responded to the reception area for a duty call and met a very tall masculine, but attractive middle-aged grayish blond lady. After the initial introduction she related her name was Grace Istanbullyan of Russian extraction. Grace related that she had been referred to us from across the street (Central Receiving Hospital). We talked in generalities for a while and I noted that she was content and pleased at what insignificant topics we discussed. We talked randomly for about twenty minutes and Grace alerted me that I was not complying with BNDD policy regarding interviewing females. Grace related that there are aliens invading California and zapping people with ray guns. She raised her long shirt up to her pelvic area and tried to show me a mark on her inner left thigh where she had been zapped. I immediately excused myself for a few minutes, got another agent to witness the interview and rejoined Grace in the interview room.

Grace again raised her skirt up to her pubic area and tried to show us the mark where she had been zapped by the aliens. She wore no panties and pointed to an imaginary scar about 2" below where her left leg joined her hip. We looked but could see nothing irregular on her skin. Her conversation went on and on about how other women were being zapped by aliens. When I asked Grace if the aliens were possibly using laser beams to cause abortions, she immediately dropped her skirt, looked at both of us with extra wide open eyes and asked, "How do you know? You guys don't have anything to do with them do you?" We were both somewhat dumb founded because the other agent was aware of the assertions made by the Truman look-a-like.

I recalled a similar incident when I was a policeman, where my partner used a flashlight beam on a man who was seeing a little man flitting about the floor with sparks flying from his shoes. I went upstairs got a flashlight and asked Grace if she wanted us to remove the zapped scar from her thigh. She agreed. We had her hold up her skirt and we turned the lights out I flashed the beam of the flashlight on the imaginary scar advising Grace that when I flicked the light beam off and on three times that the scar would disappear. After three flicks, according to Grace, the scar had disappeared. She remarked, "That's amazing, you know my doctor tried all kinds of medicines and he could not heal the scar. That's amazing." Grace left the office very appreciative of the cure. I felt certain that we would never see her again.

A week later I received a ten-page letter from Grace that had apparently been slid under the entrance door. The handwriting was legible and appeared to be that of a teacher. I failed to find a complete sentence in the entire letter. I was able to discern that Grace was a friend that we had helped in a way she could never repay. I surmised that Grace was one of those non compos mentis persons who had no family, no friends and certainly posed no significant threat to herself and only a bother, not a physical threat, to others.

The BNDD office became plagued with visitors from Central Receiving Hospital; became a referral from the hospital staff. During my second duty agent assignment, I was called to the reception area to meet another walk-in source of information. I met a neatly dressed Black male and escorted him into the interview room. I called another agent in to assist. I introduced myself as Agent Sutton to the walk-in. He introduced himself as "Bonny."

"Bonny what can we do for you?" I asked.

"It is a long story. Do you have the time?"

"Yes, all we have is time Bonny. What's on your mind'?" I asked.

"Well, there is this little rich Mexican motherf____r named El Flacco that lives up in Altadena. He's been dealing dope like forty going west. You know he's going huckly-buck dealing all kinds of dope. He'll sell anything as long as it is dope, heroin, cocaine, marijuana, pills—you name it as long as it is dope. Man I tell you he's going huckly buck and he's brazen. He seems to get some sort of sexual thrill out of it and he likes to deal dope right around police stations. He told me he just did a 5 kilo coke case in front of Parker Center, that it went as smooth as owl shit."

"Do you know him well enough to duke (introduce) someone into him?" I asked.

"Yeah, I could duke you or this white guy or both of you into him. The guy will sell dope to the police. He's just that bold. Man this guy has balls bigger than a brass ass monkey. He's easy to take down."

"Bonny, let us process you. We will do a background on this guy El Flacco. Try to set up a deal to introduce me to him for a multiple kilogram heroin or cocaine deal. Give me a six-hour notice, that is, give me enough time in advance to put a good posse together and we will do the deal. Bonny have you been cracked before?" I asked.

"Only for traffic tickets and child support, nothing major."

"What is your connection to El Flacco?" I asked.

"He was my oldest boys connect. My boy took a fall for him

Thin White Lines

and now he doesn't want to pay him as he promised. That's my connection with the motherf_____r."

"Okay, Bonny go ahead and make the arrangements and we'll take this shit bird down okay?" I said.

We ran a preliminary to identify Flacco. The next day, at noon, Bonny telephoned and advised that Flacco had a shipment of drugs in and was ready to do business. According to Bonny, Flacco would not advise if he had heroin, cocaine or pills other than he had a significant shipment and he was ready to do business. I instructed Bonny to determine the type of drugs Flacco had and schedule a meeting for 6:00 p.m. that day.

Bonny called back and advised that Flacco wanted to have a sit down chat before finalizing a deal. Flacco had agreed to meet with us at LIPO's Restaurant in Chinatown at 3:00 p.m.

I met with Bonny at 2:20 p.m. He was unable to determine the kind of drug that Flacco had for sale. We entered a flashy Cadillac Eldora do with wide whitewall tires and drove over to LI PO's and entered at about 2:40 p.m. to await the arrival of Flacco. At about 2:55 p.m., two neatly dressed well polished, Mexican males wearing sunglasses, one tall and muscular, the other medium height and stocky like a weight lifter, entered the restaurant and without being seated, walked over to the walls, returned to the front and exited. Each had a noticeably bulge under their left armpit. Bonny advised that they were likely Flacco's bodyguards or henchmen. A few minutes later, the two males re-entered the restaurant and requested seats to our rear. A neatly dressed well-groomed Mexican male entered with a very attractive; young Mexican female with dyed blond hair. Bonny advised, "That's him with the cute chick in the red dress." Flacco spoke softly paused with the Host for a few seconds then joined us at the table. Close up the female was more attractive than at first glance and smelled perfumy.

After exchanging pleasantries, Bonny introduced me as Beenum to Flacco. After a brief general conversation I advised,

"I hear you got the girl (cocaine) and boy (heroin) good Flacco. I just raised and I am trying to get down again (fresh out of prison trying to re-enter the drug trafficking business)."

Flacco's response was shocking to me and almost caused me to gag on a cup of coffee.

"Yeah what's you name again, Bee, Bee, Bee..."

"Beenum. Beenum, Flacco. Beenum," I advised.

"Yeah, Beenum, I got it all good heroin, coke, uppers, downers, and on occasions I have PCP and LSD. I'm what the feds call a polydrug trafficker, a major violator," he advised.

My immediate reaction was that I was dealing with an undercover officer from State Bureau of Narcotic Enforcement (BNE), Los Angeles Police Department, Los Angeles Sheriff's office or maybe even U.S. Customs.

I directed the conversation to not wanting to be busted that Flacco appeared to be the police to me. Flacco countered by accusing me of possibly being the police. The subject went on for about five minutes until I suggested that we were having a nice Chinese meal and suggested that we forget the deal. Flacco disagreed and related that when he moves it's for money, that he had come down to meet and finalize a deal. He then related that I probably would like the product that he wanted to move right away. I told Flacco that I did not want to ever discuss business with him until I was assured that he was not the police. Bonny tried to vouch that Flacco was not the police. I insisted that I was not certain that he was not; that the phrase he had said about the feds caused me a lot of concern.

After bickering back and forth, even after ordering food, Flacco had a solution. He asked his girlfriend for her Bible. She reached inside of a red purse and handed Flacco a small Bible. Flacco placed his left hand on the Bible, raised his right hand and stated, "I swear before God almighty that I am not the police, nor am I working for the police, so help me God."

He then handed me the Bible and asked me to swear to the

same. I complied. Afterwards, Flacco related that if either turned out to be the police that little ritual would prevent prosecution. I became more alarmed of Flacco's identity but let it fade and asked him how much good coke and heroin he had available for sale. Flacco related that he had not yet restocked his supply. He further related that a biker and a trucker had just stood him up. As a result, he had a lot of pills that he would sell dirt cheap to get them off his hands.

"What kind are they?" I asked.

"Mini-bennies, made in the U.S.A., shipped to Mexico, then smuggled back up to Los Angeles. The best you can buy Amigo, Dextroamphetamine sulfates. They'll keep a motherf____r awake for weeks. Why don't you take them off my hands, Beenum? I'll give you a good deal for them." He advised.

"How much? How much do you want for them?" I asked.

"Well, I was supposed to get $150 per thousand from the trucker and $160 per thousand from the biker for about $300,000. I'll let you have the whole shipment for $200,000. All 2,000,000 pills, 2,000 jars, a thou to the jar."

"I'll take them, if you will give me a good deal on five kilos of cocaine and two kilos of heroin when your shipment comes in." I advised. I wondered if this was some kind of test.

"It's a deal. When do you want to do it?" He asked.

"Hey, Flacco, let's get it over as soon as possible. Let's do it tonight." I urged.

Flacco agreed to do the deal that night and requested that I bring only $100 and $50 notes.

"Okay, Beenum, let's do it tonight at 7:30 p.m. Let's meet on the parking lot at 7:30 p.m. at Charlie Brown's restaurant off the Pomona Freeway and Rosemead Boulevard." We exchanged farewells. Bonny and I drove from the area, met with surveillant agents and advised them what had transpired.

We went back to the office where a heated discussion occurred regarding the unavailability of a $200,000 flash roll that day. I convinced surveillance that I would convince Flacco to deliver the 2,000,000 mini-bennies without the need of a flash roll. Bonny thought I was crazy and strongly advised that the deal would not go without the money. He was afraid of getting "waxed" (killed), if things did not go right. Bonny was certain the two subjects that entered the restaurant before Flacco were his henchmen, "stone killers." I tried to calm him by advising that if any fireworks erupted that it would be spitting from my guns, that I would be illuminating the sky with fireworks, not Flacco or his henchmen. I instructed Bonny that if fireworks erupted to immediately fall to the ground, that I would take it from there. Despite my encouragement and confidence, I believe Bonny viewed my remarks as the false bravado of a seemingly self-assured undercover agent.

I stressed to Bonny that I was not afraid—that if he wanted to he could sit in the undercover car and that I would take it from there. Bonny nervously joined me in the undercover Cadillac and we drove over to Charlie Brown's restaurant on Rosemead Boulevard, just off the Pomona Freeway in Montebello. Shortly after we parked, Flacco and the female drove up in a black, white topped Mercedes SL190. Two Mexican males, driving a Dodge Challenger, followed them onto the lot. There appeared to be a trail car cruising the area. The trail car, a 1964 Chevrolet, occupied by two male Mexicans pulled into the parking lot, proceeded to the rear and parked in the southwest corner facing the Pomona Freeway. The two occupants exited and entered the restaurant as Flacco drove gingerly around the parking lot. They parked next to the undercover car. I yelled over, "I am ready Flacco, you got the materials?"

"Yeah, I am ready do you have the ducats?' he asked.

"Yeah, I got it let me see the material and we can get it over very quickly." Flacco continued to gaze at passers-by in the lot and related that the material was in the Chevrolet. From the undercover car, I could see boxes in the rear seat area and the rear of the Chevrolet set low on the ground like a low rider. When I exited the undercover vehicle Flacco told me to get back into my car and stand by for a few minutes. I rejoined Bonny in the undercover car and sat for about five minutes watching Flacco inspect the parking lot. The two occupants of the Challenger parked on the northwest corner of the parking lot facing the load car remained in the car with the engine running. A few minutes later the occupants of the Chevrolet, exited Charlie Brown's, entered the Chevrolet (load car) and drove from the area. Flacco told me to follow him and drove from the parking lot. I followed Flacco westbound on the Pomona Freeway for a distance. We pulled off the freeway then drove north in a circuitous route until we arrived about a block and a half from East Los Angeles Sheriff's station.

Flacco parked and walked up to the undercover car and told me to walk with him. I got out and waked with Flacco toward the Sheriff's station about half way up the street, I saw the load car park on the street ahead. We walked up to the load car. Flacco handed me the keys. I entered the rear seat area, inspected the boxes in the rear and noted approximately 700,000 or more mini-bennies. I opened the trunk and examined six large boxes of mini- bennies approximately 1,300,000. 1 closed the trunk and advised Flacco that I would go back to get the $200,000, pay him and make arrangements for the cocaine and heroin deal in a few days. I then lit a Kool filter king cigarette, took three puffs and tossed it against the curb (arrest signal).

Almost immediately, tires screeched, agents jumped out of cars and snatched up Flacco and the occupants of the Chevrolet. The occupants of the Dodge Challenger led the agents in a brief chase but were apprehended a short distance away in heavy traffic.

Two million mini- bennies were seized, believed to be the largest undercover seizure of mini- bennies.

Unbeknownst to me an official from Washington, D.C. Headquarters was riding along and experienced the chase. Consequently, I was recommended for a monetary Special Achievement Award for the case.

On the following day we presented Flacco et al, for arraignment before the U.S. Magistrate and requested $250,000 bail for Flacco and $100,000 bail for the other defendants. Bail for Flacco was set at $25,000 corporate surety and $15,000 C/S for the other defendants. That day Flacco posted cash bail and became an instant fugitive. The word on the streets was that Flacco had gone into the interior of Mexico, grew a beard, put on a lot weight and would never be apprehended.

A lot of out-of-staters came to California, saw a laid back life style, a kind of "laissez-faire" lifestyle where even the police were neatly dressed and rode around in highly polished clean cars, very few were fat and only a few security guards were seen on foot patrol.

Opportunists from Texas, Arkansas, Louisiana, Oklahoma, Tennessee, Missouri, Illinois, Michigan, Minnesota, Wisconsin, Indiana, Ohio and other places in the Midwest and East moved west to sunny Southern California, a place where the sun shone long hours, almost all year.

With this crowd came bands of expatriated Cubans that had entered the U.S. via Miami and were developing anonymity with a fast moving young crowd. Some were murielitos; others were remnants of the Bay of Pigs invasion, the alternate income acquirers.

Drugs became fashionable all over California, spread north and deliberated into a pandemic. Out of the drug culture developed a major cancer, an underground economy that continues to eat at the very core of the American economy. Numerous entrepreneurs dropped legitimate businesses and entered into a more profiting enterprise—drug trafficking. Farmers in various parts of the U. S. stopped harvesting corn and started harvesting marijuana and/or leasing fertile land to marijuana growers for large amounts of money. Some growers took to growing marijuana on abandoned land; land involved in crop rotation (restoration) programs, U.S. Park, U.S. Forest, state and city lands.

Prior to this time, Mexico had produced the best marijuana. Most of it was smuggled into the U.S. via small aircraft that made clandestine landings at various airports, some manned, some unmanned, some with illuminated landing strips, others unlighted. Rialto, Compton, Hawthorne, Barstow, Daggett, Elsinore, Flabob, and Riverside were some of the major smuggling ports of entry from Mexico. World War II pilots, new pilots, and novices, purchased, leased and/or stole vintage DC-3 aircraft, went south and returned back to the states with ton quantities of marijuana and 100 pound quantities of cocaine and lesser quantities of heroin. When airports became hot, the smugglers resorted to landing/smuggling drugs into the U.S. from Mexico by landing on dry lake beds in the Mojave Dessert around Apple Valley, Lucerne, Hesperia, Adelanto, Victorville, El Mirage, Helendale, Hodge, Lenwood, Vermo, Newberry Springs, Yucca Valley, Joshua Tree and Twenty-nine Palms. Soggy dry lake beds were frequent landing strips during the day and during various night hours from sunset to early sunrise. During darkness the dry lake beds were illuminated with high beam lights of delivery campers on each end awaiting their loads. Small aircraft often arrived loaded with marijuana from the end of the fuselage to the dashboard of the right co-pilot's seat, providing the pilot that often flew on vision only a 90 degree scope of vision.

After smuggling a big load, the pilots secured their aircraft at a legitimate airport, drove down to one of the beach towns, had a drink, flashed a little coke to a barfly then bedded down with her for the night. The amount of money produced in this underground economy was in the hundred billions, mostly U.S. dollars in $100 and $50 denominations. In batches of millions they flowed from the United States into foreign bank accounts like an unregulated river; the monies flowed out of the country with no tangible asset realized. Often these multiple 100 millions changed hands four, five and sometimes six times before the U.S. came close to realizing any tax benefit. Even today there is still an uncontrolled large amount of U.S. dollars flowing in the underground economy with a significant quantity flowing out of the country into secret, clandestine accounts of traffickers committing offenses against the United States.

Along with the huge amounts of money involved in the underground economy came crimes of omissions and corruption. Our South and Central American law enforcement counterparts began to acquire large amounts of money, often more than they could legally make in a lifetime, to not see a particular act or not be at a location at a designated time. Bribery became widespread and spilled over into the U.S.

As it related to the amount of U.S. money flowing in the underground drug economy, the Central Intelligence Agency (CIA) was burdened with that responsibility. The CIA was also tasked with the responsibility of determining marijuana, coca, and opium production in source countries; to supplement its budget, it is believed in certain circles that the CIA has the responsibility to be involved in alternative income acquiring activities.

In part, because of the appearance of a lack of adequate police in California, its geographical makeup, cosmopolitan makeup, drug dealers, potential drug dealers, influencers and financiers moved into California in hordes. The dismantling of the French heroin producers and smugglers by law enforcement made Mexico ideal for the production of lower grade heroin for importation into the United States, Canada and throughout the world market. Heroin production in laboratories in Culiacan and Matzatlan caused these cities to become known as heroin producing capitals in Mexico.

Of the hordes of newcomers to California, some attempted legal jobs; others tried to get rich quickly by dealing dope. Several arrestees, when questioned regarding how they got into the dope business, related being disenchanted trying to be a movie star. Some had been bit actors in subplots; others were passersby in atmospheric scenes. They went into the dope business to make up for failed acting careers. Several related they wanted to make enough money dealing dope to produce their own movie; some related having drug addictions and habituations beyond their means to sustain.

One of the oddest newcomers to California was one Edward Kassaka also known as Hollywood Eddie, (AKA) Eddie. Eddie was one of the dumbest, slowest talking New Yorkers I ever met. He appeared shy and when he spoke he was most naive and wanting to please. Eddie did not like confrontations and would have been a very good customer service officer for some big department store like Sears, J.C. Penny or K-Mart.

Eddie had moved to California from New York. It was unknown what he did in New York. He came to California with a little money and with the intent of making several big scores in the drug business. He was an avowed Catholic. In reviewing background information on him, he had the misfortune to be praying aloud in a Catholic Church in San Fernando Valley. Next to Eddie at the time was an U.S. Customs CI. The CI heard Eddie praying to the Almighty to allow him to make several big scores in the dope business and he promised to retire, amend his ways and be a good tithing Catholic thereafter, that he would thereafter say ten Hail Mary's daily and walk, rather go in the way of our savior Jesus Christ.. The CI thought it was hilarious to one point and realizing that Eddie was not an intoxicated person and was joking with his friend who was praying with him. The CI became very irate and decided that he would assist Eddie for a broker's fee, and then turn him into U.S. Customs for a moiety.

After they exited the church, the CI befriended Eddie and inquired about how serious he was. Eddie assured him that he was serious, invited the CI to his apartment where he flashed $15,000 to substantiate his seriousness about the dope trade.

The CI made the necessary contacts with U.S. Customs, then traveled to Tijuana, B.C. Mexico and brokered a 200 pound marijuana deal between Eddie, Eddie's friend and a local Tijuana marijuana trafficker. Eddie and his friend paid the CI $1,500 for his services. The CI went back to the Tijuana dealer and was paid a $1,000 finder's fee. The CI contacted U.S. Customs and dimed Eddie out (informed on him-talked the police) and was promised $2500 upon the arrest and seizure in the case. Eddie left his Chevrolet in Tijuana. On the next day, he was telephoned at a hotel in National City and told where to pickup his car loaded with 200 lbs. of marijuana. Eddie and his friend took a taxi over to Chula Vista picked up his marijuana-laden car and then drove northbound on Interstate 5.

About two miles north of Encinitas, U.S. Custom's agents surveilling Eddie and his friend, activated a cut-off switch that caused Eddie's car to lose all electricity and stop. Surveilling customs agents approached Eddie and his friend and noted a strong order of marijuana coming from the car. Eddie and his friend were placed under arrest; 200 pounds of marijuana and the car were seized.

About two months later, I received a telephone call from a BNDD CI relating that Hollywood Eddie, a white boy living in an apartment on Van Nuys Boulevard in the valley, was selling multiple ounce quantities of cocaine like he had a license. According to the CI, he had never seen a multiple ounce cocaine dealer as open and loose and as Hollywood Eddie. The CI further related that Eddie would soon be busted because he has a lot of foot traffic in and out of his apartment and that he would deliver a quantity of four ounces or more to the buyer. The CI added that he was in Hollywood Eddie's apartment yesterday and saw him in possession of approximately eight pounds of coke, which he was selling on an "as-come" basis from the apartment. I told the CI to make arrangements to introduce me to Hollywood Eddie for a multiple ounce cocaine transaction.

A few minutes later the CI called back and related that I could walk into Hollywood Eddie's cold and cite the name of anybody as a referral; Hollywood Eddie would sell to me. The CI further advised that an ounce of uncut cocaine cost $750, that I could buy three ounces for about $2,000 to $2,100. The CI provided the address and telephone number where Hollywood Eddie could be reached. I put together a lightweight posse and pre-surveillance was initiated on Hollywood Eddie's apartment. A lot of vehicle and foot traffic was observed arriving, entering for a short while then leaving the area.

About two hours later I telephoned Hollywood Eddie and related, "H. E. — Hello" Beenum—"Hello, may I speak to Hollywood Eddie?"

"H.E. — You're talking to him, you sound like a bro. What can I do for you bro?"

"Yeah, I am Beenum, I am a bro. One of my non-bro friends tells me you got the girl real good (has cocaine)", I remarked.

"What if I do have the girl? What do you want to do, just talk about it?"

"No man, I want to cop (buy) three or four pieces (ounces)," I advised.

"Hey bro, if you want to cop then you had better hurry on over here. These things are going like Nathan's hot dogs. Shit, you don't know about Nathan's at Coney Island, so that's Greek to you, huh bro?"

"No, I've been to Coney Island. I like the frog legs at Nathan's better than the hot dogs. Hey, what does this have to do with buying three or four pieces?"

Nothing, bro. Why don't you saddle up and ride over before I run out of stock."

"Hey, when you run out of stock, will you be out of business or will you be restocked?" I asked.

"I get my stock in sometimes twice a week. I am not a fly-by-night man. I'm in business for the long haul."

"Okay, I'm on my way. I'll see you in thirty."

About thirty minutes later I arrived at Hollywood Eddie's apartment building, rang the bell to his apartment and identified myself as Beenum to see Hollywood Eddie. I was buzzed into the apartment complex. While approaching Hollywood Eddie's apartment, three males exited examining what appeared to be several ounces of cocaine packaged in rubber contraceptives. As I started to ring the doorbell, a male and female exited Eddie's apartment with cocaine. I walked into the apartment as they were exiting. I could see a man in the kitchen as described as Hollywood Eddie by the CI finishing up a two piece sale to a slick black male and a beautiful longhaired blond in the kitchen. He looked up briefly at me and asked, "How many pieces do you want? What's your name?"

I am Beenum, I called you earlier about the four piece sale." I advised.

"Yeah, yeah, I remember. I am glad you came right over for these things are going faster than I can ounce them out man. I'm going to be out of stock in a little while. My stock boy won't be here for three days," Eddie remarked

I told Hollywood Eddie that he should watch himself that he seemed kind of lax dealing dope. He told me to call him Eddie, not Hollywood Eddie and remarked that the police in California could not catch a dealer if he fell out of the sky. I agreed and found his remark interesting. I was glad I came over as soon as possible for I feared that Hollywood Eddie, so loose with his operation, would certainly be busted in a short while. It was like the CI explained; Hollywood Eddie had opened a cocaine supermarket and was dealing dope like he was immune from arrest. I surmised the slick black guy and the blond with the long hair were from LAPD major narcotic crew.

I copped (purchased) four pieces (ounces) from Hollywood Eddie and made arrangements to buy a pound from him the following week. After copping, I hung around and engaged him in conversation to determine his source. Hollywood Eddie advised that his source were Cubans in New York. He further related that on two previous occasions the couriers ran off with the coke. As a consequence, he had to fly back to New York to score more coke. I advised Hollywood Eddie that I had a partner and that we wanted to cop five or seven kilograms of cocaine. He advised that he could handle the order and advised me to give him a one-day notice when ready. Hollywood Eddie was very straightforward, rather had no problem discussing his operation. He was a slow talker but did not hesitate or show any aversion to discussing drugs. After I had elicited as much information about his operation, I told him that I would bring my partner with me on the next deal. Hollywood Eddie related that he would like to have a sit down negotiations prior to doing a multiple kilogram transaction. We exchanged farewells. I gave Hollywood Eddie a telephone number where I could be reached. While walking to the elevator, two other customers got off and walked to Hollywood Eddie's apartment.

Two days later Special Agent G. Robert "Bob" Warren was putting together a surveillant posse for a pending three-ounce cocaine purchase he had scheduled that afternoon in San Fernando Valley. I joined up with Bob's crew and we initiated surveillance on Denny's restaurant on Van Nuys Boulevard, San Fernando Valley at about 11:30 a.m. At about 11:50 a.m., undercover agent (U/A) Warren arrived entered the restaurant and joined the purported dealer in a booth in the southeast corner of the restaurant. I entered the restaurant to cover Bob and noted that he was sitting with Hollywood Eddie. I immediately left the dining area called a waitress and instructed her to give Bob a note. Bob noted my rapid exit and conversation with the waitress, took a trip to the restroom. I joined him in the restroom and advised that his defendant Eddie was actually Hollywood Eddie a defendant in my case.

Bob rejoined Hollywood Eddie and tried to kill the deal by

asking Eddie to front him a half-pound of cocaine for two weeks. Bob negotiated up to a one pound front thinking this would send Hollywood Eddie en route. Hollywood Eddie told Bob to wait for him a few minutes and left the restaurant. Shortly after he departed, Bob left and put the deal down. Surveillant agents followed Hollywood Eddie from the restaurant to his apartment, then back to Denny's restaurant where he entered carrying a brown paper bag. After not finding U/A Warren, he returned back to his apartment.

Upon returning to the office, I found a message that Hollywood Eddie had called. I placed a telephone call to Hollywood Eddie. He related that he had just been stood up by a guy he was about to front a pound of coke. I asked Hollywood Eddie if he had done business with the guy before and he related that he had not. I then stated, "Hey Eddie, you have done business with me, why not front the pound to me for about a week?"

"Okay. Come on over and I'll front it to you for not more than two weeks okay?"

"Okay, I'll be there in forty-five or an hour, make it an hour." I stated.

"Okay, I'll see you then, bye."

"Bye."

I drove over and took delivery of the pound of coke and decided to introduce another agent to Eddie regarding purchasing five kilograms of coke. I got back to Eddie three days later and introduced him to Special Agent Larry Lusardi. We ordered five kilos of coke from Eddie advising that we had to have it within four days. Eddie placed a telephone call to his source in New York. S/A Lusardi peeked over his shoulder and got the number he dialed and wrote it down in the palm of his hand. Eddie ordered five kilograms of cocaine and advised that he would be traveling to New York for delivery. If we wanted we could travel to New York. Agent Lusardi and I agreed to meet Eddie in New York a day after he arrived. We got a telephone number where

Eddie could be reached in New and agreed on the price of $75,000 for five kilos of cocaine. We exchanged farewells and left.

Agent Lusardi and I drove back to the office and made arrangements to fly a TWA .747 flight non-stop from Los Angeles to JFK International Airport, New York. Two days later we boarded the flight to New York and met with Bob Manning's group at the JFK Hilton hotel.

We obtained a $40,000 flash roll, secured the undercover, surveillant rooms and placed surveillance around the hotel and the location of the telephone number where we were to call Eddie. I placed a telephone call to Eddie at the number and advised, "Hey Eddie we just got in, freshened up, had a bite and we are now ready to roll. We want to cop the five kilos and do a turn around back to L.A. We got hungry customers standing by...."

"Okay Beenum, give me a few minutes to raise up and I'll bring the merchandise right over, okay..."

Agent Lusardi interrupted, "Hey Beenum let me holler at Eddie." I gave Lusardi the telephone and he belted out, 'Hey Eddie my man it is good to hear your voice. Hey man we are ready for Freddy, you are not going to hang us up are you?"

"Oh hell no man, what kind of dope peddler do you think I am? Do you think I'll have you guys come all the way, 3,000 miles to hang you, no, no way."

"Okay, we'll stand by here for a bell from you. Give us a Bell (telephone call) when you are on your way. You know we don't want to let anybody in the room especially since we are carrying all these ducats (dollars), you know what I mean?"

"Yeah, man you know it pays to be careful. New York is five times faster and slicker than L.A. Hey just give me your room number. The only telephone call you will receive will be when I am on my way, okay?" "Okay Eddie, we'll stand by, please don't hang us up 'cause we want to sky up as soon as we cop okay! We are in 16-42."

"16-42 okay, I'll call you when I am on my way to you. It won't be long, so just sit tight. I'll see you later, okay?"

"Okay Eddie, bye, we'll see you later."

"Bye."

Surveillant agents followed Eddie in a rented Mercedes over the Triboro Bridge into Queens, to a high rise apartment building on Sanford Avenue, two blocks off Main, where he entered. About ten minutes later, he exited with two Latin males that appeared to be of Cuban or Puerto Rican descent. They entered the Mercedes and proceeded over toward the JFK Hilton. About ten miles from the Hilton, they pulled over to a pay phone and placed a telephone call to the undercover room.

"Hello."

"Hey Beenum, this is Eddie. I am on my way. There is a small change. We will deliver two kilos now and deliver three more about two hours later okay? My connect is with me, I'll do all of the deal so you guys don't have to worry about meeting anybody strange okay?"

"Sure Eddie, we are standing by. We'll separate $30,000 for two kilos and await your arrival."

About thirty minutes later, Eddie called from the hotel lobby advising that he was coming up. A few minutes later I let him into the room. Immediately upon walking into the room, Eddie handed me a brown paper bag containing a package about the size of a football covered with white adhesive tape. He related that there were four and a half pounds of uncut cocaine in the two-kilo package. Larry and I inspected the package, determined that it possibly contained cocaine and then both gave a prearranged arrest signal. Agents converged into the room from both adjoining rooms and the front door screaming, "Freeze, motherf____r, federal agents, if you move, we'll blow your God D___n brains out!"

We were placed under arrest, handcuffed and taken down to the BNDD office at 90 Church Street. While sitting in the hold-

Thin White Lines

ing cell at 90 Church Street feigning being arrested a white agent, not related to the caper, commenced calling me a dope dealing no good black sleazy motherf___r. When I did not respond to his angry outburst he screamed, "You are one of those quiet black no good motherf___rs. Now you don't want to talk. On the streets you think you are king riding around in Cadillacs with that loud colored fucked up crushed velvet seats and shit."

When I did not react to his outburst, he became angrier. I thought he was over playing his role but there was an aura about this face that indicated he was serious. I had always been told that silence is golden. I remained silent as he continued to lambaste me with unpleasant remarks. Twice he threatened to come in and "kick your black ass, you no good motherf___r". I remained quiet. Eddie, the two Cubans, in adjoining holding cells remained quiet. The agent ranted on and his angered intensified. "Answer me you motherf___r. Don't you hear me talking to you motherf___r?"

I remained quiet, thinking—rather wishing—that he would go away. It was apparent that he was totally unaware of my identity. I remained quiet and on one occasion looked at him as he, screamed at me. This angered him more. After cursing me again, calling me a series of profane names, he never used the big N word; he accused me of "casting spears" at him. I then looked up and asked, "I am doing what to you?" "Casting spears motherf___r, casting spears at me", he yelled back.

I knew then this white agent was not white, that he was a very light complexioned Creole or mulatto with a small portion of black blood flowing in his veins. I remained silent—did not answer or respond to his shouts and questions. He became angrier, opened the holding cage, entered and struck me hard in the stomach just below my solar plexus. I folded forward and caught another blow in my left kidney area. I realized that my assailant was not role-playing or if so, had played his role beyond the level I was willing to accept. When he pulled his right fist back, threatening to bust my nose if I did not answer him, I started stuttering, confused him, moved to his right pushing his right hand away from me and grabbed him from the back and locked his neck in the fold of my left arm. I then squeezed it tight until I felt the pulse of his carotid artery, arched it up diagonally and braced and tightened it with my right hand. I held him in that position, cutting off his breathing and the flow of blow to and from his head, until his body went limp. I released the hold and watched him fall limp to the floor. I backed into the corner and waited. A few minutes later several agents came into the holding area just as the unconscious agent was getting up off the floor. One asked, "Hey what happened to you?" I told them that he had fainted. The freshly unconscious agent echoed that he had fainted. He then left the area staring gingerly back at me. I don't believe out of lost pride that he ever learned that a brother federal agent had choked him out.

I later told the other agents I had had enough of being an arrestee that I had telephonically introduced myself to Eddie so there was no need for a further ruse. Additionally, I wanted to flip Eddie and work him in California. He had displayed good potential for a CI. Afterwards, I talked for a half-hour convincing him that I was a federal narcotic agent, not a bona fide crook. It must have been the undercover role that had upset him for Eddie refused to cooperate with me or any other agent. One agent threatened to have his bail set at $2,000,000. The threat went unheeded. Eddie refused to cooperate. We took Eddie and his cohorts before the U.S. Magistrate and bail for each was set at $50,000 corporate surety. I was certain Eddie would post bail and possibly beat us back to Los Angeles.

About a month later another group was putting a posse together to do a take down with Pasadena PD narcotic unit and asked for assistance. I joined the posse and during the briefing was advised that Pasadena PD had a CI with two crooks in an undercover capacity. The crooks and CI in two cars were en

Thin White Lines

route to Pasadena to deliver a quarter ton of marijuana to a PPD undercover officer. The delivery was scheduled to take place at 3 00 p m that date. A birddog monitor had been placed on the load car.

We drove up to Pasadena, met with the PD narcotic unit, participated in the briefing then drove over to an apartment complex off Colorado Boulevard to await the delivery. About thirty minutes later a surveillant unit advised other units that the load car and U/C car were now northbound on the Pasadena freeway from Interstate five. We waited and heard the units arrive in our area.

"This is PD-1. I got the eyeball; the vehicles are entering the area five minutes from your 10-20"

"10-4. PD 3 and other units are standing by."

"10-4."

"I got eyeball of vehicles pulling into the target area, PD-1 you can drop off if you want"

"10-4. I'll peel off and take a pit-stop. I'll been 10-7 for 5."

"10-4."

As the load car turned the corner and drove pass my location, I got a quick glance of the passenger in the front seat and immediately noted how he resembled Hollywood Eddie. They pulled up to the apartment complex exited and entered the apartment. About five minutes later the undercover officer advised, "I just received a telephone call from suspect Eddie advising we have a green light. I am saddling up and riding your way with an ETA of 2 minutes. The bust signal is the open trunk of the U/C vehicle. Bust signal number 2 will be my gun drawn on the suspect or suspects at the load vehicle. The trouble signal will be the removal of sunglasses and hat. 10-4."

"10-4. We got you U/C."

The undercover agent arrived at the location, parked in the front of the apartment and entered the apartment complex.

"The Kel is working perfectly. The U/C and Eddie will be coming down to see the dope and flash in a short while."

A few minutes later the U/C and two crooks exited the apartment complex, walked to the rear parking lot where the U/C looked into the rear seat area, removed a package and shook and examined it.

PD-5 relayed "The U/C is advising the crooks the marijuana package he has in his hands appears to be lighter than 20 pounds. The crooks are advising the U/C that some are 21,22,23 and as much as 25 pounds, none of them are under 20 pounds."

The U/C and two crooks then walked around the front of the apartment to the undercover car. The U/C waked back to the rear of the U/C car and opened the trunk. Immediately Eddie took off running between the apartments. I jumped out of my car and chased him through several yards, between apartments for three blocks until he became exhausted and fell to the ground. As I approached Eddie to handcuff him, he looked up and saw me and screamed "All fuck, no not you again. This is some kind of fucking nightmare."

"Yeah, Eddie, this is your friend Beenum again. Why did you run?" I asked.

"When that guy popped that trunk, I knew I had been had. I was busted two times before when the trunk was opened. That is the silliest fucking thing I ever heard of. In the middle of doing big dope deals involving thousands of dollars, some motherf___r has to open a god d__n trunk" Eddie shouted.

I could not help but laugh and feel sorry for poor old Eddie. The United States Attorney's office for the Central District of California had charged him with four ounce sale and one pound cocaine case he had with me, Eddie had two U.S. Customs cases involving marijuana smuggling; LAPD, LASO and state narcotic each had multiple hand-to-hand ounce buys from him and he had a two kilo cocaine case in New York.

If it were not for bad luck, Eddie would have no luck. It seems almost everybody he met upon his move to California was either a CI or an undercover agent. When Eddie raises up out of prison, dope dealing and drug abuse could well be a thing in the past

CHAPTER 5

WHILE MARIJUANA, heroin, cocaine and dangerous drugs were still entering the U. S. from Mexico, the undercover role was one of the most effective investigative techniques for penetrating the core of organizations. Almost always, one of the prerequisites for a wiretap, Title III, was via an undercover penetration by an agent preferably or a CI. The wiretap was granted when all other conventional methods of drug investigative efforts had failed to immobilize an organization or penetrate its highest level of operation.

I developed an informant (CI) with information about major marijuana smugglers. According to the CI, the organization would only deal ton quantities of marijuana and that most of the deliveries took place along the Mexican border. After facilitating the delivery, the main players always left the area on motorcycles at a high rate of speed. The organization had a reputation of running away from law enforcement officials. I instructed the informant to arrange for the delivery of two tons of marijuana to three white longhaired dudes (federal undercover agents) at Calexico, Imperial, Brawley or El Centro California.

The CI negotiated with the identified members for a week. We shot (introduced) an undercover agent and his girlfriend (another agent) into them at Indio, California. The undercover agents negotiated for two hours with three longhaired bikers. We picked up counter surveillance outside of the restaurant and on one occasion one of the crooks met with the three bad guys inside. Surveillance of the negotiations indicated the need for motorcycles, longhair undercover agents, a van, several cars and a helicopter. During the negotiations, it was intimated that one of the crooks had a brother in the Imperial County Sheriffs office that was believed to be a source of information regarding police activities in the area. The crooks related they had a large cache of marijuana in Mexicali guarded by corrupt Baja State policemen. The crooks wanted to meet in three days at a restaurant in Brawley, California to negotiate the delivery of two tons of marijuana for $200,000. A plan was formulated to seize two tons of marijuana in Brawley, California.

A day before the scheduled meet a posse of ten agents in six cars, three on motorcycles, a single engine airplane and a mobile home were sent to Brawley and into Mexicali as an advance party. We were at a disadvantage, unable to coordinate the investigation with the Imperial County Sheriffs Office or the Baja State police or the MFJP out of Mexico City in fear of the deal being compromised. Late that afternoon, surveillance observed the three primary suspects arrive in town on motorcycles with "ape bars" (high rise handle bars). They checked into a hotel, had a meal and drinks then rode across the border into Mexicali. The surveillant aircraft was put in the air and three surveillant cars were sent into Mexico, but lost the suspects. Surveillance was terminated and returned back to Brawley. Early the next morning the helicopter, eighteen agents in fifteen cars and two campers arrived in Brawley. It was the middle of July. 1 drove down following the undercover agents. En route we stopped to gas up at a town outside of Indio and Coachella called Thermal. The temperature in the alcove of the service station read 119 degrees and 124 degrees in the sun.

We drove on to Brawley, California. We all checked into new, neatly decorated white stucco hotel, met and I finalized surveillant plans. The undercover agents met with the primary crooks at 12:30 p.m. at the Brawley Inn restaurant and negotiated. At 1:30 p.m. two undercover agents exited the restaurant to their undercover money car, removed the $200,000 flash roll, and re-entered the restaurant where they flashed (showed) the money to the crooks. After the flash, the agents returned the flash roll and secured it in the car. One agent stayed with the flash roll. At 2:00 p.m. the three bad guys exited the restaurant, got on motorcycles and drove across the border into Mexicali. Surveillance went airborne and mobile. Several mobile units were left behind with the undercover agents. Agents Gil Mora, Larry Johnson and I remained as point surveillance of the undercover agents and flash roll. The undercover agents advised they had another meeting with the bad guys at 7:30 that evening. It was 120 degrees in Brawley, and heat waves danced across the streets and highway.

We decided to take a nap, relax and meet at 6:00 for a slight repast in preparation for the pending undercover meeting. I stripped down to my shorts, turned up the air conditioning and fell into a deep sleep. I got up at 4:45 p.m., took a quick shower, dressed and walked over to the room across the hall where agents Mora and Johnson were residing. I knocked on the door twice. When Agent Johnson admitted me into the room, he was clad in a white T-shirt and white cotton shorts and drenching wet all over. Agent Mora was clad in only boxer shorts and perspiration was pouring down both of their faces. They were drinking cold water, toweling themselves and fanning their faces.

Agent Johnson remarked, "Man it is hotter than an oven in this goddamn town, why didn't you tell us it was this hot?"

"It isn't that hot," I responded and could not help but laugh. I then asked, "Larry, Gil do you guys know why it is so hot here?"

"No, why smart ass—why is it so hot here?" Larry asked.

Because you guys have turned your heat up high," I advised. I then walked over, turned the heat off, and then turned the air conditioning on high. I got a death threat from both agents regarding ever discussing that this ever occurred.

Surveillance took the crooks outside of Mexicali to a large barn. At that location, a forty-pound hermetically sealed bale of marijuana was removed, placed on the passenger seat of one of the motorcycles and driven back across the border.

The marijuana was delivered to the undercover agents that night as a sample. Undercover negotiations continued with the intent to stall to allow time to bring up a special group of MFJP agents from Mexico City to make the arrests and seizure in Mexicali, Baja California, Mexico.

Mexico City advised that MFJP personnel could not arrive in Mexicali inside of three days. Negotiations continued with the bad guys with the undercover agents stalling the delivery time to facilitate for Mexico City MFJP arrival. The marriage between the MFJP and the crooks could not be made inside of three days. The bad guys became antsy and the deal was put down. We shut down and went into Mexicali for food, drinks and booze run (purchase of liquor at low prices). On the morning of the next day, at sunrise, we had breakfast and pulled out and drove back up to Los Angeles. Neither the supposed relationship with the Baja State Police at Mexicali nor the relationship with the Imperial County Sheriff's Office was tarnished. Four days later Mexico City MFJP agents arrived in Mexicali and raided the barn. Approximately 200 pounds of marijuana debris was collected. The MFJP estimated from the wrappings and storage area that there had been approximately 20 tons of marijuana recently stored in the barn.

Undercover work is fascinating, highly stressful, and dangerous and has significant negative impact on the undercover agent if not managed properly. During the early years, many undercover agents develop major drinking problems, some to the degree that they were fired, or placed on stress leave. Firing was the most economical and consequently many undercover agents were unfairly treated because of the malady. There was no employee assistance program to provide guidance or assistance despite the sickness stemmed mainly from undercover work.

Finding undercover work intriguing, encouraged me to mix it with other cases. There was a brief consensus of many white special agents that black special agents were hired mainly for undercover purposes, for penetrating the black, white, red, yellow and brown organizations. It was very difficult for all agents except Asian agents to penetrate the yellow community because of the language barrier. Several black special agents lost their jobs and/or fell on the bad side of management for refusal to work undercover on a non-black agent's case.

Some of the best white undercover agents like Raymond Chemes, G. Robert Warren, George Clemente, Robert Sternaman, were never promoted beyond the first line supervision level, perhaps due to their early careers in undercover work. On the other hand, a number of agents that never really "crushed a grape" (made a significant case) had meteoric careers.

Not understanding the foregoing, I continued to work as hard and dedicated as possible in all federal drug investigative capacities. I worked undercover throughout the State of California and various parts of Baja California, Mexico. At Lake Elsinore, California defendant Douglas Bjorian delivered two kilograms of 97 percent cocaine to me and was arrested in lieu of payment. He later fugitated. He was subsequently arrested and during his trial he was arrested again involving a larger amount of cocaine. Bjorian made bail and again fugitated was not apprehended until about 18 years later. At Inglewood, California, I made undercover purchases of multiple ounces of cocaine and heroin from a double leg amputee as his wife aided and abetted the sales. During the take down, I had $6900 flash for a one-pound coke, four-ounce deal. The amputee's connection, a former underclassman and his henchman were present. Also present at the house were the elderly parents of the amputee. During the flash, the henchman stood in the door well of the bedroom brandishing a .12 gauge shotgun. The size of the henchman covered almost the entire door well. At one point he locked a shell in the chamber. I was glad that he held the shotgun at port arms and trail arms, for had he raised it in my direction I was prepared to let him quickly experience the effects of 3 to5 rounds of 150 grain, hollow point soft lead jacket rounds in his torso area. When the henchman locked the shell into the chamber, I instinctively positioned myself behind the double leg amputee while flashing the $6900. Although I did not have authority to spend the $6900, I spent $6700 for the purchase in lieu of causing a major shootout in the house.

Like the textbooks, marijuana had spread throughout most college campuses. Its use had replaced the old fraternity house beer bust. Students were engaged in marijuana smoke and smoke-ins. Part of growing up in college life was experiencing panty raids, drunk from beer parties and experimenting with marijuana. Young white adults who had flunked out of college became marijuana entrepreneurs. They frequented colleges and high schools like bees and made tons of money selling marijuana in ounce and on occasion pound quantities. Several police departments requested federal assistance and some requested state and other local assistance. Those cases that did not meet the federal threshold for prosecution were not immediately pursued.

Another enforcement group in the Los Angeles office developed a two-ton marijuana case and requested assistance. We joined up and drove down to San Diego and conducted surveillance of two undercover meetings, one at Anthony's on the pier and the other aboard the restaurant The "Rubin E Lee." It was determined from surveillance that the sources were young white adult males, some still in college and ex-college students. The primary defendant was named Martin B. West, a student at California Western College, located on part of the beach area of San Diego. The undercover meetings and surveillance was put down for a week. We drove back up to Los Angeles with the understanding that we would be available to assist when the deal was ready to take place the next week.

The crooks called the undercover agents six days later and advised they were ready to deliver two tons of high-grade marijuana to the agents that day. Arrangements were made to meet the crooks at a topless bar in La Jolla California. We initiated pre-surveillance at the topless bar an hour prior to the 1:00 p.m. meet schedule. No significant unusual activity was noted. At 1:05 p.m. the undercover agents arrived and entered the bar. About five minutes later two suspects arrived and met with the undercover agents. They remained in the bar until 2:10 p.m. They exited. The crooks got into their car and the undercover agents followed in their car. They were followed to a house in a nice neighborhood on the outskirts of San Diego. The passenger exited, entered the house and backed a huge camper out of a large garage. The camper took the lead, followed by the other crook and further followed by the undercover agents. Surveillant agents in a leapfrog manner followed them to a Denny's restaurant, where another car containing four males (chase car), joined the caravan and proceeded to Cal-Western College campus on the beach. The driver of the camper exited, joined the driver in the car, then they joined the undercover agents and walked over to the Cafeteria. Three crooks got out of the chase car, and walked over to the crooks car and two walked over and stood by the camper as though they were students milling about in the area.

They took positions as lookouts and caused our radio traffic to be reduced to the bare minimum. The lookout at the rear of the camper was approximately 6'1" tall, very muscularly built. He wore a white T-shirt displaying well-defined muscular triceps and biceps, and a well-molded pectoral area. His head was not as wide as his neck, rather the muscles in his neck were wider than his head and muscles could be seen in his upper legs. This specimen had a "Body by Fisher" and put Arnold to shame.

Agent Johnny Grenados had volunteered to take down one of the lookouts. Agents Mike McGlone and Miguel Acuna were scheduled to take down the other one. Granados came on the air, "This is 103, and I got eyeball of a huge muscular male rear of the load vehicle. He is standing folding his arms looking around the area. Other units with eyeball of the load vehicle identify."

McGlone and Acuna responded. "105 and 110 have eyeball of the front. We'll take down the bad guy in the front when the word is given."

"10-4." Said Granados.

This was followed by a long pause, then, "Is there another unit that can assist 103 with the bad guy in the rear?"

I chuckled when under my breath, I had eyeball of the big bad guy at the rear of the car.

I remained mute to see his reaction. Other surveillant units reported the undercover and two bad guys were out of the cafeteria walking back toward the load car, one agent shouted, "It is about to go down."

Agent Granados shouted, "Any unit other than 105 or 110 that can assist me at the load car identify."

I remained quiet until Granados hurriedly and anxiously repeated the request three more times. I responded, "I got you 103."

Hearing my voice, Granados blew a sigh of relief over the

radio and remarked, "I think we are going to have a fight with this big mother____r." I agreed.

The undercover agents and two crooks walked back to the van. One agent entered the rear for a few minutes, exited and gave the bust signal. Agent Granados and I ran over to the Captain Marvel-like lookout and each agent placed a gun in his ear, yelled in unison, "Freeze motherf____r, federal agents, if you move I'll blow your goddamn brains out."

We were both disappointed; the Captain Marvel-built lookout urinated and defecated on himself. I made Agent Granados transport him to the San Diego office.

At Salt Lake City, Utah, I worked undercover on one Billy Charles Harris, Charles Joshua and Lorenzo Hubbard, sources of supply for heroin and cocaine in the greater Salt Lake City area. I remember the deal as though it was yesterday.

The pilot on the United Airline flight alerted us to see on our right side the Great St. Lake, a lake with a reputation that had no drown victims and advised to fasten the seat belts, that we were making our final approach into the Salt Lake City area. As we came over the mountain starting our descent into the valley, we were shaken by a little turbulence. The plane landed and I was introduced to Harry Sumega, the Resident Agent in Charge (RAC).

Harry was apologetic advising that the crooks were out of town, believed to be in the Los Angeles area, where I had just departed, and would be returning to Salt Lake City in a few days. Harry took me to his residence for dinner. During the visit he stated he was Polish and commenced telling "Pollack Jokes" to no end. One joke Harry told involved two Pollocks staring at tracks and debating whether they were deer or bear tracks, while discussing the tracks further, one Pollack told the other one to bend over, and you will see these are deer tracks. They both bent over and were run over by a train (railroad tracks).

After dinner, I was driven down to the BNDD office given an

undercover car and introduced to Agents Charles Bullock and Drew Moren. Later I checked into my hotel room and drove back to West Second South and walked the streets to become familiar with the Salt Lake drug area.

The next day I drove to the office met with Agents Bullock and Moren and assumed a light undercover role on West Second South Street. I frequented Adolph's restaurant and several bars, cafes and businesses in the area. That evening I was introduced to a CI named Rex. Rex was black approximately 6'9" tall, 290 pounds and he related that he was a "bad motherf___r," that nobody; I mean nobody fucked with him.

I liked Rex from the onset for I noted that despite his huge stature that underneath there was a degree of tenderness, kindness and love. Additionally, he loved cowboy movies. While frequenting the haunts of Salt Lake City, I casually asked Rex why he had gone to jail about two weeks before my arrival.

Rex broke out in an uncontrollable laughter, laughing so hard that he almost deflated his lungs. Tears, apparently tears of joy welled in his eyes. As he almost caught his breath he laughed again. This went on for about five minutes. When he calmed down, Rex advised that he had "killed a motherf___r. "That the motherf____r attacked me in a gambling joint with a knife. I took one stab in the left hand, took the knife away from that motherf____r, downed him to the floor and stabbed that cocks___r until he couldn't move. Then I laid that son-of-a-bitch wide open like a hog from throat to asshole. As two cops would say, I took his Black ass 10-7, out of service. That's why I went to jail."

I did not know whether he was serious or not. I remarked, "That is very interesting Rex."

Why don't you ask me how I got out of jail?' Rex asked.

"Why?" I asked.

"Because I killed a nigger. I took a nigger 10-7. You see if it had been a white boy you would have to pump sunshine into me."

"Well Rex, it seems like it was in self-defense to me," I stated.

"Yeah Beenum, I think I can beat the case on the self defense thing. Even if I get convicted for murder, I will only do a bullet (one year) cause I killed only a nigger," Rex advised.

Rex related that Utah was a Mormon state, different from any other state, that the Mormons controlled everything—the liquor stores, schools, banks, police department and every legitimate establishment that was making money. According to Rex, the statute on top of the Mormon Church in downtown Salt Lake City was solid gold. I found Rex interesting and got to know him better after we had had several meals together. We frequented the West Second South Street location for three days on the third night; Rex took me to one of the target heroin houses. Rex knocked on the door, identified himself as Rex with his friend Beenum. A white female named Kitty responded and talked to us behind closed doors. Kitty related that someone named Red had robbed the dope house. She had been instructed not to allow anyone into the dope house without the approval of "Sammy, the henchman." Kitty related that she had telephoned Sammy and that he was coming over.

Rex advised Kitty that we would walk out to the sidewalk and await the arrival of Sammy. We walked out to the sidewalk. A few minutes later we saw a black male who appeared to be 7' tall walking down the center of the street carrying a long barrel nickel-plated pistol in his right hand. As he walked from under the trees and under the lamppost the pistol glittered and appeared larger.

Rex stated, "Look at this crazy motherf___r walking down the middle of the street like John Wayne or Clint Eastwood trying to scare somebody. As soon as he gets close to us I am going to light into his ass to see how bad this motherf___r really is.

This motherf____r knows me, he knows not to come at me like this."

"No Rex, don't bother him if he comes up with the gun toward us, just fall to the ground. I'll take him, 10-7. I advised. Rex insisted that he was going to "tear into his ass to see how bad he really is."

Rex and I started to debate during this dangerous time, I finally convinced him that he should fall to the ground if Sammy pointed the gun toward us; that I would take him out quickly. I assured Rex that I could shoot Sammy in the chest at least three times before he could get the first round off. I watched Sammy walk down the middle of the street toward us, when he was approximately 30 yards, he walked over to the east sidewalk, then walked under a tree until he reached our position. He kept the barrel of the pistol pointed toward the ground. Rex stated, "Hey Sammy how're you doing? This is my cousin Beenum. What's all this for man?"

"I am sorry man, Kitty didn't tell me it was you. The dope house was robbed today man. There were several customers inside copping when "Red" came in with a shotgun, held everybody up, took all the money, all the dope, then shot in the ceiling and shouted that he would be back. That's why we are on alert. It is very bad man. You know Billy and Lorenzo kept most of their dope here. The other dope houses are almost empty. There's going to be a lot of sick motherf____rs around here when the other three dope houses run out. We are not scheduled to get a shipment until four days from now. That's why Billy went back to L.A."

I asked, "Do you mean to tell me that you guys let a dude rob the dope house? Man what kind of business are you guys running up here?"

"Salt Lake City is different, we've never had this sort of thing happen before. See most of our customers are white. I don't believe there are over 400 black people in Salt Lake. This sort of thing just doesn't happen. You see we know everybody around here. Even Red knows he can't come back around here without some fireworks."

Rex remarked, "Yeah man, you guys are acting like you are scared shitless. Red must have really put the fear in you."

"No, not me man. It was Kitty," Sammy said. "I wasn't even there. He picked the time he knew I wouldn't be there to avoid any fireworks. Come on in the house man there is no need to stand out here in the streets."

Rex remarked, "I don't know Sammy. Red might come back through here. I don't have a gun."

Sammy assured us that he was well armed and had armed Kitty and others in all of the dope houses. Sammy related they had been instructed to kill.

We joined Kitty inside of the dope house. I noted the shotgun blast damage on the ceiling. Apparently Red had fired two shots in the ceiling. Kitty had not yet regained composure. She scurried around the house nervously mumbling that she needed to find another line of work—something less dangerous.

I could not help but sympathize for Kitty. She, by now with a deteriorating appearance, had once been a fairly attractive white female with hair that spread over her shoulders. She was in denial that she was heavily addicted to heroin. She remarked that she "chipped every now and then" (was an occasional heroin user) but was unaware of the extent of her drug addiction. Despite being a "chipper" I could tell by her mannerism and walk that she had experienced the pain of the "Yenshee baby." Perhaps more alarming, she had opted to shoot heroin in her juggler veins. White scared tissue was visible through her see-through turtleneck blouse marking both sides of her neck. To add to her woes, Kitty had a young daughter that lived in the dope house with her and her stomach protruded like that of a four month pregnant teenager. Kitty could not quit her job if she wanted to; she had no place to go and unbeknownst she had been made a slave, a slave to the great and super powerful heroin. King heroin, a drug that turns the mildest of humans into the wildest of animals.

Knowing that the undercover role I was playing would in someway immobilize these traffickers was awe-inspiring; the danger was merely a job related possible injury. Rex and I conversed with Sammy and Kitty for about an hour—Red's name came up numerous times. Kitty and Sammy were in agreement that he was a bad motherf__r for robbing a dope house and that he was marked for death.

Rex and I left with Sammy and drove over to a "shooting gallery" operated by the organization. It was a frame house in a partially run down section. All of the occupants inside were white. There were three addicts sitting on the sofa of the west wall of the living room. On the north wall a young blond male had strapped his left arm and was injecting heroin in his vein, using a makeshift needle with an eye drop sponge on the end. He was a professional for I watched him aspirate (remove the air from the makeshift syringe) before he plunged it into his arm. A skinny white female sat next to him urging him to hurry up so she could shoot up. Two white females and a white male nodded in a sofa chair in the corner next to the front door. Blood was oozing from the veins of the female and a stench of burnt heroin, fresh blood, cigarette smoke and the smell of unwashed female that had recently had sex filled the room.

As we stood in the center of the front room, apparently unnoticed by the occupants, Sammy remarked, "See there is big money here. We don't even have to have a henchman here for all they do is come in pay their $20 get their shot and kit all ready, shoot up and go on the nod. Sometimes there are as many as 40 or 50 people in here shooting up and nodding at one time. This goes on 24-7, 365 (all day, all week, all year)." Sammy related that that particular dope pad cleared a minimum of $1500 daily everyday to include Christmas. Sammy further related that they were selling something (heroin) that the customers could not do without—that the biggest problem was keeping them supplied. Sammy then added that the other dope houses average about $1000 a day. I quickly computed that $3000 plus 1500 times 365 equaled over $1,500,000 per year and that there were two main operators, Harris and Hubbard. Two main henchmen Sammy and Joshua and four dope house managers, Kitty, et al, — that this operation had all of the ingredients of an 848 investigation, Continuing Criminal Enterprise (CCE). The more Sammy talked, he revealed, rather identified other members of the organization. I had originally believed that there was no dope, especially heroin in Salt Lake City. I was surprised to learn that two black dope dealers had the heroin franchise in Utah.

We went to another shooting gallery and the scene was a replica of the last one. A short time later, I drove Sammy and Rex back to their house and retired to my hotel room. I telephoned two surveillant agents and advised them what had transpired. I then prepared a preliminary report and retired for the night.

The next morning I received a telephone call from RAC Sumega advising that the three major crooks, Hubbard, Harris and Joshua, were back in town. I met with Agent Bullock and we drove by Hubbard's apartment complex and noted three new Cadillac Eldorados parked in the rear. I felt more relieved realizing my trip to Salt Lake City was no longer humming along.

I met with Rex that afternoon and we drove over to Hubbard's apartment and were let into the apartment by Charles Joshua, a.k.a. Big Josh. Josh answered the door with a .357 Magnum that had a barrel that appeared eight inches long. He toyed with it before admitting us into the apartment and related that he thought Rex was possibly Red. A short time later, Hubbard, Harris, and two blond moderately attractive females joined us in the living room. Rex introduced me as his cousin Beenum that I had just raised out of jail and was trying to get down again. Big Josh related that he had just raised up a few months ago and inquired about where I had done time. I started to say San Quentin, but changed to Joliet Illinois. Big Josh related that he had just raised up from San Quentin after doing six years of a "dime stretch."

Big Josh toyed with the pistol and talked out of the side of his mouth as though trying to somehow intimidate Rex and myself. He related that he had just arrived back in Salt Lake City from Pocatello, Idaho. That he had gone up there to find Red and kill him. According to Big Josh, "You can't let a mothetf___r rob your dope house and walk away like nothing happened. Otherwise every motherf___r and his mother and cousin would try to rob the dope house."

For about five minutes Big Josh did all the talking. Hubbard, Harris and the females toyed around for a while went into the kitchen area and made snorting sounds as though snorting cocaine. When I stood up and started walking toward the kitchen area simultaneously asking for a drink of water, Big Josh told me to remain seated, that he would get the water for me. He left the living room, returned with a glass of water and a small portion of white powdery substance on his mustache/nostril. I stated, "I see you guys got the girl good too?"

"Naw, we ain't got nothing good. That motherf_r Red took everything we had. What is bothering me is that I can't find him to kill him. That bothers the shit out of me." Big Josh said. He then toyed with the .357 Magnum by aiming it at me and Rex and dry firing. When I advised him not to do it he asked, "Why not?" and continued to dry fire at Rex and myself and out the window. I walked over to where he was seated, remarked that his pistol was pretty and asked if I could see it and he stated, "Naw motherf___r. I just met you and you think I am going to let you play with my gun. Shit you could be Red's cousin or brother or something."

Rex broke out in uncontrollable laughter advising Big Josh what a crazy motherf___r he was. I removed a 6" nickel-plated model 19 Smith and Wesson revolver from the small of my back unloaded it and handed it to Big Josh. "You see Big Josh my gun is prettier than yours." I remarked. I had caught him by total surprise, caught him with an empty gun trying to be menacing. He was extremely impressed and surprised that I did not wimp him out. I knew thereafter he would never dry fire at me or try to be menacing. I made him believe that he was not the only convicted felon with a firearm.

A short time later Hubbard, Harris and the females came back into the living room. Both Hubbard and Harris reiterated their anger at Red for robbing the dope house. It had become clearer that Red had instilled fear in their minds and hearts.

We talked in generalities about the drug trade and it was related that there are many white heroin addicts and only two or three black addicts in the Salt Lake City area. According to Harris, the white addicts paid timely for their dope and never complained or caused a hassle. Additionally, they did not cause "heat waves" (hordes of police frequenting an area probing) and were not prone to stick ups, complaints, fights, disagreements and chaos.

It was ironic learning that Hubbard and Harris were in fact black dope dealers that had a strong aversion to selling dope to Black addicts. They had found a lucrative market where the police were light years behind knowing anything about drugs—plus Salt Lake City did not have black policemen and when they did get one or two, they would be recognized right away. According to Harris, "I could sell an ounce of heroin right in front of the police here. They don't know their ass from a hole in the ground. It's easy picking up here man. Just don't get any ideas about moving up here." I assured him that I was not about to get involved with their action there; that I was trying to set up shop in Las Vegas, Boise and Pocatello, Idaho. Both Hubbard and Hams chuckled and wished me luck. I advised that I was trying to cop an ounce to take to Las Vegas in a few days. Harris advised he would get back with us later. Harris further bragged about how good business was and how they were insulated from the police. I wanted badly to tell them how wrong they were, how they had three things that throughout the United States attracted the police like flies to a dead animal: Cadillacs, white women, and dope. I wanted badly to advise them that two of those things had caused my first trip to the great city of Salt Lake City. He then elicited Rex and my services to lean on a guy named Jelly who was late paying him for an ounce of heroin.

When Rex and I talked about what was in it for us to lean on Jelly or other people, Harris advised that he would pay us in heroin.

Rex and I left the apartment and drove down to West Second South where we met "Jelly" inside of Adolph's. We threatened to kick Jelly's ass if he did not come up with $600 that he owed Harris. Jelly confirmed that he had gotten two 1/2 ounces of heroin from Harris, which he had not yet paid. Rex accused Jelly of shooting up the heroin.

After threatening Jelly, I stood out on West Second South Street chatting with passers-by and ignoring a flirt that a black prostitute was putting on me. I looked diagonally across the street at the intersection and saw Agents Bullock and Moren (surveillant agents) staring in my direction. On the corner to my right stood shapely blond wearing red leather short shorts, red boots, a pink sweater and a red leather tam. She peered briefly in my direction and appeared to moisten her red lips with her tongue. I started walking in her direction to chat with her but was by passed by a black male that dashed out of one of the businesses ahead of me. I watched them engage in conversation. I gazed at the surveillant unit and noted that Agent Moren was waiving his hands as though trying to give me a signal. I watched the blond and black male then walk around the corner south bound out of view. I walked up to the corner, looked in their direction. A few seconds later a four-door sedan pulled up, two tall white males grabbed the black male, handcuffed him and placed him in the rear seat. The blond joined the driver in the front seat and they drove from the area. I walked back and joined Rex inside of Adolph's, had a slight repast and exited without Rex. I noticed the same blond was on the corner flaunting again. I stood in front of Adolph's, chatted with another black whore and watched the same scenario but with a white male. I had no idea what was transpiring and about thirty minutes later the blond reappeared on the corner. Again, I walked toward her to chat and before I got to her location, surveillant agents flashed their headlights off and on several times then drove slowly from the area. I walked back to Adolph's, advised Rex I would be back in a few, entered the undercover car and drove to a prearranged location and met with surveillant agents and RAC Sumega. RAC Sumega laughed so hard until he turned red in the face and water flooded his eyes. When he gained his composure, he related, "Beenum you could just smell that sweet white pussy on the corner and could not help but try to talk to her huh? You are lucky that those two Johns beat you to her. The blond hooker is one of Salt Lake City finest officers. Vice/narcotics is working decoys in the area. They were not supposed to be on West Second South. I was preparing to bail you out for soliciting prostitution. They are supposed to put all of the arrestee's names in the newspaper the following day."

We shut the operation down. The next day, about noon Rex and I drove upon the Boulevard (West Second South). Immediately upon our arrival we met Jesus. Jesus was crying like a baby and snot oozed out of his nose like water. I had been introduced to Jesus, a short black male heroin addict in his early thirties and his whore "little mama," my first day in Salt Lake City. Jesus then denied that he was a heroin addict despite the welts, scars and keloids on his skin. Jesus was a one-whore pimp/heroin addict and his whore "Little Mama" was with him. Little Mama wore extremely short and tight blue shorts that cut into her rectum and vagina. She wore red high heel shoes and a matching red cap. Whoring had broken her body down. She was not as fairly attractive as she once appeared to be. Jesus had stated, "1 have pimped from Maine to the San Francisco Bay, when a whore gets on my hook she plays hell trying to get off." I knew the reality was that "Little Mama" was all Jesus had. Heroin had enslaved him so that he was too weak to commit the type of crimes that addicts commit to support an addiction like his.

Jesus cried incoherently like a baby. Snot oozed from his nose and dripped string-like to the ground. On occasion he wiped long strings of snot with the sleeve of his shirt. Rex yelled, "Hell Jesus, you are sounding like a pussy. 1 thought you pimped from Maine to the Frisco Bay. What in the hell happened to you?"

Jesus cried more, wiped the mucous flowing freely from his nose and screamed, "Man those pigs have gone berserk. They came down here and busted Little Mama before she could clock in on her job. I ought to go uptown and burn that goddamn church down."

"Jesus if you go up there fucking around with that Mormon Church, those Mormons will have something for your black ass." Rex warned.

Jesus cried incessantly, incoherently and uttered begging pleas. Mucous flowed from his nose in long string-like patterns, like freezing water oozing from a faucet. He whined, begged, moaned, grimaced, urinated on himself and even offered to perform a homosexual act for $20 to relieve his pain. I had a $5,000 flash roll in one pocket and $600 of personal money in a wallet in my left sock. I felt extremely sad, sorry and pity for Jesus but I could not reduce myself to enabling him to continue to use heroin. I offered to buy him food at Adolph's in lieu of giving him money, but he refused. Jesus, pleaded, whined, moaned and shouted, "Man-n-n-n n, I'm-m sicker than-n-er motherf____r. Please hel-l-l-p me."

Rex began to sympathize with Jesus but had no money to give. Out of pride, he never asked me for money to give and never recommended it. Rex recommended that Jesus go into the department store, shoplift, get arrested and then he could kick the habit "cold turkey" in jail. Jesus disagreed. We left him standing in the street, just off the sidewalk begging to imaginary passers.

For three days we negotiated with Harris and Hubbard to no avail. I was convinced that their prejudices against other black drug dealers were very deep, unending and that possibly they had been burned before, or maybe Red had pissed them off to the point of being irrational. During the last meeting with Harris, I advised that I would never beg a person to sell me anything, that I am a buyer not a beggar. Harris stated, "That's good, that's a good way to be." It was obvious that he was not going to do a hand-to-hand deal with me. I then wore a nagra recorder and negotiated with him for payment for leaning on Jelly to pay his dope debt. Harris would not part with any and stated he would take care of the matter with Rex. That Rex would settle with me.

Two days later, Harris called Rex; we drove over to his apartment. Harris then asked what he owed us for leaning on Jelly. Rex told him 1/2 ounce of heroin. Harris left the room briefly, returned and handed a 1/2-ounce heroin package toward Rex. I immediately reached up and took the heroin from Harris, advising, "I'll take it. We'll split it even okay Rex?" Rex agreed. We left Harris' apartment, met with surveillance agents and advised them what had transpired. The heroin was processed as evidence and sent to the laboratory for analysis.

The Assistant United States Attorney advised that due to the senility level of the Chief Federal Judge, some of the antics he was known to pull and his aversion to conspiracy cases, he would take the case to state court. Consequently there was no need to do a financial work up, additional investigation and witness development and presenting before a special grand jury in order to pursue a Continuing Criminal Enterprise case against Harris et al.

Only four defendants were indicted in state court. Three months later I flew back up to Salt Lake City. During pretrial, I went with the Assistant U. S. Attorney and other agents and officers, chemist and secretary to several private clubs in Salt Lake City where hard liquor was sold over the counter. During these visits, I noted that the BNDD chemist was kind of an unfriendly person, rather he did not speak much and when he did he never talked to me and seemed to be unconcerned and disinterested in everything I said. He was from the BNDD laboratory in Dallas.

On the day of the trial, I was standing outside of the courtroom during the jury selection. The chemist surprisingly walked up to me and started a general conversation. He asked me what I thought of rattlesnakes. I admitted that they are dangerous, evil and that I did not like them. At that time he showed me the open mouth of a rattlesnake that was an ornament on his cowboy hat. I told him his hat was very nice and that I believed it was expensive. He related that it cost $200.

The chemist seemed shocked that I was a BNDD agent and related that he thought I was a "snitch." He did not know why BNDD would ever hire "a nigger" —I mean Negro agent or a Negro to do anything," he stated. The chemist was a melanochri approximately 5'9' tall, 160 pounds with a slight ruddy, hairy, infested area below the level of his nose. He stated that all of his life he has had a strong hatred for Negroes, never liked them, never associated with them and had stepped wide of them on every opportunity. The chemist looked me firmly in the eyes as he talked and related that Negroes are inferior to all other races and always will be. He related that he was a reserve Texas Ranger and member of the Ku Klux Klan. When I readjusted my gun in my shoulder holster the chemist seemed alarmed that I was armed. He later related that law enforcement officers are not allowed to carry guns in the federal court in Ft. Worth, Texas. According to the chemist, of all the Negroes he had seen, he could begin to like me and to get along with me. He extended his hand in a handshake and gripped my hand very hard during the shake.

I was very versed in my testimony, having studied it last night before going to bed, but now I was completely stunned. I had never had a racist tell me he was a racist and had never before experienced a black drug trafficker refusing to sell me drugs because I was black. On the next day I testified in a six-man jury trial, was excused and immediately went to the airport and flew back to Los Angeles. I knew Harris et. al. had been found guilty but I never thereafter checked on the case. I did promise myself to never travel to Dallas, Texas.

About a year later, I was busy at my desk working a kojak conspiracy (a conspiracy based on numerous documented overt acts and witnesses), when someone dropped a hermetically sealed kilogram package of heroin on my desk on the paper where I was writing. 1 looked up and saw a young blond, southern drawl-talking agent smiling down on me, Bobby Mueller. He stated, "Here's a present for you."

"A present for me? What the hell you mean a damn present for me?" I asked.

Agent Mueller continued smiling and stated, "Everybody's been telling me what a good undercover agent you are and I told them they were full of shit. I told them that you couldn't even buy dope from a black dope peddler, which I could. They didn't believe me so here's the proof this is a kilo I bought last night from Billy Charles Harris. He wouldn't sell a brother an ounce of heroin but he sold this little ol' slo' southern talking white boy a kilo."

I stood up, shook Bobby's hand and congratulated him. He made a very good conspiracy and substantial case against Harris and his cohorts. They went to jail for a long time.

CHAPTER 6

DRUG ABUSE escalated to a level where there was no need for turf wars as often erroneously reported via the media. Numerous entrepreneurs dropped legitimate businesses and went into the dope business; some used legitimate businesses to camouflage their drug trafficking activities; others used legal businesses to launder drug profits. Many of the newcomers, some could not find good jobs; others came specifically to enter into the drug trafficking business, found it yielded lucrative income with a low overhead.

One of the noted Beverly Hills based black drug traffickers, believed to have come to California from Texas or Arkansas, via Fresno, California was one Joseph Levi Ethridge, a.k.a. Fresno Billy.

Fresno Billy sold dope, heroin and cocaine, like he had a license. He made a mistake— having no business front, no visible means of support. Fresno Billy purchased two residences in Beverly Hills, hired a maid for each and purchased several cars that were typical to the neighborhood. Perhaps one of the most inquisitive and professional police departments is Beverly Hills Police Department.

Fresno Billy had an entourage. Some lived between the two residences others were relatives and friends that were out of tune with urban living. Because of the foregoing, the police buzzed around his residences like flies and some deployed CI's and tried to penetrate his organization. He was flamboyant and had a penchant for Caucasian women over Black women. The FBI, BNDD, LAPD, LASO, State Narcotics, Office of Drug Abuse and Law Enforcement (ODALE), Beverly Hills Police Department and IRS were targeting Fresno Billy.

I developed intelligence that indicated that Fresno Billy was the source of supply for a Philadelphia based drug trafficker named Harry Jones. I further developed a CI from New York that could purchase heroin from Fresno Billy. While preparing to immobilize his organization, I learned that ODALE had devoted significant efforts investigating his organization but was devoid of any meaningful CI or method to really penetrate the organization. One of my state BNE investigator friends was assigned to ODALE and my partner Agent Roland Talton and I decided to share our investigation with him and do a joint investigation in the true spirit of good law enforcement interaction/cooperation.

We brought the newly developed CI from New York to Los Angeles and had a strategy meeting, leaving with the agreement to do a joint ODALE-BNDD investigation to immobilize Fresno Billy, who had a reputation on the streets of "riding high" (prospering from dealing dope without law enforcement interception -no pending cases) and being "fly" (street vernacular for flamboyant). We agreed to obtain a Title III, wiretap or non-consensual court authorized telephone intercept.

ODALE, one of President Nixon's pork barrel projects, was a task force of LAPD, State BNE, LASO, DEA, LASO, U.S.

Customs, IRS and a few other state and local agencies. When initially established, it was directed at the level of drug traffic that did not meet the federal prosecutorial threshold. Because of its makeup, it became very competitive and directed its efforts toward the major violators. There were ODALE offices in many cities and as usual, the director was a political appointee devoid of elementary knowledge of law enforcement and was lesser knowledgeable about drug trafficking or the law. They were very dangerous, that is, they were in charge of an activity, a dangerous activity, that they had little to no training other than from feeling their way by reacting or being naive to anything and everything that was transpiring in their unit.

Agent Talton and I assisted ODALE, utilizing our CI, in purchasing a quantity of heroin from the Fresno Billy's organization as a prelude for a court authorized telephone intercept. As the case developed further toward obtaining the intercept, a breakdown in communication between ODALE and BNDD erupted regarding ODALE's authority to conduct Title III investigations. Some Phi Beta Kappa attorney convinced the Department of Justice that it did by citing or misciting a particular law.

ODALE broke away from BNDD and tried to pursue the investigations alone but was thwarted by the U.S. Attorney's Office relating the need for experienced federal agents to monitor, transcribe tapes, minimize and provide the needed direction that a Title 111 case required.

My partner and I, isolated, rather cut out of the case up to that point, were re- contacted and assigned to minor roles in the case. A degree of hostility developed between the numerous agencies working the case and one afternoon upon reporting to duty at the command post, a state BNE Supervisor, an appointed case supervisor, tried to demean my partner and me. He made the mistake of cursing me three times in front of one LAPD

Sergeant Segar, a cop that had a long history of directing and expressing racial hatred toward blacks.

I advised the BNE supervisor that if he cursed my partner or me again that I would physically beat him to a pulp in front of his subordinates, right there in the command post. He ceased cursing but never apologized.

That same date, the prejudiced sergeant (Segar) advised my partner, Agent Talton, to steer clear of me and to watch himself around me "because he's going to take a fall," meaning that I was going to be set up on false charges to be either fired or/and arrested. Not believing that this officer was serious, I did not prepare a report or have my partner prepare a report of the sergeant's statement. I, at that time, believed the threat to be merely the false bravado of a frustrated narcotic officer.

Later we took down Fresno Billy and his cohorts based on evidence obtained from the Title III. During the arrest, one of the defendants had copies of the arrest plan, which was reported by the arresters that saw the plan. I do not believe that there was an Internal Affairs or BNDD inspection investigation regarding the matter.

Over the last several years aside from other investigations, I had conducted a lengthy investigation of major narcotic trafficker—Thomas "Tootie" Reese and cohorts. Shortly after the conclusion of the Fresno Billy investigation, I was called in by Inspections (Internal Affairs) regarding allegations that I had frequented a residence of a member of the Thomas Reese organization on several occasions and that I had taken a $7,500 bribe from Reese.

I was interviewed and prepared a candid affidavit. I was later exonerated. I noted that the complaint against me had old addresses where I supposedly had attended parties and stated a period when I was on temporary assignment (TDY) out of state. I was somewhat encouraged by a statement made by Ted Hunter, the Chief Inspector and one of my former supervisors, "John we don't believe there is anything to this. I know you are disappointed but don't be. It is the hard workers like you that always come to our attention. The lazy or non-working agents always stay hidden in the woodworks" he assured.

About two years after being cleared from the allegations, I was again called over to Inspections. I met with Inspector Murray Mahan, who was somewhat cryptic about the allegation. In a talkative and kidding manner I blurted out, "Hey Murray you are insinuating that the allegation involves money. I was over here on the last allegation that in part alleged that I had taken $7500 from a dope dealer. You guys must think I have $50,000 stashed somewhere. I don't. I just applied for food stamps yesterday" I kidded. I noticed that when I mentioned $50,000 Inspector Mahan fell back in his swivel chair and almost fell to the floor. He asked me to excuse him and left his office for a few minutes. When he returned, he was accompanied by Chief Inspector, Ted Hunter. Hunter related, "This is a serous allegation involving a lot of money, rather involving an allegation that you took a $50,000 bribe from major narcotic trafficker Thomas Reese."

"This is not true rather, it is preposterous," I assured. After using the word preposterous, I realized from Interrogation training that that is one of the words most often used by a guilty person. Nothing was going right for me today. I further added, "Ted the only thing I ever took from a defendant or suspect was his freedom and that on most cases was pursuant to a warrant, complaint or I got one after the arrest."

Inspector Hunter stated, "You know this type of allegation about you came up before involving money. Would you take a polygraph test?" he asked.

"Sure, I'll take a polygraph, lie detector test or even sodium pentothal," I blurted out. Inspector Hunter, "1 think this would be the best way of clearing this matter up."

I was then advised by Inspector Mahan that the allegation

was that one George Reese, a person I do not believe I had ever seen and the brother of major narcotic violator Thomas Reese had reported that Thomas Reese, his attorney Burton Marks, George Reese and I were sitting at a table. There was $50,000 on the table. Thomas Reese told his brother George to leave the room for a few minutes. George left the room and returned in a short while. Upon his return, the $50,000 was gone and I had left. In reality what he described is a supposed situation wherein inference could be drawn suggesting that I took the $50,000 and that I had an improper association with a drug trafficker

I went up to Big Bear Lake in San Bemadino County for Labor Day with my brother, sister-in-law and family and fished, camped, barbecued and had a few drinks.

On the next day, I drove to the Inspection Office in Los Angeles located in the U.S. Courthouse building and took the polygraph examination regarding these allegations. The polygrapher ripped the tape off the machine, left the room for about twenty minutes, returned and advised me that I had passed the examination. Inspector Hunter advised me that I should receive a letter of clearance in about two weeks.

I was somewhat dismayed that someone had lodged false allegations against me. I knew that I was not obligated to take the polygraph and that no inference could be drawn from my refusal and that the refusal could not be mentioned in the Inspection Report. I continued to do my job of putting drug pushers in jail.

There were not many black agents in BNDD or U.S. Customs and there were only a handful of blacks working narcotics at state BND, LAPD, and LASO. Many white agents were reluctant to work undercover. Often they asked black agents to work undercover in assisting them in their cases. I was very cooperative and often overextended myself helping others. It seemed the more I helped, the more they asked. Many white agents believe that a black agent, by virtue of his race, could purchase drugs undercover in the white, black, brown (Hispanic), yellow (Asian/Pacific rim) and red (Native American) communities. Consequently, black agents were over-tasked with requests to work undercover on a non-black agent's case. Many police departments in California did not have black officers working undercover and they too made the same requests.

On one occasion, I was asked to do an undercover caper in Lompoc, California. My partner, Bill Taylor and I drove up to Lompoc where I then purchased a quantity of cocaine and heroin from a black trafficker that was supplying heroin and cocaine to the Air Force base and nearby cities in that area.

We had a Strike Force (SF) in the office made up of state and local officers, of BNDD agents and U.S. Customs. Shortly after arriving at the office one morning, I was approached by a S.F. agent and asked if I would assist them in an investigation. I knew by the tone of his voice that the assistance entailed undercover. I was dressed in a dark green velvet long sleeve leisure suit and green shoes and agreed. The SF was investigating one Juan Hernandez and one George Mejia, two major heroin dealers in the LaPuente-Montebello area. A CI had been developed that could introduce an undercover agent to Hernandez and Mejia for a multiple pound heroin transaction. I met and debriefed the CI and we got our roles worked out. I tried to determine how much heroin they had wherein I would order up all of it to obviate the need for a search warrant. The CI believed that an order of more than four pounds would spook them. The Cl placed a telephone call to Hernandez and advised that he had a customer that wanted to purchase four pounds of heroin for delivery back to San Fernando that day. Arrangements were made to meet with the crooks that morning on the parking lot of a supermarket in La Puente, California. I obtained a $75,000 flash roll and the CI and I, via undercover car (a flashy Cadillac El Dorado) drove over to the supermarket parking lot. A few minutes later Hernandez and Mejia arrived via a ragged Chevrolet and joined us at the undercover car. Two male Mexicans in another car followed them. They exited and conducted counter-surveillance. After a brief introduction, I told Mejia and Hernandez that I wanted to purchase four pounds of heroin. If it was good heroin that I would be back to purchase six or seven pounds within a few days. When Hernandez tried to play the suspicious of police role, I put his mind focused on the proposed subsequent six to seven-pound heroin purchase. Hernandez asked if I was ready to do the deal then. I advised that I was, that I had the money. I asked him if he wanted to see the money. He agreed. I went to the trunk, removed $75,000 rejoined them in the undercover car and flashed the money. I then told Hernandez and Mejia that I had a lot of money, made a lot of money and was looking to do a lot of business with them. Hernandez advised that he could supply as much heroin as I could buy.

In a short while, Hernandez and Mejia left to pick up the heroin for delivery. Counter-surveillance remained in the parking lot. I placed the flash roll in the trunk, exited the car advising the CI to watch the flash roll—that I was going into the supermarket to take a comfort break. I made a small purchase and asked the female cashier if they had a public restroom. She directed me to one in the southeast corner of the store. As I walked back to the rest room, I noticed that the cashier shut down the register and walked toward the back. After returning from the restroom I walked past a surveillant agent in the store and advised him that the crooks had left to pick up the heroin. I further advised that the second trip to the trunk would be the "Bust Signal." It was agreed that the CI and I would be arrested along with the crooks to protect his identify.

I rejoined the CI in the undercover vehicle and told him that I had met with a surveillant agent and apprised him what was transpiring. We chatted awaiting the arrival of the crooks with the heroin. The CI related that Hernandez had advised that he had approximately ten kilograms of heroin for sale when he had talked with him telephonically the day before. He did not believe they had sold all of it.

About thirty minutes later, Hernandez and Mejia arrived back at the parking lot, drove up to the counter-surveillant vehicle for a few moments, and then drove slowly around in the parking lot for about two minutes. They then drove up to our left, parked and walked over to the undercover car with Mejia carrying a bag. Both entered the undercover car. Mejia handed me the bag relating it contained four pounds of good heroin. I examined the heroin advised them that I would get the money out of the trunk, pay them and look forward to doing another deal with them in a few days. I walked back to the back with the heroin and opened the trunk. Instantaneously, surveillant units drove up to the undercover car. Agents/officers jumped out with guns screaming, "Federal Agent, freeze motherf___r. If you move, we'll blow your goddamn brains out. You're under arrest."

All of us were placed on the ground in a prone position and handcuffed. While on the ground, an arresting agent mumbled, "Man you are sure fucking up your velvet suit." I agreed. While in the arrest prone position, the female cashier ran out of the supermarket and identified me as having a gun. The transporting agent later asked me how she knew that I had a gun. I related that she had just identified herself as a peeping Tom. The only way she could have known that I had a gun was to see me urinate and adjust it in the restroom.

A search warrant was executed on Mejia's house and an additional eleven pounds of heroin were seized. There was no doubt that the immobilization of this organization caused a significant impact on the reduction of heroin in the San Gabriel Valley area.

As a promise for working undercover in other agents' cases, I requested the choice of the first or best CI developed out of the case. I later learned that two very good CIs were developed, however, I was never subsequently contacted or given the courtesy to be advised that they had been developed. This did not deter, impede or thwart my efforts. There were enough drug dealers and CIs around for all of us. I was pleased to learn that the investigation was being furthered beyond the initial seizure, that efforts were being made to identify and develop prosecution against the ultimate source of supply and cohorts.

About a week afterwards, my partner Roland Talton and I developed information that a major black heroin trafficker from Indianapolis, Indiana traveled to Los Angeles on a frequent basis, purchased a kilogram of heroin and he personally took back to Indianapolis for distribution. We determined his pattern from the CI and timed his arrival in the Los Angeles area, watching him deplane from a non-stop flight. We conducted surveillance of his activities and saw him meet with a male Mexican. Shortly after the meet, he went back to his hotel, checked out then drove toward Los Angeles International Airport. En route we popped him (arrested) at the light, noting that he had a neatly wrapped bag on the front seat. I shouted, "Freeze motherf__r Federal Agents. You are under arrest for violation of federal narcotic laws. What's in the bag?" He responded, "h-hh-h-h-h-her-rion."

His arrest, apparently shocked by being arrested by the Feds and being told that he was going to jail for twenty to forty years made him stutter badly, it took two hours to flip him into being a CI. He later advised that had we not scared him so during the arrest, he would have immediately cooperated. The CI further advised that when initially arrested, having a gun in each ear, caused him to defecate on himself He was somewhat hilarious and stated, "You sure know how to take a motherf___r down.'

We processed and presented him before the Magistrate and obtained a low bail that he could make. After a thorough debriefing, we allowed him to travel back to Indianapolis and to return back to Los Angeles, as he would usually do. The CI's source of supply was identified as Roberto Ram, a significant heroin trafficker that masqueraded as a common laborer. He drove an old model pick-up truck with a camper shell.

A week later, we coordinated, supervised and arranged for the CI to order two kilograms of heroin and a pound of cocaine from Ram, advising that he would travel to Los Angeles the next day to take delivery. My partner Talton and the CI were undercover in an undercover room at the Holiday Inn, Olympic and Figueroa. Surveillant agents saw Ram exit his residence with a package, enter the camper and drive to a Catholic Church. He entered the church where he prayed for a few minutes, entered the camper then drove to the Holiday Inn where he delivered the heroin and cocaine to the CI and undercover agent Talton and was immediately arrested in lieu of payment. During the post arrest interview, Agent Gary Elliot continuously asked Ram what he was praying for in the church. Ram never responded and seemed to get angry each time he was asked but he never responded. We tried to flip him but he hired an attorney, was advised not to cooperate. Ram paid his attorney a lot of money for a case he could not win. He paid more money on the promise of a victory during appeal. Ram went to prison for a long time. His little quiet, nice, neatly manicured lawn neighborhood was shocked of his arrest and sentencing.

I continued to travel all over California working undercover and conducting surveillance. I remember the first time I met Enrique "Cookie" Camarena, a DEA agent later brutally murdered in Mexico. The Calexico resident office had requested assistance in two cases. The RAC was Guillermo "Bill" Ortiz, one of my former supervisors, a man for whom I will always have a lot of respect and admiration. The Calexico office had two drug traffickers that were causing them heartburn. One was a youngster named, Manuel Olague. Olague sold multiple ounces of cocaine out of his residence in Calexico as though he had a license. U.S. Customs reported that he was a thorn in their side. He crossed the border from Calexico into Mexicali, Mexico two, three and sometimes as much as six times a day. On each time he was taken into secondary and searched and a dog scanned his vehicle. He came up clean. U.S. Customs had information that he was scoring (purchasing) four to eight ounces of cocaine and delivering it back to customers on the U.S. side. U.S. Customs had a CI in jail that related he could make a telephone introduction of an undercover agent for a cocaine transaction.

When I first talked to RAC Ortiz, I asked him to have the CI order a pound or two. RAC Ortiz disagreed and I realized that I had made a mistake by telling such a well-seasoned veteran like Ortiz how to proceed in a case. He had worked undercover before I could spell undercover, was bilingual, a native Californian and certainly was more cognizant of the drug dealers in his area of responsibility. Ortiz was one of the nicest agents I ever met. He had one of those faces that made him seem angry all the time, he seldom smiled, was very business like and very seldom questioned authority, a truly duty oriented organization man.

I drove down to Calexico, met with Ortiz, other BNDD agents, U.S. Customs and Imperial County Sheriffs Deputy. One deputy that seemed to admire me, asked a lot of questions, was introduced to me as Enrique Camera. We chatted for a long time. A plan was formulated to take Olaque down (arrest him). U.S. Customs had a new camper that had just come out of seizure and it was deployed across the street from Olaque's residence with two U.S. Customs surveillant agents. I telephoned Olaque, ordered four ounces of cocaine, telling him that I was the friend of the CI, had just gotten out of jail in Imperial County and wanted to take the cocaine back to Los Angeles. I advised I had originally come down for a pound but got ripped off by a courier. Olaque agreed to sell me four ounces that day two hours later. I made arrangements to meet him at his house to do the deal.

About two hours later, I arrived at Olaque's house and knocked. When he came to the door, I advised I was there to buy the coke. Olaque told me to wait and went back into the house momentarily. He then joined me at the porch with four ounces of cocaine in his right hand. Each contained a rubber contraceptive. When I asked to see it he extended it to me asking for the money in direct exchange. I asked if he had the coke (a bust signal for the U.S. Customs agents on point in the camper). He responded that he did. I asked to inspect the coke; he refused and continued to hold it in his right hand. I stated here is the money, immediately clasp his right hand with my left hand, pulled out my .38 Colt Cobra revolver and pointed at him and shouted, "Federal agent, you are under arrest."

Olaque attempted to go back into the house and I grabbed him around the neck and physically lifted him off the porch toward the camper to await the arrival of assistance from surveillant units. I struggled with him off the porch around the right side of the house where we tore down a wooden fence that bordered his house. I put the gun in his ear and shouted, "Federal agent, freeze you cocks___r or I will blow you goddamn brains out."

He did not relent and continued to kick and strike me with his free hand. I squeezed his neck tight in the fold of my left arm and tried to choke him out. He continued to fight. I took him to the ground and pushed his head forward and placed the gun in his ear again screaming, "Freeze, you are under arrest, federal agent." With me on his back, Olaque crawled the width of the neighbor's yard where we tore down another picket fence and struggled to the sidewalk. At the sidewalk, Olaque tore open one of the ounces of cocaine and tossed it back into my face, before I became temporarily blinded a group of male Mexicans drove up in a car and shouted, "What in the fuck is he doing to Manny?" I could vaguely see two of them exiting the car and walking toward me. I then fired two shots in the air and shouted, "Get out of here, federal agent, get out of here motherf___r." Olaque tore open another ounce package of cocaine and tossed it back into my face. I became blind and my whole face went numb. I released my grip around his neck and heard the sound of footsteps on the sidewalk running away from me and the car at the curb closed to me peel rubber and speed away. A few seconds later, I heard surveillance agents arrive asking what had happened. I was blind, not knowing whether it was permanent or temporary. Ortiz arrived and advised that it was not permanent; that after washing my eyes with cold to lukewarm water I would be okay. We scrapped up as much of the discarded cocaine as possible and forwarded it to the laboratory.

At the office, RAC Ortiz apologized for the ineptness of the customs agents. He advised that they had heard the bust signal, saw the fight but did not want to make an arrest from a new camper, did not want to burn the camper—that in their ineptness, they had placed the identity of the camper over the safety of a federal agent. Ortiz stated he would burn them to a crisp if that were my desire. I told Ortiz that I could never burn a brother law enforcement officer for doing what he believed was right to do. I prepared an affidavit for a warrant charging Qlaque with possession of cocaine, possession of cocaine for sale and assault on a federal agent. An intensive search was initiated for Olaque for three days without luck. Two weeks later he was popped crossing the border into the U.S. from Mexicali, Mexico.

My next trip down to Calexico about two months later involved major heroin trafficker Efrem Osuna Romero. Osuna sold 1/2 kilogram and higher quantities of heroin that, unknown to us at the time, he personally smuggled into the United States concealed in auto parts, machinery, etc. Agent Taylor and I drove over, ordered five ounces of heroin from Osuna. He instructed us to meet him on an isolated road outside of Calexico. We drove up, met with him, and were instructed to follow him. We followed Osuna around the deserted roads for about twenty minutes, then we drove drown a dirt road about five miles outside of the city. Osuna then told us the heroin was at a light post, requested that we pay him and walk over and take delivery of it. I paid Osuna and Agent Taylor and I watched him drive away as we walked to the telephone pole. We did not see any heroin.

We immediately surmised we had been burned. We drove over to three other telephone poles and found nothing. We drove back to the office, met with RAC Ortiz and advised him what had transpired. We then telephoned Osuna in Mexicali and advised him that we did not see the heroin. He advised us that the heroin was in the "juice can." It was then that we realized that the heroin was in the voltage regulator. There was a voltage regulator resting against the post. I had instinctively picked up the voltage regulator tossed it in the back of the undercover car.

A month later I telephoned Osuna, ordered a kilogram of heroin advising that I was in Brawley and would meet with him in three hours in Calixico. Osuna was arrested that day as he came into the United States at the port of entry at Calexico. Three kilograms of heroin were seized from auto parts found in the bed of his truck.

The next time I went to Calexico, was about six months later. My identity had somewhat faded from the memories of crooks and suspects in the area. I negotiated with one Pedro Belmontes-Lopez for the proposed seizure of two kilograms of heroin. Belmontes delivered one kilogram of heroin to me and was arrested in lieu of payment.

The request for a black undercover agent continued to be made by numerous police departments, some that had no narcotic units and some that had not yet progressed to hiring black law enforcement officers. Additionally, there were areas, certain parts of California where the black population was either sparse or non existent.

On one request, I drove up to Oxnard, California—the first time I met Gustavo Vasquez, who later left the Ventura Sheriffs Department and became a federal narcotic agent with BNDD. At Oxnard, a major heroin dealer called El Lobo had operated in the La Colonia area with impunity. He was a native of Oxnard, knew all of the police, drug users, and dealers and would not deal with a total stranger. For some reason, I had the idea that I could make an undercover purchase of heroin from him. It did not matter what quantity. The sale of heroin would have resulted in a lot of time for him due to his history. Ventura sheriffs had a black informant (CI) that believed he could introduce an undercover agent to El Lobo. The CI had been in custody for two months and had been released only a day before my arrival in Oxnard. I met with the CI and discussed the pending deal and he seemed capable but a bit uncertain. I obtained a $1000 purchase of evidence (PE) funds, searched the CI and thereafter we drove over to the La Colonia section and entered a bar. I ordered a couple of beers and tried to engage in conversation with the bartender and a couple patrons sitting at the bar. There were approximately 15 to 20 patrons in the bar, 8 sitting at the bar and others sitting at tables. When we first entered the bar, two males on my right and a male and female on the CI's left were seated at the bar speaking English. After ordering the beers, they started speaking Spanish. In a very short while, the first man on my right stated, "Yo tengo que ir a mi casa (I have to go home) es muy caliente aqui (it is very hot in here)." His partner responded, "Y yo tambien" (me too). They both left the bar.

A short time later the couple on our left departed. Before we finished half of the beer, I looked around. The CI and I were the only customers left. We left, drove over to another bar and the customers left even sooner. We then went to the last bar in the La Colonia section and the same scenario happened. At that bar I decided to try to speak Spanish with the bartender, a plump female. "Que pasa?" (What's happening), I asked. She responded in English, "Nothing but heat and beer, nada mas" (nothing more).

After a short while, we drove back to the first bar and upon arrival saw El Lobo sitting on a BSA motorcycle with large tires. We parked and walked up toward El Lobo. When the CI said "El Lobo this____" before he could complete the introduction El Lobo peeled rubber leaving the area.

Thin White Lines

We drove back to the sheriff's office, met with surveillant units and advised them what had transpired. I told Vasquez sarcastically to call me back when he had a good kilo heroin case.

Drugs had been so prevalent in the U.S. parks and forests, at Yosemite, Eldorado, Stanislaus, Lassen, Shasta-Trinity, Plumas, Joshua Tree and Los Padres. Of all the parks and forests, Yosemite had become a doper's haven. While communes were springing up in Big Sur, Cleveland, San Bernardino, Los Padres, Kings/Sequoia, Los Angeles and San Bernardino, Yosemite had become a hot bed for drug cultivation, selling, using and producing. Acid heads and flower children running behind Bob Dylan, the Grateful Dead, Blood, Sweat and Tears, Janis Joplin, Jimmy Hendrix, Joan Baez, Sonny and Cher and Timmi Yuro quit good jobs, moved out of nice apartments and moved up into those areas and started communes. Some moved into Laguna Canyon and set up camps in caves, shacks, mobile homes and lean-tos.

At Laguna Canyon, I assisted undercover Agent G. Robert Warren in the take down of a major LSD manufacturer/dealer known as "Crazy Horse." Crazy Horse was the source of supply for LSD from Costa Mesa down to San Diego.

During the day of the take down, Agent Billy Waters made the mistake of wearing a light blue shirt and trying to hide in green bushes as point unit while Warren was undercover. He was flushed out when the acidheads set off a long string of firecrackers. Perhaps the thing that blew the surveillance was the sight of a big black surveillant agents walking, casually into the all white acid valley commune. We thought we were going to have to call El Toro Marines but we managed to affect the arrest with the posse we had at hand.

At Yosemite a year previous, the acid heads, bikers, druggers, fugitives and eremites had remained sober enough to realize that the uninformed officers were naturalist, not law enforcement personnel; that they could smoke marijuana, hashish, take acid, get drunk rowdy, and urinate on the camp fire without being warned or arrested. A big fight broke out that turned into a major riot. The naturalists and few law enforcement personnel on hand could only stand by and watch innocent families and children get caught up in a disturbance that escalated into an imbroglio. The riot quelled when the druggies, some passed out from exhaustion others so under the influence that they just quit.

Yosemite had become a major attraction for would be mountain climbers. People flocked there in hordes to learn mountain climbing and attempt to climb the face of El Capitan, the 7,569 feet Yosemite Point, Glazier Point, Sentinel Rock, and Sentinel Point. Ginger bears became friendly and on occasion walked into camps and ate along with campers.

As a result of the riot, the U.S. Park Police requested assistance from the FBI, BNDD, US. Marshals, state and local police during the Fourth of July weekend. Rumors of another riot sprang up and Department of Interior Secretary Herzog was planning a visit. Additionally, there were rumors that possibly President Nixon would also arrive for some sort of ceremonial presentation.

Agent Arthur Barnes and I were detailed to assist the park rangers and park police at Yosemite National Park. I drove up to Fresno, stopped had a hamburger, French fries and a beer. I drank all of the beer but kept half of hamburger and some fries for a late snack. While driving up to the park, I became sleepy. I drove until I entered the U.S. Park property and passed two turnouts noticing that there were campers. Several cars pulled into the turnouts. I became sleepier and nervous going around curves and the next vacant turnout I pulled into, cracked the windows about 2" from the top and fell asleep. I was awakened in pitch darkness from scratches and pawing at the front right passenger door. While awakening, I could slightly see the movement of a huge figure at the door that initially I though was a man. I immediately grabbed my service revolver and prepared to shoot until I realized/recognized it was a huge bear. I started the engine and drove away with the bear still trying to get into the car. I was so frightened that I was no longer sleepy. I drove down into the village and slept next to the park police station. En route down to the village I saw two sets of bears cross the road in front of me.

One of the most beautiful sights I have ever seen was that night when I first saw the vertical face of El Capitan silhouetted by the moon against a darkened sky. The large granite-like face was awesome, eerie and majestic to behold. It was even prettier during the day and when viewed at an angle with flitting clouds, it looked like a huge piece of beautiful art moving in front of you.

Art arrived late that morning and we were housed in a barrack in the village. We met an U.S. Marshal in the barracks that morning and I knew I would not be having breakfast with him. It was apparent he drank his breakfast and that it consisted of scotch whiskey. I had seen some drinkers in my days and had had my fill of brown water. I did not shy away from a good "pop" (cocktail) but I always had difficulties trying to have a "pop" before 6:00 p.m. and after 1:00 am. We were scheduled to work with the Marshal and the amount of whiskey I watched him consume on our first arrival convinced me that Art and I would be working alone.

The next day, we parked one car and drove through the village and visited several campsites in one car. Later that day, we had a briefing and Art and I decided to take a few dopers down for the arrest to be printed in the local newspaper to deter and reduce drug trafficking in the park. Art and I drove to a restaurant, had a slight repast and upon leaving were asked by two white males if we wanted to buy some "smokes" (marijuana). We advised that we wanted to buy a couple pounds for a campfire party that night. The two males agreed and entered a truck, advising that they had the marijuana with them. Art and I had them follow us in a circuitous route to the parking lot of the ranger station. They delivered two pounds of marijuana to us and were immediately arrested and walked about 25 yards into the ranger station where they were booked.

The next day while walking in the village, a young white female, approximately 19 to 20 years old asked us if we wanted to buy some acid (LSD). We agreed and she told us to wait for her, that she had to go home. We advised her that we would take her home. We then got in the car and drove her over to an area where she entered a cave and rejoined us in the car. We drove around toward the ranger station chatting about the quality of the acid until we reached the parking lot of the station. The female delivered 100 hits of acid and we placed her under arrest. Art and I had to physically carry her into the ranger station. She cursed, kicked, scratched and screamed. We had the arrests reported in the local newspaper and indicated that there were approximately 1000 federal narcotic agents conducting undercover raids and arrests in the park. There was no riot as rumored in Yosemite Park that year.

Of all the places I have visited, Yosemite National Park has a beauty that is beyond words to describe, the mountains, vegetation, waterfalls, streams, campsites, animals, especially the Ginger bears with their beautiful brown coats. All kinds of birds are seen during the day and many chirp, sing and coo during the night.

Our office was then located on the eighth and seventh floors in the World Trade Center on Figueroa and Third Street—a nice location. The U.S. Passport Office was located there. Although I was never a movie star fan, I had the opportunity to see the comings and goings of numerous movie stars: Angie Dickinson and her police crew including Earl Holiman film a scene in the garage of the World Trade Center. On passing I saw Eva Gabor, Telly Savalas, Loretta Swit, Eddie Fisher, Dennis Cole, Richard Pryor, James Arness, Grady (Sanford and Son), Red Foxx, Bob Hope and others. On one occasion while walking casually on the main floor showing a gentleman the location of the U.S. Passport Office, Supervisory Agents George Heard and William Alden asked me how long had I been a friend of Dane Clark. I told them I did not know him. They chuckled and advised that I was walking and talking to him like old friends.

One day shortly after I had exited the elevator on the 8th floor, a black male that was waiting in the reception area looked at me as though shocked to see me. He waived, called my name and advised that he would contact me later. I learned from another agent on the elevator going down, that the black male was a once very famous singer that had a single record that sold several millions, that he was a CI of Agent Robert Lucido. Later that day I contacted Agent Lucido and learned the true identity of the black male and Agent Lucido provided a telephone number where the CI could be reached.

On the following day, the CI telephoned and advised that he wanted to meet with me briefly, that he was coming to the office to talk to Agent Lucido. He advised that upon arrival, he would call me before advising Agent Lucido that he had arrived. When I met the CI in the reception area, he gave me a surprising hug and immediately asked me to forgive him. He then related that LAPD Sergeant James L. Segar, Badge #11550 had stopped him on a "humbug" (non-existing charge or reason) and physically punished and abused him. Segar referred to him continuously as a "nigger" and forced him to fabricate a story about me. According to the CI, he had never seen me before but was shown a photo of me by Segar. Segar and his partner forced him to sign a false statement. The CI then asked what you would do if someone were beating you. intimidating and threatening you. At this point his eyes were filled with tears. He again asked for forgiveness, relating that he had been forced by Segar et al to do something that could have caused me to be arrested, jailed and to lose my job. The CI swore that he would take a polygraph examination to verify his truthfulness. He further related that Sergeant

Segar openly displays a strong hatred for all blacks; a hatred that was deeper than any that he had ever experienced. The CI added that Sergeant Segar was one of the "crookedest cops" that he had ever seen. He assured me that he would cooperate fully and related that he believed that based on the foregoing, that there were a lot of innocent blacks in jail on "trumped up charges" by Sergeant Segar.

I felt very sad learning that the CI related that he had provided the information to one of my white brother agents to tell me; that I was never informed, that I was subjected to not one but two unwarranted internal security investigations based solely on the racially contrived, concocted and perjurious false documents perpetrated by another brother law enforcement officer. Perhaps more saddening is the fact that a brother agent, a person I would under an enforcement situation have to rely on to protect my life, a person, by virtue of our occupation, training and dedication I would have to put my life on the line to protect, had remained mute. It was more disheartening realizing that he did so advertently.

I conducted a preliminary investigation, which disclosed that Sgt. Segar was the presenter of the first false allegation. I met with an Assistant U.S. Attorney (AUSA) and apprised him what had transpired. The AUSA advised that Sgt. Segar could be charged with I8USC 1001; furnishing false information to a federal agency, perjury, obstruction of justice, subordination of perjury, conspiracy of all of the foregoing and civil right violations involving their CI and equal charges involving the allegations lodge supposedly by one George Reese.

I directed a three-page letter to my supervisor relating that I was contemplating filing criminal and civil charges against Sergeant Segar for conspiracy to commit perjury, perjury, solicitation of perjury, defamation of character, obstruction of justice and civil rights violation; that he had done this on two separate occasions, involving two alleged informants. I conferred with an

AUSA who advised he would pursue the charges and recommended that if they were to be pursued that a letter should be forwarded to the U.S. Attorney's office by top management to initiate it. Additionally, I talked with two LAPD officers and they described Sergeant Segar as a reckless racist cop with a reputation within his department of having extremely strong racial biases that he often openly displayed at work.

I suggested that corrective action be taken against Sgt. Segar to prevent him from further committing perjury, solicitation of perjury and other crimes and malpractices. I recommended that the informant that was forced to commit the first false charges be interviewed by inspections, deactivated and blacklisted.

A short time later, I was called into DRD Azzam's office where I was introduced to LAPD Commander Reese, the supposedly then apparent next LAPD Chief of Police. Commander Reese related that he had written his master's thesis on prejudices; he further related that he had been cognizant for some time that Sgt. Segar possessed unacceptable prejudices against Blacks and Hispanics that often spilled over into his work. He also related that he had sent Sgt. Segar to a behavior modification course. I explained that the behavior/acts committed by Segar were serious enough to warrant corrective action. I knew from the tones of Commander Reese and DRD Azzam's voices that they were both predetermined that nothing was going to happen to Sgt. Segar. I began to think of the two police officers whose action encouraged me to choose law enforcement as a profession and then realized that they were LASO deputies not LAPD, that even LASO and my parent agency had employees whose morals and ethics were shocking.

I had become highly skilled in undercover investigations that often resulted in request for my assistance in numerous cities. I was scheduled to go to New York City for a 90-day special operation dealing with police corruption and major black drug dealers, The Knapp Commission, in Harlem and the Bedford

Styverson sections. I had traveled to Seattle, Washington and worked undercover with narcotic detective Janet Schrader on the Humphrey Ross et al. al. organization.

On the first day of arrival with Det. Schrader, I made a hand-to-hand purchase of cocaine from Richard Rovine Stewart, a prior convicted felon, who at the time of the purchase, was in violation of federal parole for being outside of the Central District of California. The organization was busted and when they went to trial, they were stunned to learn that the little blond naive female they were selling dope to was really a redhead Seattle PD narcotic officer and that she was married to a Seattle policeman, who was a sergeant in the homicide division. They were also stunned to learn that her supposedly boyfriend was a federal narcotic agent out of Los Angeles. The work that previous black undercover agents and I did in Seattle was instrumental in black agents being recruited and assigned there. Two of the first were Alice Shuemate and Greg Williams.

It was a request for a black undercover agent that caused some of my travel to Los Vegas, Nevada. Agents George Clemente and Robert Sternaman had worked numerous major cases. One case involved a major drug trafficker named Smokey Joe Lovato. Attendant to his arrest, they seized a blue/white Buick Electra-225. It had a horn that when depressed, played the song "La Cucaracha." I was assigned to work undercover in Las Vegas. I drove the Buick Electra 225 up to Las Vegas, met with the RAC Richard Robinson, checked into the Villa Roma Motel off the Las Vegas strip, had dinner at RAC Robinson's residence then drove back to my lodging.

On the next day, I met with RAC Robinson and Agent Sam Ozment. A plan was formulated to make an undercover purchase of heroin from John Doe Slim, a black heroin trafficker that resided in North Las Vegas, a predominately black neighborhood. I was wondering how two white agents were going to cover me on surveillance in a predominantly black neighborhood. Agent

Ozment assured me that they would have the point and that he would be close enough to me on surveillance that he could hear me "fart." I searched the CI, found him devoid of narcotics. He had a small amount of money he was allowed to keep. We entered the Buick Electra and drove over to Slim's house and joined six other black males in the living room. The CI introduced me to Slim as his cousin Beenum from Henderson, Nevada. After the introduction and speaking in generalities for a few minutes, I asked Slim if we could talk business. He stated, "Sure these are all my customers, feel free to talk." I told Slim I wanted to purchase an ounce or two of heroin if the heroin was good quality heroin. I talked about future deals, advised Slim that my cousin (CI) and I would leave, return in about an hour to purchase either an ounce or two ounces of heroin. Slim advised that he would have the heroin ready upon our return. He further advised that depending on how much his other customers wanted, that he would at least have an ounce and more than likely he would have two ounces of heroin available upon my return.

    The CI and I entered the undercover car and was driving away when I saw a funny looking black guy sitting in a car that I believed to be Agent Sam Ozment's official government car. I turned the radio on and heard Agent Ozment broadcast, "The u/c has just departed the crooks house eastbound." I got on the radio and advised that Slim was expecting his source within a half-hour and that we were going to return in an hour to complete the deal. We drove from the area, met with RAC Robinson at a park and chatted from car to car. While chatting, SA Ozment advised that a Thunderbird with a California license plate had arrived at Slim's house. A black male got out and entered Slim's residence.

    A few minutes later the CI and I went back to Slim's house and joined Slim and six of his customers in the living room. Slim advised that his man had arrived and he could do the two piece (ounce) deal with me. A man walked out of the back room into the living room. Immediately when he crossed the door well I recognized him to be Charles Gary, a defendant I had purchased drugs from resulting in his arrest in Lompoc, California; I had caused his first federal case for which he was out on bail. I was dressed like a gangster with a wide brim hat and ankle length leather coat. Before Gary could make facial contact I tilted my head to the side somewhat shielding my face from him. Gary walked over to the area where I was seated and I carefully spoke in a false street voice, "Hey what it is my man, what it bee's like?" still partially shielding my face. Gary did not return the greeting and walked back into the back room motioning for Slim to join him. While they were in the back room, I readied myself to draw and shoot quickly. I reached down into the slit of my leather jacket pocket into my crotch and removed a 5-shot .38 Colt Cobra, loaded with 150 grain soft lead, hollow point, jacketed rounds. I reached into my left pocket and removed my speed loader and prepared to if necessary engage in some heavy fireworks if the situation dictated it.

Only Slim came back into the living room and immediately asked me how many dozens of eggs I wanted. "Two- dozen, two that will take a 3 or 4" (realizing that Slim had been told that I was a federal agent I told him, thinking in jargon, that eggs heroin, that I wanted two ounces of heroin that could be cut 3 or 4 times). I could see Slim was nervous by the crackle in his voice. It changed from a baritone to almost a first tenor and he had difficulties selecting his words.

I then stated, "Is your heroin brown heroin or white heroin? I was told you got both of them good."

I thought Slim was going to choke on his tongue when he slurringly responded "Her- he-he-her-he-her-roin? What are you talking about man? Don't talk about no dope in my house. Wh-wh-wh-wh-what are ya-ya-ya talkin' bout, I-I-I-I don't know no-no nothin' about no, no drugs."

When I asked Slim what was he going to sell me for $600 a

piece, his mouth went dry and his eyes widened. Poor Slim was petrified that a federal agent was in his house and so was his connection. While Slim was stuttering I heard a continuous flushing of a toilet in the back.

A big, dark-complexioned male black customer that was dozing off to sleep yelled, "Yeah Slim what in the fuck are you talking about some goddamn eggs. When am I getting my dope motherf___r? I paid you for it yesterday."

Another customer yelled, "Heah Slim, I was here first, when am I getting my dope?"

Slim yelled back, "Wh wh wh what the fuck y'all talkin 'bout? I don't do no dope."

All six customers tore into Slim for their dope. A big urination match erupted. Apparently three customers fronted their money (paid in advance) and they were not about to leave Slim's residence without their dope.

One customer yelled, "Slim I have been buying dope from you for a couple of years and you still make me front my money. Most of these guys here are new customers and only two of them had to front. Now motherf___r you trying to play this shit off. You sound like you are scared or something. Did your connect bring the dope or not?"

Slim had no answer. To make matters worse, the CI asked, "Slim what the fuck's going on man? Why are you acting like that?" Slim looked at the CI, shook his head in a sad and disgustingly manner and stated, "Of all people, you should know why I'm acting like this. Why me?"

The CI played it off, "What the fuck's wrong with you Slim? What are you talking about?"

Slim did not answer and looked at me as though somewhat in disbelief that this was happening to him. He did not know whether his arrest was eminent and was apparently afraid to tell us to leave. From his demeanor, I knew that we were in no danger so I decided to make him sweat bullets and maybe I could build a conspiracy case around our conversation with Gary and Slim's customers. It was very apparent that Gary had recognized me and was sitting in the back room petrified.

I asked Slim for permission to use his bathroom in an effort to check Gary out in the back room. At first Slim denied me but after his customers complained he consented, advising that the bathroom was in the back to the left. I walked into the hall then opened the door to my immediate right and saw Gary sitting on the bed. When he saw me he shied away.

I walked into the bathroom and returned in a short while and again asked Slim, "Yeah Slim why don't you cut this shit out, sell me the two ounces of heroin and I'll get out of your hair." Apparently I struck a soft spot. Slim was a tall thin bodied, thin face, mustachioed black that had his hair done up in a Marcel. Slim started cursing me and told me to get the "fuck out of my house motherf___r." He seemed shocked that he had blurted out at me like that and became apologetic.

The CI and I exchanged farewells with Slim and left the residence. As soon as we left the residence, Gary entered the Thunderbird and was followed southbound on Interstate 15 at 85 mph. I turned on the radio and heard the local surveillant agents following him. The first transmission we heard, "He's barreling ass, and he's barreling ass southbound on 15 at 85." A few minutes later another unit, "He's still barreling ass southbound at 85, shall we stay with him?"

"Stay with him until LV-2 connect with the u/c"

All units responded, "10-4." "10-4." "10-4."

While driving to a prearranged meet location, the strange looking black guy in the car like LV-2 pulled up along side of us and yelled "follow me" and motioned with his white forearm and white hand. It was LV-2 donned up like a medium complexion black man and wearing an Afro wig. Despite the make up, it was his non-black facial features that made him look different and a bit funny.

After advising LV-1 and LV-2 what had transpired, I drove the CI to his residence, went back to the hotel and freshened up. I decided to drive around the city and find some nice little place to eat. I knew it would not be prudent to eat in West Las Vega. I drove down the Las Vegas strip. At a busy cross street I sounded the horn, let it play "La Cucaracha" for almost three minutes. Cars screeched, putting on brakes. Drivers and passengers peeked out of cars up toward the sky. I did the same while stopped at the light and saw cars crossing the intersection with startled and amused drivers and passengers.

CHAPTER 7

ABOUT SIX MONTHS LATER, I traveled back to Las Vegas, met with the RAC, Agent Ozment and a CI. During the debriefing, the CI related that "Sonny" Liston, the former world heavyweight champion was dealing $50 and $100 bags of cocaine in the Keno area of the International Hotel on a daily basis. According to the CI, Liston could be contacted at the Keno area for an introduction as a prelude for a cocaine purchase. The CI further advised that he could introduce an undercover agent to Liston for cocaine purchases.

Prior to starting the investigation of Liston, I went with RAC Robinson and we surveilled a short black male and his entourage from New York as they arrived at McCarren Airport, were picked up by a limousine and transported to the hotel. When an inquiry was made with the desk, we learned the black male was Frank Matthews, a.k.a. PeeWee, a major drug trafficker from New York linked to "the Mafia." Frank reportedly was a frequent visitor to the hotel and dropped $50,000 to $100,000 per visit.

The next day I searched the informant and found him devoid of any narcotics. He had a moderate amount of money that he was allowed to keep. I obtained a $1,000 flash roll, mostly $50s and a few $100s, marked the bills for identification. The CI and I then drove over to the International Hotel and tried to contact Sonny Liston. We spent five hours in the casino and did not find Sonny Liston. We then contacted a cocktail waitress who related that Liston would not be in today. We terminated the operation. I drove, per the CI's instructions, to 2058 Ottawa Way, where Liston lived according to the CI. The CI related that he had purchased $50 bag of cocaine from Liston at the hotel and at his residence. The CI advised that we could do a cold knock on his door. I put that idea aside advising that we could try the house approach later.

The next day, the CI and I went over to the International Hotel and as we entered the Keno area, we could see Liston walking back toward the cashier area. We waited for about an hour and a half and Liston had not returned to the Keno area. I then called on the house telephone and requested the operator to page Mr. Charles "Sonny" Liston and left a message for him to meet his friends in the Keno area. After the second page I saw Liston hurriedly walk outside enter a Cadillac and sped from the area. We put the deal down that day. On the following day we went back to the International Hotel and paged "Mr. Charles Sonny Liston." There was no response. We waited in the area for three hours, paged him again and got no response. We got into the undercover car, drove over to 2058 Ottawa Way and knocked. I was dressed gangster-like with a wide brim hat. Liston answered the door and spoke briefly with the CI. The CI told Liston that I was his cousin Big John from Salt Lake City. Liston invited us into his house. His wife was moving about in the kitchen. There was an almost human size teddy bear with the heavyweight title belt wrapped around the waist in the living room. Liston turned and shook my hand and invited us to follow him into the den.

I had a 47" chest and 17?" biceps but felt like a much smaller man next to Liston. His shoulders appeared to be at least 54" wide and his hands were the largest I had ever seen; they resembled boxing gloves but were hard and callous. He appeared plump but had an appearance of being made of rugged solid muscle. I had heard a prior story about the police in St. Louis striking Liston on the head so hard that the baton broke and the blow reportedly only angered him. I had always had confidence in my 5-shot .38 Colt Cobra with the hollow point supervels. In the presence of Liston, I had a doubt that they could stop him immediately. I relaxed seeing his demeanor and the respect he gave his wife and the respect that she displayed for him. All while conversing Liston, seemed assured that she was not trying to overhear any of the conversation. He respected her by talking in a soft low voice when talking about drugs or women.

Liston related often in the conversation "how much pussy I was getting", when he was actively fighting. In a sly way, the CI tried to mention the Mafia on two or three occasions. Liston ignored him each time. Frequently, in the conversation, he referred back to "how much pussy I used to get" and spoke quietly and on occasion peered toward the kitchen where his wife was.

After a brief general conversation, Liston related that he had run out of cocaine yesterday. He suspected that the police was looking for him at the International Hotel. I asked him if the police had contacted him. He said he had not, but that he knew it was the police because, "A white friend of mine and I was in the bathroom doing a line (snorting cocaine). I don't know how long it was but it was a long time. I think we went through about ten packs, I felt so good I even gave some away. You know I had a pocketful of 'em when I went in there. I only had one left that I musta missed...."

Thin White Lines

The CI asked, "Did the police come into the bathroom?"

Liston answered "Naw man. While in the shitter—now check this out—somebody paged me calling me Charles. Ain't no motherf___r in the world but the police calls me Charles. The motherf__r paged me several times, calling me Charles. The first time my buddy had to tell me I was being paged. I was so high; I even forgot my name was Charles. You ain't never seen nothing about nobody calling me no Charles in the damn news 'cause my name is Sonny. You know a buddy of mine, a little White dude that works in the hotel, he told me that the place was crawlin' with police. I thanked him but I didn't give a fuck..."

The CI asked, "Sonny do you have a little taste, a stamp for your man?"

"Wait a minute," Sonny said, "I might have a little something laying around somewhere if my old lady ain't throwed it in the trash. She's so clean she don't even know what it is."

He left the room for a little while, and then returned relating that he didn't have any. Liston then related that he had been in a bad car accident and pointed at several vertical scars on his face. He stated that while in the hospital, the medication kept him so high and feeling good that he didn't want to get out. He believed he was given morphine or dilaudid. Liston related that he drives to Los Angeles picks up from 1/2 to a pound of cocaine on a regular basis. When he arrives back in Las Vegas, he packages some of it up and stashes it in a hole next to a telephone pole on the golf course at the rear of his house. Liston related that on one occasion, he drove to Los Angeles, picked up 8 ounces of cocaine and was in his Cadillac driving back to Las Vegas on Interstate 15; he had snorted a little coke in Los Angeles, stopped several times on his way back and snorted a little more and was feeling good. He was driving along feeling good when the red lights of a police car came on behind him. He looked at the speedometer and he was doing 85 miles per hour. Liston stated he immediately grabbed the cocaine from under the seat "wrapped in two condoms." He placed one on the left door and burst it with his fingernail and let it blow in the wind. He did the same with the other package, dropping both empty "rubbers." He then pulled over and stopped. According to Liston, when the Nevada Highway Patrolman walked up on him, he could see cocaine on the police car like it had snowed. The patrolman approached, recognized him, and told him to slow it down and let him go without giving him a ticket. According to Liston, "the police around here are nice motherf___rs man, if they know you. You know I'm a big nigger in this town. All the big white folks here like me" and laughed.

Liston rambled about how much white pussy he had gotten and how for some reason before his fights all of the white women wanted to give him some pussy. According to Liston, they came out of the woodwork but after the fight, he couldn't even buy pussy.

I told Liston that I was really from Henderson, Nevada, not Salt Lake City, and that I wanted to get an ounce coke connection in Las Vegas to prevent having to drive all the way to Los Angeles. Liston advised that he would be traveling back to Los Angeles to "cop" (purchase) and he would reserve an ounce for the CI and me. All while talking, Liston shielded the contents of the conversation from his wife; she remained in the kitchen. He related that he just made enough from the coke business to get by, have a little cocaine for his own use and pay a few bills; he had no pension, no money saved and no real future ahead of him.

I began to somewhat empathize with Liston, recognizing that he was merely a small town fellow, a country boy that got caught up in a world of trickeration, deceit, chicanery, skullduggery, shenanigans and scams. Because of his physical strength, he had been exalted to a level of world attention, the heavyweight champion of the world. While he rejoiced and jubilated, a large segment viewed him with a degree of disdain, viewed him as an undesirable, a non-role model, and a hoodlum. It was apparent that he was being exploited beyond his ability to comprehend and at this point in his life, he is proving to be what he was earlier believed to be—a crook, a hoodlum, and a contracultralist to the core.

We discontinued the negotiations with the promise that Liston would sell me an ounce of cocaine at a later date. Liston stated he would let the Cl know when he had copped. We discontinued the undercover negotiations, exchanged farewells and departed Liston's residence. We then drove over to a prearranged meet location and advised surveillance what had transpired. I had to be back in Los Angeles for a trial that Monday.

I drove back and about five days later, the Nevada Police found Liston dead from an alleged overdose of heroin. I am convinced that he was given a "hot shot" (a dose of high-grade heroin) for during the undercover negotiations and according to the CI, Sonny would never shoot heroin. One of the things he had related was how afraid he was of needles. I believe that had he decided to use heroin, because of his fear of needles, he would have snorted it. Sonny Liston was murdered. Like almost all deaths from heroin overdoses, the police throughout America exert little to no effort toward pursuing them as a possible murder; they view the deceased as a resolution to a major evil, heroin addiction. I telephoned the CI and he related that he was certain that "the Mafia" had killed Sonny.

A short time later, New York made a good case on Frank Matthew and a search warrant was executed on a safety deposit box in Las Vegas. $1,000,000 in cash was seized.

I traveled to the Beach cities, worked surveillance and undercover. On one occasion, Special Agent Larry Shoemaker was undercover on a group of longhaired marijuana traffickers in Costa Mesa, California. We surveilled the crooks involved for two days, dropped off after midnight the first day and started up again at 6:00 a.m. the following day. We watched two crooks leave a house with a quantity of marijuana and deliver it to undercover agent Shoemaker. Eight other agents and I remained on surveillance of the stash house. When the bust signal was given at the delivery location we decided to secure the stash house, detained about eight subjects inside until we got a search warrant. With my service revolver drawn, I knocked and announced our authority and identity. Silence fell from within and heavy footsteps could be heard moving around in the house and nobody answered the knock. I caved the front door in with my shoulder, taking it completely off the hinges and jam. I entered the residence with five agents simultaneously as two agents entered the side door. We screamed "Federal agents, get up against the wall with your hands held high!" We fanned out to secure the house. In the southwest bedroom I saw what appeared to be a man hiding in the closet. I screamed, "Come out with your hands raised high, federal agents!" There was no movement. Another agent joined me to flush the subject out of the closet. We hollered for about two minutes, the legs of the subject did not move. After becoming frustrated I reached into the closet, grabbed the subject by the belt and snatched a prosthetic leg dressed in blue jeans partially hidden in the closet.

I went back into the living room and it was then, all eight agents realized that one of the defendants leaning on the wall was an amputee with his right leg amputated at the hip area. We allowed him to sit instead of standing. We later asked him how he had gotten to the wall. He related that almost contemporaneous with the front door being knocked down he fled to the wall and obtained a front leaning rest position. The amputee further related that the excitement and fear caused him to have an accident.

We worked all over doing take downs (making arrests and seizures) in Culver City, Santa Monica, Compton, Lynwood, Bellflower, Lakewood, Torrance, San Pedro, San Bernandino,

Colton, Rialto, Riverside, Manhattan Beach, Redondo Beach, Hermosa Beach, Anaheim, San Luis Obispo, San Francisco.

On one occasion, Agent Talton and I went TDY to San Francisco to work undercover on a high-ranking black political official. We went into numerous locations, debriefed numerous CI's and conferred undercover with close friends and relatives only to learn that the suspicion was all concocted in the mind of the alleging agent.

At Long Beach, California I worked undercover on a tattoo artist, purchased 10,000 seconals and had him taken down that same day trying to "sky up and deliver a batch to my customer in Denver." He was taken down at Los Angeles International Airport with 200,000 seconals, a briefcase of marijuana, a small amount of speed and a little personal coke. He tried to fight but was immediately subdued. He was a skuzzy fellow that had a big reputation as a tattoo artist and had his studio next to the Long Beach pier where all of the sailors visited and bikers frequented. I guess he wanted to make all of the money.

At Palm Springs, California, I worked undercover on a plastic surgeon that wanted to make all of the money. Besides doing facelifts and breast enhancements, he decided to sell pharmaceutical cocaine in liquid and powdery form. He sold the liquid to certain men involved in premature ejaculation. The surgeon had developed a solution of liquid cocaine, water and a mild lubricant. I learned from the U.S. Attorney's office that the procedure was questionable whether criminal or whether he could include his unconventional treatment as plastic surgery. The powder cocaine as "nose candy" was a different story; it was illegal.

I was working with Sgt. Grobe of the Palm Springs Police Department and Detectives from the Riverside Sheriff's office. Sgt. Grobe had developed a young attractive female CI that cut me into (introduced) the surgeon. He was a very inquisitive person. Rather than sell me an ounce of pharmaceutical cocaine, he preferred to ask questions, especially questions about my sexual prowess. I put the deal down with the understanding that the surgeon would check me out and if I were legitimate he would sell me multiple ounces of coke.

As luck would have it, two weeks later Sgt. Grobe got hired by Elvis Presley, the female CI could not be found and the surgeon left town. I was unable to find registration records of him in our indices.

The next undercover caper involved a white heroin addict CI that was supposed to introduce me to several young cocaine dealers in the Palm Springs, Cathedral City, Cabazon, Desert Hot Springs and Rancho Mirage areas. I made arrangements for a Riverside County detective and I to pick up the CI, drive to a trendy club in Palm Springs where the CI was going to introduce us to several cocaine traffickers for undercover drug purchases. We drove over to Palm Desert to the CI's house and per his instructions blew the horn. The CI peeked out the window then yelled, "Hey sit tight. I'll be out in a second." The CI had company.

After we waited about five minutes, the CI exited the house carrying a sweater. Blood was oozing from the vein of his left arm down to the fold of his left hand. He swabbed it with the sweater, then put on the sweater and entered the rear of the undercover car. Immediately I became angry but shielded it from the CI.

I asked, "Hey what did you just shoot up, boy or girl?"

"Nothing man. I cut myself shaving," the CI answered.

"I know it is possible to cut yourself in the fold of the arm, but I doubt that you did it shaving," I remarked.

The CI stated, "Aw man get off my case. Let's go and do the deal. I told Bucky I don't like working with black guys anyway and here I am getting ready to do a caper with you."

We drove back to Palm Springs and pulled up in front of a club. En route I noted that the CI dozed off and swayed from side to side and his head fell down a few times and he jerked it forward. We had turned on the radio to a hard rock station. While sitting in the car giving the CI last minute instructions, do's and don'ts, a song was playing and part of the lyric went "I can't go back there, Indiana wants me." The music played then the song continued, "This is the police, you are surrounded get out of the car!"

The CI, not realizing he was listening to a song stated, "Well I guess we'd betta do what he said we are busted again." He then mumbled something about bail and stumbling and mumbling attempted to get out of the undercover car.

"Hey just sit tight, we are not busted," I assured.

"Th-th-that- that's what the m-m-m-man said," he uttered.

I started the car and drove the CI back to his residence. Bucky, the Riverside Deputy helped the CI stagger to his house. We put the deal down.

The next trip in that area was an undercover caper with a drug trafficker named "Blood," a black dealer that had a history of dealing heroin in the Indio, Coachella, La Quinta and Thermal area. The first night undercover, Blood brought a sample of heroin and two addicts. I watched them fix and shoot up. When I asked the male addict how he felt, he related the following; 'Heroin is the king and queen of all drugs. It gradually takes over your body, thrilling you from the hair on your head and floats down into your body like a smooth salve, soothing and thrilling you as it flows. It settles in your stomach like ten orgasms, with the thrill circulating all over your chest and stomach; it flows down to your toenails making your whole body feel good, better than you can ever dream you could feel, but when it wears off, when you need it, you will do anything to get it."

I watched both addicts fall into deep slumber-walk, staggering about like in some kind of locomotive ataxia. Blood stated, "Is this some good shit or is this some good shit?" I agreed and purchased a one-ounce sample as a prelude to a proposed two-kilo seizure the following day.

On the following day, I checked into a u-shaped hotel in Indio, with adjoining surveillant rooms and a jump out crew (surveillant agents) two rooms across the hall. I telephoned Blood and gave him my hotel and room number and advised that I was ready to purchase the two kilos. Blood advised he would meet with me in two hours. After waiting about an hour and a half, I heard a gunshot in the adjacent surveillance room. I grabbed my revolver and entered the room with it drawn at waist level. The narcotic deputies advised me that everything was okay, that one of the surveillant officers had "killed a mattress" and the surveillant officers broke out in laughter.

A short time later, Blood and two henchmen arrived and delivered two kilos of heroin to me in the room and were arrested in lieu of payment for violation of federal narcotic laws. Surveillant agents had located the stash pad, a house in Coachella. In the process of taking the house, the surveilling helicopter flew around and eventually landed on a hard sand bed. It seemed as though the whole town came out to see what had transpired.

While in the office one day, my partner and I got a walk-in CI that gave us some valuable information about drug trafficking in the Los Angeles "Sugar Hill" and "Jungle" areas. The CI claimed to know Ike and Tina Turner, relating that he had attended several parties at their house. According to the CI, when Ike and Tina came back into town from a tour, Ike would purchase two pounds of cocaine and have cocaine parties with quarter ounce mounds of coke all over the house for consumption. When asked if he could introduce an undercover agent to Ike Turner for an undercover purchase, he related that Ike was a user not a seller. He believed that we could sell Ike a couple pounds of coke. Federal drug enforcement had not yet progressed to reverse undercover operations. Conversely, there were many instances where black undercover agents in an undercover capacity inside of crooks residences had given unwitting defendants a pinch of the drugs and were nearly charged with distribution of a controlled substance. In several cases corrective actions were taken against the agent.

The CI related knowing several major Detroit-based drug traffickers and related that one of the biggest drug traffickers in Detroit was a black dealer named, Marzette, a former Detroit narcotic officer. Marzette sold 1/8 kilograms or higher quantities of heroin because he believed that the police would not let that kind of money ride.

The CI knew Big Eddie Jackson, "Boogie Bear" Ernest Jackson Jr., Lester Ramsey, John Classen, and many other major black drug dealers. According to the CI, there was a large black Mafia dealing large quantities of drugs, operating "blind pigs, chop shops, booking numbers, booking horses, hijacking shipments, murder for hire, organized prostitution and that they get a piece of the action from prostitutes in the Cass Corridor and The Mack." He named Chester Campbell, a black male, as one of the biggest contract killers in Detroit.

According to the CI, the "Eyetalian Mafia" from the swank Grosse Pointe area controls the black Mafia. Campbell was a non-discriminating hitman. He would kill anybody as long as they paid his price. The CI further related that Campbell always wore black clothing—the mourning colors most often worn at funerals, wakes, and sad and suffering occasions. He further described Campbell as "the most baddest motherf___r I ever saw." The CI related that a big Detroit dope dealer had had a party with lots of food, liquor and coke and was relaxing in the den of his basement when a heroin addict forced his way into the house. The addict hijacked his money, dope and raped his 16-year-old daughter. The dealer knew the identity of the addict and was surprised that he did not try to disguise himself. The dealer put a $5,000 death contract on the addict and a $10,000 contract for him live, tied up and delivered to his house.

The CI further related that a man in the fast life went out one night with the addict to a bar called "The Pink Lady" where they, despite the cost of $4.00 per cocktail, drank Remy Martin like it was water. They left "The Pink Lady" and went to "The Twenty Grand Night Club." Afterward they went to a "Blind Pig" where they had more drinks and cocaine. The addict seemed to become more alert per drink. After snorting two lines of coke, he really woke up. The man got a Mickey (chloral hydrate) from the owner and slipped it in the addict's drink. A few minutes later the addict finally passed out. The man then advised the owner and patrons that he was taking his friend home, lugged him to the car buckled him down in the front and drove away.

Unbeknownst to the man until later, he drove over to a street behind the 10th precinct off Livernois where he tied the addict's hands behind him and tied his legs together with thick duct tape. He then taped his mouth with duct tape and put him in the trunk of the car. The man then called the dope dealer at 5:30 in the morning and advised that he had the robber/rapist. The first question the dope dealer asked "is he alive?" When the man stated yes, the dope dealer told him to come on over and pull into the garage. The man drove over and pulled the car into the garage.

The man took the addict down into the basement and seated him in a metal chair in front of a chaise lounge occupied by the dope dealer. The dope dealer tied the addict to the chair and went up stairs with the man. The dope dealer paid the man $10,000 and told him to come back later, that day and agreed to pay the man $3,000 more for a little job three days later.

The dope dealer then sent his wife and daughter that day down to Miami. About noon that day the man returned and joined the dope dealer in the basement.

The dope dealer fed the addict coffee, doused him with cold water, placed ice cubes in a wet towel and placed them on his face. He then got a washbasin of ice and water and submerged the addict face in the ice water until he became fully conscious.

The dope dealer then forced two tablets of speed down the addict's throat and fed him coffee until he was fully awake, fully alert.

The dope dealer left the basement and returned with drinks, snacks, a quantity of cocaine and a box of Cuban cigars. He lit a Cuban cigar, smoked it for about two minutes then put it out in the addict's eye. The addict screamed, hollered, begged, cried and moaned, but no relief came. For three days the dope dealer punished the addict in every cruel way he could think, even placing a hot poker iron up his rectum. The addict died from excessive punishment and torture. He was tortured beyond recognition.

The dope dealer then paid the man $3,000 to remove the body from his house and dispose of it. The man loaded the addict's body into the trunk of his car drove over to Belle Isle and dumped the addict body into the Detroit river just over the bridge off Jefferson.

When my partner asked the CI how he knew so much detail about the incident, the CI laughed, looked at me, winked his eye and stated, "I heard about it. That's how I know about it. You know you hear a lot of things on the streets."

We prepared a report and forwarded to the Detroit and other affected offices.

CHAPTER 8

DRUG LAW ENFORCEMENT for some agents often proves boring from routine and repetitive tasks. Some could not grow with the time; they became bored from the lack of any newness in duties, coupled with unending paperwork. There was very little to do other than pursue investigations via conventional methods.

We were all happy when the federal wiretap law was passed, and too, like most people we were not readily acceptable to the change, it took a while to catch on. Prior to the law a few enterprising agents initiated their own unauthorized wiretaps that caused their demise from law enforcement. Some went to jail. I recall the first wiretap investigation I worked was on Vincente Guzman-Zuniga, a major heroin trafficker. I was impressed that we were afforded a room and part of a bank as a stationary observation post.

My first trip into Tijuana as an agent was with a posse of about 25 agents trying to arrest Guzman in Tijuana. He was a slick dope peddler, old and worn, but cagey. He made our surveillance in Tijuana and slipped out from under us the second night.

As a young agent, I was assigned a number of details, some interesting, many dull, and others with memories that last a lifetime. I remember my first visit to the Federal Reserve Bank on Olympic Boulevard in Los Angeles, the first time I really saw wall-to-wall dollars; wall-to-wall $100 bills, not notes but hundred dollar bills. It was then that I finally realized that the U.S. Government actually printed money. For some reason I had envisioned that money came from heaven or some other place. Maybe it was because I was not fortunate to have easy access to large amounts of it. Perhaps one of the most memorable details I pulled was when I was assigned to chaperon a Nigerian Interpol officer. We called it "baby sitting," or "holding hands."

I was detailed to pick up one Michael Okeyede, an Interpol Officer (IO) arriving on a non-stop TWA flight from New York, JFK Airport. IO Okeyede had visited Washington, DC, Chicago and New York. He was arriving in Los Angeles for a five-day tour. His trip was being sponsored by the US Department of State (State Department) and we were requested to provide the utmost courtesy to I0 Okeyede and to make his visit to the Los Angeles area pleasant.

I waited at the TWA gate and watched approximately 300 passengers disembark a TWA 747 flight. Shortly I saw IO Okeyede walk out of the ramp into the terminal. I walked up to him and stated, "Michael Okeyede, I am John Sutton. Welcome to Los Angeles!"

I was wearing a black dashiki at the time. IO Qkeyede appeared perplexed that I knew him and a bit apprehensive. I tried to smile often but not too much, not wanting to make him more apprehensive. En route to the luggage area, IO Okeyede demanded that I call him Michael and finally got the nerve to ask me how I recognized him, if I had seen him before and how did I learn to pronounce his name correctly.

"Michael, I caught your eyes, you caught mine when you came off the plane so I knew you were the right person," I lied. I could not tell him that he had just deplaned from the world's largest commercial passenger aircraft, out of over 350 deplaning passengers, that he was the only black male. Additionally, it would have been too much to further advise him that of all the passengers, he was the only one with three vertical tribal scars on each cheek. I knew the next five days with Michael was going to be very interesting.

I don't know who made his hotel accommodations. He had reservations at a "flea bag" hotel off of Fifth and Los Angeles streets. The room was small, equipped with cheap furniture, dirty carpeting and the bed smelled of dry urine. I tried to make an exchange for a better room but Michael was adamant about keeping the room. I would not relent until he agreed to spend the first two nights at my residence. He agreed. I took Michael over to the BNDD office, LAPD, L.A. Sheriffs Office, the U.S. Attorney's Office, the US Marshall's Office, and then to Hollywood. On Hollywood Boulevard, he walked the Avenue of the Stars and saw certain names that he knew written on the sidewalk. At Hollywood and Vine he peered across the intersection speechless for several hours. Michael watched the thinly clad women walking the Boulevard, some tourist, workers, visitors, passers by and hookers. We took photos, even a photo of him hugging a 300-pound blond wearing a yellow blouse, red polyester pants and yellow shoes. I then took him to my residence.

While having dinner, Michael related that his country, Nigeria had the largest black population in the world. He talked about large snakes that could almost swallow humans and that several were large enough to swallow small babies. I began to think that maybe the beer he had consumed was too strong.

Michael related that he was surprised that there was topless

Thin White Lines

dancing in the United States and that he had heard that there were a few bars where there was nude dancing. Apparently he had seen one on Century Boulevard when we exited Los Angeles International Airport. After mentioning it three more times, I asked Michael if he was sleepy. He advised he was not.

I said, "Michael, let's go. I have something I want to show you."

"Where are we going? Is it far?" he asked.

"No, less than ten minutes from here," I assured.

I drove Michael up to the Golden Garter, a nude bar on Long Beach Boulevard and Rosecrans. I knew the bartenders, some of the dancers, the owner and a few customers from my days on the police department.

We were escorted to a table next to the stage. A beautiful blond, fully clad in a blue evening dress and high heels danced on the stage as topless waitresses attended customers at tables. I ordered two beers and Michael and I sat at center stage. The dancer danced fully clothed the first song, and then drank water during the changing of the music. Even then she held her head down, stared at the crowd sultry like and moved her tongue in and out of her mouth in a sexy suggestive, but coy manner. Michael took a drink from the beer glass and related that he liked American beer.

During the second dance, the dancer stripped down to a bathing suit, displaying a well-defined voluptuous, sexy body that was devoid of an ounce of fat. On several occasions, customers threw dollars upon the stage; some slipped them inside her bra and panties. As she danced, I noticed that Michael sat quietly starring and on occasion, sipping his beer. The dancer apparently sensed that Michael was a foreigner, danced at both ends of the oblong stage, but always came back to center stage and danced a little special number for Michael. He clapped almost unendingly when the music stopped and the dancer walked over to the corner to await the next song. While drinking water, she stared at Michael and gesticulated with her tongue. A customer sitting next to Michael believed she was directing her actions, motions, suggestions at him and started running his tongue out of his mouth every chance he thought not many customers were looking. He was unaware that almost every move he made was mirrored in the dark mirror behind the stage.

Before the next song, the dancer removed the dollars from her bra, panties and the stage; put them in a wicker basket. The next song she came out danced a few seconds then removed her bra, displaying large solid grapefruit-like breast that seemed as though they were difficult to shake. She had a body that even sculptors admired. All the customers around the bar screamed and yelled and watched in awe. Midway through the song, the dancer gyrated in front of Michael, danced provocatively, grabbed her breast on occasions, pointed them like guns at him and then ran her tongue over her bright red lips making them wet, shinny, thicker and sexy. I noticed Michael squirm in his seat like a little boy indicating he has to urinate. During the trailing end of the song, the dancer raised her right leg, danced on her left leg, appearing to move her bikini-clad vagina toward Michael. I noticed his eyes grew wider as though he was about to enter into a gran mal epileptic seizure. The song ended, the dancer removed the dollars from the stage and walked back to the corner and again stared at Michael. Michael stared back at her unendingly.

On the next dance, she came center stage danced provocatively in front of Michael, then slowly removed her panties and threw them on the floor. She then squatted in front of Michael and spread her legs exposing her vagina. She moved her stomach in an upward wave-like motion then, placed her hands on her labia majors and parted her vagina, exposing blond hair and pink flesh within three feet of Michael's face. Michael's eyes grew wide, perspiration beaded up on his brow and he screamed at the peak of his voice, "M-mmmy G-God, John, my God."

Michael then passed out and fell from his chair to the floor. The manager ran up screaming, "Step back! We've a sick man here." Michael was coiled into a fetal position and trembling. The manager and I picked him up from the floor and placed him on the stage and placed him in a supine position, with his legs elevated higher than the level of his head.

The manager asked, "Do you think we should call an ambulance? Is he okay? What happened? Is your friend okay?"

"I believe he is just exhausted and the beer is probably new to him." I assured. I toweled his face with cold water and ice, noting only the white of his eyes. After a few minutes, Michael awakened. He stared upon the stage and saw the dancer bending down nude in front of him and passed out again. I asked the manager if he had a first aid kit, which he later provided. I got an ammonia ampule, broke it in half and held it to Michael's nose. He came to and I sat him upright in a chair and forced him to drink black coffee. Michael became wide-awake and started talking about how beautiful the dancer is and how beautiful she looked between her legs.

The dancer left the stage, changed and joined us at the table. After learning that Michael was an African, the dancer had a desire to have sex with Michael relating that she had never had an African before and that Michael was "very hot, hotter than a firecracker." When I advised Michael of the dancer's desire, he begged off relating that he was forever truthful to his wife. Michael was the only law enforcement officer I ever knew that gracefully turned down a wonderful gift.

A couple days later, I took Michael to a nude bar featuring mostly black female dancers. A beautiful light complexioned female dancer also thought Michael was "Hot. He's something else" and wanted to have sex with him. Again, Michael begged off relating that he was truthful to his wife. Michael was the only man I ever saw turn down two gifts from beautiful women.

On the last day of his visit, Michael became more talkative

and related many things about Nigeria, his form of government, the over two hundred different tribes, that he was from the Hausa, a tribe known for its horsemanship, and that one day Nigeria had strong hopes for a democratic government just like we have in the United States.

I asked Michael if he was as true to his wife that he had mentioned in the bars. He confessed that he had four wives; that in Nigeria a man can have as many wives as he can support. When asked why he did not consort with the women at the bar and even the single lady in our office that had shown a desire for him, Michael related that he was afraid, afraid of the American lovemaking trends. Although I did not openly agree, I understood what my little friend was trying to explain.

After Michael left, I began to miss him because I had gotten accustomed to him being around. However, in another sense I was glad he had left, for babysitting does become boring at times. Three months later, I got a letter from Michael thanking me for a wonderful time. Enclosed in the letter were photographs of his wives. Three of them appeared to be under 18; very beautiful, sexy and had smooth black skin and beautiful breast.

I was asked to work undercover in Detroit, Michigan. When the request came I recalled how one CI had described the dope dealer punishing an addict to death. I further remember how he described how quick the crooks would kill and how everybody in Detroit had a gun or two or three guns, how he had described them as "outlaws"; people with a hatred for law and order. Perhaps more importantly, how they would "kill you at the drop of a hat."

The big airplane taxied to the terminal at Detroit Metropolitan Airport after a long 3? -hour turbulent flight from Los Angeles. I suspected the pilot was either drunk or angry for it seemed as though he flew into every turbulent area en route. I was traveling to Detroit to work a 30-day special undercover assignment. The office had had two very good black undercover agents that had apparently burned themselves out, Garfield Hammed and Claude Smith.

A young agent met me at the terminal with a penchant for crime fighting. En route to the baggage area he asked me several times if I was truly an agent or an informant. After I showed him my badge and credentials then he proceeded to tell me that he thought my only duties involved flying around the country buying dope from "every scumbag and his brother." He was a very talkative agent. I got the sense that he admired undercover work but doubted his ability to perform it, and that he had never been placed in a position to volunteer to work undercover. I suspected the agent had been a local law enforcement officer for he seemed to know a lot of officers in the airport. When we departed the parking lot, an officer yelled over, "Hey Al, we got a good one over here do you want to seen what we got?"

"I can't. I am in sort of a hurry. Whatcha got?" he asked.

"A beaut. You'll like this one, if you can take it. Come on, it'll only take a minute," the officer assured.

Al looked at me askingly, "Do you mind, I sure in the hell would like to see what he's got that he's so excited about," he pleaded.

"No, I am with you. You are driving; wherever you go I'll have to go. Go ahead. I don't mind," I assured.

Al drove in tandem with the police unit in a circuitous route up the ramp of the multilevel parking structure until we reached the top level. The police officer exited his car, as his partner talked on the radio, and joined us at our car. He had a smirky smile on his face and winked at me when telling us to follow him. We walked over toward the corner of the parking lot where a black and a dark green car were parked. I could see flies buzzing about both cars and as we came within thirty feet, I knew what we were about to see from the strong stench emanating from the two cars.

While walking toward the cars Al yelled, "Man what the fuck is that awful smell. I ain't never smelt no shit like this before?"

The second officer had exited the patrol car walking behind us yelled, "I don't know either Al, maybe some Chinaman left some sushi in his car before he took off," and laughed.

The first officer stated, "Al come on over here. Al, we'll see how this sushi looks in this hot ass car." He then took out a ring of keys tried them several times until he opened the trunk of the black car. The stench was strong enough to knock us down. Inside the truck was a decaying body of a once blue silk suit clad black male. Maggots swarmed about his facial orifices and the puss like mass about his face moved from the crawl of maggots. Al stared into the trunk and immediately vomited all over himself. The other officer popped the other trunk of the other car, displaying the body of a decaying maggot, fly infested black male.

Al, still vomiting, peered into the trunk of the other car and became sicker. The two officers yelled, "Look at this little candy ass pussy fed. He's puking his goddamn hemorrhoids out of his mouth. Al, what the hell's wrong with you? You can't get sick on us now," he yelled. The more they talked the sicker Al got. He was trying to vomit but his stomach was empty.

Although I had seen death like this before and had developed an iron skin, I felt an urge to vomit but braved it. I would not wimp up in front of two local Wayne County deputies. I watched the rookie agent almost vomit his intestines outside of his body, the worse vomiting of all, the dry one, saliva dropped from his mouth and he passed out. I grabbed him before he hit the ground and placed him in a sitting position, resting against the front right tire of his car. The smell of the vomituse on his clothing coupled with the foul odor of the two bodies, two maggot infested bodies rotting close by gave me the strong urge to vomit, to puke. While giving the rookie water and coffee, I lit a Kool filter king cigarette, inhaled it deep into my lungs and exhaled slowly. The urge to vomit passed, momentarily and I resumed conversing with the officers in a normal manner.

The shorter officer stated, "I know this guy is dead, what about the one in the other car? Do you think he's dead?"

I found no humor in his remark but took it for what it was - an old officer about to puke in front of other brother law enforcement officers playing a macho role, a flash role of well being while strongly fighting the urge within to do the normal thing, to vomit, to react humanly to a very inhuman situation.

His partner played it off too. I guess the vomiting rookie was the only one really being himself. The three of us inflated our egos beyond any level ever expected of us as humans, and too, merely in the presence of each other, devoid of a pubic that expects superhuman acts from its public servants. In reality, we would all have felt better vomiting and maybe even better if we cried; cried at seeing human existence reduced to a level of murder, storing bodies in car trunks to rot and and become maggot infested with blue tail flies soaring and flying about like airplanes at an air show.

Detroit was one of the most violent crime and drug-ridden cities in the United States. The previous year there were 755 homicides; robberies, murders, dope dealers, mayhem specialist and hit men roamed the streets at will. The worst of them all was the heroin addict in dire need of a fix. He would kill his own mother for a fix to alleviate the pain, which awful pain that drove him like a slave master, each period of existence brought on deeper pain, making the addict a mad dog, mad enough to do anything for release.

Detroit—the motor city of the world—also known as the murder capital of the world. The scene at the airport will forever be a computer chip in my brain easily recallable and vividly. I checked into the Ramada Inn off I-94, close to the world's largest tire. I was given the keys to a flashy Cadillac undercover car that was parked out front. After I checked into my room, the smell of the decayed bodies filled my nostrils and clothing. I took a hot bath, soaked for an hour but the stench would not go away. I took a shower after the bath, washed the inside of my nostrils with soap, rinsed them thoroughly with water. The stench would not abate. I smelled my clothing—it appeared to have permeated my suit, my socks and even the leather of my shoes. I began to think the smell was imaginary, that what I had sensed was a play on my mind. I sprayed cologne and aftershave lotion all over my face, on the bed, on my shoes, clothing, luggage and even the carpeting. The smell did not abate. I called for room service and asked the bellman if he smelled anything unusual. "No nothing but a lot of aftershave lotion, that's all," he remarked. I requested two bottles of deodorizer. When the bellman returned, he placed one on the air conditioning unit and adjusted the fan to high. The smell of the deodorizer filled the room but failed to shield the smell of the deaths I had seen earlier. The smell lingered.

 I got in the undercover car and drove downtown and ended up on Cass Street and drove opposite of downtown. There were prostitutes all over the place, walking in scantily clad shorts, short skirts and short dresses. They all had two things in common, too much make up and their sex organ almost uncovered. Heroin addicts walked sleepily on the sidewalks. Some nodded in the alley and against buildings. Several pink Cadillacs were parked at the curb. In one, a black male wearing a crush velvet hat smiled at passers-by displaying a mouth full of gold teeth that he was apparently proud of and wanted to display.

 I got stopped at a traffic light. A prostitute walked up to the right door and asked, "Whose your whores? Why don't you choose me?" I was speechless; she had a pound of make up on her face and two missing front teeth, one at the top and the other off set at the bottom of her mouth. She smelled of cheap perfume mixed with a strong body odor. I stared speechless at her until the light changed. I peeled rubber leaving her at the curb.

I drove down on Lafayette Street, stopped at a Coney Island and attempted to eat a bowl of chili. When the waiter handed it to me I could only focus on the black rotting flesh I had seen earlier. Instead, I drank several strong cups of black coffee. The warmth from the coffee soothed my stomach and took the crawling maggots away from my mind. When I left Coney Island, a car sped by chased by another car with men hanging out both sides shooting and cursing. I watched, drove around in the circle and a man in the car in front started shooting back at the chasing car.

I drove back toward my hotel and saw two more shootings en route. I checked my wristwatch; it was only 11:30 p.m. I went up to room and tried to sleep, but sleep would not come.

I went downstairs to the bar, ordered a double shot of "Old Granddad" and soda with a twist of lime. I drank it in three gulps and ordered two more. It was the third drink that took the smell away. I staggered up to my room and fell asleep upon the bed fully clothed.

I woke up about 9:30 a.m. the next day with a headache and hangover; at least that awful stench had gone away, but the site of maggots crawling and blue tail flies flying about was as clear as a television screen. The site, the smell, the joviality of the Wayne County deputies left an imprint on my mind, rather a sense of fear for the city. I knew that there was an average of two murders per day in Detroit and had never expected to see remnants of it my first day.

I thought of the danger I was about to enter into especially in an unfamiliar city. I remember the remark that one deputy had made, "This is two less ass hole dope dealers we don't have to worry about." I was perplexed how he concluded that only dope dealers were shot in the head, driven to Detroit Metropolitan Airport and left in the trunk of stolen cars. Maybe they were good citizens and possibly a thorough investigation would be conducted by the homicide division. I doubt it.

I remembered what a college professor had once told the class about how often in the midst of a malady or something evil, bad, askew, awry, or surprising, that there is something positive; how many positive things could emanate from a bad thing. The only positive thing I could think of was possibly dietary, for I knew I would not be able to eat for a long time, realizing that scrambled eggs would likely remind me of the sight of maggots all over the faces of the deceased.

I had lost all thought of my purpose for the temporary assignment at Detroit and could not focus my mind on who or what kind of person could or would do such an awful thing to another human being. Maybe the deceased were the mad dogs, the heroin addicts - those that would do anything to alleviate that awful pain—anything to alleviate that awful feeling that drives them insane, pushes them into criminal acts that even they don't know why or how they did it other than to alleviate a monster that has taken over their whole body, mind and soul.

Even they, despite the evil deeds and acts they perpetrated against the innocent, did not deserve to die so inhumanely. I often wonder if there was a possibility that they could have been innocent, family-oriented, God-fearing good citizens devoid of any record or reputation of any criminal activity or association. The mere fact that they had been shot in the head, put in the trunk of a stolen car, driven to the airport to rot did not necessarily indicate to me that they were former drug dealers. Could they have been informants or CI's – or could they have been innocent men suspected of being associated with the police or innocent men caught in the wrong place at the wrong time and possibly saw something that they should or should not have? Who makes that determination? America is supposed to be a free country. Who has the right to take one's life for being in the wrong place or seeing something?

The sight of the two bodies would become a permanent template. One that during good times, sad times, happy times and fun times would force its reflection up front to forever remind me how awful, how filthy, how ugly, how brutal, how inhumane and how shocking it was intended to be.

One reason for the temporary assignment to Detroit was to investigate one Marzette, a former Detroit Police officer that worked narcotics. It seemed that the drug dealers made more money than police officers. Since he knew how DPD and the feds worked, especially since he knew most of them, Marzette went into the dope dealing business. He hired a boy out of Milwaukee, "Milwaukee Jack," as his main lieutenant. Milwaukee Jack was "rolling big" (selling heroin like he had a franchise) for Marzette, who would not talk dope or codes on the telephone because he had seen the feds operate on wiretaps. None of his lieutenants were allowed to talk drugs or use codes on the telephone and had been taught counter surveillance techniques. They sold heroin in increments of 1/8-kilogram quantities (5 ounces) with the misconception that the feds would never let that kind of money ride. They only dealt with established customers and knew that meeting a stranger would most likely result in meeting the police.

There were the Jacksons, Big Eddie Jackson, Devil Jackson, and Ernest Jackson Jr. a.k.a. Boogie Bear, identified and documented as major drug traffickers. It seemed that Detroit, a predominant black city, had only black drug traffickers. Their method of operating was very similar to that of the Mafia. Deaths, assaults, kidnappings, arson and mayhem were merely acts of the trade. They were the black Mafia. The two black agents previously assigned to Detroit had worked undercover to the extent that their identities were known and contracts were placed on their lives.

I was equipped with a black Cadillac El Dorado with a sunroof for an undercover car and given instructions on how to get to the office. With the airport still fresh on my mind I drove to downtown Detroit. I drove around the area to ease my mind again listening to a new Marvin Gaye tape "What's Going On." While driving and meditating I ended up in the area of 12500 blocks of Livernois. While driving slowly and casually staring at women driving and on the streets, I heard what appeared to be firecrackers or gunshots ringing out. I knew they were not firecrackers from the sound and that the 4th of July was at least two months away. I was driving down Livernois at about 35 miles per hour when a black male dressed in a maroon and black velvet jumpsuit dashed across Livernois in front of my car and was nearly struck by the passing car on my left. A shorter man running with something in his hand followed him.

As the shorter man came abreast to my car he raised the item in his right hand and fired three shots at the fleeing man and screamed, "Stop you low-lifed cocksucker. I'll blow your goddamn brains out."

The fleeing man ran between two buildings out of view with the shorter man in pursuit with the pistol in his hand.

I circled the block to see this festivity, but with caution of the shooter's aim. As I came up on a back street, I saw the fleeing man scaling fences – wooden, chain link, brick and concrete — moving out quickly as though shortness of breath was alien to him. He was "low flying." The short pursuing man's loud voice, filled with profanity was faintly heard in the distance.

I drove back upon Livernois and noted that I was only a few blocks from Detroit PD 10th precinct. I drove down Livernois until I saw a party store on three corners of the intersection. I pulled over to the one past the light on my right. While walking to the entrance I noticed a young adult sprawled out on the sidewalk grimacing, moaning, whining, and begging, "Oh, please help me! Please help me!" I thought he might have been part of some kind of scam, noticing that none of the customers coming and going from the store even paused to ask questions or assist. I could see that he was bleeding slightly about the stomach.

Thin White Lines

A departing customer remarked, "It's a crying shame for this little dope fiend to get shot trying to rob a party store."

Another man responded, "Yeah, he is so high, rather so sick, he musta thought that thick bullet proof plastic was thin glass." Both chuckled.

"Yeah, these dope fiends are some crazy dudes. They don't think a bullet can stop 'em, they think they're like superman, bullets just bounce off them."

I entered the party store and wondered how anyone could possibly rob or attempt to rob it. The whole counter area was covered with thick bulletproof plastic, more than an inch thick. All alcoholic beverages were stored behind the counter. There were three apertures with rotating wheels like a lazy Susan where the money and whisky were exchanged. The employees were well protected in a cage behind the counter.

I drove in a lost manner until I came upon an entrance to the Lodge Freeway that I guessed would take me downtown. I got on the Lodge and was driving about 55 miles per hour when a blue Cadillac Fleetwood brougham, with three black males drove up parallel. The two passengers each brandished a .45 automatic to show that they were armed gave the 'power to the people' hand symbol and drove hurriedly from the area. I parked the undercover car on the lot of the Howard Johnson Hotel downtown.

At the intersection in front a tall white male wearing a burnt orange raincoat blew a whistle and waived cars in both directions. His gesticulation, dress, beard and mannerism indicated to me that he was not the police, not a city employee, not officially involved in traffic control. I entered the lobby of the hotel.

I forced down a breakfast of ham, eggs, coffee and orange juice, smoked a cigarette and tried to relax. I was alerted after overhearing one of the waitresses tell someone that Devil Jackson had gotten killed last night, that he had gotten shot in the face twice with a shotgun.

The male customer sitting with a female in the adjacent booth stated, "1 just can't wait until my transfer comes through. I'm getting the hell outta this town. It's too tough for me. There are three and four killings every night and people shoot all day all night in my neighborhood like it's a combat zone. These crazy fools are now doing like they did back with the cowboys. They now will ride by and shoot at you on the sidewalk or spray your house with bullets. It's all cause of this dope thing. Detroit is now worse than New York...."

"You really think so honey?" his female companion asked.

"Think so? Hell I know so. I didn't want to upset you and make you all nervous, but they killed a boy on our street the other day in broad daylight. Somebody just walked up and shot him in the back of the head in front of his house, while he was just sitting in his car, just like that. There is so much dope in this town that's pitiful. We need to get the hell outta here," he said.

"Honey, those are just isolated incidents. Those sorts of things do happen in bad neighborhoods."

"Bad neighborhoods," he interrupted, "All Detroit is a bad neighborhood. There ain't no place in this big city where there ain't got bad neighborhoods. They's even shooting in some of the white neighborhoods," he ranted.

"Honey, if we moved to Palmer Park we wouldn't have those sort of problems," she assured.

"Palmer Park—you still got in your mind buying one of them big houses in Palmer Park. I told you we can't afford it honey. We're just factory workers, plus I'm getting a transfer to one of our Ohio plants. I told you didn't I?"

Unlike other places, small cafes, restaurants and bars are newsrooms for the world, places where you can sit quietly and learn about the things in the city, county, state and other countries. I checked my watch, it was ten minutes to eleven and the

Thin White Lines

hotel bar was already open. From my booth I could see several customers drinking their lunch.

A short time later I saw something that rarely existed in California—a beat policeman—a policeman actually walking a beat. In California, policemen rode everywhere in highly cleaned and waxed black and white squad cars. Their uniforms were always neatly pressed, brass polished and shoes spit shined. This beat officer was an old timer, somewhat rotund, pants were slightly soiled and his shoes were dirty and unpolished. He walked into the bar, spoke and chatted with a few patrons. The bartender secretly mixed him a drink and handed it to him in a coffee cup. The officer drank the whiskey in two gulps and stayed at the end of the bar until the bartender finished working on customers and refilled his cup two more times. The officer, not paying for the drinks, thanked the bartender, referring to him in a friendly manner by his first name, then walked into the adjacent restaurant and chatted with the cashier. In a short while one of the waitresses took a Styrofoam cup of coffee up to the cashier and handed it to the officer. I discerned from the conversation his name was Al.

I overheard the cashier ask, "Al, do you want me to sweeten it (put a little whiskey in it) for you?"

"No, I'm fine Sally, I am okay."

He took a few drinks of the coffee, cleared his throat loudly then ambled out of the restaurant toward the Radisson Cadillac Hotel across the street. I surmised that he would repeat the same at that location. My first day in Detroit was becoming a memorable experience.

After breakfast, I walked over to the BNDD office. I was advised that Marzette, one of the primary targets had died and that Devil Jackson, another target had in fact been gunned down last night. I was further advised that there was a drug war on in Detroit. Those dopers were killing each other, innocent people, informants and even people they suspected of being informants.

I was also advised to be extremely careful for Detroit dopers would kill merely based on suspicion or distrust. I met several of the agents. I saw a male with long brown shoulder length hair and a beard, platform shoes and tight bell bottom pants moving about in one of the group areas talking loudly. I asked one of the agents "Who is that guy; he switches like some kind of a fag, what is he a CI?"

"No," the agent replied. "That's Doug Wankel. He's an agent working the Detroit Joint Narcotic Task Force (DJNTF). He buys a lot of dope."

My initial thought was if this fag looking agent is buying a lot of dope then why do I have to come to Detroit. I was further advised that Wankel worked undercover in all communities, buying dope from blacks, whites and browns, that he had not been fortunate to meet a yellow or red CI to penetrate the Asiatic and Native American drug rings.

I was later introduced to Wankel, Dennis Schoenrock, another agent working undercover in the DJNTF. They were both new agents and offered their assistance. I was later introduced to the head of the DJNTF, Group Supervisor, Raymond McKinnon, surprisingly one of my former college classmates.

I met other members of the DJNTF, one a Wayne County Sheriff's deputy, J.W. West. He also offered to assist in any way that he could. J.W. advised that Detroit is the most dangerous city in the U.S.; that the dopers kill you at the drop of a hat. He warned me to be careful and most attentive especially when undercover. According to J.W., many dope dealers use addicts as protection. They are known to actually go on the nod for long periods of time. They have a reputation of shooting, maiming, kidnapping and intimidating innocent and older people. They were also described as mean and would "shoot you at the drop of a hat." "You have to always watch those motherf___rs."

J.W. added that another problem they caused is that sometimes while on the nod they were known to accidentally shoot people and sometimes themselves. I thanked J.W. for the information and went back into the group I area. I was advised that we had a caper scheduled for that afternoon. I welcomed it. I wanted to get the first buy down to see how different things were in Detroit.

Late that afternoon, the CI and I got together and formulated plans to purchase two ounces of heroin from Sweets, a dealer in the Livernois and Tireman area. After the initial telephone call, pre-surveillance was initiated on the crook's house. The CI and I, after getting our roles in sync, entered the undercover car and drove over to the crooks house and knocked. Two young heroin addicts admitted us into the residence both wielding long barreled pistols.

As I entered the door well, the addict on my right pointed his pistol at me and stated, "You got to give up the Roscoe before you can come in."

I assumed he meant pistol for I had never heard it referred to as a Roscoe before. I ignored him and continued to walk up the small steps. He pressed the pistol against my chest and repeated, "You got to give up the Roscoe."

I said, "What're you trying to do, test me?"

When the addict attempted to pat me down, I backed up and advised, "Hey you don't have to do all of that, what kind of dope house is this?" I asked.

"It don't matter you gotta give up the Roscoe before you can go back there, that's what I'm saying. You know Sweets is in charge and he don't want nobody but his people with guns in here," the addict advised.

The addict to my left gave the CI a quick pat down, stated "He's clean" and stood by with his gun casually pointed in my direction. I reached inside of my waistband, removed a .38 caliber 5-shot Colt Cobra, unloaded the shells and handed it to the addict on my right. He looked at it and asked, "What kinda fuckin' gun is this? It looks like a police gun to me. It's so light it don't even look real."

"It is," I responded. "I had to shoot a double crossing cop twice in the head to get it. He won't be missing it now. Dead cops, like dead niggers, they don't need guns do they?" I then stared the addict sternly in the eyes. He was not fully satisfied and still tried to search me. I walked on past him, stating "Hey man that's all I got. What do you want to do feel my cock?" The addict backed down.

The CI and I walked into the back of the house. There were about 15 customers in a large sparsely furnished room off the kitchen. Sweets had a platter full of heroin and a make shift condom stretcher. He dipped a quarter ounce-measuring ladle into the mound, and then used a playing card to scrape off the excess. When the customer was not attentive, Sweets bent the card and dipped beyond the level of the edges and hurriedly tossed the heroin into the stretched condom. He was selling four tablespoons of heroin to the ounce.

Sweets, apparently seeing me with the informant, peered up at me and asked, "How many pieces do you want motha fucka?"

The CI started to introduce me to Sweets. I motioned for his silence, the less he was involved eliminated the requirement that he testify. Sweets was so carried away he basically thought I was a regular. He was selling heroin like selling groceries in a store. The armed guards at the door were his perceived security from the police and hijackers. Sweets' mannerism and conversation indicated he had been dealing dope, heroin, for a long time, had never been caught and he perceived that his operation was fool proof.

Sweets wore a painter's mask when measuring the heroin and talked badly with it on as well as when he tilted it under his chin. He was running a dope store. For smaller customers, he had his henchman issuing McDonald spoons of heroin. It was because of Sweets et al., that the McDonald Corporation changed their coffee stirring spoons to a flat spatula.

I purchased two ounces of heroin from Sweets for $1500 and engaged him in a conversation about large quantities at a later date. According to Sweets, he was the heroin man in Detroit. He advised that given the proper time and notification that he could sell multiple kilograms of good heroin. Sweets alluded to having a few kilogram customers that he took special care of when they came to town. He reiterated, "For heroin, I am the man. I got the boy good, gooder than any other motha fucka in Detroit — nigga or honky, I got it damn good."

I assured him that I believed he had it good and alluded to not wanting to be searched or having to give up my "Roscoe" when I came to cop (purchase). Sweets response was "Well don't ever come over here armed and after I get to know you better, I'll have your shit delivered to you like they deliver the Detroit Free Press. How's that for a country boy that is a good dope peddling motha fucka?"

I wanted badly to tell Sweets that he was now bought and paid for; that his dope peddling days were soon coming to an end. I made arrangements to purchase 1/8 kilogram of heroin from Sweets at a later date. When exiting Sweets', I noted both addicts were on the nod. I had to wake the lead addict to get my weapon back. While coming out of his stupor, the addict slowly pointed the long barreled pistol in my direction, confused as to whether to shoot or not.

I yelled, "Hey, I am a friendly guy! I'm with you! Wake up! Give me my Roscoe back."

He left the room for a few minutes, returned with about eight weapons and asked, "Which one is yourn?" I retrieved it and left advising both addicts that I was going to pray that they did not have an accident and shoot each other. The CI and I left.

While leaving the area, gunshots rang out, stopped and continued like a series of firecrackers. I asked the CI if they celebrated the 4th of July early in Detroit. The CI advised that the bangs were gunshots—that we were in the 10th precinct area of Detroit known as the DMZ.

"What does DMZ mean?" I asked.

He stated, "Demilitarized zone, there is always gun play over here. It is so bad in some areas; people sleep in old-fashioned bathtubs to avoid getting hit by stray flying bullets. It is badder than a motherfucker here."

We drove to the office where I went to the basement of the building with the CI and we took the freight elevator up to the second floor. I completed all required reports, paid the CI, mailed the evidence and secured for the day. I got Detroit News and a Detroit Free Press newspaper and drove back to my hotel. The gist of both newspapers depicted a violence-plagued Detroit, where two and three people are killed violently on a daily basis. Killings and shootings were taking place inside of the automotive plants parking lots, suburban areas and downtown, causing many inner city blacks, whites and browns to move north of Eight Mile Road fleeing from a city that was growing wild.

The violence grew unbearable on Belle Isle and there was talk in the newspaper of a stricter curfew on the Isle. There were shootings all over the place.

Of all the places where I had worked undercover, albeit there was always caution and a degree of nervousness, there was something about Detroit that was terrifying and frightening. There was concern that the drug traffickers and would-be's or wannabes were more dangerous than any place I had been, whether on vacation or working. I had seen the 14th U&T Streets and Southeastern Washington D.C., the Los Angeles Watts, Nickerson, Jordan Downs and Aliso Village projects of Los Angeles, Jefferson Street in Seattle, West Las Vegas, south side of Chicago, Cottonwood Row in Bakersfield, Harlem in New York, the Desire housing project of New Orleans, Pruitt-Igo housing project of St. Louis, the Robert Taylor and Cabrini Green projects of Chicago, West Second South Street of Salt Lake City, bad areas in Memphis, Nashville, San Francisco, Atlanta, Cleveland, the Front in Baltimore, Miami, Kansas City, Dallas, Houston, Commerce Street in San Antonio, the water front in Long Beach and many other cities' sections with bad reputations, been there either working, visiting or sightseeing and never once was I as leery as I was of being in Detroit. Maybe it was the site of the two bodies rotting in the trunk of cars that was causing all the apprehension. There was no doubt; Detroit was the most violent city I had ever seen. The two-armed addicts in the dope house did not really scare me as much as the thought of the violence they could accidentally perpetrate while enslaved by heroin. Perhaps all the dopers would be hiring addicts, knowing that they would take a life without fear or afterthought.

The next day I met with a CI. We got our roles in sync and drove over to 14400 block of Coyle Street in Detroit to buy two ounces of heroin. A guy admitted us into the residence the CI called Jerry, who was carrying a pistol in one hand and a rifle strapped over his shoulder. Four customers were seated and milling around in the company of three henchmen. The three henchmen sat around wearing pistols in their waistbands and talking about how many people they had killed. One hench related that the had shot a "little dude three times in the head and that little crazy motha fucka still didn't die. He lived six months before he finally kicked the bucket." He further told how the dope man did not want to pay him and that he had gone to several hospitals to find him and finish him off but finally gave up.

The CI asked if Denard was available. Jerry advised that he was. I heard several customers in the back room having a discussion about the quantity and quality of drugs they were purchasing. A customer left the house exchanging a look at the customers in the living room by exchanging pleasantries with all of us. I suspected that he was an undercover policeman.

A few minutes later Denard and a very attractive, beautiful-bodied female arrived at the residence. The CI introduced me to Denard as his cousin "Big John" from Toledo. Denard stared at me coldly, did not return my greeting and walked back into the rear room. A few minutes later, he called the CI back into the room.

When the CI and I walked back to the room, Denard asked me to give him a few minutes alone with the CI. I went back into the living room.

The henchmen were still talking about how many people they had killed. A black male about 5'10" tall 200 pounds, wearing a black cap, black shoes, black shirt and pants was admitted into the residence by Jerry who referred to him as Chester. Chester glanced at everybody and walked into the back room. When he initially entered, the henchmen became silent and looked at him surprisingly. There was eeriness about him that was indescribable.

After Chester left the residence, one henchman asked, "You motha fuckas don't know who that guy is do you?"

One remarked, "Naw man, who give a rat's ass, who is the mothafucka?"

"That's Chester Campbell," he advised.

The other two henchmen echoed "Chester Campbell, you're shitting me man, that was not Chester Campbell."

Jerry advised, "Yeah that's him alright."

The henchmen then got in a heated discussion about how many people Chester had killed, one swore it was over 300 and related that they call Chester "the Death Angel" and remarked how cold and silent it got when Chester had entered the room. There was an aura about Chester that is difficult to describe. The henchmen went on telling how Chester always wears black.

One of the henchmen wants to be like Chester when he grows up. Chester reportedly earns $10,000 a hit. He is the best hitman in Detroit and has gotten filthy rich killing people.

After a short while, the CI came back into the living room.

Thin White Lines

He appeared frightened and mumbled that Denard wanted me to come back into the back room. As soon as I entered the back room, two armed addicts that were guarding the heroin packaging and cutting, focused their attention on me and each placed a gun at my head and screamed a series of profanity about my identity possibly being the police. I removed each gun with my hands three times stating that I was not the police only to have them placed them back on my head. I finally told Denard, "I came here to buy two or three pieces of heroin but your guys can't do any business for trying to figure out who is and who is not the police. I'll just leave and go spend my money where they are selling dope instead of trying to scare the hell out of somebody."

Denard waived the two addicts off and then took a seat across the room from us and stared. The cutter continued cutting the little heroin that was left and was bagging it in quarter ounce pieces of aluminum foil. Several customers copped and left. Others waited their turn.

Denard stated he had a feeling that I was the police and that he would have his girlfriend Jeanie deliver the heroin to me and asked me to front the money for two ounces. I disagreed. After bickering for several minutes about the front, Denard advised that that would be the only way he would do business with me. He related that if I were not the police, then I would front the money without any problem. I disagreed, told Denard to keep his dope that I did not like the over cut dope he was selling and left the room. I joined the CI and other customers and henchmen in the living room and told him we were leaving.

When we got out to the undercover car, Jeanie ran out and told us she would get the heroin for us; that she would go to Denard's source. I disagreed, not wanting to make an unwilling drug dealer out of Jeanie and not knowing beforehand whether she would go to Denard's source or not.

Jeanie jumped in the undercover car and pulled her skirt up

showing a very beautiful left thigh. She was adamant about getting the heroin from Denard's source and related that his name was Al and that he was one of the largest heroin dealers in Detroit. According to Jeanie, Al got his heroin "straight from the Eyetalians (sic) from Gross Pointe." I drove Jeanie to her residence, a two-story brick home on Coyle, where she lived with her mother. She had a five-year old daughter that was being raised by her mother as she ran the streets with Denard and others. She had no occupation, no job, no intent or finding one and to add to her woes, she was not receiving child support or state or county aid. Jeanie pleaded to do the deal advising that the heroin would be purer and more per ounce than what Denard was selling. Jeanie then tried to get me to front the money advising that I could wait at her house to take delivery. I declined. Jeanie then tried to get me to trip with her to Al's to take delivery of the heroin. I refused. She then telephoned a cab, advised me to wait at her house that she would deliver two ounces of heroin to me in a short while.

The CI and I sat on the porch and conversed with Jeanie's mother and daughter. About a half hour later a blue Cadillac El Dorado with two black males pulled up to the curb opposite Jeanie's house. The passenger neatly dressed, stared at me for about two minutes, blandished what appeared to be Thompson machine gun and then they drove away. The CI did not know Al or the guys in the Cadillac.

About 30 minutes later, Jeanie arrived back driving the blue Cadillac, called me over and handed me two ounces of heroin. I paid Jeanie $1500 and advised I would contact her in a few days for a larger purchase. I was sure that surveillant agents had made the connection. After I returned to the office, I telephoned Jeanie and advised her that before she came back with the heroin two guys had come over to her house, parked and brandished an automatic rifle. Jeanie stated that Al was the passenger with the gun. Al wanted to see me and if he believed I was the police, he

Thin White Lines

was going to shoot me when I left her house. That bit of information was helpful. A new federal law had been enacted providing additional penalties for armed defendants in the commission of a federal drug offense. For the little intimidation tactic, Al deserved as much time that he could get.

I got back with Jeanie, Jerry and Denard on two subsequent occasions and purchased four ounces of heroin on each. Al was further implicated in the sale.

Everyday I read the newspaper, there were two and three people reportedly shot gangland style in Detroit. A black female agent named Linda (the first), was assigned to the Detroit office and on her second undercover role, she was robbed and almost murdered. When the robber found her identification, they came within an inch of killing her. She quit.

Shortly thereafter, the same robbers, mad dog heroin addicts, kidnapped a six-year old boy and demanded $50,000. When the ransom was not paid they shot the little boy in the back of the head and dumped his body on a deserted road in Romulus. A few weeks later, they kidnapped an eight-year old boy, and again demanded $50,000. Some enterprising police official decided to put excelsior in the drop moneybag. The kidnappers came into the area on foot, picked up the purported ransom and eluded a horde of surveillance officers. The eight-year old boy's body was found on a deserted road in Romulus, Michigan. He had also been shot in the head. Dead bodies continued showing up in the trunk of cars at the Detroit Metropolitan Airport.

I had not seen the CI in the Denard case in about ten days. One day we got a telephone call that his body was found outside of Toledo. I saw the gruesome photos. The field rats had devoured almost all of him and identification was made from his uneaten left thumb. I was surprised that the murder case had little significance over the drug case. The first and only federal preliminary hearing I ever attended was in the Denard case. Denard and his cohorts were bad plus. I often believed even now that the CI's death resulted from my identity as an agent was somehow compromised.

Early during this TDY, I hooked up with a homosexual CI named Dixie. He introduced me to Tyrone Mountain, a cripple dope dealing little guy. On the first deal, Dixie and I drove over to Tyrone's house and were admitted into the residence by his wife, a major heroin abettor. On the first occasion, there were 19 customers inside the living room, dining room and kitchen. Tyrone was waiting until the number reached 25.

When Dixie introduced me to Tyrone, Tyrone merely remarked that he would sell me three or four ounces of heroin but I had to wait in line. While waiting, I calculated that Tyrone was selling approximately a little over a kilogram of commercial grade heroin per day. He was a cantankerous little puke who talked to his one-ounce customer with a bit of disdain. He was king and he well knew that his wares were king maker and enslaver. The customers needed him. Tyrone had a product that was in great demand. His neighbors were in actuality held somewhat hostage, they feared calling the police believing that "one day somebody will get the nerves to call the police." They could not get involved for it would require testifying, time off from work, threats, intimidation and possible violence or harm would come to them. Nobody called. An enterprising agent had developed Dixie into a CI, and consequently Dixie and I were sitting in Tyrone's house preparing to send him to jail for a long time.

When the magic number 25 came into the residence, Tyrone limped out of the house into his Lincoln Mark IV and drove away. Tyrone was smart. He did not keep drugs in his house because he had children. He conducted business Monday through Friday during normal school hours. Tyrone shut down when school let out and played father and husband.

While Tyrone was picking up the heroin, I engaged several males in general conversation. One had just raised up from Jackson prison. He related that Jackson prison is the largest walled prison in the United States that housed some very bad inmates. Two other customers had recently raised up from some camp in Ionia, Michigan. Unbeknownst them, they were all preparing to return to prison.

Tyrone returned about an hour later and entered the house carrying a heavy shopping bag. Several of us followed him into the kitchen. The shopping bag was filled almost to the top with heroin, white heroin, contained in one, two, and five-ounce rubber contraceptives. I was at the bottom pecking order and watched Tyrone sell more heroin, collect more money than I had ever seen in a single dope house.

One of the purchasers called Tyrone an ORN. Tyrone asked, "What the hell you mean by calling me an Orange, what did you say?"

"An ORN, an ORN haven't you ever heard about ORNs?" He asked.

"Naw, motha fucka, what is a goddamn ORN?"

"One rich nigger, that's what an ORN is Tyrone, that's an acronym for one rich nigger, you know like those orns moving out to Palmer Park..." he related.

"I be being one rich motha fucka", Tyrone stated and continued dealing dope at the table like he had carte blanche.

Tyrone was one of the fastest money counters I had ever seen. He would rapidly count $1,000 or even $3,000 only once, gives the customer the heroin just like selling goods in a supermarket.

I bought five ounces of heroin from Tyrone and doubled back on him a week later.

On the next occasion while waiting for Tyrone to return from his cache, his cousin Buddy, I had met on the first occasion drove up in a new Lincoln. On the first occasion Buddy bragged that he had just purchased a black new Lincoln Mark IV. I knew his vehicle would be a good undercover car.

I engaged Buddy in a conversation, "I hear you got the girl good Buddy?" I asked.

"I got her decently, just recreationally, nothing major," he replied.

"I was trying to get a stamp for my lady. What size stamps do you have?" I asked. "I got $50, $100, $200 stamps. The $200 stamp is almost a quarter ounce and she's good too", he assured.

"Let me have a $200 stamp."

Buddy handed me about six grams of cocaine contained in a small plastic bag. I paid Buddy four $50 notes and thanked him for giving his new Lincoln over to the U.S. Government in a subsequent seizure.

Tyrone's wife saw the transaction and became irate with Buddy. She accused Buddy of disrespecting her house for which she was going to tell Tyrone. It was puzzling to me how 25 customers waiting to purchase heroin from Tyrone and this little transaction was deemed disrespectful. I tried to apologize and found Tyrone's wife further implicated herself by stating, "Tyrone and I are the only dope dealers in this house."

In a short while, Tyrone arrived back at the house with a shopping bag full of heroin. The bag was so heavy it caused him to rock to the side. He limped on into the house mumbling.

I copped five ounces of heroin from Tyrone and stayed around for a few minutes engaging him and his wife in a conversation. Tyrone then asked about the CI (Dixie). Having cut Dixie out of this deal, I told Tyrone that he was sick, had a hangover and possible rectal problems. They both chuckled relating that Dixie had been a homosexual all his life.

When I asked Tyrone if he could do kilograms of heroin, he became a little indignant relating that he had just sold three kilograms of heroin that day. When I asked Tyrone if he was afraid of the police he shrugged his shoulders and asked, "What for? All of us are making money. I'm making money, they are making money." He further related that he had been dealing dope for several years, had purchased a home for his mother, his grandmother, favorite aunt, sister and his wife's mother and father.

Thin White Lines

It was hard to estimate how much money Tyrone had made and was making. He related that Cadillac cars, flashy clothing, flashy cars and jewelry and white women were the main reason many black dealers were being arrested. Tyrone related where the "feds busted a boy and the IRS levied $500,000 on him. Without talking to his mouthpiece, the fool went to the IRS tax office and paid $500,000 in cash. They then put a 1? million dollar tax levy on that nigger."

I was familiar with the case from conversations in the Detroit office. Tyrone further related that there was a dope dealer living in Southfield. He had just moved out there and was having "white folks, about ten of them working around his house everyday and he never went to work. He had a lot of traffic coming and going. The feds took him down with ten kilograms of pure cocaine." According to Tyrone, the guy had the cocaine better than anybody in Detroit. Somebody had snitched him off. I was familiar with the case. Unbeknownst to Tyrone, the Southfield dealer was busted twice and not how he described it.

Tyrone related that he had "insurance." He related that the feds could not make a case if it fell out of the sky. I knew that Tyrone was in for a rude awakening. I knew his take down would occur when he had picked up his heroin for delivery and traveling back to his residence. I made a decision that there was no need to spend more money on him for he was a walking case.

When I was leaving, Tyrone remarked that he had a friend that had a Cadillac just like mine that had copped a federal case.

When I got back to the Detroit office, I learned that the Cadillac I was driving had been seized and forfeited from major heroin trafficker John Classen. It did not really matter, there were a lot of black Cadillac El Dorado's in Detroit.

That same date, a white CI came into the office and identified a white drug trafficker living in a penthouse in the Jeffersonian apartments who was selling cocaine like he had a license. He believed he could introduce a black agent to him for an undercover dope transaction. The CI and I went over to the apartment and were introduced as Big John wanting to buy five ounces of cocaine from one "Cowboy Bob." He seemed to be grateful being called "Cowboy Bob." He had a penthouse that faces the Detroit River, with a view of the Detroit skyline and a better view of Windsor Canada and Belle Isle. From the veranda you could see the Bob-lo boat anchored on the river.

Cowboy Bob was "way out there" and had his whole penthouse decorated in white, eggshell white, beige and trimmed in Corinthian green. He wore white cotton pants, white shirt, and beige house shoes. The carpeting was beige, furniture beige, with white trim, legs and pedestals. He had a white telephone, white clock; white refrigerator, stove, dishwasher, coffee table and the legs of his glass top breakfast table were white wrought iron. The wall of the living room was beige with white spotted wallpaper. A thin white wainscot adorned the living and dining room walls.

Cowboy Bob's Lincoln Mark IV was white. The leather upholstery was white. A white beige trimmed welcome mat covered the white tiled entranceway. There was no doubt about his favorite color.

Cowboy Bob appeared somewhat effeminate, maybe because of his earrings. His left ear was pierced with a medium size gold ring; a one-carat diamond stud was affixed to right ear lobe.

Cowboy Bob snorted cocaine like he had one hell of a habit. He wore a small gold coke spoon affixed to a thick baht chain around his neck. He also wore a gold metal coke jar-like container around his neck. He vowed to have the best coke in town and displayed no concern for the police. It appeared as though the cocaine made his favorite color white.

Cowboy Bob believed he could hear ants crawling on the ground from his veranda. He believed he could see musical notes when they are played. According to Cowboy Bob, the best thing that ever happened to him was when he discovered cocaine.

"Coke made me. Coke made this lovely apartment, my fine clothing, my jewelry, my cars, and my big bank account. Yeah coke made me. Now I am king. I make people move, dance, and perform for me. I'm now taking applications for a maid. I'm thinking about getting a chauffeur."

With that remark, Cowboy Bob asked me if I would be his chauffeur, if I wanted to apply for the job.

"Naw Cowboy Bob, I got the boy good." I bragged. "I make just as much money as you do."

Coke had really affected Cowboy Bob's mind. He related being a student at the University of Michigan cramming for a final when a California big titty, big ass, blue eyed blond gave him his first hit. He snorted coke and studied all night. On the next day he "maxed the final."

According to Cowboy Bob, coke affected each user differently. Some become sleepy, some lazy but alert, more alert than when not under the influence, for some it peaks their sexual prowess. For him, cocaine lifted his mind to a mountain of bliss, where all beautiful thoughts flowed; where he dreamed in beautiful Technicolor, flowing musically through a space, seeing every color in existence appearing in front of him, "moving in some magnificent form of kaleidoscopic wizardry", thrilling him beyond his wildest imagination.

Yeah Cowboy Bob was way out there. I suspected that he was experimenting with cocaine, LSD and heroin, possibly injecting a concoction that is lethal for most mortals. I almost lost my purpose of being in his penthouse and had to state five times that I wanted to buy the coke and get on our way. Cowboy Bob was dealing cocaine like a doctor or dentist treating patients. He looked at his appointment book and related that we were spilling over into the time for his "next client." Almost simultaneously, the next "client" rang the buzzer. I purchased five ounces of cocaine from Cowboy Bob for $3,000 and agreed to meet with him a week later.

The next week I went without the CI and purchased five ounces of cocaine from Cowboy Bob. He was as weird then as he was the first time and was still taking appointments. As laissez faire he was, I was surprised that he had not been cracked. He was into heavy metal and always played his music loud at night. Detroit PD had had a number of reports but never checked him out further. I guess a good take down of Cowboy Bob could take place with a five-kilo order.

Detroit frightened me with the two and three murders every day; sometimes there would be two days and no murders, then the weekend would come and there would be twelve or fourteen murders over the weekend. During my last week of the 30-day TDY, I ran out of cash and went to three banks, four party stores and two super markets—none would cash an American Express traveler's check. At one party store, I showed the Caldean owner my credentials and badge, driver's license and credit cards; his remark was "How do I know any of this is for real?"

Dead bodies continued to show up in the trunk of cars at Detroit Metro airport. While driving on the streets passers-by and idlers brandished firearms. Every dope house I entered was full of guns. Only Cowboy Bob was without a henchman. He believed that he could have a robber killed before he could reach the bottom floor. Cowboy Bob had an arsenal of guns on display. For some reason, all the dopers in Detroit believed that guns were necessary tools of the drug trade. Murder, mayhem, kidnapping, arson, abduction and ambushing were ways of doing business in a world caught up with the greed for money. For some reason, I had the fear that all Detroit dope dealers would kill at the drop of a hat. My belief was fortified when I learned that there was no death penalty in the State of Michigan.

I was glad to board the big 747 back to Los Angeles. Leaving Detroit was like shedding a heavy burden. The thirty days I was there, I made strong cases against twenty-two defendants. I had a strong suspicion that they would request my undercover services again.

CHAPTER 9

GOING BACK to Los Angeles provided a sigh of relief from Detroit. Perhaps it was the first two letters in Detroit that made me often think of death or the two bodies in the car trunks at the Detroit airport that caused it to frequently surface in my mind. If it were left up to me, I would never return to Detroit to live or work. It seemed that every other car I passed in Detroit had a popped trunk. It was common for addicts to pop trunks and steal the spare tire for an instant exchange for money for a fix of heroin. I suspected that the locksmiths in Detroit were making a lot of money.

I was sitting at my desk in the Los Angeles office when advised that the work I had done in Detroit was so impressive that I had been requested to return for a sixty day special operation— "Operation Skyhook", an operation directed at immobilizing Detroit based black heroin/cocaine traffickers known as "The Black Mafia." I was not too thrilled at the request but took it as a call to duty. I took another big jet to Detroit and checked into the same Ramada Inn. When I went into the office the next day, I was advised that Dixie, the CI in the Tyrone Mountain case, had been brutally murdered. He was found dead, clad in a white baby doll-sleeping gown. It was speculated that a passing homosexual or an old lover murdered him. I knew that little effort would be devoted to bringing his killer to justice, for like dope addicts, homosexuals were also an unwanted lot.

Despite his sexual preferences, I had grown to like Dixie as a CI, a person and certainly as a human being. It was sad seeing a young person like him murdered. I could recall the first time I met him at the BNDD office; Dixie stood back, stared me up and down, flipped his left wrist limply and stated, "My, my, my, what a magnificent black Mandingo warrior specimen you are. If you weren't straight, you would definitely be my nigger." Dixie is no longer around to make those types of comments.

Another CI I had worked with during the same time had been killed. Three dead, all inside of two months. All died at the hands of another. It was unknown whether by the dope dealer or just a routine Detroit killing. In Detroit, a new thing was cropping up all over the city. Just like the cowboys and crooks bushwhacked and ambushed one another, Detroit crooks started the drive-by shootings. They also started decapitating victims. On my first week back in the Detroit area, there were several rotting bodies discovered in car trunks at Metro airport. A couple of headless bodies were found and on one occasion, only the head of a man was found. There was a strong sense of fear intended for each murder, a message of fear, intimidation, a wake up call for the intruders, betrayers, untrusted—that this is what will happen to you if you go astray, if you join forces with law enforcement; perhaps more importantly if you betray the dope man that only bad things would happen to you.

The next undercover caper seemed boring, not of sufficient quantity, and too, it involved cocaine. I met with the agents and CI and learned that one Frederick Burges, aka Fred, was a midlevel cocaine trafficker, scoring his coke from one of the Jacksons. The CI made the case seem interesting when he described how Fred made the delivery. After getting our roles in sync, the CI and I got into the black Cadillac Eldorado undercover car and drove over to Fred's house. I was introduced to Fred as Big John from Toledo. Almost immediately after the introduction, I engaged Fred in a conversation about cocaine in the presence of his wife and two smaller children.

I was contemplating that Fred would tell his children to go into another room. After he seemed too dense to take my hints, I finally asked, "Fred it isn't too cool to be talking about coke in front of your kids is it?"

"Why not, only the police has a problem talking about dope in front of children, you

Aren't the police are you?" he asked.

"Aw man, come on, what in the hell are you talking bout?" I responded. The conversation about being the police or a snitch came out of Fred's mouth rapidly and frequently. Each time he used the word "snitch" the CI unconsciously and nervously rose up slightly from his seat as though he was ready to run. We played the police game for several minutes and I shut it down by putting Fred's mind focused on the second drug deal rather than the one pending; put his mind off into the next week.

After settling down, Fred related that he wanted his children to grow up and be just like him, a dope dealer and refused to tell them to leave the room. He did relate that he did not want them to use drugs but indeed wanted them to be the best dope dealers around. Fred related that he did not keep drugs in his house in fear of his children accidentally taking it. Consequently, he stored drugs at his mother's house about five or six miles "across town." Fred also related that he had been dealing drugs for ten years and never caught a case. I noticed the CI again rose up from his seat and sat back down. Under my breath, I was about to tell Fred that he was on the right track to catching a case like no other case he had ever seen or heard. I told him 1 wanted to purchase two ounces of good coke and flashed $3,000.

Fred advised it would cost $700 per ounce of cocaine. I negotiated and he agreed to sell me two ounces of cocaine for $1300. A short time later Fred left the residence, taking his five-year-old daughter with him. He advised that he would return in about thirty minutes and told us to wait at his house until he returned. Shortly after Fred left, I left the residence en route to the store. I advised surveillant agents what was transpiring and returned back to the residence. About fifteen minutes later Fred and his five-year old daughter arrived back at the house. Fred called me into the dining room and asked if I was ready to do this deal. I removed the $3,000 official government funds from my pocket and counted $1300 and showed it to Fred asking if he had the coke. Fred stated, "Yes" then called his five year old daughter into the dining room, reached under her dress and removed two ounces of coke concealed inside of her panties and handed it to me. I handed him the $1300 and went into a Blue funk for a few seconds.

When I came out, I heard Fred asking, "Hey Big John, are you alright, hey, hey are you okay?"

"Yeah, I'm okay, I just felt a little faint. Have you been painting around here?" I asked and feigned that I had had an allergic reaction to paint thinner. The reality of it was I had stopped short of queering the deal and short of kicking Fred's ass to a pulp for utilizing his daughter as he had. When I looked into his face, all I could see was the disgust of purported parenthood. I thought of a phrase from the Watts Hood, "I was a half inch off his ass" (provoked to the degree of initiating a fist fight). Apparently Fred saw the disgust in my expression and related, "Hey, she is the best little insurance I got. I have been stopped eight times and they never found a grain of coke, how about that?"

With that remark I became 1/32 of an inch off Fred's ass, but had to refrain myself, had to refocus on the big picture. I knew then that I would have to double up on Fred and set him up for about a two-kilo take-down. That would ensure his incarceration for ten years or more. Too bad the mandatory sentences had been eliminated; otherwise Fred would have been exposed to more time. Instead of becoming angrier, the CI and I hurriedly left the residence, advising that I would contact him in a few days for a four-ounce deal. Inside the undercover car en route to the office, the CI related what a lousy motherf___r Fred was. I knew I had to get two more buys on Fred without the presence of the CI.

Late that same afternoon another CI advised that he could introduce me to a John Doe Ralph, who lived on Outer Drive, a lieutenant for major heroin trafficker Cleveland Clay. That night, just at sunset, the CI and I drove over to Ralph's house on Outer Drive subsequent to a taped telephone call to Ralph. He admitted us into the residence and became suspicious that I was the police. We bantered back and forth for fifteen minutes. Ralph left the room and returned with two ak-47s and placed them on the table and asked if I knew what they were.

"Yeah, these are some fucked up foreign guns do they shoot?" I asked.

"Do they shoot, hell these're AK47s man you must be crazy. You can piss down the barrel of 'em and they'll still fire. These motherf___rs will tear a motherf__ r's ass up" Ralph remarked. By not identifying the guns, apparently proved to Ralph that I was not the police for I was too "stupid to be the police," he remarked. I told Ralph that I was there to meet him, to buy five ounces of good heroin that could take a four, not to play police games.

Ralph then became somewhat indignant, placed one of the AK-47s on the table with the barrel pointed toward me as he fooled around with the other one. He stated, "Hey this is my house, a motherf___r plays whatever game I am playing in my house, you know what I mean?"

"Hey Ralph, I thought you were the dope man, I didn't know you were into guns, I must have the wrong man." I related.

The CI blurted in, "Naw, Ralph is Clay's main man. He's got good heroin don't you Ralph?"

Ralph looked at the CI angrily and stated, "Now don't you try to punk me out motherf___r."

It became obvious that we would have to listen to Ralph for he certainly wanted to be king in his house. Ralph wanted to show us something and went into the bathroom and filled the tub with water. He then had us accompany him into the bathroom. He loaded both AK-47s and placed them in the tub of water and we walked back into the dining room.

Ralph then related that he would sell five ounces of heroin for $3500 but he had to wait for Clay. We talked about dope, dopers, women, pussy, cocaine, the Pink Lady club and the white folks now allowing blacks to move into Palmer Park. About about twenty minutes, we followed Ralph back into the bathroom. He removed the two AK-47s from the water and we followed him into his back yard. I held one wet AK-47 as Ralph fired several rounds in the air. The sound of the gunshot deadened my ears and the smell of spent rifle rounds filled the air. I heard cars speeding away in the front and some braking, with doors opening and shutting quickly. The first thought that came to mind was surveillant agents storming Ralph's house. I saw the profile of an agent walk pass Ralph's house peering in the direction of the rear yard. I spoke loudly about the guns in a friendly manner to alert the surveillant agent that all was well. I handed him the other wet AK-47 and he fired several rounds in the air and related, "This is the baddest "motherf——r in the world and I got a hundred of 'me. I'm a most bad motherf___r," he spouted.

After the little ritual, we went back into the house and started negotiating for future drug deals. Ralph was somewhat astute; he wanted to consummate the first deal without problems without dealing with future deals. In all the prior times I had used the focusing on the next transaction, Ralph was the only dealer that remained focused on the deal at hand. He came back with the police thing, relating that he had been busted before for a "sale to the man." The man (police) had gotten him confused about future deals and he had lost sight of his initial suspicion by focusing on future deals.

Again we went around about the police, who is the police, or working for the police and if I was the police or working for the police. I finally told Ralph that he was in the police search business and I thought he was in the dope business. He became indignant and left the room. Ralph returned in a short while and advised that his connection would be there in a short while and he would do the deal. About ten minutes later a Cadillac Fleetwood Brougham pulled up in front of Ralph's house and he went outside and met with the occupant briefly and came back into the residence. He went into another room for a few seconds returned and advised he was ready to do the deal. I asked, "Do you have the heroin?"

"Yeah, I got it, give me the money first and I'll give you the dope," he insisted. We argued back and forth for a while until Ralph finally handed me the heroin and placed both of his hands on his hips. I looked in the smoked glass wall mirror and saw that he had two .45 automatics, one in each Levi hip pocket. When I reached into my left pant pocket to get the money, I noticed that Ralph had placed his right hand on the automatic in his right rear pocket as though ready to draw and shoot. I pondered for a few minutes thinking that I should light this ass hole up (kill him). He was about 6'4", 250 lbs. and appeared muscular. When retrieving the money, I touched the .38 in my crotch and started to get the drop of Ralph just to let him know that he was not as bad as he was purporting himself to be. I noted that beads of sweat had formed on the Call's brow and his lips had turned white.

I asked Ralph if the 1/8 kilo cost $3,000 or what price he had quoted. He responded, "$3500 mothef___r don't try to start no shit up in here."

I removed $5,000 and counted $3500 and handed it to Ralph. He then relaxed and related that he thought I was trying to rip him off. I realized then that Ralph, although in his own house, was really afraid of me. All of the drama he had engaged in did not frighten me to the point that he had anticipated. After the deal, I exchanged farewells with him and his wife and advised that I would get back with him in a short while for another 1/8 or 1/5-kilo heroin deal. When the CI and I left Ralph's house, we saw a short black male seated in the driver's position of the Fleetwood Brougham parked out front.

A few days later I telephoned Fred and ordered four ounces of cocaine. Per his instruction, almost (without the CI), I drove over to Fred's house and met with him and his wife. I tried to elicit whether Fred was actually buying the cocaine and reselling to me. He related again that he kept a cache of cocaine at his mother's residence somewhat close by. All while talking to Fred, his wife sat in the background wearing skimpy shorts exposing her privates to me. On one occasion she put her hand in her crotch and then placed it in her mouth while making eyes at me. She was a cute little petite big breasted well-built young woman that child bearing had not affected.

After Fred and his daughter and son left, his wife came on to me and asked how could I respect a fool like Fred, "a fool who hides his dope in his little daughter's panties." She sat on the couch next to me and buried her head in my crotch and blew her warm breath over me. I pushed her away thinking that she was equally as guilty as Fred for allowing him to use their daughter. I wrestled her away from me for what seemed like hours. I felt relieved when I heard Fred pull into the driveway.

Fred came into to the living room carrying his son in one arm and leading his daughter by the hand. He then raised her little dress and removed four ounces of cocaine from her panties contained in a rubber contraceptive and handed them to me. I counted $2500 and handed it to Fred. I stared at the innocent face of his daughter and wanted to cry. It was not time but I wanted to arrest Fred and his wife to stop their utilization of a five-year old daughter in their drug business. Immediately a number of disgusting names, like puke ball, sleaze ball, slime ball, doorbell, tirdball, shit bird, scumbag, maggot ball, buzzard cake, hemorrhoid mouth, and other unlikable names came to mind. As far as I was concerned, they all fit Fred. He was the lowest man I had ever met. All while a policeman, I had never struck a person needlessly and the same while an agent. Fred was one person I wanted to fight—I wanted to strike. I wanted to put the cold aluminum barrel of my gun in his ear, pull the trigger hammer back and pray that he engaged me in a struggle.

Sometimes when working undercover you begin to like the defendant as a person, not what he is doing, maybe that is the nature of human contact, human interaction. There was not a single doubt about how I felt about Fred. He had disappointed me, of all the dope dealers I had met in Detroit, he was the only one unarmed. During our first meeting he related how he had a dislike for guns. A throw away officer would have a difficult time dealing with him. Maybe he would use a knife as justification for killing him.

It was in Detroit that I learned what a throw away is to some policemen. It was explained that despite being human, the police is viewed by the public as being fair, strong, a good American and consequently everything the police does has to be just right, just and there is no margin for human errors. The police has to be empowered to take a citizen's freedom and if necessary to take a citizen's life. In all life taking incidents, the police has to be right, the right equation or ingredients must exist. In the past a poster for a criminal would read, "Wanted dead or alive." This gave the police carte blanche to kill whether the wanted person was armed, posed a threat or was fleeing from arrest. As time evolved many outlaws were shot in the back by good citizens and by good policemen. This procedure became an anchor for one's back had long been considered sacred, that is, sportsmen had touted that a man's back afforded him a disadvantage from an attacker. Even professional fighters were often penalized for striking a boxer whose back was turned.

After this changed, so did the consensus change that even an outlaw's back should be respected. Police then had to be extremely cautious on taking a life and back shootings went out like horseback travel giving in to the automobile.

In those instances where an officer mistakenly took a life, the public outcry failed to accept the fact that the officer, like all humans, made an honest mistake in judgment. As a result, many officers were terminated, prosecuted, found guilty and criminally libel for making an honest mistake in judgment. To alleviate this and to establish some sort of insurance against these types of incidents, officers nationwide started arming themselves with unregistered guns, knives and weapons. When they made an honest mistake and shot a citizen or suspect that was unarmed, or a deaf mute or for whatever reason, to justify the shooting the officer tossed a "throw away" next to the injured or deceased to justify the shooting.

Realizing this to be extremely wrong, unlawful, and unethical and truly a violation of one's rights, I could not help but contemplate that Fred would meet his demise in that manner. Maybe, as luck would happen, it would be at the hands of Detroit's finest men and women in blue.

I had always been fascinated with cars and admired mechanics, autoworkers and being in Detroit, the motor capital of the world, was certainly a new experience. I admired, even on my first trip, seeing the factory workers going to and fro during all hours of the day; seeing the pride on their faces, the beautiful cars they drove, the type of money they earned and how they lived.

John P. Sutton

I recall on my first assignment an interesting article about a family's success story about a man, wife and three sons, how they worked at an auto factory with a household annual income of almost $200,000. Perhaps most interesting was how they had started a family savings club where each member saved $50 per week over a number of years, how they had accumulated over 1/2 million dollars, had purchased a party store, several homes and were on their way to becoming rich. The family was described as an average family with no formal education beyond the high school level.

The article went further describing the positive impact of the automotive industry that started in Detroit and now worldwide, had on the American as well as the world economy. Perhaps most interesting was crediting Ford, the major pioneer, for the establishment of the "Installment Plan", a plan that allowed the unrich to own an automobile and to gain wider access to employment and money making ventures. The article described them as "Blue Collar workers."

I had always wanted to tour an auto plant, especially when passing and seeing how huge they are, some larger than many towns.

I was introduced to the CI, called RR, as a blue-collar worker, at Dodge Main in Hamtramck, Michigan. When I asked him what RR meant, he advised that it was for Redneck Red and that he was from West Memphis, Arkansas. RR related that he personally knew Black blues singer Little Junior Parker that was from his hometown. After we exchanged general conversations of generalities and chitchat, I asked RR why he wanted to see a black agent. RR related that there was heavy drug dealings at the Dodge Main plant in Hamtramck on the part of a "bunch of Hoosiers." He described a Hoosier as a rural white Americans with less than a high school diploma, a low lifer, a snuff dipper, tobacco chewer that came from a long line of not to well educated parents and fore parents. According to RR, some were even Klansmen or white power, white supremacy advocates that did not really know what to believe or who to follow.

When asked how I fit in with them, RR related that he thought one of the most evil things he could think of was dope dealing. He could not understand how someone with a good job at Chrysler or any major automaker could stoop so low as to deal drugs. RR believed that drug dealing and drug use inside of the automotive industry would completely destroy it, causing him to one day lose his job. He wanted to introduce a black agent to several for drug deals. According to RR, they would really be hurt being arrested by a black and he wanted to hurt them as much as possible. RR believed that I would have to work for the Dodge Main plant in order to buy drugs from two of the biggest polydrug dealers, Biff and HB, who worked at Dodge Main. I convinced RR to introduce me to both dealers without all the fanfare of working for Dodge Main.

The next day at lunch break I met RR on the B parking lot at Dodge Main and saw him walk up with a monstrous looking man with a beard. I stirred around my truck (undercover vehicle) trying to act normal. RR introduced me as Big John to Biff and related that I was handling the drug business in the northeast area of the plant.

Biff looked me over curiously and stated, "He don't look that big ta me, why you call him Big John, Hell I expected ta see a bigun."

"I can hold my own Biff. I ain't as big as you but I've been known to kick a little ass too ya know," I blurted out trying to fit the role.

Biff replied, "Ya know I'd rather fight than fuck. Thas somethin' 'bout a good ass fight that makes ya feel good ya know what I mean? The reason I'as lookin atcha so hard ya look like a guy's ass I kicked at a bar a few days ago. Ya sure you ain't him?" He asked and smiled. Biff had large even teeth in his mouth that made him look larger than life; rather he had the largest teeth I've ever seen.

"Naw Biff, I ain't the guy. I heard you got the boy and girl (heroin and cocaine) good, I'm here to buy a little something if it is as good as RR says it is." I advised.

Biff replied, "RR didn't tell ya I got it all—good weed, salad bowl, ya know almost any kinda goddamn pill ya can think of. Yeah I'm the man at Dodge Main and other places. If you buy dope from anybody at any Chrysler plant, then you are buying my products. How much of what ever you want do ya want ta buy today?"

"I want one piece of each if you can do it now." I related. Biff seemed to become indignant. Without quoting prices he advised, "Wait right here a few minutes" and walked away in the parking lot out of my view in the area of a blue Dodge truck. He returned in a short while with a lunch box, opened the lunch box, displaying approximately eight ounces of heroin and eight ounces of cocaine contained in rubber contraceptives. Biff then stated, "Take how many you want, they're $700 a piece."

I reached into the lunch box removed one ounce of each shook them and told Biff they appeared to be an ounce each.

Biff related, "They're 28 grams on the nose, we don't worry about the point 3-7-5 do we? That'll be $1400 big ones my friend."

I counted $1400 from a $5000 roll and handed it to Biff. Without counting the $1400 Biff placed it inside his overall pocket, closed his lunch pail, and left the area stating, "It's nice doing business with ya. See RR when you want ta do business again."

I tried unsuccessfully to get Biff's telephone number at home and at the plant in order to cut RR out of the next transaction. RR had emphatically stated that he did not want to testify. We decided to make the case and if necessary convince RR to testify.

RR and I went back to the undercover truck and secured the

heroin and cocaine. We then drove over to the D parking lot where RR walked into the plant. A short time later he returned with a short rotund, pear shaped, round head white male that seemed to rock from side to side when he walked. As he came closer, I noted that he was bow legged. As RR had described he had to be HB. RR was right; HB would have difficulties trying to corner any animal.

HB related that he could do the ounces then, but I would have to buy them in 1/2-ounce packages, that he had packaged them in 1/2-ounce packages. He agreed to sell me an ounce of heroin and an ounce of cocaine for $1500. After I agreed, HB told us to wait for him in the parking lot and left the area. HB returned and handed me a letter and told me I had to take care of the letter before he would complete the sale. I opened the envelope, removed a piece of paper and almost busted out laughing. HB wanted me to sign the letter, a kind of contract that read,

"I _____- being duly sworn, do solemnly state that I am not the police, not a snitch and am not working for the police in any capacity."

_____

_____ Date

I told HB that I believed he was the police based on how the contract was written. I signed it Willie Lee Henderson and handed it to HB. HB then became alarmed that if I was Big John then why I was signing the contract differently. I argued with HB for a while regarding showing him some identification. I had read his from his plant identification tag, yet I insisted that he show me some ID and that I would do likewise. HB refused and started to walk away stating the "deal is off."

I called HB back and handed him my undercover driver's license in the name of Willie Lee Henderson. After giving me my license, HB reached into his left pants pocket and handed me two 1/2 ounces of heroin. He then reached into his right pants pocket and handed me two 1/2 ounces of cocaine, and then advised that the total price was $1400. I counted $1400 of official government funds and handed it to HB. He recounted it and secured it in his left sock. I advised HB that I wanted to purchase two ounces of each the next week and got a telephone number where he could be contacted. HB related that he was a big dealer and could provide large amounts of cocaine and heroin if given sufficient notice. He related that he was the second biggest drug dealer working for Chrysler and when asked who was the biggest, RB referred to him as a motherf___r and related that the other dealer had stolen some of his customers, that he was trying to make all of the money. I agreed to meet with HB in a week, the CI and I exchanged farewells and left.

En route to the office, the CI related that all auto plants had drug dealers, whores, number bookers, number runners, fences, hit men, arsonist, real estate brokers and pawn brokers. He further related that they are cities within walls where almost everybody is involved in some kind of hustle other than working for the auto industry. He also stated that the unions really started in the auto industry. Now unions, most of them, are just as crooked as some of the drug dealers that even they represent. I made two subsequent large buys from Biff and HB and let them hang around for a subsequent arrest.

Agents Moffett and Adams were also buying dope all over Detroit. When we were not simultaneous undercover, we were the point surveillant unit in predominant black areas. On occasion, we worked joint undercover cases, that is, two of us went undercover. They were witnessing the same thing undercover that I had, that is, that there were more firearms in the hands of the dope dealers, their henchmen and lookouts than they had ever experienced. Agent Adams was stationed in Chicago and Agent Moffett was stationed in Pittsburgh. The three of us agreed to be on the safe side, we had to carry at least three guns undercover. On some occasions, three did not seem enough. Most of the dope houses we went into were crowded like supermarkets; rather the dealers were dealing dope like they had a legitimate business, devoid of the slightest fear of the police. The "Feds" were unheard of as far as they were concerned. Most of the dealers were poorly educated but hell-bent on doing the best that they knew how-selling dope. Consequently, their shortest and quickest solution to a problem was murder, mayhem and arson.

In Detroit besides putting bodies in trunks at the airport, some dealers believed that to be too nice and started decapitating double crossers, CIs and enemies and placing the head in a conspicuous place and secreting the torso in another location. Some even took to dousing with gasoline and throwing a book of matches or a Zippo lighter on the soaked body.

One night while terminating an undercover deal and driving back to the office on Woodward Avenue a human fireball ran across Woodward in front of me as a shooter ran behind him shooting and screaming. One of the rounds came close to me sounding like a fast moving plane.

SA Ken Adams requested that I assist him in an undercover deal wherein the primary suspect was reportedly very dangerous and unpredictable. Ken had purchased one ounce of heroin from the subject, one Royal Burton with the assistance of a CI. The CI was being cut out and the amount of heroin had been increased to three ounces. I met with Ken and we got our roles in sync and dressed for the occasion. Under the surveillance of all white agents we entered a green Cadillac Fleetwood Brougham undercover car with Ohio plates and drove over to Royal Burton's house and parked. There were three rough looking black males standing in the yard conversing and the bulges in their waistbands indicated they were packing some heavy artillery. When Ken and I got out and approached the house, we noted a tall black male wearing a Jesus Christ-type robe tailored out of a bed sheet. He had a web belt around his waist and was wearing black military boots. He had a large leather tote bag with a strap that went around his neck. He held the tote bag meticulously in both hands. He wore a black beret with an odd logo. Ken and I walked up to the porch and spoke simultaneously to the Jesus-clad subject and got no response. He stared at us until we knocked and entered the residence. Ken stated," That crazy MF was here on the first buy. Keep an eye on him. I have a strong suspicion that he has something hellacious in that tote bag."

We were greeted in the living room by Royal Burton, who despite his color immediately reminded me of Roy Rogers. Shortly after Ken introduced me to Royal, I made the mistake and called him Roy. Royal was wearing two guns in holsters just like Roy Rogers, but without the fancy rhinestones. There were about 17 customers inside of the house, some had just purchased drugs and leaving, others were waiting. Royal then announced to the customers, "You quarter ounce, half ounce and one ounce customers will have to wait until I take care of my multiple ounce customers from Ohio. See my dope is so good I got customers coming from as far as Cleveland to cop from me."

Ken whispered, "Can you believe this crazy m.f.? He's running a dope house here."

Royal left the living room area for a short while then returned with a platter full of heroin stacked in a mound approximately 6" high. He had the platter in his left hand and an old .45 automatic in his right hand plus the two guns on his sides. Two young heroin addicts sporting .12 gauge shotguns followed him. I whispered to Ken, "If anything funky goes down, I'll take out the two shotgun riders, you take Royal and the Jesus Christ."

Royal set the heroin on the dining room table and sat facing customers in the dining room and living room. The two shot gunners took a position to his right and left rear. Royal set the .45 on the table and started stirring the heroin with a playing card simultaneously stating, "I hope ain't none of you MFs getting sick or thinking about ripping me off 'cause I got enough firepower to start a young fucking war up in here." The Jesus Christ dressed male stood at the left of the front door facing Royal.

Ken ordered two ounces of heroin and I ordered one. Royal measured the heroin out in tablespoons. He gave us five tablespoons to the ounce and packaged each ounce in a rubber contraceptive, looped back over the ball and tied it a knot at the end. Ken paid Royal $1300 official funds and I paid $700 official funds for the one ounce. We secured the heroin in our sock and stood around and chatted with Royal as he sold to other customers. We watched the Jesus Christ subject. He watched us intently and never uttered a word. After several minutes Ken and I exchanged farewells with Royal advising that we would contact him in a few days for another deal. When we left, we attempted to make conversation with the Jesus Christ like man and he did not utter a word but stared at us menacingly. I attempted to trick him into a handshake by extending my hand simultaneously stating, "Let's shake to a good day my friend." Instead of extending his hand the JC grabbed the tote bag with his left hand and placed his right hand inside of the flap.

Ken remarked, "Hey can't you see that MF can't talk that's it maybe he can do sign language." The JC did not respond.

We drove from the area and picked up on what we believed was counter surveillance, not our surveillant agents. One car passed us and two unknown white males both stared at us and sped away. We wrote down the license number and at the office met with our surveillant agents and ran a record check and learned that it was not in file, an indication that it was a law enforcement vehicle.

Later that day and two days afterward, we tried to determine what other law enforcement agency was involved. We tossed it aside thinking that maybe our own inspection was in the area checking.

About five days later, Ken and I got back with Royal Burton for a five-ounce buy. The scene in his house was a duplication of the last one. The JC was positioned at the same location. His robe, fashioned out of a sheet, was white and spotless. We noted that his tote bag seemed to bulge more. Again he never spoke but stared at us from our arrival to our departure. Again our surveillant units peeled off as we advised that we were en route to the office. Shortly thereafter, we picked up on a black car following us. We made several turns and did a yo-yo (u-turn) and came back in its direction, noting a salt-pepper team this time. We noted they u-turned and continued to follow us. We took them hurriedly into a cul-de-sac and blocked them as they attempted to exit. Four agents, two facing two drew weapons and shouted in unison "federal agents." We reholstered our weapons and laughed uproariously, relieved that the other was not a crook. They were from Alcohol, Tobacco and Firearms (ATF) agents.

The non-black ATF agent asked, "Do you guys have anything on the Jesus Christ guy?"

"No, he sure looks mean as hell. I don't believe he can talk," I stated.

"Yeah, we tried to talk to the MF but he has never said a word. I've seen him there three times, but never heard him say a word even when people try to speak to his crazy ass," Ken related.

"This guy is a real winner, his elevator does not go up to the top floor. He is a walking time bomb. We know that he has between eight and a dozen frag grenades in his fag bag. We believe that he will not hesitate to pop a few off," the other ATF agent advised.

"All along I suspected this guy had a weapon of some sort, possibly a sawed off shotgun but I never suspected grenades," I related.

I began to think about the damage this nut could inflict if

angered and how Ken and I in a routine gangster role-play had mother fucked him a couple times inside of his earshot trying to elicit a response. Had we known he had grenades in the tote bag, we would have bowed and said worship to him and his Jesus Christ robe and all. ATF advised that they would be taking him down possibly tomorrow or the next day and invited us along. They suspected that he had an arsenal in his basement. We declined the ride along due to our undercover roles.

The next day, ATF saw the Jesus Christ figure walking from his residence toward the neighborhood store. They popped him at the milk container; cuffed him tight, walked him back to his house and executed a federal search warrant. They removed a crate of fragmentation grenades, C-4 plastics, dynamite, two light antitank weapons (LAW) dozens of LAWs rockets, 12 AK-47s, over 100,000 rounds of ammunition, numerous other weapons from the basement of his house.

The tote bag was seized from the bedroom nightstand. It was filled with 10 frag grenades and a .32 caliber Iver-Johnson pistol.

Ken and I shivered from reading the write up about the arrest and seizure and seeing the photograph of his tote bag with grenades and a pistol. That same night two Detroit based drug dealers were shotgun and several other murders transpired the next day that was all reported as drug related.

The 4th of July came around and gunshots, not firecrackers rang out all over Detroit except in the Palmer Park and Outer Drive areas. Even the hotel where I resided, the other customers and some of the hotel workers began to show a different attitude toward me. I detected crassness in their voices and a bit of rudeness in their mannerism. At the front desk certain employees would not cash American Express traveler's checks and even the bellman looked at me with a disgusting stare.

To gain some sense of relaxation and comfort, I rented a car and drove to Toronto and checked into a nice hotel ironically named Suttons Place. I took a walk through Yonge Street and ate at several nearby cafes. On the second evening, after obtaining directions twice, I drove to a three story frame house-restaurant called, "The Underground" and consumed a delicious soul food meal of ham hocks and pinto beans over a bed of rice arid corn bread. I watched two ladies at the table adjacent to me order chitterling hors d'oeuvres. We all drank either strawberry or grape cool-aid with lemon and lots of sugar from a mason jar. It was a nice meal, reasonable and one of the tourist advised that Bill Cosby owned the restaurant.

The next day I took a bus tour along the water front to a beautiful flower garden and to various parts of the beautiful city of Toronto. En route back to the hotel, from the bus I saw a man making love to a double leg female amputee in the park off Yonge Street. They did not try to conceal themselves as they struggled nude in the open grass far from any bush or tree.

In the hotel lobby and cafe, I heard the laughter and chatter of the French Canadian women and men. They all seemed happier, devoid of a worry or care in the world, living a life of fun, enjoyment, gaiety and pleasure, while enjoying both the simple and complex things about them. Perhaps the most unusual thing I saw was a policeman. A few were unarmed. It was then that I realized how wonderful it must be to live in a world, apparently so full of peace, serenity and quietude, where gunshots did not ring out, dead bodies rotting in trunks did not exist, neither did human fireballs, decapitations, mayhem, arson and other bad crime frequently occur. Certainly they existed, but not to the extent as in Detroit a few hundred miles away.

Perhaps their answer to all the violence was centered on their firearms laws. Citizens reportedly could not carry or own firearms in Canada, especially not as easy as in the United States. Carrying a firearm was a serious offense. With that thought, I then realized that I had forgotten about the prohibition of bringing handguns into Canada. There I was in Toronto, Canada, out-

Thin White Lines

side of United States, a US agent carrying two handguns concealed upon my person. I was never one to test laws or ask for special dispensation. Driving to Toronto, Canada armed was strictly an oversight on my part, an honest mistake. I went back to the hotel, packed and slept until 6:00 a.m. I checked out at 7:00 a.m. and drove back to Detroit that Sunday. Shortly after I came out of the tunnel upon Jefferson, I saw a car chasing another car east on Jefferson with a man each hanging out of the windows shooting at each other. The sound of sirens sounded in the air and the acceleration and fading of the police engines rang in the air. While driving on I-94 toward the hotel, a black Cadillac pulled up next to me, the driver, front right and rear right passengers were each smoking a marijuana cigarette about the size of a large cigar. The front passenger took a deep draw, held it for a while then exhaled and shook his head. He then motioned to me offering it to me, I smiled shook my head to the side and pulled away from them. I drove back to the airport, turned in the rental car and took a taxi back to the hotel.

I went to the front desk to check for messages. The clerk advised nonchalantly, without looking in my box or at me, "No, you don't have any messages. Is there anything else sir?" I thanked him, went up to my room and noted the red light blinking on the telephone. I called down and had two messages, both from the office.

I went down to the newsstand and got a Sunday newspaper. On the front page was a report of two decaying bodies found at Detroit Metro Airport. There was a joke asking the name of the busiest cemetery or burial ground in the Detroit Metropolitan area. The answer: The Detroit Metro Airport. There was a picture of two-car trunks open, an airplane flying above, and an unknown voice in one trunk asked, "Why do you always drive? Why don't you fly?" The other trunk answers, "I'd rather die than fly."

The murders, dead bodies, suspects with gun shots ringing

out, seeing passers-by flashing guns, drugs, seeing guns in almost every dope dealers house, three CIs murdered, all within less than three months was about to take its toll on me. Perhaps seeing Fred utilize his five year old daughter to conceal drugs in her crotch, seeing dope dealers deal dope like they had immunity from arrest, hearing ex-convicts talk about how much time they had served and vowing not to go back to jail yet doing crimes with fervor as though they could not be arrested certainly portrayed Detroit as the reputation it had gained, the "murder capital of the world" caused me great concern.

On each undercover endeavor, there was always the potential of possible gunplay. Perhaps more alarming was the possibility of being accidentally shot by a heroin addict henchman while on the nod or coming out of a nod. Additionally, there were hijackers, also known on the streets as "jackers." They hijacked drug pushers, stash pads, and runners. Since the drug dealer could not call the police, he had to handle hijackers on his own. They kept the likes of Chester Campbell busy.

One day a new agent, trying to get his feet wet on his first case, asked for my assistance in identifying a subject reportedly dealing cocaine from a service station on Warren. I agreed, met with the agent and CI and agreed to meet with the suspect to identify him for a subsequent transaction. The CI joined me in the undercover car and we drove over to the service station on Warren. As we parked on the lot, I could see the back of a black male, wearing a black coat, black pants and a black derby hat, sitting behind the counter as a tall young male worked the register and two men outside pumped gasoline and attended cars.

We walked into the office and the CI introduced me to the male in black as Big John, his cousin. Immediately I recognized that he was the notorious hit man Chester Campbell. His first word was, "Yeah, I'm glad to metcha. What can I do fer you motherf____rs?"

Thin White Lines

"I'm new here in Detroit, just raised up (got out of jail) and trying to get down again," I advised.

"What do you mean, you trying to do like Marvin Gaye, trying to dance motherf___r?" he asked.

"Hey, why do I have to be a motherf___r I just met you man? Why would you come on to me a stranger like that?" I asked.

Chester stated, "'Cause if you really knew who I am man you would be scared to even talk to me. Especially talk to me about getting down", he said.

"What are you, some kinda police or snitch or something?" I asked.

"Naw motherf___r, I am a killa of policemen. I kill policemen for a living, that's what I do. Do you want me to kill somebody fer you?" Chester asked.

"Naw why should I have to get somebody to kill for me. I can kill for myself," I bluffed.

I noticed the CI apparently recognized that he had unknowingly introduced me to Chester Campbell, a guy he had had a general conversation with a few days earlier about drugs. The CI had been popped by DPD and was dying to initiate a case for some relief. I watched his mouth turn dry, lips white, perspiration bead upon his forehead and he moved nervously about like he had to urinate badly. When he talked his voice was nervous and squeaky. Chester realizing the CI was scared directed his conversation at the CI, calling him a "candy assed punk" on every other occasion.

"Hey man I see you are the baddest motherf___r in all Detroit. I am trying to get down. I am not here trying to make a mean motherf___r meaner or to piss anyone off. I got a little money I want to spend but not with somebody that can only get madder and try to punk somebody out," I advised.

"You know, you got a point. I had a chat with your boy here a couple days ago about some coke. I was just pulling his leg. I don't do no drugs. I make enough money doing what I do. You never heard of me huh?" He asked.

"How could I say whether I have or not you never told me your name, yet I told you mine." I related.

"I am Chester Campbell man. I am the Chester Campbell. I have seen you before but I can't put my finger on it. My name don't mean nothing to ya huh?" he said.

"No it doesn't. Like I said I am not from around here so your name wouldn't mean nothing to me." I advised. I then asked, "Are you some ex-boxer, football player or something."

"Naw man, just ask around and they will tell you who I am", he related. The more we talked, the more the CI became nervous and frightened. Seeing the CI frightened, Chester stated, "I think your boy knows who I am. I can tell by his reaction. Ask him who I am. He'll tell ya."

I asked the CI, "Who is this guy, is he somebody special or important, is he the police?

"Naw, he-e-e-e-e's Chester C-C-Campbell that's who he is. He-e-e-e is C-C-Chester C-C-Campbell", the CI uttered.

"Who is this Chester Campbell man, why is he so important?" I asked.

The CI stated, "He-eee-ees, su-u-uposed to be a killer man tha-t-ts who-o-o-o-oo-o he-ee-ees supposed to be."

"Hey Chester, I'm glad to know you're a killer too." I walked outside of the service station, took my .45 automatic and fired eight rounds into the air, unloaded the clip quickly reloaded another clip and popped a round in the chamber. I heard cars peeling rubber leaving the service station and several cars ran the red light across the street. I put the safety on, placed the .45 back into my waist and waked back into the office.

I looked at Chester and said, "You ain't the baddest motherf—— r in the world are you?" I stared him directly in the eyes with the grip of my .45 exposed from under my shirt and repeated, "You ain't the baddest motherf___r in the world are you?" Chester did not answer just stared back at me unafraid but surprised at what I had just pulled. There was no change in the tone of his voice, no nervousness, no concern for his safety or the arrival of the police. The expression on his face was that of steel—unbendable, unmovable, firmly set and projected fear. He was apparently relieved that I was not some killer that was sent there for him but he showed no emotions other than smiled coyly and stated, "I can get to like you. You're a crazy motherf__r just like me."

We talked in generalities and Chester related that he had a friend that had a black El Dorado Cadillac just like mine but he had wider Whitewall tires. According to Chester, his friend had caught a federal case, was convicted and copped a dime (got 10 years in prison). Chester laughed and related that the feds had really tricked him. They sent a sharply dressed undercover agent with a gold tooth into "John." "John bit on it, hook, line and sinker, you know he's up in the federal joint in Milan, Michigan. He still don't believe the man he was dealing with was a fed. Can you imagine a fed with a gold front tooth, that's unheard of man?" Chester related.

I tried to determine how much Chester charged for a "stop order" (murder contract) but he would not comment on whether he did them or not. On almost every little hint, he either ignored it or changed subjects immediately. Chester denied being the owner of the service station and showed two guns that the proprietor owned and kept under the counter for robbers. According to Chester, they had never been robbed.

Although his conversation was congenial, he showed concern for life, family, friends and pets, underneath there existed strongly an aura of a murderer, a man devoid of remorse, sympathy, empathy, compassion or the good in a human life. He projected an aura often displayed by seasoned doctors that some people live, some people die. Although they are healers, even the healer dies when his or her time comes.

I had seen death on many occasions, some from natural causes, others the result of violence at the hands of another. The closest thing in my mind of a death angel was Chester Campbell—Mr. Death himself. He was so bad, so feared, so evil and so reliable at what he did that even hired professional killers in the Mafia were afraid of and respected him for his trade. I suspected that he was the killer of at least one if not two of the CIs that I had worked with earlier. There was a reason for the CI to become frightened, to sweat, to lose his voice, to be totally upset for he knew Chester was all the streets reported him to be—evil, a killer, a stalker, a finder an evil force that could, would and did bring death to many.

After chatting about the street life, seeing Chester taunt the CI unmercifully, the CI and I exchanged farewells with Chester and left.

Perhaps it was self-machismo, false bravado, and the fact that I was licensed by the U.S. Government to carry a gun nationwide and into foreign countries, have been shot at, and have shot people that cause me not to fear Chester. Seeing him was no more risky than the number of armed addicted henchmen that I had encountered in the many dope houses in Detroit. The Jesus Christ character was more terrifying but only after he had been taken down did we realize the danger he projected. He was a walking time bomb just aching for a fuse to explode. I am glad he had taken our motherf___g in stride and not let us upset him.

I could not help but think about Chester. The next day I asked several agents in the office about him. They all reiterated that he was the number one murderer in town; that the FBI was working him. Several were a bit surprised that I had met and negotiated with him undercover. The young surveillant agents were more surprised at the discharging of my firearm at the service station. We all learned a lesson that is, always be prepared when working undercover, but most importantly know the identity and background of the subject before hand.

One of the agents developed a CI that was a very good drug dealer in his own rights and suspected to be the murderer of 'Devil Jackson' on my first in Detroit. He advised that he could introduce an undercover agent to John Mays, aka, Milwaukee Jack for a 1/8-kilogram heroin transaction. According to the CI, Jack only sold 1/8-kilogram quantities of heroin as a precautionary measure to avoid a bust. The CI placed a telephone call to Jack and ordered 1/8 kilo of heroin for his friend. Jack agreed to meet at a barbershop on John R Street. Pre-surveillance was initiated on Jack at the telephone location. I searched the CI and his car and found both devoid of narcotics. He had $250 in large bills that he was allowed to keep.

We entered the CI's red/white Cadillac ElDorado and drove over to a barbershop on John R Street and met with Jack. The CI introduced me as the buyer. After exchanging pleasantries and a general conversation, Jack asked if I was ready to do the deal. He then removed a flat brown paper bag from the inside of his shirt and handed it toward the CI. I took the bag from Jack's hand examined and noted it contained a quantity of white powdery substance. I asked Jack how many ounces were in the package. He stated, "five." I then asked him how many cuts it would take, simultaneously flashing $5000 official government funds. Jack stated, "It'll take a strong three or three and a half cuts. It cost $3500."

I counted $3300 and handed it to Jack telling him it was $3500. I watched him count the money several times and pause. I then counted out $200 and handed to him stating, "I think I shorted you $200."

Jack thanked me and related that he thought he was miscounting the money. "When do you want to make another purchase?" he asked.

I advised Jack that I would get back with him in a few days and asked him for a telephone number where he could be reached. Jack told me to get in contact with him through the CI.

Of all the dope dealers I had seen, Jack was one of the neatest. The first pair of white alligator shoes I ever saw was on his feet. According to the CI they cost $800 at a men's store called Cousins. According to the CI, Jack had about eight pairs. Jack's fingernails were neatly manicured, buffed into shinning and his mustache and small beard were neatly cut and styled. He wore silk pants, silk shirt and jewelry not typical of a doper. I had read about Rolex watches in Ian Fleming's books, never knew what they looked like until I saw the Rolex president style on Jack's wrist.

Jack was a drug dealer. I could only think how he was contributing to the income of the jewelers, clothing stores, nightclubs, party stores, and car dealers and in a short while he would be enriching a bail bondsman and a lawyer. Now that he had been bought and paid for by the US government, that later we would determine what he wears, eats, where he sleeps, when he goes to bed and when he arises the next day. Yeah, Jack had been purchased by Uncle Sam. We, the U. S. government would seize all those things he had acquired from drug trafficking.

I had a busy day with three separate undercover buys and completing the attendant paperwork in meticulous detail. I went to the hotel bar after dinner and had several bourbon and soda until I felt a slight buzz. While consuming the last drink, I noticed a strange looking white adult sitting alone at a table in the corner making friendly gestures at me. I hurriedly finished the drink, paid the tab and went up to my room to avoid him. I suspected that he was possibly some kind of freak or a very talkative lonely person. I had planned to sleep late the next day.

About 7:00 o'clock the next morning, I heard a lot of shouting in unison like loud cheering at an athletic event. I tried to go back to sleep but the shouting and cheering subsided for a few moments then started up again. It appeared as though the shouting was becoming louder after each period of silence. It was impossible to go back to sleep. I telephoned the front desk and

Thin White Lines

complained about all the noise and was advised that there was a national convention held by some guy named Turner espousing "A Dare to be Rich." The clerk advises that I could expect the shouting and cheering all week; the conventioneers had booked the entire hotel. I was the only non-participant and the only thing the hotel could do was apologizing.

While having breakfast, the strange man from the bar last night walked over to my table, sat down and asked if he could join me. Realizing that he had already done so, I agreed. He stated his name as Bernie something, an investor from Bloomfield Hills. Bernie stated that he thought what I did for a living was one of the vilest things a person could inflict upon society. When I asked what he thought I did for a livelihood, he stated, "Drug dealer. Everybody here knows you are a drug dealer—your clothing, your car, your jewelry, your mannerism, plus you don't have any visible means of support and you travel around with a pocket full of $100 bills like you own the world." When I asked Bernie several times if he was certain that he knew what my profession was he replied, "Without a doubt. I would bet my house on it." It finally registered why certain clerks in the hotel were treating me with such disdain. Perhaps they were visioning that I was part of the dead bodies in car trunks activities. Apparently they were not as astute as I thought.

My hotel room was at a government discount and I am sure they knew that I was from California, not Detroit. Maybe it was my mannerism.

I did not have the nerve or desire to identify myself to Bernie for I did not know if he was who he was purporting himself to be. When I inquired if he was with the " Dare to be Rich" noisemakers, he stated that he was not. That he was merely there to siphon off whatever innovative money making ventures he could.

After talking about how disgusting my supposed profession was, Bernie finally got around to the real reason he wanted to talk to me—money, investments. He related that he had approached me as people see me, as a no good dope dealer. Bernie had a scheme to "launder money." When he first mentioned laundering money, I thought he was crazy, rather I was somewhat sure he was. He related the incident involving the dope dealer that paid the IRS $500,000 cash penalty assessment only to be assessed an additional $1,500,000. After relating what a fool the dealer was Bernie related how he could have "legitimatize the money" to allow the trafficker to justify having it.

Bernie related having access to a foreign bank somewhere in the Caribbean where he, for a 1-5% fee, could take several million dollars down, get a cashier's check and loan papers showing that the money was borrowed and that interest was being paid on the loan that could also be deducted from legitimate US income taxes. He related that he had an MBA, had handled money for many people before and found that his services are major money savers, keeps IRS, US Customs and other government agents intact, rather away from large sums of money.

Bernie also related how he could take large sums of money; invest it and yield as much as 50% in nine months. There was a slight catch—he related that there would be no records indicating the investment, the investor would not know where his/her money is invested but would be guaranteed high interest payments every 91st day, that the interest rate would average 50% per year. According to Bernie, a lot of drug dealers were investing in those types of ventures. Some had made enough money that they gave up drug trafficking and are now full time investors. He related that the key ingredient was having a large sum of money for the initial investment, a minimum of $500,000. Bernie advised that only poor people paid taxes and that dope dealers and number runners and bookies had the ideal mechanism for evading taxes; they deal in cash with no traceable documents.

I was adamant about not getting involved with Bernie but he

was persistent. He even asked me, "How much are you worth? Tell me how much are you worth?"

I thought about what he was asking and the way he asked it caused me to realize that

That was something I had never thought about. It became eerie just the thought of it. It was eerier when Bernie started throwing numbers, "$100,000, and $500,000, a million dollars? What are you actually worth?" he asked loudly. Despite not having that kind of money, I began to strongly realize that for some people, one's monetary worth is paramount, especially in terms of readily available cash dollars contrasted to property, stocks and bonds. Bernie knew that all dope peddlers deal in cash, not credit too often but cash, and cash in increments of $50 and $100 notes.

The more I resisted investing multiple hundred thousands of dollars (money that I did not have) with Bernie, the more persistent he became. He used profanity, switched from bad guy, good guy, back to bad guy and back to the good guy only trying to "make a lot of money for all of us." According to Bernie, the Mafia for investment purposes frequently utilizes him. He related how he had invested union pension funds that the mafia had some how acquired. Supposedly, the pension fund was returned only after the mafia had collected significant interest. We talked for over two hours and I was steadfast about not revealing my identity to Bernie.

During the end of our meeting, Bernie, I believe unconsciously, stated, "Everybody can use some alternative income acquiring modalities." I was immediately alarmed for Bernie had slipped and disclosed his true identity, he was a spook.

CHAPTER 10

I HAD A HARD CRIMINAL LOOK about my carriage. Often when I walked the streets in Detroit, I noticed fear on the faces of women Black and White and their suspicious eyes until I passed and often they would switch their purses to the other side, away from me, and clutch it tighter. Robberies of men and women occurred all over the city. Tourism was falling off. Inner city blacks, whites, Caldeans, Macedonians, Albanians, Poles, Germans, Frenchmen, Lebanese, Italians et al, were fleeing the inner city rapidly citing the high crime rate. Downtown stores were suffering from fewer city shoppers' fear of robberies, purse snatches, car burglaries and thefts. One of the most amazing crimes, "chop shop operations" emanated in the motor capital of the world.

Cars were stolen, taken to a garage (chop shop) where they were dismantled into various parts and sold on the illicit market. Sometimes the stolen parts were placed into the legal market. The thief usually sold the car for $500 -$1,000. When parceled

Thin White Lines

out in parts a $15,000 car would bring as much as $15,000 or more with the motor and transmission bringing the top selling price.

The news media, in reporting frequent robberies as they occurred and where, further instilled fear of the inner city. At night, downtown Detroit became a ghost town, where only a handful of people dared to venture. Citizens groups sprang up requesting police action to bring the city back to a peaceful living environment.

Out of desperation, the Detroit Police Department deployed undercover operations coded STRESS, an acronym for Stop The Robberies and Enjoy Safe Streets. STRESS deployed groups of young undercover officers in teams throughout various parts of the city to suppress crime wherever they occurred. At the initial inception, STRESS caused a noticeable reduction in certain crimes. Most of their undercover operators were insufficiently trained and lacked adequate coordination.

One night a CI and I went undercover in a blind pig operated by a John Doe A.K.A. Sugarman on Dexter. All the description and telephone subscriber information, plus photos failed to truly identify Sugarman.

It was amazing how Sugarman was able to operate a blind pig, especially in a residential neighborhood, where heavy traffic of people came and went all hours of the night until around sunrise or six o'clock in the morning.

The police were often called, but seldom came. When they did, they did not address the issue and the drinking, cursing, loud music, cars parked all over the area, even on private lawns, the curb, in front of fire hydrants, driveways double and triple parked. According to the CI on a few occasions someone drove by and shot at the blind pig. Sugarman got fed up and built a little guardroom on the second level sun porch, hired and placed a sniper with a rifle and scope inside. On a few occasions the sniper fired at passing shooters. The whole neighborhood for several blocks was terrified. During the day, 20-30 young boys sold heroin and coke out front for Sugarman. The block on either side of the blind pig looked like a major sports arena, but was always filled with crooks, thugs, dopers and pushers. The neighbors lived in fear. Some had fortified their homes with brick retainer walls and steel plates covered some front porches. The CI further related that the used appliance dealers were making a fortune selling old-fashioned bathtubs that were used for beds for protection from stray bullets.

The night we went to Sugarman's blind pig we could not find a parking space. We found a spot two blocks away and walked up. Cars were parked all over the street, some double parked, on adjoining lawns, blocking driveways, on the grass abutment, and headed in the wrong direction. When we first arrived on the street, we had to wait several minutes while a driver stopped in front of us casually talked to a man standing at the passenger side of his car. After waiting a while, I sounded the horn. The driver flipped the bird then motioned for us to go over the top of his car. Immediately I became angry and contemplated putting a cylindrical blue steel object (the muzzle of my gun) in his left ear but realized it was an un-agent-like thing to do.

En route I thought how difficult it would be for surveillant agents to assist if something went awry. The sniper sat in the cabana smoking. The aperture at his head level lit up like a candle each time he inhaled. As we approached the two-story blind pig, I prayed silently that he was not a heroin addict on the nod. Perhaps the worst way to die is at the hands of a heroin addict on the nod, not really knowing what he is doing, about to do or will do when fluctuating in and out of the nod.

Before we approached the entrance I pondered why crime was so high in Detroit, thought of the human fireball I had seen and my mind slowly drifted back to the decaying bodies in the car trunks. I rationalized that the criminals in Detroit or Michigan did not respect the law and were prone to lawlessness because they don't gas or fry murderers in Michigan-there is no death penalty.

The CI knocked on the front door, waited about 30 seconds, and then rang the doorbell. A male peeked out of a hole displaying only his eyes and responded, "Yeah, what do you want?" Loud music and dancing could be heard within the front room.

The CI stated, "Lemonade, we want to buy some lemonade."

The lookout said, "That will be $10 a piece."

I handed the lookout $20 and he let us in. The front rooms resembled a dance hall, extending the length and width of the house with two bathrooms and a bar at the rear. The smell of marijuana, whiskey, sweat, cheap perfume and cigarette smoke filled the air. All of the attendees on the first floor appeared to be under the legal drinking age and drinks were on the tables that lined the walls. A jukebox played Marvin Gaye's "What's Going On" and young couples danced and cajoled.

There were three young males without females that seemed out of place. One approached me from the front asking, "Who are you motherf___r, don't I know you?" I noted that his two partners had taken position behind me. He took a defensive position with his left leg forward as he talked, identifying to me that he was a police officer protecting himself from a possible kick in the vital area. I ignored him twice until he put his hand on my arm further asking, "Hey I'm talkin' to you. Are you dumb or something?"

I pushed his hand away and stated, "I'm your father and I am about to get into your little young ass like you have never experienced and your two little buddies behind us are also about to get an ass whipping like you and they have never experienced." I tried to engage him in a light struggle to let him know that I was a law enforcement officer and let him know that I was cognizant of his undercover identity. They backed off, with the younger one vowing that they would see me later that night.

The CI whispered, "Those guys are STRESS. I wonder what's about to go down here."

"If any thing goes down, we'll just act like crooks and take the bust that will take us even closer to Sugarman," I advised.

As we walked to the rear, the lookout asked the CI if he was going up. I turned and saw a rifleman looking out of each front corner window.

The CI and I walked up the wooden spiral stairs to a door where only one person could stand. It had apparently been specially constructed to thwart police efforts in kicking it open. It opened to the outside, making it more difficult to force entry, with a second wooden door that opened to the inside.

As we entered it was barred with a 2x4 across the middle and further barred with a steel rod anchored to the floor. There was a stack of rifles and shotguns in the little room left of the door. The whole upstairs was dim lit with an expensive wooden u-shaped bar that almost covered the width of the room.

A multiracial crowd of males and females sat at the bar with small mounds of cocaine on a mirror in front of them and a cocktail on the side. The CI introduced me as his cousin John to Sugarman, a flamboyant young white American with shoulder length hair. He was clad in a light blue velvet jump suit and snake skin cowboy boots with gold tips, a velvet belt with gold buckle and tip, a large gold chain around his neck with a large diamond pendant, large diamond rings on seven fingers, a Rolex watch on his left arm and a large, thick gold bracelet on his right wrist.

Sugarman talked black. He could say motha fucka better than blacks in the hood. I had to stare at him closely to determine if he was a mulatto or really white. Scantily clad big-breasted black and white female bartenders measured out quantities of cocaine, mixed and served drinks. Sugarman catered to only "Big time players who could pay" and had police protection for the night.

He related that the jackers (hijackers) had come through twice and took him off. The first time it was on a Sunday and he lost over $30,000. It was amusing learning that in the criminal environment, how certain criminals played policeman, how they speculated, guessed, plotted, schemed, and meted out justice. Sugarman related how he had picked up on some information that the 'jackers were coming back to rob him again but he had a nice cake baked for them this time. According to him "the lowest thing a motha-fucka could do is rob a dope man or a gambling joint 'cause they know you can't call the police. They ain't playing fair game." He went on relating that he had hired eight gunmen, four upstairs and four downstairs, for the weekend to shoot it out with the 'jackers and that none of his customers knew what was about to go down. The CI looked around the room and walked away from Sugarman signaling for me to join him.

The CI was nervous and stated, "Man STRESS is up in this mother wall-to- wall." It appeared that STRESS had introduced themselves undercover to Sugarman for two reasons—to wipe out the hijackers and arrest Sugarman and his customers. The CI identified a STRESS office upstairs and we both wondered who the fourth one was downstairs. STRESS was too new to be corrupt. The two neatly dressed beer drinking, nonsmoking young STRESS officers strutted about as though they would enjoy a good shoot out. On occasion they attempted to anger me but I remained calm. One stepped on my right outer toe. I brushed it off. I knew their identity and wondered if they were aware of mine but doubted it for certainly I would have been apprised that they were undercover to avoid the possibilities of law enforcement officers being involved in a shootout with one another. I prayed that the 'jackers did not arrive for I was not about to be in a shoot out and not be involved. If there was any killing to be done, as a law enforcement officer it was expected that I would be involved. It would be very difficult deciding who should be killed. The worst killing often involves law enforcement officers unknowingly killing each other.

Sugarman was certain they were going to hit his place that night but would not disclose the source of his information. He indicated that he had paid the source for the information. I began to think of the possibility of STRESS as the source but did not believe a new unit could be that sophisticated in undercover operations.

The cocaine flowed almost like cocktails and the women became more relaxed. At the far corner of the bar, I noticed a waitress fill several balloons from a metal cylinder and sell them to several customers for $10. They inhaled the gas both through their mouth and nose and seemed to get some euphoric feeling from it. I eliminated it as oxygen noting the waitress smoked while extracting it. At certain times there were at least two ounces of cocaine on the bar.

Sugarman was making money. According to the CI, there was a heroin shooting gallery in the basement that was only accessible through the rear yard. Yeah, Sugarman had heroin in the basement, marijuana, liquor, and pills for young adults on the first floor, cocaine, liquor and some type of gas for customers on the upstairs level.

The whole neighborhood was being traumatized and placed in strong fear of Sugarman's operation. Often neighbors would drive from their residence to a telephone booth and place anonymous telephone calls to the police complaining about Sugarman's blind pig. Because the calls were anonymous, the police seldom came and when they did they merely flashed their spotlight on several houses in the area and drove away. It was suspected that they were involved. On a few occasions the police just showed up, went into the blind pig and came out laughing and talking. On some occasions during the day a police car would stop, the officers would exit their car, chat with Sugarman for a short while then drive away. For some reason dating back several years, the police seemed to remember that it was an incident in a blind pig that had caused the worst race riot that Detroit had ever experienced. It was rumored that there was a degree of shake down activity going on, that the police were in on the action. And too, the police were fully cognizant that most of the customers in a blind pig were usually armed, prone to resist arrest, prone to violate the law, prone to escape, prone to be non-cooperative and would fight quickly and were easily provoked to violence- this they had learned from the raid that had caused the riot.

The neighborhood was convinced that the police was involved. No good citizen came forward, gave his/her name and/or really lodged a complaint; rather they took the easy way out. They lived in a hostile neighborhood in fear of what would happen to them if they complained. It was blind pigs like Sugarman's that sent many good citizens out of Detroit away from homes they had intended to die in, that they had cherished, had worked hard for and admired because it was theirs.

After a short while, I approached Sugarman and asked if it were possible to buy an ounce or two of coke from him. Unhesitantly he agreed. He related that his coke was the purest in all Detroit, that he never stepped on it, just sold it as he got it. He further related that a special courier delivers cocaine to him on a weekly basis. Some he parceled out to other dealers. Sugarman advised that an ounce would cost $800 and there would be no break in price if I purchased 1 or 10 ounces. I agreed to buy two ounces for $1600. He advised that he had a policy that all large amounts of cocaine purchased had to be either consumed on the premises or the buyer had to leave after the purchase. I agreed to leave after the buy. He instructed me to stay at the end of the bar and left for a short while, returned and handed me two rubber contraceptives of cocaine. I counted $1600 official government funds and handed to him. Sugarman reiterated that I had to leave. I talked briefly about a future purchase, joined the CI at the table briefly and we left. A block from Sugarman's, the CI and I had a little fight with two black males in a robbery attempt. We prevailed and I fired three rounds in the air to quicken their exit from the area.

Three nights later the "jackers" came through Sugarman's when STRESS was nowhere about. A big shoot-out erupted. The blind pig burned to the ground. Sugarman reportedly died inside. I never checked to see how he had died, whether shot inside or merely burned alive. It did not matter; a major drug trafficker had been immobilized. Renegade hijackers solved the problem that the police would not solve. A long traumatized neighborhood could now rest in peace. I thought a lot about Sugarman's and other blind pigs—how they exist in residential neighborhoods causing random shootings, loud noise, assaults, threats, intimidations, fear and reprisals, and how neighborhood residents accept them, not wanting to become involved; how they let one man engage in criminal activity, hold the whole neighborhood in reverent fear; how law enforcement either advertently or inadvertently could or would allow a community of good citizens, all including the young, the retirees, younger children et al, to live under such conditions; how they could or would allow a blind pig to operate so freely with such an attendant history of violence.

It was sad seeing even criminals die a violent death. There was no doubt that the death of Sugarman brought jubilation to even the Christians in the neighborhood. The only sadness I felt was that he had avoided going to Terre Haute, Indiana or Milan, Michigan federal correctional institutions.

There were many neighborhoods infested with blind pigs. The same CI gave me a telephone introduction to Downriver Don, one of the meanest white drug traffickers I had ever met. I telephoned him a few minutes later and ordered two ounces of cocaine and one ounce of heroin. No prices were quoted. He told me to "Come on down. Get the directions from Mack."

His true name was Donnie Joe Williams. Nobody ever dared

to call him Donnie or Joe. According to the CI, the DIRD had a sweet tooth for brown sugar. He had on several occasions gotten caught alone in a few predominantly black neighborhoods and had been ganged up on by several black males. Reportedly, the DIRD always kicked their asses and walked away whistling. The "Brothers were afraid to fuck with him" and in the 'hood he was referred to as the Big Crazy White Boy. He was referred to by friends as the DIRD; sometimes they substituted the D with a T.

The DIRD lived in a three-story red brick building just outside of Trenton. I had to travel a long gravel road to the entry of his property. From the entrance gate for about a quarter mile up to his house was paved asphalt. It was late at night and surveillant agents could not get within one-half mile of the entrance without being seen from the telescope the D1RD had aimed at the dirt road, and too each arriving and passing car left a mushroom of dust in its wake.

I drove up to the front door and rang the bell. A voice within asked, "What low lifed motha fucka is ringin' my door this late?"

"John, DIRD. I'm Mack's friend." I responded.

The door opened and the whole door well was filled with a massive, bearded, robust, longhaired white man. He filled the entire door well and despite being 6'10", 325 lbs., he appeared to be 7'6", 500 lbs.

"Yeah, motha fucka, whatcha want?" DIRD asked.

I repeated that I was Mack's friend and had come to cop two ounces of coke and one ounce of heroin. "Like Mack and I told you DIRD, if you have some problem, I'll just go on my way," I advised.

"Naw, it's cool. Com' on in. Are you in a hurry? I'm in the middle of a class. I thought you were coming a little later. Shit you musta tore ass on down here as soon as you got off the phone, huh?" he related.

"Yeah, I thought you wanted to do it right away, so I came on down."

"Come on down into the basement and set in on my class for a few minutes," DIRD invited.

I followed him down into the basement where there were 12 young males, eight Caucasians and four Blacks, seated in a makeshift classroom. I was shocked to learn what the DIRD was teaching the young men. All my life, I had believed that robbers sat and thought briefly how to commit a robbery, but never in my wildest imagination did I ever think that they went to school. The DIRD related, "I'm just passing on some valuable information to these youngsters like the old timers passed on to me. Ya see I'm trying to keep 'em outa jail."

The DIRD demonstrated the correct method for a stick up of one person, describing how to place the left finger in the victims back with the gun in right hand ready to shoot should the victim turn, struggle, or attempt to knock the gun out of your hand. He stressed that all resisters should be shot on the spot, shot in the back.

DIRD further described decoys, how decoys smelled of fresh whiskey. He related that no drunk or strong drinker ever spills whiskey. DIRD warned that a drunk or heavy drinker would unlikely have a lot of money on him. He gave instructions of how to rob without a gun, using a knife to kill if there is resistance.

Perhaps the most awesome of his instructions weighed heavily on having the ability to kill when confronted with resistance, that the main issue is to take money, items and articles of value, not to be beaten or manhandled by the victim. According to DIRD, robbers should be robbers not victims. He gave several examples of how several would-be robbers had been thwarted in their attempts by even little old ladies because they did not have the will to rob or to kill or harm.

The DIRD was from the old school, he believed and stressed

that a dead victim could not testify. He further stressed that witnesses are not likely to testify involving a dead victim and how the death of a victim is a major dissuader for would-be witnesses. He further instructed how to take a liquor store, how to fan out at the entrance, how to take control of all entering customers and how to kill immediately for immediate response and compliance to the orders of the robbers.

The DIRD also warned of heroes and would be heroes, how they should be killed immediately in order to gain complete control of the robbery. He had all students stretch on the floor spread from wall to wall and demonstrated how the movement of one or two could easily be detected. In the demonstration, he grabbed a large black male, flipped him in every direction he desired then grabbed his left hand and bent his finger back as he thought he was walking away and brought tears from his eyes.

I asked permission to use the restroom and was directed to a bathroom down the stairs. There were two urinals and two toilets and three washbasins that appeared newly installed. I checked the first toilet and noted that someone had urinated all over the toilet seat. The second toilet was cleaner and on the rear wall of the booth were toilet seat hygiene napkins, with a sign above that tread, "Ass Gaskets."

While relieving myself, I read the writings of toilet poets, one had written:

"I've shit in Paris
I've shat in France
Before I shit in here
I'll shit in my pants"

Another one read:

"Hear I sit here
with buns ah flexin'

Givin' birth to
One mo' Mexican"

One on the right wall read:
"Niggers and Flies I do despise
The more I see niggers
The more I like flies"

One below read:
"Black boy, black boy
Where you've been
Eating yo mamma's pussy
outa peanut butter can.

I rejoined the group upstairs and noted a smirk type grin on the DIRD's face. Maybe he was the famous poet trying to act out the role. The DIRD jumped up, yelled, screamed and gesticulated with his fist until he was able to sound somewhat convincingly that he knew what robbery was all about. He finished the class, relating that he had committed several hundred robberies and had never gotten caught, that he had given it up because it was no longer fun to him. I surmised the DIRD's number of robberies was merely the false bravado of an egotist.

He further related that the best part he had enjoyed was the passing of the police responding to a robbery that he had just committed. He refused to answer questions regarding whether he had ever robbed a bank. I noticed the asker had asked several pointed questions that the DIRD never answered, skirted around them smoother than the best politician. I noticed a familiarity about the asker that I could not immediately identify. It was the salt and pepper combination of askers that gave it away. The salt had a difficult time speaking in street vernacular but seemed to manage. I was convinced they were either FBI or STRESS. It was unlikely STRESS for although they were all over the place, this was not the city of Detroit. I did not believe they ventured outside of their area of responsibility. When asked what he had done time for, the DIRD stated that he had been arrested in an area of a robbery in possession of tools and paraphernalia used in several robberies in the area, that he did not go to jail for the robbery but for the possession charge. According to the DIRD, he made several million dollars and never had to work hard like his ancestors.

I noticed that after all the other students had departed, the salt and pepper combination stayed back. The pepper sauntered up to me and began an unsolicited conversation trying to elicit criminal information from me. I clamped up fearing if they were the FBI that they would have a hard time believing I was not who they suspected me to be, and too, some of their agents were prolific writers that could write an innocent person into a purported conspiracy. The DIRD engaged his partner in a conversation of generalities, relating nothing that could be traced. I overheard the salt ask about 30 questions that the DIRD never really answered. He asked specific instructions on how to take down a bank that had bullet proof glass in Detroit. Instead of answering, the DIRD asked why he would want to take down such a bank when there were others without the bulletproof glass. He related he thought it would be more challenging, more thrilling and that he wanted to prove to the bank that all that money they had spent bulletproofing was stupid that it could still be taken down.

The DIRD's most intelligent statement that night was, "That is really stupid, only an asshole would want to do somethin' stupid like that man; you're kinda stupid. That's a lotta banks out there that don't have bullet proof glass and here your crazy ass wants to take down one that's all glassed up, that's the most stupid thing I've ever heard of."

The salt and pepper combination exchanged farewells and left. The DIRD remarked, "That little white asshole sound like a fuckin' cop. He can't be that goddamn stupid, wanting to take down a bullet proof bank, you know the ones got all that thick plastic around the teller. Shit any fool knows they're easy to take down, all you have to do is go in like you want to open an account or safety deposit box, when they let you behind the door you then take that person, usually an older lady or man and you put the fear of God in them and ya rob the motha fucka but I wouldn't tell his little police acting ass that."

I realized then that it was guys like the DIRD that had made it almost impossible for guys like me to even cash a government check or an American Express money order in Detroit. Maybe the DIRD had something — maybe they should be taken down. I learned from the DIRD that when money is stolen from banks, that the federal government replaced it under the "FDIC or something like that", and that the federal government actually printed money.

I purchased two ounces of coke and one ounce of heroin from the DIRD for $2200 and set a prelude to purchase a large amount later. The DIIRD related that dealing dope was one of the best careers he had ever happened upon, relating that it was low risk, not dangerous and that the profit margin was very high. The DIRD believed that when you purchased a car from certain dealerships that the dealer only made $150 or less. He related that he was making at least a thousand dollar profit from me and that I would make at least the same or more from my customers. The DIRD had a rough aura about him that indicated he could hold his own in a dangerous situation. He appeared to be one of those guys that have the potential to eat five or six bullets before he was affected or slowed down, that he would or could cause a lot of damage before the lethal effect of the bullets finally caught up with him. He appeared to be the kind of guy that could walk in any black neighborhood unmolested, where the "get whitey" would immediately become mum.

After driving away from his house a distance, I pulled over

to the side of the road and started reflecting of what I had just experienced—a school for robbers conducted by a poly drug dealer. A short time later a surveillant unit pulled up. I advised them what had transpired and drove on into the office.

There was a kind of sickness about the mindset of Detroit criminals. They seemed to be without a conscience, ruthless, devoid of morals, devoid of love, envious of those appearing to have more and hell bent to lawlessness. It was symbolic of a justice system not working. How could so many criminals be up and about in mass in such a general area? How could an adult teach others, including young adults and teenagers the art of robbery, especially adding or including murder as merely a part of the robbery process? I thought of the DIRD en route back to the city. I thought of the callous policemen that time had worn to the point of "giving arrestees a little spanking" realizing the physical punishment that they sometimes delivered would likely be the only real punishment the arrestees would ever receive. I thought of personally arresting the DIRD and affording him the opportunity to resist in order to prove to him how bad he really is not. I thought of many ways to immediately immobilize him, like punching him hard in the solar plexus, breaking his hyod bone, bursting his eardrums, breaking his nose every method of inflicting intense and long lasting pain.

It was guys like the DIRD and other criminals that turned good residential neighborhoods into jails, homes laden with bars on all windows and doors; firetraps and still non-safe haven from the desperate, brazen, ruthless, non remorseful criminals.

Two days after the DIRD undercover buy, I found myself sitting in the living room in a moderate two-story house in the area of the 10th precinct station negotiating undercover with a crook for a proposed two-ounce heroin purchase. I heard a car pull up and stop across the street and two doors slam. The crook got up, walked over to the front door and stared across the street. He then moved to the window adjacent to the door and called me over stating, "Hey come over here for a second and watch this."

We watched the two males that arrived in the car emerge from the rear of a heavy metal laced window/door residence and walk two houses up the street where they removed a heavy chain from a front attached open door garage. They tied the chain to the metal front door and then backed their car upon the sidewalk and lawn, then tied the other end of the chain to the car. They then pulled the front metal front door off the hinges and jamb, taking a large part of the wall with it. Both subjects then slowly walked into the house and started loading; TVs, radio, appliances and a sheet ball full of items from the house into the car. I asked the dope dealer if we should call the police relating that they could or would likely also burglarize his house. The dope dealer stated, "Naw man, motha fuck the police, fuck that motha fucka over there too." He then sat back down on the couch and we resumed negotiating for the heroin deal.

The dealer then focused on whether I was the police or not and became alarmed that I had mentioned calling them. He further related that nobody in the neighborhood would call the police because they are scared. Then he refocused on my identity. I then accused him of being the police and placed his focus on a proposed large heroin deal next week, despite having not completed the first one. The dealer half bit on it but stayed focused on my identity. He left the room for a short while and returned with a large revolver protruding from his waist in a somewhat threatening manner. I fast-talked him by complimenting how neat his gun was and asked him if he wanted to sell it while simultaneously removing it from his waist. I then inspected it, removed the bullets, then reached into the small of my back and removed a .45 automatic, ejected the clip and one 120 grain soft lead jacketed Supervalu hollow point round and handed it to the crook and asked him, "How do you like these babies? I'll trade you all this, for yours." He disagreed and appeared slightly nervous. I then gave him his gun back and secured mine. I then flashed $2000 in 100's denominations advising that I was ready to do the deal.

The crook left the room for a short while, returned and handed me two ounces of heroin contained in two ball shaped rubber contraceptives quoting a total price of $1500. I counted 15-100's and handed it to the dealer and made arrangements to get back with him a week later.

As I drove from the neighborhood, police cars roared to and fro running Code 3 (emergency lights and siren), gunshots rang in the air, a purse snatcher ran across the street three cars ahead, got struck by a passing car but did not break much of his stride in getting away from his pursuers. Two blocks ahead the roar of fire engines trembled the streets as they raced through intersections with emergency lights flashing, sirens sounding and horns beeping.

Perhaps many cities are like Detroit; maybe Los Angeles, Long Beach and Compton are also. Perhaps living in a different part of Los Angeles County had shielded my experience or view from the maddening streets of loud noises of passing cars, police and fire departments responding frequently in an emergency mode. I continued to think that all this mainly happened in Detroit. Maybe it was my personal prejudices causing me to dislike Detroit, perhaps coupled with some hidden fear that emanated from the event of my first arrival. I knew or believed that traumatic events often causes one to be over cautious, leery, somewhat afraid and brings on certain dislikes that are hard to overcome, especially during quiet and peaceful times when one is far from a hostile environment. For me, it seemed that all Detroit was a hostile environment, from north, west, northeast, south and downriver. Even the expression on many passing faces seemed to bear either fear, caution, hatred or a combination of the three. I could not understand the mindset of the criminals, I dealt with firsthand, the ones it the immediate criminal undercover environment or the ones I saw in passing. They all seemed to have a total willful disregard for life, health, and the well being of others and lived in an aura of fear, where fear, violence, gunshots ringing out seemed to be the order of the day. Almost everybody carried a "rosco" and some carried two and three, even including the bad guys, wannabes, good citizens and the police. Most crooks and good guys espoused that it was "better to let the police catch you carrying a gun than a Detroit fool to catch you without one."

In the predominant black neighborhoods, almost all Detroit, there seemed to be a party store, sometimes two, three and four and large churches and store front churches within each one mile radius. Many of the homes in middle to lower income areas sported burglar bars and metal antiburgulary doors. The party stores, banks, fast food outlets, also bore bullet proof plastic protectors and the attendants and tellers operated from behind what appeared to be prison solitary confinement through a type of lazy Suzan or revolving door or off set window with slits. The robbers, apparently very widespread, had wrecked terrifying fear on the workers and proprietors. Behind bulletproof walls, the openly carried guns.

One of the most ironic situations I recall involved a downtown bank that previously would not cash an American Express traveler's check for me. Although heavily fortified with bullet proof plastic, an innovative robber robbed it. The bank decided to hire security officers inside. None of the security officers were armed. I felt deep sympathy for those purported unarmed security officers for they were merely ushers and were placed in harms way by unthinking managers and executives.

On a quiet weekend, I drove up to Frankenmuth and had a heavy meal of bratwurst, beer, sour brauten and German chocolate cake. I drove back to Detroit, covertly sipping a nice German beer and smoking a menthol cigarette. A few miles outside of Flint, I felt a deep pain in my stomach and warm saliva fill

Thin White Lines

my mouth and an urge to vomit. I lit another cigarette, inhaled it deeply and held the smoke in my lungs for a long period in an attempt to off set the need to vomit. When I exhaled, the urge to vomit became stronger and the pain in my stomach became more intense. I slowed down, pulled off the highway, got out and vomited until I thought I could feel the walls of my stomach touching. I stood up and lit another cigarette and tried to relax. The pain in my stomach had somewhat subsided. As I continued to smoke, the pain reappeared and became more intense and warm saliva formed in my mouth causing me to regurgitate again, only liquid and dryness came. I puffed on the cigarette again and got the same reaction. Despite unknowingly being heavily addicted to nicotine, I did not believe that cigarettes could cause this type of reaction. Immediately I remembered a brother law enforcement officer had died at an early age from lung cancer. This became my wake up call indicating that I should go to the hospital. I drove to the nearest service station and drank a large root beer, ate several Rolaids and swallowed several pieces of ice. The pain subsided a little but would not go away. I began to reflect that I was 2000 miles from home, in a dangerous city, sick and did not have a clue how to get to the nearest hospital. I drove back to Detroit trying to determine whether to call the police for directions to a hospital or whether to ask for information and drive there. I drove down the interstate and instinctively exited on Warren. While meandering about trying to ask directions to the hospital, I pulled up next to a white couple stopped next to me at the light, I rolled down the passenger window and sounded the horn, the driver looked at me nervously, looked to his right and left then peeled rubber speeding through the intersections against the red light. A black man inched up parallel to me. As I attempted to ask him for directions, he looked in the other direction and before the light changed, he also sped through the intersection running the red light. I felt the pain grow stronger in my stomach, causing me to bend over. Almost simultaneously I heard the sound of an emergency vehicle coming in my direction from my rear. I looked in the rear view mirror but could only faintly see oncoming passenger cars. A few seconds later the light for me changed to green and the sirens and horns grew louder. I looked to my right and saw an EMS unit rolling code-3 approaching the intersection at a high rate of speed. It entered the intersection ahead of me and right turned on to Gratiot. I followed the EMS unit to a hospital, parked in the regular section and struggled into the emergency room.

I tried to grab an orderly or nurse indicating that I was very sick and needed to see a doctor. One of the orderlies screamed, "We'll get to ya when we can. We're operating on a triage now."

A fat white male was wheeled in on a stretcher with blood all over his clothing and hooked up to an IV and wheeled around. A black male was rushed in on a stretcher with no rise and fall of his chest noted, no IV, no movement. I was sure he was dead. A young black male seated next to me had been shot five times, two bullets in the thoracic area, no IV, no stretcher and he was fully conscious. At the onset he was quiet but every few minutes he rose up and screamed, "Help me! These god damn things are hot inside of me." A young heroin addict came crying to the peak of her voice and screaming, "Get this monster off of my back please, and please take these cramps away." A pregnant lady, in a wheelchair, was rushed in. Several gunshot victims sat around like being shot only required a few stitches and a tetanus shot.

I sat back in pain and counted seven gunshot victims, all fully alert, screaming for help, cursing and denying knowing where or who had shot them. One large black male sat up staring wide eyed at everybody and his dress, jewelry and mannerism identified him as what he really was - a dope dealer. The doctors, nurses and orderlies ran to and fro and ambulances arrived with patients and left like the emergency room was a bus station. The unconscious patients were treated first along with the pregnant lady. As fewer patients were wheeled back into the treatment area, newer ones arrived. When it appeared that I was being moved up in the pecking order more seriously injured, some unconscious patients arrived. I looked at my watch and an hour had passed. All conscious gunshot victims were still awaiting treatment. The five bullets in the body patient to my right had suddenly lost their heat. He cried out, "Hey when y'all gonna get these damn bullets outa me! They're cold as hell." An orderly passing with a gurney yelled, "You're next my man, we'll be cutting on your cheeks next." The five-bullet patient started to tremble and shake further complaining about being cold. A short time later he was wheeled back into the treatment area. The sirens of the EMS unit roared loud and faded as they came and went. It seemed like every five or ten minutes one or two would arrive, all carrying emergencies.

One patient, shot in the leg and hip, related that he would pass out to see how fast he could get treated. After a short while he feigned fainting and fell on the floor. The patient next to him screamed, "Hey this man is on the floor dying, y'all better help him, I know a good attorney." Two orderlies ran over and took him back into the treatment area.

Seeing all of this bedlam relaxed my stomach. While feeling somewhat sorry for myself with a stomachache and partially dehydrated, I realized that it would be hours before I would be treated.

About an hour later, the patient shot in the leg and hip, walked out of the emergency room. He had apparently been patched up, given a tetanus shot and released.

I waited another hour, fell asleep in between and noted that I had fallen behind in the pecking order. My stomach felt a tad better. A cute nurse came over and chatted with me while taking the temperatures of four patients next to me. She gave me a pain killer that somewhat eased the pain. She remarked about how amazing some black gunshot patients are, how many have taken lethal gunshots in vital areas and how unaffected they appeared to be. She further related that she had personally attended to a number of gunshot victims that had been shot on as many as eight different occasions. She added that they had earned the name of "frequent fliers." I found her most interesting and agreed to join her ten minutes later on her coffee break.

Roslyn was her name. She had graduated from Michigan State and had been a nurse there for two years. She had had her fill of the emergency room. On weekends and on some regular days during the summer she described the ER as absolute bedlam, days when she worked continuously for eight hours without even a coffee break or a snack on the run. She had been on duty for seven hours and took the 15-minute break at the direction of her supervisor. Roslyn was aware of certain fair standards in labor rights; one she explained prohibited an employer from working an employee six hours without a lunch break.

Roslyn, a single attractive nurse fed up with Detroit, had been so involved in her work that she had never really taken the time or thought of a life after work. Even on her 15 minutes break all she found to talk about was work, the horrors of gunshot wounds, cuttings, mayhem and bedlam of the ER. I felt sorry for Roslyn for her specialty was the ER. Three years out of school she inwardly was viewing herself as a failure, no marriage, no engagement, and no significant other in her life. Her job was all she had thought she wanted.

At the outset, I thought Roslyn had some sort or attraction for me. In reality, she merely needed to talk to someone, to get an unbiased opinion whether she was making the right decision to quit her job, her profession in a few days. I gave her the unbiased approval she sought. I agreed she should quit. We went back to the ER where I waited for another hour. I left realizing that I was not close to being treated. I drove back to my hotel room and crashed.

The next day I went back to the ER and found it less chaotic. A young Black intern saw me from Georgetown Medical School. Although he was very dark complexion, when he talked it was difficult realizing he was black especially using the phrases and medical terms and coupled with his New England resonant accent. The intern asked numerous questions about drug law enforcement to the extent that I thought maybe he desired a position in law enforcement over medicine. He had been in the ER for 18 months and had experienced the treatment of a number of traumatic injuries. He seemed perplexed that many of the blacks that had been shot on numerous occasions and many with multiple gunshot wounds in the vital organs, how many appear slightly affected, how they have a tendency to walk around like they are beyond dying. He related how many discharge themselves, how some walk out of intensive care units, how they disconnect monitoring machines and IVs and discharge themselves. The intern described how one gunshot victim with a .45 slug lodged next to his aorta had walked around in the ER complaining like he only had indigestion. He further related how invincible they are and how lesser injuries are more prone to be fatal to law enforcement officers. I was also perplexed. It was enriching talking with him. I learned a new word. According to the intern, the multiple incident gunshot victims were called "Frequent flyers" and the ragged hard-to-die gunshot victims were referred to by his black colleagues as "Thunderniggers." According to his colleagues, the Thunderniggers were hardcore and too mean to die. They came from a trauma/drama environment.

Many Detroiters liked Detroit, liked Michigan—talked admiringly about the changing of the seasons and the beautiful October drives up north to watch the changing of the color of the leaves, how they set against a sky magically like a God created heaven, the brisk frosty mornings of fall, the nice crispy morning of fresh fallen snow and the rivalry between the mighty Wolverines and the mighty Spartans, Belle Isle, the Bob-Lo,

Frankenmuth, the Zilwaukee Bridge, Marquette, the Upper Peninsula, the Gran Hotel, Charlevoix, the Detroit River, Lake Superior, Lake Michigan, Lake Erie, Lake Huron and Lake St. Clair that surrounded the state of Michigan; the great cities and towns like Flint, Lansing, Battle Creek, Kalamazoo, Grand Rapids, Muskegon, Ann Arbor, Troy, Warren, Southfield, Saginaw, Traverse City, Jackson, Adrian, Pontiac, Port Huron, Grosse Pointe, Mackinaw City, Mackinaw Island, and Sault Ste Marie, the Coho Salmon, Steelheads, black bears, elk, deer, farming, industrial belt from rural to big city. They even talked about going up to the Upper Peninsula and seeing one of nature's most wonderful sights, the Aurora Borealis (great northern light).

All of those cities, places and things are wonderful, many of them I have seen, experienced and enjoyed. Perhaps the seedy part of Michigan, that part of Detroit, along with all of its inhuman ruthless ways weighed heavily on my mind. With each passing day, I rejoiced realizing that that was one less day that I had to spend in the Detroit area.

About a week after my stomach problem, I saw the head of the CI that I had worked with a few weeks prior. One or ones unknown had decapitated him.

Perhaps more gruesome was the realization that Detroit seemed to be a place where a person could commit many murders and never get caught. It was fairly known that Chester Campbell had killed close to 100 people yet he was allowed to walk the streets unapprehended as though he was a good citizen gainfully employed at Dodge Main.

It did not take a rocket scientist to discover that the crime wave in Detroit was continuing to escalate because there was little indication that it did not pay. Perhaps most important was seeing criminals overtly commit offenses and go about their business as though immune from arrest and prosecution. It caused me to wonder whether the undercover work I was doing there was worthwhile or just eyewash", a phrase that had just become fashionable. I was certain that when all of the defendants I was making cases on were arrested and came to trial, that there would not be the court room insignificant drama that often occurs in state courts, that they would be indicted, tried quickly, convicted and sentenced unless they decided to cooperate. Even after extensive cooperation, they would likely do some prison time due to the extent of their involvement in the drug traffic.

While I was going in one direction undercover with several groups in the office, SAS Ken Adams and Moffet were going in another direction. Our paths seldom crossed. Wayne County Airport Police arrested a cute 19-year old white female with two ounces of heroin as she tried to go through the metal detectors at Metropolitan Airport. She had two packages of white heroin doubly wrapped in aluminum foil concealed in a waist girdle. The arresting officers informed her that she was too cute and too young to go to jail and related how the lesbians would likely take advantage of her. Extremely fearful of lesbians, she decided to cooperate with the police. Instead of turning her over to the DJNTF, the officers decided to connect her with a new agent, a former Wayne County Deputy and friend.

During the federal flipping process the female again refused to cooperate citing fear. She then tried to use her sexual skills to get rid of the case, which did not work. She refused to give up the intended recipient in Cleveland, hinting that it could be someone related to her. She finally relented to introducing an undercover agent to her source but stipulated that it had to be an out of town black agent. She further related that most of her source's customers were blacks and that they had dealt with him over a long period of time. She provided a telephone number where her source could be reached. The number was checked and found to be an unlisted number subscribed to Willie Lee Horton, in Trenton, Michigan. Initially it was believed that Horton was the black Detroit tiger baseball player. The young agents, relying on the name only and not familiar with Trenton believed the dealer was black and never asked the newly developed female CI to identify the source. The CI only knew him as Skag, ironically a street name for heroin, and gave a good description of his house, cars and henchmen. She related that when doing a deal Skag always had at least two armed henchmen present and that he was always armed. The CI related that there was a lot of traffic in and out of his house that he was a very busy dope peddler. She recanted a shoot out that Skag and his henchmen had had in the middle of town one night and nobody got shot nor was anybody arrested. I was asked to work undercover on the case.

We utilized a female Detroit police officer to assist in the case. She searched the CI and found her devoid of any narcotics. The CI had less than a hundred dollars in cash that she was allowed to keep. Pre-surveillance was initiated at Skag's residence. The CI and I entered the undercover car, a late model Cadillac El Dorado with a sunroof and drove toward the area followed by two surveillant units. As we pulled out of the Howard Street garage, the CI removed her purse from between us, let the center armrest up and slid next to me stating that we had to look like lovers in the undercover role. Before we drove upon Interstate 75 south bound, the CI reached over and grabbed my penis, squeezed it and asked, "Why do you dress on the left?" I had no idea what she was asking and her surprise action caused my arms to immediately jerk to the left, pulling the undercover car upon the down ramp curve, missing a wall by less than an inch. As I gained control of the vehicle, I noticed that she was again reaching toward my groin area. I blocked her with my right hand and instinctively swerved the car to the right. I then pulled over at the next available chance, stopped the car then instructed the CI to keep her hands off of me. It was not that I did not enjoy her feel; I knew what was expected of me as a special agent in an undercover capacity. I did not and would not sacrifice my job for a CI even though the temptation was there. I used a few profane words and referred to her as gutter slut to gain and hold her

Thin White Lines

attention that I was serious. The closest surveillant agent arrived, parked and inquired what was wrong. I advised that all was in order that we were en route. I made the CI then move over to the right side of the undercover car to avoid being stopped by local officers en route.

Prior to arriving Skag's house I picked up a police unit that followed me slowly for over 5 miles until pulled aside by one of the trailing surveillant units.

Upon arrival, the CI identified Skag talking casually with two muscular males standing out front. It was then that I was aware that Skag was not black. There was a visible bulge in all three of their waistbands indicating that they were heavily armed. As we drove up and parked, Skag spoke to me briefly and asked the CI to join him in the house. Despite not being invited I followed them into the living room. The two muscular males entered the living room behind me and one asked, "Is everything okay Skag?"

"I think so. Just stick tight." Skag advised. He and the female then left the living room for a few minutes. I sat and engaged both muscular males in a general conversation. Neither talked but agreed or just stared and mumbled "um huh."

When Skag and the CI came back into the living room, he started talking the police conversation, how he did not know me, believed I was the police and wanted me to prove to him that I was not the police by smoking a marijuana cigarette. I told Skag that I was not about to prove to him or anybody that I was not the police, that I would not smoke a marijuana cigarette or do anything to prove to him that I was not the police. At this point a black male, customer came out of the back room, exchanged farewells with Skag and his henchmen, advising that he would be back in a few days and left. The two henchmen positioned themselves in front of me, one keeping his right hand on his gun. I could hear part of a loud telephone conversation in the rear room wherein a customer was apparently complaining about the dope he had purchased. The man in the room repeated twice, "You are the one supposed to mix the heroin with the coke, we don't mix it here." Skag hollered back "Hey, hold up the talking in there until I can determine if we have a heat wave out here."

A male came out of the back room with a rifle in his left hand and asked, "What do you mean are you saying we got the police in our house?"

Skag responded, "That's what I'm trying to figure out, I'm not sure."

I talked about all of them being the police and related that I was there to buy dope, if he *was* in the detective business then I had come to the wrong place.

I looked at the CI and she then asked, "What in the hell are you talking about Skag, are you trying to say I'm some kind of snitch or something?"

Skag said, "Naw, I'm not saying nothing, I'm just trying to see who your friend is, you know. I don't just go selling to everybody. I don't know when I have ever sold to a stranger in over five years."

The more Skag talked, the more evidence he was leaking leading to possibly charging him with Continuing Criminal Enterprise. We bantered about for about another 15 minutes until I told Skag that I was not about to beg anybody to sell me anything. I reiterated that I am in the dope business not detective playing like he was. I also told Skag that I would leave and spend my money with a real dope dealer, not one too scared to make money.

I then offered him the services of my purported good attorney whenever he copped a case. The CI and I left the residence. Before we reached the undercover car, Skag called us back stating that I had passed the test. I purchased three ounces of white heroin from Skag and made arrangements to meet with him in a few days for another purchase. While leaving Skag's, two other customers were arriving. The CI was glad the deal had been consummated and screamed out in joy.

On the next purchase, I telephoned Skag and ordered six ounces of heroin. He agreed to meet with the CI and me in an hour. I went back alone. Skag tried to feign not recognizing me, asked about the CI and then went into a big discussion about the CI. After getting over that barrier with a strong conversation, Skag became more relaxed. While we sat and negotiated in the living room the two henchmen entered and exited the room almost every 30 seconds, on each occasion they looked at me as though trying to instill fear. At no time was I afraid or uneasy for I knew I could have hip shot and killed both of them with a single shot.

After talking with Skag for a few minutes and after he had become more relaxed, he left the room advising that he wanted to show me something. He returned with two little boys, one about seven and the other about eight or nine. They we dressed in black denims, cowboy boots, a plaid shirt, and cowboy hat and had Roy Rogers type 2 gun holsters and cap guns. Each wore a mask.

Skag stated, "These are my two younguns, Rick and Rickey. They got different mothers. Ain't it funny how they both look like me?"

They did. They looked as though Skag had given birth to them. Rick looked more like Skag and had a big stomach and fat face just like his dad. Rickey was developing a big stomach and seemed to be the shyer of the two. Skag asked them to go fetch the items in the room for him. Both left. Rickey returned carrying a deck of cards, a white small plastic board, and a quantity of white powdery substance and (heroin) contained in large thick plastic zip lock bag and a measuring spoon. Rick returned with a triple beam scale, a Wonder bread bag containing rubber contraceptives, a box of aluminum foil, a bottle of mannite, a coat hanger, a plastic bowl and a pair of women stockings.

Skag stated, "I want you to watch this. They are Santa Claus' little helpers. Y'all go ahead and do y'alls thing for dad and his friend now. Go ahead and put a one on it"

Methodically Rick bent the coat hanger and arched the corners. He then stretched the stocking over it like a sieve and then placed it over the bowl. Rickey placed twelve large measuring spoons of heroin on the plastic board. He and his brother then removed 12 spoons of mannite from the bottle and spread it almost evenly over the heroin. They then both mixed it with a playing card, scraping, stirring, shuffling, flipping and chopping it and swirling it around on the board, then scrapped it up into a mound. They then poured it on the stocking and sieved it into the bowl. The particles that remained on the top of the sieve were, crushed with a rolling pin, mixed with a portion of mannite then sieved into the bowl.

Skag advised that the heroin was almost pure that he had gotten it uncut and that he always cut his heroin at least once. Rick and Rickey continued mixing for a few minutes then one removed a rubber contraceptives from the bag and placed one inside the other and stretched the outside as the other measured 12 spoons of heroin into one contraceptive, secured it, and double tied the end and at the top very professional-like. They repeated the procedure with another double contraceptive, then placed them on the plate of the triple beam scale, then slid the bars until the scale read 170 grams. Skag yelled in jubilation, "how's that for dope dealers as little as them?"

I smiled, shook my head in false agreement and surprised while underneath thinking that I had met the scummiest of scumbags, how I could easily put my .45 to his head or up his rectum and discharge three to five rounds without any remorse.

Skag grinned and stated, 'I never wanted to be like my dad 'cause he was a worthless piece of shit—dirt poor, always without a job and a drunk at that. I 'member one time my brother and I got so hungry, we ate some grass to fill our bellies. Yeah, he was a worthless piece of shit. He spent more money on booze than he ever spent on groceries. I want my boys to be just like their daddy."

"I want my boys to be just like me too." I added.

"That'll be $4500." Skag stated.

I counted $4500 official government funds and handed to Sag then double wrapped the two contraceptives of heroin in a piece of aluminum foil, placed them in a McDonald bag and stated, "Thank ya sir for your business. Please come again."

An aura of sadness fell upon me. Skag stated, "I want my boys to be well off, not to want for anything. I want them to be the best dope dealers in the world. Just like their daddy, never getting a case."

I smiled, agreed with Skag and commented, "Yeah Skag, you got some fine young men there."

I exchanged farewells and left the house advising Skag that I would get back with him in a few days for a larger purchase. Total disgust, distrust and anger fell upon me, causing a degree of sadness, not for Skag but for his two boys. During all of my basic agent training only once had I seen or read how to cut heroin and that happened on a happenstance. Special Agent Arthur Lewis, one of the agency's first black supervisors, was visiting headquarters on another matter. One of the instructors asked him to speak to the class. He gave a superb speech about undercover activity, surveillance, do's and don'ts and terminated his speech by demonstrating how to adulterate (cut) heroin. Skag's two boys had cut the heroin identically as Art had demonstrated. Of all the bad people I had met over my lifetime most, if not all had espoused having their children grow up to be the best they could be. Only a few low life dopers wanted their children to be drug dealers.

I could not help but reflect on Skag, a proud father of two young boys born out of wedlock, bastards by the dictionary term, yet he could only desire that they grow up to be dope dealers like him. Little did he know that he had been bought and paid for and later, rather sooner than later, he would experience his first big case—a case he would unlikely beat—a case wherein he would have to serve a lot of jail time; a case where his name would be heard on television, radio and in the major and local newspapers.

I got back with Skag about a week later and made an undercover purchase of another six ounces of heroin. His sons did a repeat performance. His two henchmen further implicated themselves in that purchase and I learned that the dealer in the other room on the first buy on the telephone was his brother. So far there were four identifiable defendants to fulfill the requirements of a continuing criminal enterprise charge against Skag. Already there were six counts, sales, possession, and conspiracy on the second and third buys. We would not charge the first buy to obviate the need for the informant to testify.

When I entered the city from the south, I heard gunshots ringing out like the Fourth of July. The sound of EMS and police sirens rising and falling in the distance. In front of the federal building I saw a man snatch a lady's purse and run across the parking lot toward the Howard Johnson Hotel. A car sped by filled with juveniles that I suspected was stolen. As I parked in the lot across from the federal building between the Howard Johnson, I saw a car of males speed by with what appeared to be automatic weapons, not in any way involved in law enforcement.

Before entering the federal building, a loud noise, with the intensity of a howitzer fire blasted my ears and echoed off surrounding buildings. A few seconds later an explosion sounded that shook the Michigan Avenue, Lafayette, Congress and Fort Street area. After entering the federal building the loud sound of emergency sirens rolling code-3 were audible inside the thick concrete marble adorned walls of the federal building.

After securing for the night I turned on the television in my hotel room only to hear the news of shootings, robberies, murders, little children shot in an ambush intended for an adult, car thefts, police chases and shoot outs between the police and bad guys. Always I had envisioned New York City, based on its size and over crowdedness to be a crime-ridden city. Having been there several times, it was nothing like Detroit.

I tried to fall asleep about 1:00 in the morning but sleep would not come. While in bed trying to fall asleep, thinking of ways to fall asleep, sleep would not come. Almost like a frozen frame screen, the decaying bodies at the airport flashed on my mind, the dope pusher hiding cocaine in his daughters panties, Skag, the banks and convenience stores that would not cash a federal government check or an American Express traveler's check for me, the women on the street that clutch their purses and switched carrying sides when I approached or passed, the expression on the faces of passers-by reflecting fear, fright, flight and uneasiness.

I began to think that maybe the undercover roles I was constantly involved in were getting the best of me. It had become commonplace to expect the worst. Almost every undercover situation aside from being very dangerous and involving people with a mindset that murder and mayhem are merely part of the trade, involved some of the lowest living creatures that I had ever met. It was difficult to sleep and I finally fell asleep about 4:00 a.m.

To make matters worse, I had a nightmare wherein I was undercover with several guys and they were about to shoot me and take my official government funds. A shoot out erupted, I shot three crooks twice in the chest area but they did not fall they continued to pursue me with loud eerie sucking chest wounds scarring me as they came near. I fired three more times and saw each bullet traveling in slow motion to the area of their nose. It seemed a week before they made impact and all three died. I became terrified not of killing the three crooks but of the huge-mounds of paperwork I knew I would have to do.

I was awaken about 10:00 a.m. by the maid knocking on my

door. Upon awaking I noted that I was sitting on the edge of the bed with my pistol in a drawn position pointed in the direction of the door. I was cold and my pajamas were soaking wet. I knew then that I needed a break—not from undercover work, but from Detroit.

Perhaps the good part of it was that I did not have to participate in the subsequent arrest process, the rodeo. We were making cases against as many defendants as possible for later early morning major takedowns. I would be back in Los Angeles by then.

A few days later my undercover assignment in Detroit had come to an end with arrest warrants prepared for a major early morning take down in "Operation Skyhook." I had made strong multiple undercover purchases involving 65 defendants. I would be in Los Angeles when the take down took place. The westbound big jet ride was a welcomed treat.

CHAPTER 11

U. S. CUSTOMS works narcotics at U.S. Borders and on occasion ventures outside of their area of responsibility to conduct internal investigations. On occasions they seized drugs at the U. S. Port of Entry, flipped the courier into doing a control deliver of the drugs (convoy) to the intended recipient, which results in the arrest of "Mr. Big" and several of his lieutenants. Since U. S. Customs' authority basically terminates at the Ports of Entry, they were required to coordinate their investigations with BNDD. We worked convoy cases with U. S. Customs to immobilize the recipients.

On one occasion I got detailed to support a U. S. Customs convoy on a side street south of Slauson and east of Hoover. U.S. Custom sector communication center was advised of my travel to join the agents. I drove over to the rendezvous location, got out of my official government car, walked up to the U. S. Custom camper and knocked and could hear radio traffic inside. When I was approaching the camper, I heard two pistols being cocked inside of the camper. I knocked and heard the slight muffled sound of a shotgun being loaded inside. I knocked for several seconds noting complete silence inside except the sporadic transmission of the radio traffic. I started to open the door of the camper to advise the customs agents inside of my identity and purpose. Instinctively my hand moved back and I walked back to my official government car, turned up the radio volume and talked on the radio. I heard my base radio advise U. S. Customs sector that I was at the camper to assist. I walked up to the camper and before I could knock I again heard two pistols being cocked. I knocked on the door and identified myself, but there was no response from within. I stood by the door for about two minutes trying to identify myself to the U. S. Customs agents inside of the camper to no avail. I radioed base and heard Customs' sector broadcast that the BNDD agent was at the camper to make contact. I went back to the camper only to hear the pistols being cocked again. It was time to leave.

I got into my car and drove around the area until I passed two U. S. Customs agents sitting in a white rambler. When I made a u-turn and drove back past the agents, I noticed that both slid down out of sight in the rambler. I made another u-turn, and then drove back, parked behind them and walked up to the rear, and stared at two long barrel pistols pointing at me.

The passenger asked, "What do you want motherf____r?" "What're you doing around here? Show me some ID. Who are you?

I responded, "I am the motherf____r from BNDD trying to assist some shitbird custom agents on a caper but they seem to be scared shitless of me. I guess they think I am one of the bad guys. I knocked on your camper three times and I could hear the hemorrhoids of three Customs agents inside talking."

The passenger, thick-rimmed glasses wearing, bass-voiced male got out of the Rambler and introduced himself as Bill Rosenblatt. He did not hesitate to advise that he was in charge. I admired him from the beginning for he was a decision maker. Inside of 30 minutes of meeting Bill, he gave over 30 orders, some letting his men know when they could go to the restroom, get food, take point, relieve one another and to bring him a coffee and donut when they returned. I surmised that Bill was going to enjoy a meteoric career with Customs. He appeared well liked by his subordinates who looked upon him almost like some sort of savior. The Customs agents were leery of being in a predominant Black neighborhood where the "Get Whitey" hue and cry had become fashionable. Bill felt at ease in the area and consequently had captured the respect of his subordinates. I later learned that he told his agents to shoot to kill if anything happened.

Bill had a few sayings that made a lot of sense. One was that "a dead man cannot testify against you." He told his unsure subordinates that "It is better to be tried by 12 than carried by 6."

Bill was not a bad cop, for he openly showed an aversion to the "throw down weapon." I never knew from his conversation whether he was serious or merely establishing a disclaimer.

We joined the agents in the camper where he introduced me to the three agents inside. They quickly advised that I had almost gotten shot three times. One of the agents looked at me as though he still doubted my identity and attempted to pose questions to me for further proof. I ignored him.

Bill related that they were surveilling 550 pounds of marijuana in a car driven by a newly developed CI. The CI had picked up the load car in the Logan Heights area of San Diego and had been instructed to deliver it to a "bad guy" (recipient) who was not at home. Bill had a conditional search warrant that required that the trafficker be present at the time of the delivery. Additionally, a taped telephone conversation to the recipient was needed to further strengthen the case. We waited and waited and waited.

Bill and I and Customs agent Chris went to a 24-hour cafe

and grabbed a slight repast. Meeting Chris was routine until we got inside of the restaurant. It was then I noted that he was an Eskimo. Chris had slanted eyes, smooth yellow skin, and straight hair and did not grow facial hair. All during the meal, certainly unconsciously, I asked Chris many questions about his heritage—the weather, igloos, fishing, bathing, long nights, short days and how Eskimos had sex in such cold weather. Bill sat idly by listening as though he was glad that I was the asker and showed interest in all of Chris' responses.

About 4:00 a.m. the crook arrived home. A few minutes later the courier (CI) placed a taped telephone call to him. The basis of the conversation fully implicated the intended recipient as the violator. The CI drove the load car into the garage, parked it and rang the doorbell. The crook came out, paid the CI $2,000 in cash and went into the garage. We allowed him ten minutes with the marijuana then we crashed the house.

I took the side garage door off the wall with my shoulder. When I popped it, dust and debris flew inward from the impact as it was separated from the well and hinges. It was a nice experience working with another federal agency, especially agents enforcing federal narcotic laws. Bill related that they had a Black agent in his office. I was somewhat taken by his unsolicited statement and wondered why he had proffered it.

I thought Customs agents' duties were fascinating for I knew they had more cars, more airplanes, more boats, and seemed to have more of everything than we did, except minority employees. I was impressed learning that they could actually conduct a warrantless search of a car, truck or person as long as it had been under continuous surveillance from the time it entered the U.S.

One day I got a call from one of the U. S. Customs' agents that I had developed a work relationship with regarding a large marijuana smuggling venture. According to the agent, a multi-ton marijuana trafficker named Teresi was making arrangements to sail from Los Angeles to a location in Mexico where he would take on ten tons of high grade Mexican marijuana and sail back to Marina Del Rey and eventually smuggle it to a stash location up in La Canada.

The agent related that U.S. Customers, not having a large boat, was trying to use John Wayne's yacht. He further related that we would be meeting with John Wayne and discussing the borrowing of his yacht for the deal.

One of my favorite movie stars was John Wayne, even over the tough guys like George Raft, Humphrey Bogart, Edward G. Robinson and John Garfield. I had never been one for crying in a movie and always took movies for what they are – entertainment and nothing more. There was something especially sad in the "Sands of Iwo Jima" in seeing Sergeant Striker (John Wayne) killed. My eyes became watery and a sadness fell upon me, especially seeing my favorite actor sniped by a Japanese enemy on Iwo Jima. I remember the cattle drive of "Red River" with John Wayne, Montgomery Cliff and Walter Brennan. I disliked Montgomery Cliff for rebelling against John Wayne and shooting him in the palm of his hand. Yes, I had seen all of his western movies, like "The Commancheros", "Hondo", "Rio Lobo", "Rio Bravo", "Chisum", "The Undefeated", "Rio Grande", even a swashbuckling movie called, "The Wake of the Red Witch."

Yeah, John Wayne was the man—the tough guy, the hero, the all-American, who every boy wanted to be when he became a man; an All-American hero, tall, dark with lots of pretty women—a man's man! Even as kids we created new verbs from his name, "John Wayning" a guy, meaning overpowering him, taking charge, bullying and bluffing.

He was our hero. Most of our childhood friends favored John Wayne over Roy Rogers and Gene Autry. He wore only one gun did not get involved in all the kissing, smooching and guitar strumming and singing stuff. In our neighborhood there were pictures of cowboys, Roy Rogers, Gene Autry, and John Wayne. Before it was fashionable to be Black, some homes had pictures of John Wayne and a Black singing cowboy named Louis Jordan displayed on walls. Jordan took cowboying to a new dimension; he played the piano and saxophone in his cowboy movies. John Wayne stood out above all and some Black mothers named their sons John Wayne.

The day came when we went to Newport Beach to meet with John Wayne. Chris, the Eskimo, was with us. The meeting was originally scheduled at a restaurant, but we were advised by U. S. Customs sector to meet him on a pier in the area where his yacht was docked. I rode with U.S. Customs agents over to a marina where we met John Wayne in the parking lot. He was not as friendly toward me or Chris and looked at us as though we were CIs, not agents. As we walked toward the yacht, I heard John Wayne state loudly as though for me to hear, "I don't want any niggers on my boat." He repeated it to the U.S. Customs supervisor, Bill Rosenblatt twice. Before we got to the boat, Bill told Chris and me to wait for them at the entry to the marina. I watched Bill and seven U.S. Customs agents and John Wayne walk toward several yachts out of view.

Chris and I asked each other if John Wayne had said what we thought we had heard. We were certain of what he had said. I was very saddened by his remark, but not hurt. I was sad for Chris for I had never thought he was visioned or looked upon as being a "nigger."

We waited for over an hour until Bill and the other agents returned. I asked Bill what John Wayne had said about not wanting "who" on his boat. Bill stated that John Wayne was going to lend U. S. Customs his boat but he specifically did not want any Blacks on his boat. When Chris and I asked if he had referred to Blacks as Blacks, Bill stated "yes" that was what he had used. I surmised then that Bill was not as much a racist as John Wayne, but a diplomat that he would be a non-racist when the situation dictated and would change to a racist when it was demanded,

Thin White Lines

indicated, denoted to be fashionable or when the atmosphere or environment indicated it was the chic thing to do.

In college, I learned that racism, especially biasness against a particular race stemmed from three roots, ignorance, insecurity and mental sickness. The first two roots could be modified, but there was no miracle drug like Thorazine or Prozac available to modify the third cause.

I thought of Detroit, Tijuana and many of the dangerous places where I had been buying dope undercover from killers of men, women and children in an effort to protect America from the evil of the great menace of drugs only to have a noted American refer to me as a "nigger" mostly based on the color of my skin. I thought of the time when I was a soldier in Germany during the height of the cold war, thought of a placard I had read asking "Soldier why are you in Europe?" Then answering with a white soldier standing with fixed bayonet "to fight, if necessary, for the rights of free men in a free world." I thought of how unfree I was then and not so free now. I thought of how prejudices and indifference flourished in areas of poverty, in the south when hard times, drought, poor crops and recessions caused the haves to have less than they had anticipated. Perhaps most confusing, was seeing a movie star that had all, had mountains of all of the things one could want in life, to include easy access to the unending flow of alcoholic beverages and cigarettes, yet had time to pause from all of this happiness to reflect on being different toward another American, another human being. In all of our differences toward one another, sometimes we dislike for a deep-seated bad experience, whether real or imaginary; I began to wonder why I was referred to as a "nigger."

Perhaps more curious or confusing why Chris was referred to as a "nigger." I had seen John Wayne in only a few movies including Blacks. In all the ones I could recall, the Blacks played an ignorant subhuman role or a fractional person waiting on a whole person. I could never recall a Black in a strong supporting role. John Wayne was considered as American as baseball, mommy, the American Flag, Apple Pie, GI Joe, Yankee everything that America supposedly stands for, he was. I started to reflect upon my career as to how I was being perceived and finally concluded that what I had just experienced was overt, that there are many others espousing the same thoughts covertly, that I was born what I am, that I could not change and that in the minds of many I would forever be thought of as a "nigger." Regardless of what rank or status I obtained in life, that is how some would envision me, whether warranted or not or whether being treated fairly or not, it was inconsequential.

I knew then that I was more of a man than John Wayne could ever be. He was an overachiever gone mad, a heavy smoker, heavy drinker that would, because of movies, go down in history as a noted American, a folk hero, a good citizen, good American and possibly be memorialized with his stature or name on some building, road, street, bridge or airport. The world would never see him for what he really was, s sick person, sicker than what he wanted the public to know, sick to the degree that he could no longer camouflage it with booze.

Albeit every American, every human has a right to like, dislike, to favor, disfavor, to exercise rights and beliefs whether real or unreal. Being famous and rich certainly does not make one obligatory to another or even the public, despite what others deemed expected. However, there are things—likes, dislikes, disfavors and unpleasantries that do not require being aired or spoken out of drunkenness or hatred.

Upon hearing the words uttered by this racist hero, I started to physically attack him but restrained myself knowing that ignorance and sickness often beget violence. I knew then that as much as I had admired John Wayne as an actor that I would never, if I could control it, see another movie featuring him again.

U.S. Customs utilized John Wayne's yacht, sailed south to Mexico clandestinely following suspect Teresi. A few days later they sailed back following Teresi's boat and with the assistance of U.S. Coast Guards they stopped and boarded Teresi's boat and seized several tons of marijuana and arrested Teresi and eight other defendants.

About the same time, white agents in BNDD were being promoted and transferred at a high rate as Black agents remained at the GS-12 and some GS-13 levels. The merger between some U.S. Customs agents and BNDD created the Drug Enforcement Administration (DEA).

Prior to the merger, in early 1972, BNDD hired a significant number of female agents. Many supervisors openly remarked that the job was for men only, that they could not do the job that men could do. During one of the early classes, a female agent emerged as the number one trainee in the class, a class made up of mostly white males.

The same agent that was instrumental in my transition from the local level to me federal level, Joe Gordon, was an outstanding "undercover agent." He was sent twice to the White House where a group of federal agents from all over the United States frequently went and met with President Nixon.

Because of my undercover prowess, I had been selected to fly to Washington, D.C. along with other agents for a sit down chat with President Nixon. In preparation, I shaved, purchased a new blue suit, a power necktie, and new shoes, got a haircut, fingernail manicure and my yearly teeth cleaned ahead of time. I was really looking forward, for such an honor and had told all my friends, neighbors, relatives, co-workers and some passersby. My trip was suddenly canceled with no explanation given. I surmised that President Nixon was in hot water dealing with Watergate and the Vietnam War. I saw news releases where the expressions on his face reflected a worn, beaten, tired, weary man burdened from worries and problems that would not go away.

Despite losing the California Gubernatorial race to Edmund

G. "Pat" Brown shortly after I got out of the army, I kind of liked Nixon for his perseverance, plus he was from Whittier and Yorba Linda California, both all white towns. I remember how supportive he was to law enforcement despite his vice president and attorney general being unsavory characters.

By this time the French heroin connection had been immobilized, Turkey had stopped producing opium for the illicit market. The production of heroin escalated in Mexico. Because of its proximity to the United States, and easy access (entry), moderate prices, and structured organizations, low risk in country (Mexico), and bribery, brown Mexican heroin "Mexican Mud" became the heroin of choice. It seemed as though all Mexican heroin entered the United States through California, Arizona, New Mexico and Texas. Los Angeles became the hub for large shipments. Traffickers from as far away as New Hampshire came to Los Angeles to purchase heroin, establish a source of supply for heroin to be delivered to them in various cities. There were a lot of old dope dealers that operated almost with impunity. Most of them were document, under active investigation or were undergoing the procedures of prosecution or appeal.

An Italian, Philadelphia undercover agent, using the U/C, name of "Johnny D" was purchasing heroin from a Black dealer in Philadelphia that was being supplied by a dealer in the Los Angels area. After a few preliminary purchases Johnny D ordered five (5) kilograms of heroin from the Philadelphia dealer. The Philadelphia dealer agreed to deliver 5 kilograms of heroin to Johnny D at Los Angeles, California. The Philadelphia DEA office advised that the source of supply was a black male named Eddie from Altadena, California. A plan was formulated for Johnny D and the Philadelphia dealer to travel to Los Angeles to take delivery of the heroin. Johnny D and the Philadelphia doper were scheduled to meet with the Los Angeles connection upon arrival at Los Angeles International Airport (LAX). We initiated surveillance at TWA terminal at LAX. Contemporaneous with the arrival of the undercover agent and crook from Philadelphia, a blue/white Cadillac arrived at the terminal driven by a tall flashy dressed black male. We watched him park, enter the terminal and meet with the undercover agent and crook. They drove over to the Marriott Hotel on Century Boulevard where the undercover agent checked into a pre-arranged room and flashed $150,000.

The Los Angeles supplier was identified as Eddie Robinson, aka The Godfather. Robinson was not listed any DEA, state narcotics, LAPD or LASO files. He was a sleeper. The few things that indicated that he was a major drug trafficker were his police car (Cadillac), flashy dress, nice residence and no visible means of legal income.

We maintained surveillance of Robinson and the Philadelphia crook as they departed the Marriott hotel to Robinson's residence in Altadena. Later surveillance observed a late model white and yellow Mercury Cougar XR7 with Arizona plates arrived at Robinson's residence. Two male Mexicans got out and entered the residence. One male, the passenger and older of the two was carrying a shopping bag. A few minutes later, the Philadelphia dealer and Robinson telephoned undercover agent Johnny D and advised that the heroin had just arrived and that they would deliver it to him uncut in a short while. A department of Motor Vehicle checked showed the Cougar registered to Alfonso Padilla of Winterhaven, Arizona. A check with U.S. Customs revealed that the Cougar had entered the Untied States from Mexico at San Luis, Arizona Port of Entry about six hours earlier.

A few minutes later an old Chevrolet arrived at Robinson's residence and a tall blond female exited and entered the residence. About 15 minutes later, the white and blue Cadillac, followed by the white/yellow Cougar departed the residence and was followed to the Marriott Hotel on Century Boulevard. Robinson and a tall black male exited the Cadillac, walked to the Cougar containing two male Mexicans, one black female, one white blond female and the Philadelphia dealer. The blond and the Philadelphia dealer got out of the cougar. The blond had a purse and a large beach-type tote bag. She and the Philadelphia dealer got on the elevator went up the undercover room as Robinson and his sidekick entered the lounge and each ordered a Martini.

In the undercover room, the blond and Philadelphia dealer delivered five kilograms of heroin to Johnny D. The other agents, Johnny D and I arrested them for violation of federal narcotic laws. I radioed the outside surveillant agents and told them to arrest all occupants of the Cougar, then went down to the cocktail lounge with three agents and arrested Robinson and his sidekick. I spent two hours trying to flip Robinson, his sidekick, the blond and Philadelphia dealer. They were all steadfast but Robinson was the most vociferous. He used profanity with each response and alluded to not having any dope on him or being involved in dope. He even denied knowing his cohorts and last statement of refused was, "Fuck you, you motherf___r and the horse you rode in here on." I knew then that Robinson was going to jail for a significant period of time but not before he had paid lucrative attorney fees.

All arrestees were transported to the office, processed and booked. The males were transported to Los Angeles County Jail and lodged and the two females were transported to Sybil Brand Institute (jail) for Women and lodged.

The next day we went to the U.S. Attorney's Office, had to wait, wait and wait for a complaint. The complaint was finally completed about 4:10 p.m. We took the prisoners down to the Magistrate court only to find an irate Magistrate. The Magistrate held all the black males over on the charges and released the black female and the blond female and two Mexicans. When I asked the Assistant U.S. Attorney what was transpiring, he shrugged his shoulders and stated, "I don't know. I guess he's pissed at bringing them in so late." I became very irate that a Magistrate was more concerned about the time he was breaking camp (going home) than the amount of heroin involved with no consideration that we had been up all night on the case. As an agent I was compelled to shield my anger, especially before God (the Magistrate). When I asked the AUSA what could be done about the released defendants, he shrugged his shoulders again and stated, "Nothing I guess nothing you know God has spoken." I immediately went to a telephone and called a more seasoned AUSA and advised him what had transpired. Unofficially he told me to re-arrest all the released defendants except the black female and present them before the Magistrate the next day. As the releasees walked out of the Magistrate's court, several other agents and I placed them under arrest again. I watched a flaky agent apparently lacking confidence in what we were doing all of a sudden disappear to the bathroom.

On the next day we presented the blond, Alfonso Padilla and his nephew before the same Magistrate. Although still irate, he held Padilla and the female over for trial. They all made bail. We were surprised that a low bail had been set for Padilla. He had a good non-gentile Wilshire Boulevard attorney that convinced him that he could win his case.

A few months later, all five defendants were tried in the Honorable Manuel Real's court, a no-nonsense serious and competent judge. When the defense attorney strayed or erred in any way Judge Real immediately put them in order or back on track. After four days the trial was over and the jury came back with guilty verdicts on all defendants on all counts. Four non-gentile attorneys made outstanding pleas for their clients to remain out on bail pending sentencing.

Padilla's attorneys made a motion to dismiss the case reciting the evidence against his client merely placed him at the scene of the crime as not being a criminal act. Judge Real related that he would take the motion in consideration then told Padilla, "Mr.

Padilla your attorney has filed a motion for dismissal of the charges against you which I am going to consider. You are ordered to return to this court in 30 days at 1:00 p.m. for either an acquittal or sentencing do you understand?"

After conferring with his attorney, Padilla advised the court that he understood. Judge Real repeated the phrase "acquittal or sentencing" several times and allowed them to remain on bail pending sentencing. We believed that Padilla would "fugitate." All defendants later appeared for sentencing. Padilla's attorney stood up and gave a nice legal speech regarding why the case should be dismissed against his client, citing and misciting various cases of authority laid down by supposedly previous judicial decisions.

Judge Real listened to him very intently, straight forward, and on a few occasions jotted down a few notes, possibly indicating that he was being persuaded by the defense attorney. When the litany was over, Judge Real stated, "Thank you counsel, do you have anything else to add?"

Counsel, "No your honor, I think I have been more than convincing why my clients acquittal should be set aside."

Judge Real immediately stated, "Defendants motion for acquittal is denied. Counsel is your client ready for sentencing?"

"Yes your honor, I would request that the court let my client remain free on bail we are filing an appeal in this case", the attorney said.

"It is the order of this court that Alfonso Padilla is hereby sentenced to 10 years custody of the attorney general. Bail hereby canceled and he is remanded into the custody of the attorney general."

Padilla's attorney, "Your honor, again I ask that my client be allowed to remain free on bail pending appeal."

Judge Real, "Bail is denied. I think an appeal in this case would be frivolous and fruitless. The defendant is remanded into the custody of the Attorney General."

I watched Padilla and co-conspirators stare at the judge in a kind of stupor. Padilla was the funniest he attempted to feign that he did not understand the judge but the interpreter assured the judge that he understood but did not want to comprehend. The Marshall escorted all five defendants out of the court.

The amount of heroin Robinson and Padilla produced on such short notice was a wake up call that they deserved further investigation, that there was a major source out there and major dealers, numerous midlevel traffickers still out there, still engaged in significant drug trafficking, specifically heroin. I had a strong suspicion that I would see Eddie Robinson et al., again.

A Denver based major cocaine trafficker, Amos H. Walker, aka, Hippie, became very flamboyant, purchased a Rolls Royce, got personalized license plates AHW, purchased a Jensen Interceptor, a type of car we knew little to nothing about, purchased property in Hawaii and other places. Hippie's biggest problems were white women, the lack of visible income and CIs. There was something about him that made women gravitate to him and CIs envious. Almost every time he moved, a CI telephoned the police. I was working a desk conspiracy case on Hippie and almost near the point of indictment, Hippie attacked and attempted to kill an informant in a night club and was beating him unmercifully until he was shot in the chest by a Denver policeman with a .45; a slug big enough to fall an elephant but he did not die.

My first trip to Denver was to give testimony regarding Hippie's narcotic trafficking activities in his attempted murder sentencing. Hippie, a tall, dark complexion, big eyed, broad shouldered black male, strutted into the courtroom with the aura of a professional football player. One of the Denver police officers remarked, "I can't believe that I shot this motherf___r twice in the chest and he is now walking around like he is healthier than me. I can't believe it!" Hippie was with a very pretty light complexion female and a black male that I thought I recognized that was identified by a Denver PD officer as Cookie Gilchrist, an ex-professional football player for the Denver Broncos. At the sentencing, I was surprised to see two beautiful black women clinging to Hippie at the trial. A traveling judge presided over the hearing and was very meticulous about being fair and equitable, preserving Hippie's rights and denying certain evidence but allowing hearsay evidence. The Judge allowed a minister to testify in Hippie's behalf. The minister related that he had known Hippie since he was a little boy, knew him to be honest forthright and to come from a not too well to do family, rather from the other side of the tracks where the roads and paths to food and other basic necessities were limited and narrow. The minister related how at an early age Hippie had found a wallet containing money and like an honest little boy had turned it in. How he had gone to church often and participated in worthwhile church and youth activities. Of all the accolades the minister listed, at no time did he list a job, deny that Hippie was engaged in drug trafficking or list anything meaningful that Hippie had done or was doing for his community.

The judge listened intently as the minister finished and another good citizen got up and spoke on behalf of Hippie. He also failed to list a job or anything positive that Hippie had done or was doing for the community.

Prior to the hearing I met Cookie Gilchrist, and then retired running back for the Denver Broncos. Although retired, Cookie on several occasions in our brief conversation related, "how many asses he had filled the stadium seats with" as though all the fans were coming mainly to see him play. Cookie related that he was trying to set up a retirement fund for ex-professional football players. It appeared that Hippie was a source for cocaine for him and other Denver players. When he learned that Dennis Creason and I were feds, he became somewhat at a loss for words other than about football. He attended the hearing and made a generic speech about Hippie, also failing to list or point out anything that Hippie had recently done or was doing in the community. Perhaps most damaging, neither character reference listed a job that Hippie had had then or even 10 years prior. It was apparent that they were basically trying to help Hippie for his long period of drug trafficking had left a reputation that even my testimony was extremely damaging, reflecting a major drug trafficker that had eluded justice for a significant time and had done nothing positive but inflict a carcinogen upon society as he filled his pockets with money, property, jewelry, cars, women, clothing, travel; all not contributing anything positive to the community but rather tearing it down in his quest for fortune.

In the court, three very attractive white women wept, appeared to be concerned about Hippie's future. The judge, while listening to Hippie's supposedly character witnesses, occasionally glanced at him with a forced smile. Despite the smile, I could readily sense disdain, dislike, dissatisfaction, disgust, disfavor, discernment, discombobulating, discordance, disapproval, disassociation, disapprobation, discommendation, dispassionate, displeasure, disregard, disrelish, dissidence, distrust and disturbance.

After all was said in Hippie' s favor and countered by the prosecutor, the judge asked if Hippie was ready for sentencing, his attorney stood up, stated, "Yes your honor" and gave a last ditch effort re-iterating that Hippie was merely the product of the ghetto and should be given leniency. The prosecutor stood up and added, "Your honor if the ghetto produces the wealth and life style that Mr. Walker was living, then I need some of that ghetto experience."

After both the defense attorney and prosecutor settled down and Hippie stood for sentencing, the judge sentenced Hippie to a long period in custody of 30 to 40 years which meant he had to serve a minimum of 30, not more than 40 years. Several women in the court inadvertently blurted words of disbelief. The light complexion black female ran up to Hippie crying. As he was being escorted away, glassy tears filled his large eyes and Hippie stated in a loud sad voice, "It's all over honey. It's all over."

As we left the courtroom, I learned two new phrases, hearing a Denver police officer jubilantly state, "The judge sure knocked his dick in the dirt", his partner remarked, "Yeah, he cut him a new rectum."

On the Continental Airline flight back to Los Angeles that night the flight attendant believed I was having a mental collapse. I had dozed off for a short period and upon being awakened while thinking of the officer's phrases, I burst out in uncontrollable laughter. For some odd reason various phrases I had heard spoken by law enforcement officers and crooks flashed in my mind like a movie, phrases and idiomatic expressions like, "Barreling ass, sourball, pussy posse, stink finger, fly, getting down, shitting bricks, shitting palisades stones, shitting ice cream, copping a feel, copping dope, riding high, taking down, cracking, cracking hips, splitting sheets, sheet splitting contest (divorce), dump trucking (paying high child support/alimony), taking to the cleaners (getting most of the community properly in a divorce proceeding), property manager/free place to stay during a divorce procedure, fat cat, big bank (rich guy), cock taxes (alimony/child support) rolling big (prospering from criminal activity), going hackly buck (fast), the laugher continued uncontrollably when thinking of other phrases and what they meant in a contraculturalistic environment. It was even funnier thinking how a lexicographer would react to such phrases and expressions.

My first trip to Fort Worth, Texas was a result of a case I sent over to the office base on an anonymous telephone call. While on Duty Agent duty, I received a telephone call from a male caller that refused to give his name. The caller identified a young black female, Dorothy, last name unknown, transporting one to two pounds of heroin from Los Angeles to Fort Worth on a weekly basis. She was departing that date with 1? pounds of heroin contained in a gray overnight case. I probed the informant for more information and telephoned the Ft. Worth office. I then drove to the airport and placed the suspect (survielled her) on the Continental flight to Dallas/Ft. Worth. DEA agents arrested her upon her arrival and 1 3/4 pounds of heroin was seized. The agents made an all out attempt to elicit her cooperation in a controlled delivery to the intended recipient. She was unflippable, very standupish and despite being threatened with a long jail term, she advised she would take her chances in court. An attorney got to the female courier and convinced her that he could beat the case. About three months later I flew into Ft. Worth, Texas for the trial. I was surprised that federal agents were not allowed to carry firearms in the federal court. I locked my weapon in a safe in the U.S. Marshall's office and joined other DEA agents and went to the courtroom. I admired the murals on the rear wall of the court, one mural depicting the Texas Rangers at camp, another depicting the Texas Rangers taking Sam Bass. There was no doubt in my mind that the Texas Rangers were in charge there. I was more convinced when the judge entered the court. He entered wearing cowboy boots and sporting two guns bulging from underneath his robe. I don't know what possessed the female courier not to cooperate and not to have a jury trial. Almost contemporaneous to the government's closing argument, the judge found her guilty of possession of heroin, guilty of possession of heroin with the intent to distribute and remanded her to custody pending probation and sentencing report. When her attorney asked for a bail pending an appeal, the judge became angry and related that he was surprised that the defendant had not been charged with an ITAR count (Interstate Travel in Aid of Racketeering) and increased her bail to $100,000 cash. When her attorney indicated to the AUSA that his client wanted to now cooperate, he was advised that the government did not need her cooperation now, that her intended recipient would be indicted at a later date and that it was likely that the defendant would also be included in the indictment.

As the marshals walked the defendant out of the court, I could see despair, degradation, sorrow and a doleful look that seemed to ask why did you not help me coupled with the expression, I did it to myself it is not your fault.

As I exited the court with fellow agents, an agent to my rear remarked, "The judge really busted her ovaries huh?" I had learned another phrase. I had planned to spend the night in Ft. Worth or Dallas to, see a bit of the city. As I was descending the steps outside, a sad feeling fell upon me from nowhere. I looked up and almost collapsed when I saw my racist chemist friend that I had met in St. Lake City. As he walked past me toward the court entrance hatred covered his whole face and body. I caught the earliest flight available, a 12:35 a.m. red eye with stopovers in Phoenix and Las Vegas.

The next time I had duty agent detail, another unidentified informant telephoned and advised that a Pittsburgh drug trafficker had just "copped" two pounds of heroin and 20 ounces of cocaine and would be flying back to Pittsburgh that night. I got as much detail from the male caller as possible and discerned by his voice, some of the phrases he used that he was a black male. I postulated his age, merely from his voice, to be between 40-45 years of age. The caller related that the dealer owned a nightclub with two pool tables in the adjoining room. Upon arrival in Pittsburgh he would secret the drugs in a hidden compartment, like a drop door underneath one of the pool tables. The caller further gave a detail description of the suspect relating that he was a black male, fair to reddish complexion with freckles in his face.

I telephoned the DEA Pittsburgh office and provided the information to Agent Frank Schmotzer. I was immediately impressed with Frank. He asked numerous questions, was very interested in the information and asked if he could call me back later that night if he had additional questions. I gave him my home telephone number, shut down for the day at about 6:30. About 1:00 a.m., I received a telephone call from Agent Schmotzer requesting clarification of some of the details of the information. He was very apologetic, courteous and overly thanked me when terminating the conversation.

The next day Agent Schmotzer telephoned and advised that he had executed a federal search warrant, seized two pounds of heroin, 15 ounces of cocaine and had arrested three significant Pittsburgh drug dealers. According to Schmotzer, one defendant was vacillating whether to cooperate or not. Schmotzer believed he could flip (convince him to cooperate) - the defendant over in a couple of days. As a starter, he would get $250,000 cash bail set on each defendant and make him or her work for a lower bail. Schmotzer added that if the defendant cooperates that he would be able to indict 13-15 additional defendants.

That same week I handled a walk in informant who advised that "young white dude" living in a mansion up in Hollywood was dealing cocaine "Huckly Buck." According to the walk-in, he had gotten a street name of Hollywood Bob. Hollywood Bob was "house-sitting" the mansion for a couple that had gone on a one year world cruise. Instead of paying the servants, gardeners and house employees, Hollywood Bob fired all of them, used their salaries to go into the cocaine business. According to the walk-in, Hollywood Bob has let the mansion fall apart at the seams. It reportedly had been turned into a harem and a toilet. Hollywood Bob leases it out on weekends to jet setters that come and engage in orgies and coke-in and coke-outs for several days- The walk-in provided a telephone number where Hollywood Bob could be reached. He added that Hollywood Bob would deliver 2 ounces or more of cocaine to any customer on Hollywood or Sunset Boulevards.

I ran a record check of the telephone and learned the mansion belonged to a very rich man and wife that it bordered on the edge of Beverly Hills and a side street off Doheny. I made arrangements with the air wing to do a fly over and joined John Ketchum in the DEA helicopter. After clearing the LA airport-landing pattern we flew up into the Hollywood hills to Hollywood Boulevard at Vine, Cahuenga then went west to Doheny then north and back east a tad. From the air all the mansions appeared to be Gardens of Eden with huge swimming pools, tennis courts, and beautifully landscaped multicolored oleanders bordered long driveways that led from the streets up to beautiful pastel colored mostly white egg shell white, beige, pastel colored mansions, all with curved tiled coral roofs. From 400 feet you could discern the beautiful color of the bottle brush trees, the varied colored bougainvillea climbing stairs walls covering two and three-storied verandas, covering stucco fences that bordered adjacent properties. The manicured grass, beautiful dichondra looked likes carpeting.

When we banked southeast back toward Hollywood Boulevard, Hollywood Bob's place stuck out like a sore thumb. In the midst of all of the other beautiful mansions, it stood out like an unflushed toilet. The swimming pool, a 75,000-gallon pool, looked like a pond with water lilies and debris. The grass on the lawn had become patchy and the unmanicured trees and bushes that lined the driveway from the street appeared ragged, neglected overgrown and in need of trimming, watering, fertilizing and spraying. Bald patches of dirt led from an elevated fountain, birds flew about as though heavily nesting about.

From the helicopter, it appeared criminal what Hollywood Bob had allowed this to happen to this once beautiful three-storied mansion. The driveway from the mansion to the side street appeared to be 200 yards or longer. The only beautiful part of the mansion visible from the air was the stucco wrought iron plant laden fence that bordered the property. It shielded passers-by from its unflushed toilet appearance.

At noon the next day surveillance was initiated on the mansion. A short time later, I placed a telephone call to the mansion and a female answered. When I asked for Hollywood Bob, she related that he was very busy to call back in a half an hour. I called back about 35 minutes later and Hollywood Bob answered.

"Hello H.B. here, how may I help you?"

"May I speak to Hollywood Bob please?"

"What's the nature of your call please?"

"Business, I want to do a little business with Hollywood Bob. I was recommended by a friend of mine that partied with him?"

"What kind of business do you want to talk about, this is Hollywood Bob?'

"I want to discuss the candy (cocaine) business with you."

"How many bars of candy do you want? They are $750.00 a bar."

"I want to buy two bars now and if it is good candy I want to buy a pound from you in a couple of days."

"They are $7.50 a bar whether you buy two or 50 bars, they are still $7.50 a bar do you get what I mean?"

"Yeah I understand. I was told you got the candy good and long."

"You heard right. Where are you now?"

"I'm at a coffee shop on Hollywood Boulevard."

"Meet me in 30 minutes at Tiny Naylor's, do you know where that is?"

"Yes, I know, I'll meet you there in 30. I'll be wearing, white pants, white shirt and light blue shoes."

"You're a bro too aren't you?"

"Yeah, I'm a bro. You don't have a problem with that do you?"

"Hell no, as long as your green is green. I'll see you in 30."

"Okay."

Surveillance from the helicopter followed Hollywood Bob and a female down from the mansion to the meet location. He joined me at a table inside. I purchased two ounces of cocaine from Bob for $1500 and engaged him in a conversation about the mansion in order to elicit additional information for a search warrant. While talking to Hollywood Bob his girlfriend, scantily clad frequently spread her legs wide exposing blond pubic hair. On occasion she would bend over and fumble with the straps of her sandals exposing the nipples of her large breast to me. After a long conversation with Hollywood Bob, his girlfriend invited me up to party with them sometimes and talked in generalities about the nice sex orgies they have up at the mansion. I promised her I would join them if it met with Hollywood Bob's approval, knowing that there was no way I would get involved. I suspected that his girlfriend had a venereal disease based on how generous she appeared to be and the bumps around her lips. I advised Hollywood Bob that I wanted to purchase a pound of cocaine from him in two days. He agreed. I left them in the restaurant, advised surveillant agents what had transpired.

The next two days I prepared an affidavit for a search warrant on the mansion and made preparations to take Hollywood Bob down with a pound of cocaine. I telephoned Hollywood Bob and advised him that I was ready to purchase the pound of coke. I told him that I was short a thousand dollars and asked if I could pay him the thousand in two days. After being told I had $11,000, Hollywood Bob agreed to deliver the pound to me on the parking lot of Norm's restaurant on Sunset east of the Hollywood Freeway at 7:30 p.m. Hollywood Bob advised that he wanted to complete the transaction quickly because he had another pound customer standing by.

Less than an hour later, Hollywood Bob and his girlfriend delivered a pound of cocaine to me in the parking lot of Norm's restaurant and were both arrested in lieu of payment. His girlfriend was more detained than arrested for all we had on her were sexual overtures. We got the search warrant quickly and took Hollywood Bob and his girlfriend up to the mansion. As we drove up to the turn around a snake slithered across the asphalt driveway. While walking up to the side entrance next to the huge lily, water plant infested pool; I could hear the sound of frogs jumping into the water. Hollywood Bob related that there were a lot of snakes up there but they were harmless garden snakes. He further related that sometimes the rattlesnakes came down out of the foothills in search of water.

Ten agents fanned out for a systematic search of the mansion. I took two agents with me to search Hollywood Bob's rooms. He occupied what appeared to be a two- bedroom house inside of the mansion's southeast corner with a view south toward Hollywood Boulevard. From his parquet floor master bedroom you could see cars traveling east and west on Hollywood Boulevard and numerous neon signs flickering off and on in kind of magical wizardry. The walls of the master bedroom were eggshell white. The east wall, approximate 24' X 8' and did not have a window. Across from the east wall was a movie projector, an oval shaped Hollywood king size bed with, bedding strewn about the floor. Strewn about were several dildos, a 15" huge black one, and a 10" pink plastic one and several smaller dildos all with testicles attached. The room reeked of old and fresh funk that bad not been exposed to air. There were several girlie magazines and film canisters on the nightstands. Hollywood Bob's girlfriend sat staring, smiling, and making sexual gestures with her tongue. The young agent guarding them walked around uneasy and aroused. When he saw her on the first purchase he had remarked about how sexy he thought she was.

I commenced the search of the master bedroom searching the bed, mattresses and underneath, examined the dildos for secret compartments. While I was searching the room, the two agents escorted Hollywood Bob and his girlfriend to the bathroom adjacent to the master bedroom. I got a chair from the kitchen and started searching the closet and noted a door in the ceiling of the closet large enough for a person to climb through into the attic. I got a flashlight, climbed up into the chair removed the door cover, hoisted my torso up into the crawl space. I then heard what sounded like a snake falls on to the hardwood floor below with a loud rattling noise. I eased down in the chair slowly and reached into my armpit, removed my revolver, pulled the trigger hammer back, and turned in slow motion toward the rattling noise with great fear and perspiration streaking down my cheeks and forehead and into my eyes. I started thinking that the loud rattling noises were two or three rattlesnakes used by Hollywood Bob as a booby trap and grew more petrified. As I turned slowly around and aimed my gun at the noise and prepared to shoot, I felt great relief realizing the rattling was caused by a battery-operated dildo that had fallen from the bed on to the hardwood floor.

We found about three pounds of cocaine in Hollywood Bob's living area. He and his sleazy girlfriend were booked for violation of federal narcotic laws. I had a hard time convincing the Assistant U.S. Attorney (AUSA) that we did not have enough evidence on his girlfriend. The AUSA, I felt, would go along way, for he believed that the best prosecution resulted from convicting defendant with marginal or scanty evidence.

I continued to backtrack the Robinson case and discovered that Alfonso Padilla, Robinson's connection, had a nephew that was heavily involved in heroin and cocaine trafficking. The nephew, Guillermo Calvillo-Flores had been arrested with a kilogram of cocaine and was sentenced to the Los Angeles County Jail Honor Ranch. After a few months, Calvillo fugitated from the ranch. Contemporaneous with the foregoing, I received a telephone call from Agents Bill Miller and Calvin MacFarland of the DEA Baltimore office. They were investigating the wire transfer of $3,500 to Eddie Robinson by one of their suspects. They suspected the money was for a three-ounce transaction. I had developed a CI in the prison that advised that the money was the balance paid for a two-kilogram heroin sale. I conducted further investigations that disclosed that up to the date of sentencing, Robinson and Padilla et al sold as much heroin and cocaine they could to amass large amounts of funds to continue their appeal and to post proposed increased appeal bond.

The investigation disclosed that Robinson, via Alfonso Padilla as his main source, was supplying heroin and cocaine to Joseph and Julia Walker and others in Miami, Florida; James Kenner Conway, et al., and Charlie Berman et al., in the Baltimore-Washington, D.C. area; one organization in the Pittsburgh area and two in the Philadelphia area.

I further learned that on one day Calvillo-Flores had delivered 10 pounds of heroin and two kilograms of cocaine to Robinson at about 10:00 am. Robinson paid for the drugs and sent Calvillo-Flores back for another 10 pounds of heroin and two kilograms of cocaine that he delivered the same date. I further learned that while in prison, Robinson and Padilla were still trafficking in drugs; that Robinson had worked himself up to the warden's orderly position.

I made arrangements for an in-custody telephone introduction of a DEA agent to Calvillo-Flores for a 10 pound heroin transaction. SAS Roland Talton, Marilyn Johns and Sim Willis were designated as the undercover agents. We telephoned Calvillo-Flores at San Luis Rio Colorado, a town in Baja, California-Mexico across the U.S. border from San Luis, Arizona and ordered five kilograms of heroin. Calvillo-Flores agreed to deliver the heroin in San Luis, Mexico or San Luis, Arizona. We made arrangements to take delivery of the heroin in two days. We telephoned the DEA San Luis office and advised them what was transpiring and requested assistance and a $150,000 flash roll.

We drove from Los Angeles in Tandem to San Luis in two cars and a van. We made a stop at Thermal, California where the temperature was 124 degrees. It was then that I learned of Agent Willis' drinking problem. As we were refueling at a service station, I approached him in the van and smelled the strong stench of alcohol exiting the pores of his skin. The van did not have air conditioning and he was soaked, completely wet as though he had urinated and rolled over in it. Instead of drinking water all while en route, Willis drank large glasses of vodka and orange juice. I feared he would dehydrate en route and offered to drive the van and let him drive my air-conditioned government car. He refused mainly because the van afforded him unending access to his vodka.

Upon arrival at San Luis, we met with the RAC George Corley and SA Ed Cremin and were provided the $150,000 flash roll. Corley, an old-timer and former U.S. Customs border rat appeared somewhat apprehensive and wanted to see our DEA credentials despite being told by SA Cremin that he knew me. I understood that being an old border rat, Corley had unlikely seen four black federal agents in a single investigation, and too, our clothing was typical of the drug traffickers added to his suspicion.

We checked into an undercover room with adjacent surveillant rooms and the three undercover agents telephoned Calvillo-Flores and advised that they were in town. He advised that he would come and meet with the undercover agents in two hours. While awaiting his arrival, I noticed that Agent Willis had made six trips to the dumpster, dumping trash. I suspected that it was possible that he was nervous of the deal and on the 7th trip to the dumpster, I walked up to the dumpster but did not see him. I heard footsteps on paper inside of the dumpster. I raised the lid slightly and quietly peeked inside. I saw Agent Willis drinking from a fifth of vodka as though it was water. I was shocked at the large amount he consumed. He cleared his throat, reached inside his shirt pocket and ate a mouthful of Ginseng. I rushed back to the area of the undercover and surveillant rooms a few seconds before he climbed out of the dumpster.

The first time I saw Agent Willis go into the bathroom, I rushed out to the dumpster where I found one empty bottle of vodka one one-half filled bottle and a full bottle. I poured out the half-filled bottle of vodka and filled it half full with water. I then took the empty bottle and filled it completely with water and left them in the dumpster. I took the full bottle and rushed back to the surveillant room. A short time later, Calvillo-Flores arrived at the undercover room, met with the agents and was shown the $150,000 for the proposed purchase of five kilograms of heroin. Calvillo-Flores talked briefly about the incarcerated person we had utilized to get to him. After he was assured that we knew his customer, he departed advising he would deliver the heroin in two hours and left the area followed by surveillance agents.

Shortly after Calvillo-Flores left, Agent Willis came into the surveillant room emptying ashtrays and placing papers into the trash can. With a half filled trashcan he left to the dumpster. One of the surveillant agents remarked, "Man that guy really is a cleaning nut huh?" "Yeah, he has always been a very neat and tidy guy," I remarked. When Agent Willis returned, he had a surprised expression on his face as though he had seen a space alien. He walked quietly into the undercover room and dropped his head in despair. When asked by Agents Talton and Johns on several occasions if he was okay, Agent Willis merely nodded his head in an affirmative manner and stared and gazed as though he was in a stupor wondering if his chronic alcoholism had caused him to lose the sense of taste and the supposed euphoric effect that drinking produces. He was zombie-like and afraid to let his colleagues know that he was in dire need of a drink that his body systems were awry, upset and discombobulated all due to the craving and need for an alcoholic beverage. I sat in the adjoining surveillant room and watched him in his agony.

After about two hours surveillant agents advised that Calvillo-Flores was moving in the direction of the undercover agents with an expected time of arrival of ten minutes. I watched the grimacing look on Agent Willis' face realizing that he would be unable to get a drink for a significant period that he had to now go to work devoid of the alcoholic support he was accustomed to having.

About ten minutes later, Calvillo-Flores arrived at the undercover room and handed Agents Talton and Johns five kilograms of heroin securely with adhesive tape. Agent Talton inspected the heroin and gave a prearranged arrest signal. I bolted through the adjoining door into the undercover room and placed a 6" nickel plated .357magnum in Calvillo-Flores' right ear and screamed "Federal Agents, freeze motherf——r, you are under arrest. If you move, I'll blow your God D____ brains out." Calvillo-Flores immediately froze and started trembling like he had delirium tremors and urinated on himself. He was then searched, handcuffed momentarily and allowed to use the restroom while watched by two other agents.

Bill Miller, Calvin MacFarland and I conducted intense in depth investigations of this organization resulting in the indictment of 13 major heroin traffickers at Baltimore, Maryland for various violations of federal narcotic laws, including several for operating a continuing criminal enterprise.

Alfonso Padilla and Eddie Robinson were additionally charged with trafficking in heroin while in a federal correctional institution. Robinson, after realizing that he had really been had, decided to cooperate fully and related to the press that he was going to "tell it all." There were 23 unindicted co-conspirators and the investigation documented over 450 pounds of heroin trafficked by the organization in less than two years.

The case went to trial prior to President Carter's inauguration. It was one of the top seven most significant cases investigated that year and was sent to then Attorney General Griffin Bell as an example of the work DEA was doing. The famous drug defense attorney Joel Hirshorn of Miami represented Miami Base drug traffickers Joseph and Julia Walker. Of the 13 defendants indicted, 10 pleaded guilty. Charlie Berman, Joseph and Julia Walker went to trial. During the closing argument attorney Hirshorn put on a spectacular argument, referring to the witnesses as snitches and ranted on about how bells were tied around the necks of lepers to warn people that they were on the streets. According to attorney Hirshorn, the snitches should have had bells around their necks for they were like lepers upon the streets infecting people in their wake. Judge Murray was so awed by attorney Hirshorn's argument that he shielded his face and smiled several times.

The jury came back after a short period and found Berman and both Walkers guilty on all counts charged.

The immobilization of the organization caused a major impact on the drug traffic in Los Angeles, Arizona, Miami, Baltimore, Washington, D.C., Philadelphia and Pittsburgh, Pennsylvania areas.

I knew then that I had joined an outstanding organization where work was almost like play. I enjoyed the challenge of arresting or causing the arrest of those contraculturists who thought they were untouchable. I envisioned a long career in federal drug law enforcement.

Perhaps the most exciting part of the job was the shocking arrest procedures that often caused the bad guys who caused fear and intimidation among the innocent to stain their pants or wet and stain their pants contemporaneously. This was the beginning of an exciting and rewarding career.

CHAPTER 12

AS A FEDERAL NARCOTIC AGENT, your time often was not your own, rather the position required long hours, tedious task, long stints away from home, away from your duty station in strange dirty and dangerous cities. No matter how clean the cities were, seemingly always your role or duty took you into some of the dirtiest parts.

I saw many agents come and go, some to distant places I had never heard of, some switched agencies, quit, were fired or asked diplomatically to resign. Those asked to resign, did so not with a cloud but a shroud over their head. There were many very interesting agents with varied personalities, some hard workers, other regular workers and some non-workers, some were heavy drinkers, some Jehovah Witnesses, and some that believed sex was foremost with everything else secondary, tertiary and of little importance. Some agents were outstanding money managers; they sacked their lunch, ironed their own shirts and suits, and drove around in ragged personal cars and bank rolled almost every penny they made.

There were flamboyant agents that over dressed the role. Their personal car was a flashy car like their favorite undercover car. Everything about them became flashy, ostentatious or gaudy. Some agents had the Hollywood movie actor aura about them; very smooth, glib with the ability to discourse intelligently in any atmosphere from the ghetto to the elite, traversing many different occupations. They were feds, they fit a role beyond the stiffness of FBI agents and did not wear the winged toed shoes typical of most all FBI agents.

Some agents traveled extensively on official government business, returned to their duty station with nice tailored suits that fit like a glove, sold for expensive prices stateside that they unbeknownst purchased from a tailor that ran a sweatshop.

Many agents in Los Angeles went over to the Garment District around Los Angeles Street, purchased nice shirts, suits, and slacks wholesale and had them tailored close by to fit almost perfectly.

There were agents that lived the role; being an agent was like playing cowboy. They took the job home; slept with it; played with it on weekends and holidays. At the end of the day they had difficulty trying to shut down, quit work and go home. Instead, they frequented saloons where camp followers flocked to party with the cowboys. They danced, drank lots of whiskey and sometimes went home with a barfly that scared the day lights out of them the day after.

One of the most flamboyant west coast agents was Herb House. Herb came to Los Angeles from Denver or some place close by. Initially he was suspected to be a homosexual for he was one of the few white agents that often wore tight pants. Additionally, there was a kind of feminine aura about him. Herb fooled us. He was straight laced and even a good boxer that could have done well as a professional. He won the Police Olympic Heavyweight Championship two consecutive years.

Perhaps our initial suspicion was augmented or aroused by the fact that at that time a lot of homosexuals, both males and females, were going into deep undercover and entering into law enforcement professions. We also suspected Herb was possibly Jewish because of his love for money. The job was a hobby for Herb, rather an office for him to conduct all of his other side businesses. Herb related that his father-in-law was a jeweler. Consequently, he was in the jewelry business. Herb sold jewelry from his office desk to all interested federal employees. Our office was located in the World Trade Center on Third and Figueroa. That made it convenient for Herb. He sold jewelry to vendors and customers at the World Trade Center. A catwalk connected the World Trade Center to the Bonaventure Hotel across the street. It was rumored that Herb was also selling jewelry at the Bonaventure Hotel.

One day, one of my investigations involved a nightclub called "Pips" a rendy hangout for many young movie stars. Herb had never volunteered to assist our group on anything until he overheard that we were putting a surveillance together involving several agents undercover in "Pips". It was than that we learned that Herb had a Rolls Royce personal car. When he parked and entered Pips he was flashier than Liberace. Herb was the first white agent I had ever seen wear eight rings at on time. That night he wore a blue silk shirt, opened to his navel and eight rings, an eight ounce heavy gold chain, a Piaget gold diamond watch, gold tip cowboy boots, and a cowboy hat. Herb entered Pips carrying a huge tote bag that was bigger than a woman's purse. After the surveillance was over, it was rumored that Herb had sold $20, 000 worth of jewelry while on surveillance inside Pips.

Herb sold designer shoes, leather coats and seemed to have a connection for almost everything that was being sold. He tried to sell me a gold plated .45 automatic and gold plated handcuffs. I was friendly as I could be with Herb but I kept my distance. He was too busy making money selling things while on duty than doing his job as an agent. I had a suspicion that he could have an ephemeral career with DEA.

Another flamboyant agent was Sy Brandon. Sy became a federal narcotic agent from the military. He was single and had a penchant for light complexion black women. We suspected that he also liked the pink toe but he never admitted it.

Sy was one of those agents that the women seemed to like. He was a regular guy and liked to have a good time. Once as a very young agent, he allowed an unwitting defendant to take a pinch of heroin out of an ounce he had purchased. Being an honest agent, he reported everything as it transpired. A manager tried to charge him criminally with distribution of a controlled substance, despite this type of situation not ever being covered in the basic agent training. It was then that I realized that John Wayne had the same sentiments about Blacks as did certain DEA manages. It was then that I realized that DEA managers would charge a black agent criminally or administratively for an honest mistake in judgment. Sy drew a few days off for that caper and a few weeks later had had a fracas with his common law girlfriend. Sy came to me for advice and as an older more seasoned agent, I advised him to sever the common law relationship and that his involvement again would reflect poorly on his character as an agent. Sy later assured me that he had gotten out of the relationship and had began to look at some of the single females in the office.

About two months later Joe Gonzales had resigned from the Riverside Sheriff's Office and was hired by the Palm Springs Police Department as a Sergeant. I had worked with Joe several years previous. He had a caper brewing and requested our assistance. I knew that Joe was on shaky grounds at Palms Springs and trying to make a big case. We saddled up and drove 12 agents strong over to Palm Springs to assist Joe. Group Supervisor (S/S) George Heard joined us. Sy and I met undercover with three crooks for the proposed purchase of 200 kilograms of cocaine that Thursday. On the following day, Sy and I flashed $500,000 official government funds for the proposed purchased. The crooks could not put the deal together that day and requested three days, that following Monday or Tuesday. We agreed.

Joe invited five of us to dinner on him. We all agreed except Sy. Sy had a "cute little honey pie standing by for me to cut tonight". He made a telephone call, bade farewells and left. G/S Heard and I drove back to Palm Springs in tandem. I arrived home about 11:00 p.m., took a shower, got in bed and had fallen into deep sleep when the telephone rang.

Self—"hello"

G/S Heard—"Yeah John, I just got a telephone call. Sy has been shot by his girlfriend. I'm on my way over to Compton Hospital. Do you want to go along?"

Self—"Shot, is he seriously shot?"

G/S Heard—"No, I talked to him. He is in the emergency room and will be operated on soon."

Self—"Yeah, pick me up on your way, I'll be ready."

G/S—"I'll see you in ten minutes."

Enroute to the hospital, G/S Heard relieved my suspicion by relating that it was the live-in girlfriend that Sy assured me he had broken up with that shot him. She shot him with his service revolver.

When we joined Sy in the emergency room, he was in a supine position on a gurney, had been x-rayed and was getting ready for surgery. He showed us the wound, which was a shot to the left outer surface of his stomach, just below his rib cage. No vital organs had been hit.

I told Sy he would be all right, took his service revolver, badge and personal property. Sy talked normally as though he had cut a toe. When the orderly came out and advised that the surgeon was ready, Sy asked me to accompany him to the operating room. En route he talked in a normal voice and we discussed the undercover caper pending for the next week.

When we wheeled Sy into the operating room, a tall black surgeon standing over a table in full green surgical clothing and mask stated, "Bring him over here."

Sy then went into shock, started trembling, became incoherent and complained of being cold. All of the false agent bravado had left him and his voice became squeaky and his speech slurred. As I pushed him over toward the surgeon, I could see that he had voided on himself. He pleaded mumbling for me not to reveal that he was scared and had urinated. I knew from prior incidents and this incident that Sy's career with the agency would be short.

Another character was agent Pat Saunders, a rather handsome agent that the

CI's and defendants described as being Clark Gable like. Pat, I don't believe ever made a case but rather shirt-tailed on other agent's cases. At the onset, I surmised that his career would be short. He frequently flashed a smirky smile and was referred to as "The Boy Wonder".

There was another character that I met during a take down in West Hollywood, Jerry Laverones. He was working the West Hollywood jail and was highly enthused over the arrest. I thought he was possibly gay for he was very muscular and kind of switched when he walked like a lot of the gay body builders on Venice Beach. Jerry wanted to be a DEA agent and requested a recommendation letter from me. I wrote a laudatory letter of recommendation stopping a tad short of having Jerry walk on water. Shortly after he was hired, I suspected that he mostly wanted a career in the movies instead of the hard work required of a federal narcotic agent.

Another character was Pat Stewart. I don't believe Pat ever made a case. Pat was the agency's body builder. He spent more time developing his pecs, bis, abs, lats, etc. than he ever thought of making a case. Although not illegal then, I suspected that Pat was heavy into steroids, and too, he was a short little guy but was Mr. North American in his weight/height category. For some reason I visioned Pat as using the job as a hobby. I don't recall a single case that he ever made and remembered that he was inadequate as a support agent.

Another character was Agent John Jackson, a young agent that came on in the early 70's. When I first met John he impressed me a being a religious zealot, bordering on being a "Jesus Freak". I respected him for he never tried to push his religion on me but had merely inquired about the church I attended and left the conversation at that.

I learned that John was recently married, had no children and that his wife was a school teacher. He appeared to have been from a solid family, wherein there were siblings and both parents were in the household. On one occasion John had indicated that he had wanted top be a "preacher" and related that there was a lot of money in preaching.

John learned that I was a golfer. Took a few lessons, purchased a set of golf clubs and we often played golf at Quiet Canon in Montebello. He was a fairly decent golfer, especially for being new to the game. As I got to know John I found that he had a strong love for money. He was the first Amway distributor I had ever heard talk about certificates of deposits, bonds, bearer bonds, certain stocks, stock options, certain high risk and low risk investments that did not have a college degree in marketing or finance.

The first two pac-man machines I ever saw were owned by John. He had another game machine, a total of 3 located inside of a delicatessen on the first floor of the World Trade Center. According to John, he had purchased the game machines for $3,000 each. In on month, the profits he retrieved after sharing

40% with the owner of the deli, the machines paid for themselves.

In the office, it was rumored that John was making money "hand over fist" in his legitimate side ventures. I noted that his production as an agent was marginal and most of his energies were directed toward his business ventures. I had a belief that John's career with DEA would also be short.

About the same time John was hired another agent, Darnell Garcia came on board. Darnell was a flamboyant glib Mexican American that liked the Hollywood life style. Initially we secretly called him Hollywood. He drove a Rolls Royce and had published a book on martial arts.

Darnell had come on board from Los Angeles Police Department. On each occasion I had a discourse with Darnell, he referred to his old comrades at LAPD as "those mother fuckes". He made a point to stress the pronunciation and would never relate why he felt that way about them. I recalled the first time I shook Darnell's hand, I could not believe he was a karate instructor or a rugged agent. His hands were extremely soft, softer than some females. Over a period of time I, on passing, noticed Darnell floating about the office very low key and seldom engaged in any enforcement activity other than from a low key supportive role. Seldom was his voice ever heard on the air waves during the day or at night. I had a suspicion that his career would not be long with the agency.

Another agent came on was Wayne Countryman. For some reason, perhaps based upon his bulkiness, I did not believe Wayne had the physical ability to perform as an agent. I recalled that he made a few cases, small cases and was not much of an initiator. I had a suspicion that his career would not be long with the agency.

There were other agents, some very charismatic, some weird, some so low keyed, you did not know they existed. Another different agent was Walter Erhorn, one of the nicest guys you could ever meet. Walt was very talkative. It was reported that he had been clocked at spouting out 1,000 words per minute. Walt was what is termed "disaster prone". When I first met him, he was examining an automatic personal weapon that had been recently purchased by another agent. Before the agent could tell Walt not to dry fire the weapon, Walt had pulled the trigger and fired the weapon over the shoulder of the agent, barely missing him. Management had attempted to fire Walt but he prevailed.

On bright sunny day Walt asked me to join him on surveillance. I jumped into his official government car and he drove up the Pasadena freeway. En route to the Pasadena Police Department, we immediately ran into a dark cloudy area and hail, about the size of big marbles, fell from the sky with such intensity, we could not see in front of us. This lasted approximately forty seconds, then it stopped, the sky was clear as though it never occurred. All during the hail storm, Erhorn talked incessantly and as it cleared, remarked, "John did you see that shit, man it's unbelievable". Other agents reported strange events and incidents happening when they were with Walt.

For some reason, almost everything Walt did went awry. He had a reputation of stepping on his dork with every step he took. I believe Walt has the record for the most fired or attempted fired agent within the agency. I never knew what happened to him, whether he honorably retired or was eventually fired.

Sim Willis, the undercover agent in the Calvillo Flores case, had stepped up his chronic alcoholism. In the past he had been one of the agency's best undercover agents and had worked undercover in New York on the Knapp Commission. He was one of those undercover agents that were termed "Caged Agent". The roles he constantly played undercover made it difficult for him to come back to reality. His undercover name was "Jimmy

Harris" and his drinking habit, rather addiction, made it difficult for him to distinguish between the two.

Sim was a little guy, about 5'6" tall, not more than 150 pounds. Even in the early days he was believed to have had a hollow leg for he had such a capacity to consume very large amounts of alcoholic beverages and work without swaying or staggering. His famous haunt was "Little Joe's" Restaurant in Chinatown, where he had established an outstanding liaison with the bartenders and often got numerous drinks poured strong and free. Sometimes on Saturday and Sunday nights his official government car could be seen parked in the area.

Sim had graduated up to two fifths of vodka per day and he was the only person I knew that was still using Sen Sens as a breathe refresher. He had always been a meticulous dresser and would never be caught with unshined shoes. I realized that Sim had gone into a dysfunctional level when he came to work wearing the same green leisure suit three consecutive days and his elevated Cuban shoes were dirty. I had somewhat kept in touch with him, last seeing him with his girlfriend Sandy, with whom he had moved and set up house at the Oakwood Apartment complex off Third Street, just west of the Civic Center.

Sandy was part of Sim's problem in that she was a bartender and always fed him free drinks during her shift. Sim took Sandy to work and took her home after work. During her shift, he consumed between 12 and 16 double shots of vodka.

One night I received a telephone call from base radio advising that LRPD had been called to Sim's second home and were possibly arresting him for assault. I intervened and learned that Sim was drunker than two sailors combined, had initiated a fight with his paramour. The fight got out of hand when Sim tried to burn her elbow with a Zippo cigarette lighter. LAPD advised that Sim was "1/16th inch shy of an ass whipping". In his drunken state, he told the police they could do nothing to him. Accosted them referring to them as a "sack full of honkey mother f____rs".

Sim had identified himself as Jimmy Harris, a federal agent, but had also flashed his badge and credentials in the name of Sim Willis. The officers were somewhat concerned that he was in possession of an agent's credentials for all of his other identification bore Jimmy Harris, his undercover name. I convinced Sandy and Sim to make peace until I arrived and assured the officers that all would be well.

I arrived at Sim's house and found him passed out drunk. His girlfriend Sandy took me on a tour of their two bedroom apartment, sowed me eight partial bottles of vodka that Sim had stashed around the house. She related that Sim was one of the worst drunks that she had seen or met, that they merely lived together and had not been intimate for over four months. She then asked if she could perform fellatio on me. I refused, not accepting the first refusal she came back offering to make my eyes pop and to knock the socks off my feet. The smell of dried urine, where Sim, in his drunken state, had urinated on the thick shag carpeting too all peripheral thoughts of sex with her out of my mind.

Sandy talked on and on about Sim, how he was jealous, how he wakes between 4:00 and 5:00 in the morning dresses and drives to the liquor store to buy a fifth of vodka on a daily basis. How he was so far gone that he could never buy three fifths to alleviate the anxiety of the liquor store opening on time, how bad his delirious tremors were, how on those occasions that she had felt sorry for him and purchased three fifths only to see him stay up and pickle himself in booze. Yeah, Sim had gone far out there. When I attempted to leave, advising Sandy that I would come back later in the day to force Sim into a detoxification center, she followed me to the door, grabbed my member and wrapped her mouth around my fully clothed member and begged me to make love to her. I again refused and left very sad of both of their plights, sadder for Sim for he had been AWOL for several days and the telephone call to base was an incident that could not and would not be swept under the rug.

The next day I went into the office early and telephoned DEA's Chief Medical Officer in Washington, D.C. for advice about Sim's alcoholism. The Chief Medical Officer, a medical doctor, advised to "fire him, fire his ass". After advising the doctor that I was not a supervisor but a street agent merely trying to assist a sick agent, he reiterated that firing was the only recourse.

I met with a recovering agent and explained Sin's condition. Later that day we kidnapped him, rather forced him against his will, to go to a detox center. The recovering agent kept a 48 hour vigil over Sim in the detox center. I went over the third day only to be called a sack full of motherf___rs by Sim. I saw him at his worst, trembling, soaking wet with sweat, nervous and fidgety, and eyes bouncing around wildly in his head like a demon.

Sim took the cure rather survived the detoxification and came over to my desk and thanked me for saving him. He related how he had graduated up to three fifths of vodka per day and could continue to walk around like he was normal. He surprised me by admitting that he had a very serious drinking problem. Sim promised that that was the end of his drinking, that he would be clean and dry forever. About two months later while driving to dinner in Chinatown, I saw Sim's official government car parked at "Little Joe's". I knew then that he had had a relapse. I suspected that drinking would eventually cost him his job and eventually his life.

Seeing a once outstanding agent away to nothingness was a kind of wake up call for me. I, like many other agents and law enforcement officers, enjoyed a little brown water too, however, I somehow managed my drinking, I thought, a tad better than others. Over time I had met many agents, good agents, interesting agents, well educated agents and some that had merely graduated from high school. Most of them where charismatic in their own way. I had learned early in my career that there were four main destroyers of a law enforcement officer's career, excessive drinking, loose women, informants and money.

On the federal level there was no true or real mechanism in place to predict an applicant's suitability for the job, like the six steps utilized in hiring most police officers; the written exam, physical ability, physical exam (medical) panel interview, background and psychiatric. The written exam sometimes was waived and only the background and panel interview were utilized. In many instances on the federal level politics and association played major roles in the hiring process. On occasions nepotism disguised or overlooked played a major role in the hiring process. Because of the lack of a meaningful pre-employment system, bringing with them undesirable work habits from the private sector. Despite a few bad apples, overall most DEA employees are very hard workers and very dedicated employees, especially the agents.

Another interesting agent I met was Jack Enoch. I had met him about the time I met USCS Agent Rosenblatt at a saloon at terminal island called Joe Biff's. On that occasion I noticed his nose was almost as red as a beet and he was then described by another U.S. Customs as having a serious "brown water" problem (a heavy drinker). Shortly after the merger of the Bureau of Narcotics and Dangerous Drugs (BNDD) with certain elements of U.S. Customs, Enoch transferred over to the new agency, the Drug Enforcement Administration (DEA) as a group supervisor. Although a nice person with a good heart, the transfer placed him in a position similar to a fish out of water. While he had vast knowledge of U.S. Customs laws, he had little knowledge of domestic narcotic enforcement and it was difficult for him to supervise agents more knowledgeable than him.

Jack took the easy way out. He appointed a back up group supervisor to run the group then he left his office daily about 10:00a.m. to a saloon called the Stockyard, where he consumed brown water from about 10:30a.m. to 4:00p.m. daily. In addition to his brown water problem, Jack was a chain smoker. He had the highest tolerance for alcoholic beverage consumption I had ever seen. At about 4:00p.m., Jack would walk back into his office pickled with booze but his gait was slow, somewhat steady and the only indications that he was heavily under the influence reflected in the redness of his face. If you were close to him you could see the redness of the arteries and capillaries in his face and more visible in his nose. His voice had a kind of cackle, shrill sound as though fluctuating between baritone, tenor, and soprano.

Many of the old BNDD agents referred to Jack behind his back as a robber, indicating that he had a gun that he wore, did not work but received a significant amount of money biweekly. Like most chronic alcoholics, Jack did not have a harmful bone in his body and he knew that management was well cognizant of his alcoholism and was letting him ride along with the tide.

On the few occasions he was in the office and was called up to the front office, Jack chained smoked and became very nervous as though he was going up front for some extremely bad news. We worried that he would have a heart attack or if given some bad news like being terminated and that Jack would bite a bullet from his service revolver.

On a few occasions, I assisted Jack's group on surveillance and noted that he had a penchant for flying as an observer in the helicopter when under the influence. The cackle in his voice became more pronounced and his misdirection of travel of the suspect's vehicle as often hilarious. Jack meant well, was harmless, but performed acceptably considering his chronic alcoholism. While assisting his group in Orange County, Jack insisted that I ride with him. I surmised it was to assist in a heavy decision making process if something went awry. After the caper was shut down, Jack took me by his residence for "a pop" (alcoholic beverage) at about 1:00p.m. I thought he would surprise me with a treat for lunch at his residence. I met his wife and he brought out several fifths of whiskey and offered me a drink. I could never consume an alcoholic beverage prior to 5:00p.m. and diplomatically refused the drink. I was praying that he would offer coffee or a soda but we sat at the kitchen table and I drank water as Jack and his wife drank their lunch. His wife appeared to have had her share of brown water in her days. I was glad when Jack finished the third drink. He got up gave his wife an affectionate kiss on the cheek relating that we had to go back to fighting crime. En route back up to Los Angeles, I made a small talk while thinking of number of acceptable ways to tell Jack that he had a severe drinking problem that would cause him problems on the job one day. I could not bring one to mind. Despite his drinking, I believe Jack was a fair person perhaps fairer because he was an alcoholic and did not want to cause any turbulence.

During those days we all lived from paycheck to paycheck and had accepted that fact that it was improbable, but certainly impossible to ever become rich working for the U.S. Government. We also accepted the fact that if anything could go wrong that certainly it would go wrong with the U.S. Government. We had accepted the fact that there were a lot of unworthy people feeding uncontrollably at the federal trough. So when nebulous complaints and charges were filed against us as federal agents, we took them with a grain of salt. Even when our paychecks failed to arrive on the due dates and when they were as much as a week late.

One week after a holiday, the paychecks did not arrive for several days, leaving most agents broke and living off of their credit cards. It was then that I became aware of a very unique talent of Jack's. He was a master hypnotist. Jack and an old drinking buddy did not have enough funds to go out to the saloon for their normal brown water meal. Jack got a pitcher of water and two glasses. He sat in his office, hypnotized his old buddy and then hypnotized himself. They then sat and drank water under the hypnotic suggestion that they were drinking whiskey. After finishing three glasses of water, I was certain that Jack was under the influence for his voice started to develop the same cackle that I had witnessed on several prior occasions. His old buddy later staggered out of is office mumbling something incoherent. A former custom agent verified that they had through hypnosis obtained a somewhat drunken state from drinking water.

As an agent especially a macho agent as we all were, it was still hard for me to believe that Jack, especially seeing him so often pickled from booze could actually hypnotize someone.

The Crossroads Restaurant bar was on the first floor of the World Trade Center and all of the drinkers in the office stopped in for an occasional pop. One night I was partaking a beverage after a high speed chase take down arrest. Jack and a few of his good old boys (GOBS) were having few pops and like many agents each were exaggerating certain war stories. When I entered, Jack invited me to join then at their table but I refused. I was not about to sit down to a 6 or 7 round tab on my first pop. I buzzed off telling Jack and his GOBS that I was only having one throat clearer for the road and I would be shutting down for the night. I noticed a very attractive red head sitting at the bar chatting with Mike the bartender. On occasions she stared over in my direction moistened her lips and puffed on a cigarette. I decided to finish my pop, only one and head home. I did not want to sit and have several drinks and after each one thinking that of all of the men in the bar that this red head was interested in me. I finished my pop and went home.

The next day at about noon, Mike the bartender from Crossroads called to verify that I was in the office. He then told me that within the next two hours something very weird would happen to me and requested that I call him as soon as it happened. Mike advised that he would lose $50 if it did happen, but would not explain what was suppose to happen to me. About an hour later I got a telephone call from the 8th floor receptionist advising that I had a visitor in the waiting room. I ran up the stairs toward the reception area and saw the red head from the Crossroads standing in the waiting room, she turned before I entered walked up put her arms around me, pulled me toward her and kissed me on the mouth. She then stood back, apologized and stated, "I don't know why I did that. I think it has something to do with one of your agents in the bar last night. You see, he was hypnotizing me and maybe that is what this is all about".

I accepted her apology and made friendly conversation asking her name and inquiring how she knew my name. She could not recall ever calling my name. After a few more apologies, she left. When I got back to my desk, Jack came over and held his hands out. "What is it Jack?" I asked. "You owe me $5 for the lovely kiss you just got", he replied. Jack then related that after I left the Crossroads, he hypnotized the red head. She did not believe that she could be hypnotized and neither did Mike the bartender. "Mike was so sure that I could not even after I had hypnotized her and made her hand elevate, stick to the table, made her forget her name momentarily, and Mike thought she was going along with the joke. So I bet him $50 that I could give her a post hypnotic suggestion to kiss you the next day but she would not know why. Now Mike owes me $50", Jack explained.

Jack related that he was going to hypnotize her again after work. I could not wait until 5:30. About 6:00p.m., the red head came into the restaurant and joined us. Despite loud noise, music from the jukebox, Jack hypnotized the red head and told her that his finger was hot. When he touched her forearm she reacted as though burned by his finger.

Most interesting was the prelude during the beginning when Jack was hypnotizing the red head, three of the GOBS had apparently consumed a significant amount of liquor. Jack started out after having the red head inhale hold it for several seconds then exhale, told her to relax. Then he took her on an imaginary trip to the beach where the weather was so perfect, pleasant, mild, and pleasing. I noticed the three GOBS fell asleep or either passed out under the influence of liquor and from the voice of Jack telling the red head to relax. After several other agents saw Jack's ability to hypnotize, he was held in high esteem despite his chronic alcoholism. We suspected that he was drunk daily on the job but his hypnotizing process kept him from stumbling and falling like most alcoholics. Realizing that he was a chronic alcoholic, we often discussed and debated and guessed how long his liver would take the punishment.

Within the Los Angeles office there were numerous good coworkers, good agents, fair agents, good support personnel, poor support personnel, Christians, Jehovah Witnesses, Baptist, Agnostics, Atheists, Catholics, Protestant, Mormon, rather every religion you could think existed. One from the Pacific Rim was actually a prince. Perhaps we could say that we were a cosmopolitan group all purportedly working for a good cause, removing that great evil-drugs-from the streets of America. There were the back stabbers and the undercover racist, there were those who were ambitious and believed that they could enhance their careers by eliminating other coworkers by whatever means, whether justified or not. Despite the foregoing, all were very interesting.

One of the interesting secretaries was a red head named Brenda, rather she wore a red wig and lots of makeup. Brenda could not let a telephone ring without answering it. Unfortunately, her desk was located in the corner next to the undercover room, where we used a blackboard to identify agents by undercover name. There were instructions next to the undercover agent's name for the answer to relay certain messages. The undercover room was off limits to non-agent personnel. I had made an initial purchase of heroin and a second purchased twice larger than the first one from one Charles Barnett, aka Blood. When I placed an order for a kilo of heroin, Barnett became suspicious and requested a sit down chat. I met undercover with him at a café in the Baldwin Hills (the jungle) area. Blood advised that he suspected that I was not the police but a federal agent. He went on and related that if I was a federal agent that I had him a two hand-to-hand sales of heroin. I told Barnett that I was not a federal agent and thought he was scamming me. He insisted relating that he had copped a federal case by selling one ounce, two ounces then eight ounces to a federal agent. He related that the feds called it "1,2,3 and cloud of dust" technique that he had been had by the feds.

One of the most interesting secretaries was Margaret C. Popper. Margaret was a Jewish lady that had been in a German concentration camp and by some means that she never explained she and her mother came to the United States. According to Margaret, I was the only DEA employee that had ever seen her interment identification number (number tattooed on her arm). She had come from a wealthy German family that owned some sort of factory in German. Margaret spoke German, French, English, and Spanish. She had a hump on her back that I suspected was the result of torture or experimentation when she was in the concentration camp. Margaret never married, had no relatives, and lived alone in a house that she and her mother purchased some years ago on 41st Street west of Western Avenue. At the time they purchased the house, the neighborhood was all white but had now become 99.999% black, with Margaret being the only white spot in the middle of an all black neighborhood.

Margaret was treated differently by some agents, supervisors, and managers. All of the support personnel liked her. She had a low speaking pattern and appeared scared all the time. I remembered the first time I really met her I had come in from undercover and got on the elevator with her. I thought Margaret was going to have a massive cardiac arrest. Noting that she was extremely petrified of me, I told her who I was and apologized for scaring her. Margaret relaxed and thereafter always told new agents of our first encounter.

During several Christmas holidays when getting off the bus and walking home, Margaret was robbed several times by black males. Many agents became concerned for her safety and we took turns shuttling her home during the Christmas holidays or watching her get off the bus and walk safely home.

One year Margaret got called to jury duty and was being selected as a juror involving three black males that were charged with robbery. During the voir dire, Margaret was called into the jury box, the Judge stated, "You have heard all of the questions posed to the prospective jurors, if those same questions were posed to you, would they by any different?"

"No your honor", she responded.

The Judge, "Do you think that you could render a just and fair verdict in this case?".

Margaret, "Yes your honor, I am sure I could for I know they did it."

The Judge, "Thank you Ms. Popper, you may be excused."

Margaret was disenchanted that she was excused from jury duty.

In the office of the United States Attorney at Los Angeles, I met a lot of good assistants, worked a lot of cases and was in constant contact with them from a business and professional level. Additionally, I met a lot of criminal attorneys, beat a lot of them, rather most of them in court on drug cases.

One Assistant U.S. Attorney I grew fond of, I noted was very capable, very talented, respected federal narcotic agents, smiled all the time, and was always working and willing to help in anyway that he could. I learned that he was from Georgia, had aspirations of being the U.S. Attorney, and rather was certain he would get the job after Carter was elected president. To his dismay, Carter appointed the first female United States Attorney for the Central District of California.

One day while preparing for a drug trial, the assistant brought up the conversation about marriage. When asked if he was married, he got up from his desk, walked over to a credenza and set his wife's photo upright on the credenza. He then related that his wife had gone Hollywood on him, trying to become a movie star. What he really meant was she was in Hollywood trying to outdo Linda Lovelace in order to become a movie star. She had no talent, was not a looker, and could only garner non-speaking bit acting parts in subplots and atmosphere scenes. I could surmise that having his wife whoring around the movie studios for meager insignificant roles in bad movies was eating him to the core. I could tell by the expression on his face that he could not handle the pain that was eating him alive inside. Shortly after the conversation and trial, the AUSA committed suicide. It was very sad seeing your coworker dying at their own hands and at the hands of another, especially seeing them die at such a young age, not really experiencing the wholeness what life seem to have to offer. I often imagined those who took their own lives, did so to ease a kind of pain that no medicine could obviate or a kind of mental pain that hurt more intensely.

There were deaths of law enforcement personnel, some natural and on each occasion they seemed sadder. Wearing black tape over your badge became frequent occurrence, maybe it was from knowing so many people involved. Blackie Sawyer's death was cold and sad. It made you reflect that even you were not out of harms way if a scumbag desired to take you out.

CHAPTER 13

OUR GROUP arrested unheralded movie actors, rather a bit actor in subplots pursuant to a warrant out of San Diego. The bit actor had moved from the Washington, D.C. area to Hollywood in pursuance of an acting career. Upon his arrival and several years thereafter he barely made enough money to pay his transportation to and from the various studios in pursuit of his dream. He became very discouraged and went into the drug trafficking business.

After we took him down, as always, I asked him what caused him to go into the drug business. He related the foregoing and added that he wanted to make enough money to produce his own movies but we (DEA) had "put power brakes" on his plan. We flipped him into a good CI and a short while he assisted in taking down his source of supply, a matron looking Mexican female from San Diego. When she delivered three kilograms of heroin to us undercover, I was shocked at her carriage. Never in my wildest imagination could I vision her as a drug dealer.

We did a historical conspiracy, documenting that she had over three years sold approximately six hundred pounds of heroin to the CI who in turn delivered the heroin to Alfonso Jackson et al, couriers for the infamous D.C. heroin trafficker Milton Charles Smith, aka Creep. I worked the case with Ron Hubbard and Bob Lee two D.C. metropolitan police officers assigned to the Washington, D.C. DEA office. Ron and Bob were interesting. Bob was a very huge black male with massive hands. His partial claim to fame was that he has spared with professional famous heavyweight fighters. Both were very professional and reflected highly and represented their parent department in an outstanding manner.

It was often stated that the Milton Charles Smith case was a major catalyst in cementing or promoting a work relationship between DEA and the Washington D.C. Metropolitan Police Department.

Creep and twelve other defendants were indicted in a major conspiracy. Creep, a mean looking defendant, prior to the indictment, had at one time placed a fuel bomb on the lawn of the CI regarding the low purity of heroin he had been receiving. Despite the CI telling Creep the heroin was purer when he delivered it to his courier, Creep threatened his couriers and the CI.

Creep was convicted on conspiracy, sales and possession of heroin, multiple counts and locked down that day. He was later sentenced to forty years custody of the Attorney General.

One day I got a telephone call from an Agent Bill Tucker from DEA in Nashville, Tennessee regarding an arrest warrant for a U.S. Postman in the Los Angeles area. I almost had to get an interpreter to understand Bill for he had such a deep whining type Tennessee accent. Bill faxed a copy of the warrant and photograph of the postman over and I agreed that we would arrest him for the Nashville office. The postman was charged with delivery of twenty ounces of heroin.

I and my partner, Roland Talton contacted the Postal Inspectors office and apprised them of the warrant. They agreed to assist in the take down and requested that we conduct surveillance of the postman on his route and take him down before he finish his route. We initiated surveillance of the postman watching him arrive at work. He drove a late model Cadillac, wore a tailored postman suit, expensive alligator shoes and a president Rolex watch and a big diamond ring. His fingernails were manicured and everything about him appeared expensive.

We surveilled him for two and a half hours on his route, then took him down and transported him immediately to the Los Angles office where he was searched. He had three letters addressed to "Meals for Millions" in his front left jacket pocket. I held each up to a light and could not discern that there was money in them. The Senior Postal Inspector related that some postmen can feel an envelope and determine that there is cash inside. He then opened all three envelopes and there was cash in each. The postal inspector related tat they would also charge the postman with theft from U.S. mail administratively and use the charges to terminate him. I tried to flip the postman but he would not turn at that time. I advised him that he would be indicted in Nashville, Tennessee where they would almost lynch him for drugs. The postman would not bite and refused to turn at that time.

A few weeks later I attended a personnel termination hearing on the postman. During the hearing the union representative screamed and hollered at me several times before I had uttered a word and made a mistake and called me a son of a bitch, contemporaneously spurting saliva. I asked the hearing judge to restrain the union representative but he ignored me. The union representative made another mistake and referred to me as a son of a bitch with no restraint coming from the judge. I removed my .38 Colt Cobra pistol and placed the muzzle in the left ear of the union representative, cocked the hammer, then dared him to call me anther son of a bitch. I then asked the effeminate administrative judge what kind of hearing was he attempting to run and related that it appeared to be very much out of order to me. The union representative sat down and apologized relating that he had gotten overly excited trying to represent the postman. The postman was terminated that day.

While walking from the hearing, I again asked the postman to cooperate, relating that the charges against him were serious and if I were in his position I would prefer to have a seat next to the prosecutor than one opposite of him with the defense. The ex-postman still refused to cooperate. As we departed in different directions in the parking lot I yelled out, "Remember the first person on the bus gets a seat." The ex-postman stopped and had me repeat the statement. He smiled then agreed to cooperate. Two days later I took a thorough debriefing and jogged his memory for accuracy and ended up with a significant organization based in Los Angeles that was supplying heroin to Nashville.

I flew to Nashville and worked with Bill on the conspiracy and learned that the main AUSA handling the case last name was Lynch. We indicted six defendants and charged two with 21 USC 848; Continuing Criminal Enterprise (CCE). This was the first CCE case ever charged in the U.S. District Court at Nashville, Tennessee.

During the trial, I had the pleasure of meeting Attorney Leo Branton, whose claim to fame was the acquittal of his client Angela Davis. Five of the defendants were from Los Angeles and they had attorney from the Los Angeles. Branton unquestionably was the best. During the trial AUSA Lynch made an objection and started a cite a 9th Circuit case as authority, but the judge took a short recess.

Attorney Branton told AUSA Lynch, "Counsel you were saved by the bell. You were about to cite, rather miscite that 9th Circuit case. That was my case. Lynch thereafter was highly intimidated by the sharp Los Angeles attorney. He had initially rejected my initial recommendation that he request assistance from Main Justice Narcotic and Dangerous Drugs Section. I reiterated the offer and he relented. I put him in contact with the chief of that section. That following Monday, an attorney was in Nashville ready to assist at the start up of the trial. All defendants were convicted as charged. They went to jail for a long time and lost every piece of identifiable property we could find.

At the Los Angeles office, I got a telephone call from a prospective CI relating that a new drug dealer had about ten pounds of heroin for sale. According to the CI, the dealer only wanted to deal with black traffickers that he would only sell to a black. I advised the CI that I was black but had a white business partner (Agent Kay Lameraux), but that I won't be in charge and controlling every part of our operation. The dealer was an unidentified white male residing in Newport Beach. I made arrangements with the CI to meet with the dealer that day for negotiations for the whole ten pounds.

Later that day SA Kay Lamareaux and I and the CI met undercover with the dealer at the restaurant in Newport Beach. We immediately discerned that he was a novist in the drug business based mostly on his naiveté. When we asked for a sample, he gave us about an ounce and a half as a sample. When we inquired about establishing a business relationship purchasing heroin from him on a regular basis, the dealer advised that he did not know when he would be able to get additional heroin. We advised the dealer that we would buy the whole ten pounds and made arrangements to meet with him in five days. Just enough time to get a quick analysis of the substance, a partially rocky granular substance, that was gummy and tarry on the inside. After the undercover meeting, we rushed a portion of the sample to Los Angeles sheriff's laboratory and forwarded the rest to our lab in San Francisco. It was found to be opium. The sheriff's lab believed that it was once heroin, had gotten wet somehow and had changed back to opium.

The fifth day, I telephone the dealer and advised that my partner (Agent Lamareaux) and I were ready to do the deal. He agreed to meet with us on the parking lot of a hotel located on Olympic and Figueron at 2:00p.m. SA Lamareaux and I designated the opening of the trunk as the best signal. At about 2:30p.m., we arrived on the parking lot simultaneously with the dealer. He was accompanied by a white male that immediately caught my attention. UI had seen him somewhere but could not recall where.

His partner took position outside the undercover car as though acting as a lookout. The crook exited his car with a large shopping bag and joined us in the undercover car and handed me the shopping bag. I examined it. I then told SA Lamareaux to get the money and we would pay for the dope and go on our way. SA Lamareaux exited the undercover car and opened the trunk. Surveillant agents converged on the undercover car with guns drawn screaming, "Federal agents, freeze mother fuckers, you're under arrest, if you move, we'll blow your god damn brains out." The main crook urinated all over himself in the rear seat of the undercover car. To protect the identity of the CI, SA Lamareaux and I took the arrest along with the crooks. They were transported to the Los Angeles office handcuffed to the rear. After they were taken from the scene, SA Lamareaux and I were driven around the corner and uncuffed. It was then that I recalled I had met the other suspect a few years prior in Detroit. I had suspected then that he was possibly a CIA agent or operative.

During the booking process, the partner denied even being in Detroit. I watched him through a two-way mirror and noted that he had the finesse to tell a lie as though it was the truth and to recall in detail supporting facts he had cited when lying, there wasn't heavy breathing, dryness of the mouth and notable swelling or rapid pulse about his neck. Additionally, he looked his questioner straight in the face when answering each question devoid of pausing or showing any hesitation for selecting his words. This guy was a professional. Toward the end of the interview, he volunteered that the dealer was a friend of his that had found something that he believed was heroin. His friend wanted to sell the heroin to somebody Black thinking that Blacks were the only abusers of heroin. His friend had asked him to come along for the ride because he was afraid of the big black guy he was dealing with and wanted some kind of protection. Consequently, he accompanied his friend merely for the ride. When the interviewing agent advised that he would be charged with aiding and abetting the sale of a controlled substance, the partner stated, "If riding with a friend is aiding and abetting then I am guilty. I did not even speak to the black dealer with the white girlfriend. They did what they did. I merely played outside of the car for I told my friend I would only come for the ride."

The dealer substantiated his statement and admitted, rather related that he had found drugs and had tried to make some money. The dealer agreed to make a sworn statement to that effect. He was released on his own recognizant and without any assistance made arrangements with the U.S, Attorney's office to plead guilty. He was provided a federal public defender. The U.S, Attorney's office declined to prosecute his partner. We suspected his partner was the main mover in the whole caper. We also suspected that his partner was involved with the CIA.

During this period, I assisted the Riverside Sheriff's office working undercover as a pimp at Eagle Mountain Mining Camp. Whores, pimps, and panders frequented the camp at an off-on premise liquor store on the facility. It was suspected that the owner was a major promoter of the operations. The good miners were repulsed on many occasions, often returning from the mine from a twelve hour shift, entering in their quarters taking a shower and finding a prostitute sitting upon their bed. According to the miners, the prostitutes, pimps, and panders were tenacious, overbearing and did not readily take no for an answer. Riverside advised that the liquor store was a focal point for the "Johns" to facilitate the transportation of prostitutes to the mining facility.

During the brain storm it was postulated that despite many prostitutes being sporadically arrested at the mining camp that the "Hungry Johns" (male customers who catered to the prostitutes) were the main problem. A plan was formulated to conduct a sting directed at the "Johns." The Riverside Sheriff requested that I assist them in an undercover role as a pimp in their sting operation.

Pursuant to the sting, I dressed in a white suit, white shoes, champagne colored shirt with ruffles and a matching handkerchief, a fake bid diamond ring on my left small finger and a fake Rolex watch. I had a fake large gold chain around my neck and had my shirt opened almost to my navel. I met with three attractive white sheriff's deputies, a blond, a red head, and one brown haired female. The female deputies were dressed in tight leather short hot pants, matching leather boots and purses. I obtained undercover red convertible Cadillac and met at a rendezvous location in Riverside where we were briefed. The Riverside Sheriff's office had stationed two large mobile homes around the liquor store at Eagle Mountain; each was equipped with an arrest team consisting of four large deputies. A large prisoner transportation bus was secreted in a large garage on the mining camp.

The three undercover deputies and I entered the Cadillac, I sat in the right rear and we proceeded up to Eagle Mountain. Despite having a surveillant undercover unit in the front and one in the back, we were pulled over two times on route by the California Highway Patrol.

When we arrived at the mining camp liquor store, I draped my suit coat over my shoulders (arm out of sleeves) and was escorted pimp-like into the liquor store. I walked over and asked the bartender for a roll of quarters for the jukebox and peeled off a $100 bill from a $2000 flash roll and handed it to him. After the undercover deputies and I played several songs, they loudly called me "Sweet Jay", lit my cigarette, held the beer up for me

Thin White Lines

to drink and sat close to me. One deputy invited me to a game of pool. Shortly after I broke the balls, the bartender pulled me over to the side and stared asking a lot of questions. He then got around to advising me that it was customary for him to get a cut of the action that I was not part of the regular crew that came down. He further related that his cut would be 20% and that it was high because I was not part of the regular crew. When I asked him how did he know that I was not part of the regular crew, he related that he had not placed an order for the ladies for that night. While talking to the bartender, several johns came in and two left with the undercover deputies. I could not help but laugh inside, realizing the johns were in for a rude awakening, the undercover deputies had been instructed to let the johns do all of the soliciting. I could not help but laugh uncontrollably inside thinking of the reaction of the johns, thinking that they were about to enjoy a nice sexual encounter but in lieu of reaching coitus they would probably void or defecate when arrested by the big deputies inside of the mobile home. I suddenly laughed out loud realizing that Riverside Sheriff's deputies had a knack of placing the cold steel muzzle of their revolver in a suspect's ear when taking him down in close quarters.

After eighteen johns had been arrested, a spectator walked up to me and stated, "God damn partner, them gals must have some dynamite snatch, I don't see none of them dudes coming back in here. Most of them left their drinks here."

"Yeah, they are known to knock a guy out you know their pussies are just that good. My little blond, they call her thunderpussy. Almost all of the guys that go with her want to marry her, what about you; do you want a shot?" I asked. I realized then that I had made a mistake that the sexual soliciting had come from me. Instead of stopping at that point, I told the spectator that the redhead gave the best head, that if she could not make a customer climax in five minutes then it was free and asked if he wanted to try her when she came back. He demurred, moved closer to me and started calling me a potpourri of profane names with the word nigger intermitted. I inhaled deeply several times to ward off my anger and tried to ignore him. I noted that there were no undercover deputies in the liquor store. He then raised from the stool put his right hand lightly on my left forearm and yelled, "I'm going to ride your afterbirth eating black ass outta here, you low life cocksucker." I eased my right hand down into my pocket, pushed the snapper off the bottom and retrieved my .38 Colt Cobra and placed gently on the forehead of the spectator and asked, "Now motherfucker, how would you like to ride five of these hot super vet out of here?" The spectator cowered, dropped down on his knees and begged me not to shoot him. I let him go and hurriedly left the liquor store, walked over to the nearest mobile home as they were taking down a john and advised them what had transpired. We then terminated the operation and drove back to Riverside jubilating.

The work I did over those years far surpassed what many agents would do in a lifetime career within the agency. After applying for over 100 Group Supervisor (GS) positions, I was finally promoted to a GS position in Detroit, of all places.

I sat at my desk and exchanged thanks with well wishers congratulating me on my promotion. They sounded like a stuck record; all asked who I pissed off to get promoted to Detroit. I began to wonder how I would adjust to a cold climate, especially having lived almost all my life in sunny southern California. I recalled from history that Detroit was a heavy union town and as a consequence everything involving the cost of living was as expected to be high. I began to feel like the fox and the sour grapes, especially realizing that I would be 2,000 miles away from my three children. As the days came closer to my transfer date, I almost ran out of things to do, trying not to become heavily involved in enforcement activity that would delay my transfer thereby delaying the promotion. Since the promotion was a position in Detroit, it would not be effective until I was physically there.

I began to feel a tad sorry for myself, especially when it finally registered how dangerous Detroit really is, how ruthless and lawless criminals trod the streets committing a potpourri of crimes as though they have immunity. Then the two bodies in the trunk immediately flashed in my mind, commensurate with the foul smell of maggot infested rotting human flesh. The smell filled my nostrils as though real, close by and appeared to last forever. I closed my eyes, inhaled deeply several times, held the air in for a long period, then exhaled unsuccessful convincing myself that this was merely a daytime nightmare. Shortly after closing my eyes, I began to see the maggots crawl in wave-like motion over the two deceased faces, flitting in and out of their occipital foramen as though in joyful play with one another. The dead rotting bodies were as visual as could be and even appeared closer to me. I opened my eyes and the site would not go away. When I finally focused, I could smell the awful stench even stronger. I felt an uneasiness about my stomach; the rush of warm fluid and mild pain, saliva filled my mouth and became warm indicating a need to vomit. I did a breathing exercise again and my stomach felt better, but the smell and picture of the decaying bodies stayed in my mind like a froze frame movie scene. I thought of the times I was undercover when danger and death seemed eminent, even times that I had suppressed and could not and had not recalled. I thought of the death look on the face of the Jesus Christ suspect at Royal Burton's house, the heroin addicts at the dope houses. In thinking of the heroin addicts, the thought of them coming out of a nod accidentally killing someone seemed to return often. I thought of the human fireball, the 10th precinct where gunshots rang in the air almost like a combat zone. To add to all the bad thoughts I had of Detroit, there were rumors that the police were corrupt and "on the take." That among the ranks there were robbers, dope dealers, murders, burglars, and officers that would do anything for a price.

In almost 15 years of law enforcement, I had developed and iron skin, wherein death, violent deaths, murders, mayhem, arson, and mutilations were all part of the job, supposedly not affecting you at all. Additionally, I had developed a sense of bravado that even I could not and would not be killed at the hands of some crook; that there is a protector out there. An invisible protector shielding all law enforcements officers from the evil of ruthless and lawless criminals who roam the streets with wanton disregard for law and order; criminals devoid of a conscious of right and wrong, devoid of the meaning of remorse with compassion as alien to them as a bag of diamonds.

While sitting, feeling sorry for myself, I paused and thought that I should be rejoicing, jubilating and proud that I had gotten promoted, despite having to move to Detroit. I then recalled some of the "hell holes" where I could have been transferred, like Brownsville or Eagle Pass, Texas; Tecate, California, Chicago, Illinois; Cleveland, Ohio. I recalled the disgusting expression on the face of an agent who was transferred to Cleveland. His wife immediately apprised him that Cleveland was a "shit hole", average 84 inches of snow per year, the wind off Lake Erie is forever chilling and cold, the summers are short and the winters are long and cold. I could have been transferred to Calexico, where the smell of stockyard fills the air daily. During the long summer heat waves float across in front of you like a mist, where from the outskirts of town you can see miles and miles of nothing but cropland, desert land, Joshua trees and sand.

I saw agents frowning from being transferring to Amarillo, El Paso, Lubbock, Tyler, Galveston, Loredo, McAllen, Alpine, Beaumont, Waco, Houston, Corpus Christi, and Midland, Texas. Some retired or quit when transferred to New York. Hammond and Gary, Indiana were undesirable towns, so was Minneapolis. Perhaps it was the stress of moving from a Mediterranean climate of long hot summers and short dry winters had caused all of us to be complacent; we were spoiled.

I saw agents jubilating when transferred to Miami or any city in Florida; Dallas, Texas; Seattle, Washington; Portland, Oregon; Las Vegas; Atlanta; New Orleans; Salt Lake City; Denver; Washington, D.C., Philadelphia; Boston; Hartford; San Antonio; San Diego; San Francisco; Phoenix; Albuquerque, and Los Cruces, New Mexico.

There were overseas offices where only the non-blacks were transferred. They all broke camp and departed smiling when transferred to Nassau, Bahamas, Kingston Jamaica, San Juan, Puerto Rico; San Jose; Costa Rica; Paris and Lyon France; Milan and Rome, Italy; Frankfurt and Bonn, Germany; Hong Kong, Bangkok, Thailand; London, Madrid, Brussels, Athens and Ankara, Turkey.

I had a junior partner who had never traveled overseas and the only foreign countries he had visited were Mexico and Canada. A vacancy came out for Ankara, Turkey; a place merely based on how it was pronounced fascinated him. He asked me a thousand and one questions about overseas. I had been in the Army stationed in Ausbach and Bamberg, Germany. While there, I had traveled to Norway, Denmark, Sweden, Austria, and Amsterdam, Holland on leave. Perhaps it was the 5 to 6' tulip garden of Holland that I had described that further increased his interest to be transferred to a foreign post. Having never been to Turkey, I assumed it was as nice as the few countries where I had been. After much badgering by him, I finally related that I could apply for the position but I was realistic in my thinking, Black agents were not being transferred overseas, instead, we were being heavily assigned to cities with the highest crime rate like New York, Los Angeles, Detroit, Chicago, Cleveland, Houston, Philadelphia, Pittsburgh, New Orleans, Atlanta, Washington, D.C., Baltimore, Kansas City, St. Louis, Newark, Gary and

Hammond, Indians, all of the cities that were deemed major crime beds.

Many white agents and most Hispanic agents were transferred to Buenos Aires; Argentina; Brasilia, and Sao Paulo, Brazil; Santiago, Chile; Quito, Ecuador; Mexico City. Monterey, Mazatlan, Hermosillo, Merida and Guadalajara, Mexico; Lima, Peru; Caracas, Venezuela; Curacao, Netherlands, Antilles; Guatemala City,Guatemala; Bogota, Columbia; LaPaz and Santa Cruz, Bolivia; San Salvador, El Salvador; Panama City, Panama; Montevideo, Uruguay; Asuncion, Paraguay, Tegucigalpa, Honduras; Madrid, Spain, and Rome, Italy.

Posts of Duty like Vienna, Austria; Tokyo, Japan; Seoul, Korea; Rangoon, Burma; New Delhi and Bombay, India; Nicosia, Cyprus; Montreal and Ottawa, Canada; Copenhagen, Denmark; London, England; Brussels, Belgium; Bern, Switzerland; Athens, Greece and Ankara, Turkey were reserved especially for white agents.

DEA managers had a mind set that Black agents would not be effective in these countries and utilized the rationale that a Black agent's identity would be immediately compromised. This fallacy was premised on the undercover role we had been thrust into so often and made "cage agents." They never use this when sending WASP agents to Central and South America and the Caribbean. Instead they provided language training to facilitate their transfers and opportunities for overseas posts of duty.

I began to look at some of the positive sided of being promoted and transferred to Detroit and could only bring to mind two. I would no longer be a "cage agent" relegated to working mostly undercover in the Black, Brown, Yellow, Red and White communities; I would be a supervisor and a step above performing line functions. Instead of following orders, I would be giving them. I really should not be disappointed after all it was a promotion, about a $2500 annual increase in salary. It would take at least $2500 to purchase clothing and make preparations for the cold winters in Detroit.

I began to ponder how many transfers would I be subjected to in my career. Already some agents had voiced that I had spent too long in Los Angeles; ten years was unusual for a DEA agent with a transfer clause as a condition of employment. We were all under a mobility clause, which subjected us to a move anywhere in the conterminous United States. I was really familiar with the mobility clause; unlike another black agent. He was transferred from Atlanta to Puerto Rico at the behest of management. Managers had a lot of power then; they were god-like and many of them were heavy drinkers, heavy carousers, heavy smokers, and heavy in debt from drinking good and expensive whiskey.

Manages could hire, fire, suspend and most incarcerate an agent and consequently they were often feared more than the drug traffickers. Some of the old mangers could not really discipline subordinate because of their history of violating policy procedures and the law. Most infractions involved the law entailed driving while under the influence of alcohol, drunk driving, drunk and disorderly and other minor infractions.

Some managers wondered how young non-drinkers and non-smokers ever became agents. It was common to hear them relate that they could not and did not trust a man or women that did not drink. They meted out punishment devoid of any real guidance and consequently a GOB, who would do no wrong, seldom was subjected to corrective action and when their infraction were outlandish, they were reinterpreted established policy. The unauthorized use of an official government vehicle carried, by law, a mandatory minimum 30-day suspension without pay. Often unauthorized use of the OGV by a GOB was ruled misuse and the GOB walked away with merely a reprimand or a 1-3 day suspension.

When non-GOB's committed the same offense, they were

suspended for 30 days without pay. When a Black agent committed the same offense, he/she received from a 45-day suspension to termination. When a GOB was arrested for driving while under the influence, (DWI) it was often quashed. A telephone call would be made and management would arrange for the GOB to be picked up, transported home and no paperwork would be created. When a Black agent on non-GOB was arrested for DWI, he/she went to jail and stayed until bail was posted or released by the judge. Shortly thereafter some were terminated for criminal conduct or conduct unbecoming of an agent.

Many police departments, as well as federal, state and other local agencies had GOBs. It is believed that LAPD, while trying to curry a favor for a drunken GOB actually happened upon a major discovery involving an occupational hazard typical to law enforcement, STRESS. This discovery was a catalyst for forming help groups that eventually created the forming of Employee Assistance Programs that have now spread widely into government and the private sectors.

Peter Bensinger, a republican, was the administrator of DEA during the Nixon/Ford era and survived the Jimmy Carter regime. He was a glib short conservative dresser from the private sector with little knowledge of federal drug law enforcement. Bensinger, a well to do and intelligent man, was called a bush league law enforcement, which surrounded himself with unsavory and marginally qualified cronies. The GOB system proliferated under his administration. Professional and technical employee Jesse Gallegos was DEA's first Equal Employment Opportunity (EEO) Office Officer and first Hispanic officer, positions he occupied initially on an ad hoc basis. Jesse, highly knowledgeable of Department of Justice and Civil Service Policy and Procedures, was a stickler and tried to keep management in compliance with the fair employment practices delineated in the Civil Rights Act of 1964 and subsequent amendments and modifications. It was related to me that he had ruffled a few feathers and angered several egotistical managers. As a consequence, his career was placed on a plateau and he was labeled a "rubble rouser, non-team player, militant, activist, a crusader" and other names. During a headquarters staff meeting a discussion ensued regarding what could be done about Jesse to keep harmony and "edify morale to an acceptable maximum proficiency level, thereby increasing productivity while sustaining a strong and profound management workable interpersonal relationship, requiring less modifications of current standards and policy."

The manger cleared his throat and peered around for a comment. Another manager remarked, "Y'all can deploy all the polysyllabic sesquipedalian substitutes and buzz words you want about Jesse, we know we got to do something about that guy we all know he is a 4-S." Another manager asked, "What's a 4-S?" "A super sonic shit stirrer", he was told. Reportedly it was shortly thereafter Jesse was removed from the EEO and Hispanic Officer position and was given some fancy title with no increase in pay and a smaller desk. Under the direction of Bensinger, a full time EEO officer position was established and a national search was made to fill the position. DEA selected the most docile and non-assertive Black that applied for the position as the agency EEO officer and gave him a big desk. Office and a small staff. He knew from the demeanor of top management including Administrator Bensinger, what his duties entailed and what was expected of him. Openly they talked about Jesse as troublemaker and how he had to be reassigned

CHAPTER 14

WHILE AWAITING ORDER to make my house hunting trip to Detroit, I got a call from an old CI relating that killer cocaine had just hit the street that is smoked in a pipe or cigarette in rock form. According to the CI, it appeared to be very addictive and causes the smoker to develop a hostile and combative attitude that often results in violence. The CI further advised that he could introduce me undercover to one of the main dealers. I initially hesitated realizing that I had now been promoted to a supervisory position and would no longer be expected to work undercover. I decided to give it my last shot and put together a surveillant team of DEA agents and LAPD narcotic agents. The CI placed a telephone call to a Renaldo Reyes and advised that he and his brother were coming over for a little business. The CI and I then drove over to Reyes residence on Hobart Street just south of Washington Boulevard.

As we entered Reyes residence I noted several male Hispanics placing what appeared to be broken pieces of soap in glassine envelopes. Several customers departed as we entered. The CI introduced me to Reyes and advised that we wanted to purchase three ounces of the Death Cocaine, the rocks. Reyes quoted a price of $2700, relating that he had to take a few minutes to rock it up for us. I told Reyes that I wanted to try to market the rocks, but that I had never sold it in rocks before. At that time, a tall suave, neatly dressed, well polished Hispanic male with noticeable dimples in his cheeks and no facial hair peeked into the room and beckoned for Reyes. Reyes left the room with the suave male for a few minutes and returned and asked if I wanted to learn how to rock it up and related that it was very simple. Reyes further advised that he had been instructed to sell the cocaine in less than ? ounce quantities. He agreed to sell me a half ounce of rock cocaine for $475.

The CI and I followed Reyes into the kitchen and watched him take several small quantities of cocaine, mix it with baking soda and a solution and water and placed it in a vial. He then heated a pot of water and swirled the vial around in the boiling water until the solution became hard like pieces of soap. He then placed them on a paper napkin and took a hair dryer and blew them dry until they were like rocks. Reyes placed 30 rocks in a zip lock glassine envelop and handed it to me. I noted it appeared about a half ounce and paid Reyes for the rocks then engaged him in a conversation about another transaction trying to get him to sell me 3 to 5 ounces. The neatly dressed tall Hispanic male again walked into the room and gave a nod of disapproval.

Reyes then related that he would get back with me and walked us outside to the undercover car. Reyes related that the suave Hispanic male was in charge and that he had shown him how to turn the cocaine into rocks. Reyes related that turning the cocaine into rock form and smoking it makes the smoker an instant addict. He further related that the rocks were similar to the "Patillo" and "Bazuko" smoked in Bolivia, Columbia and Peru, but the rock is more addicting. According to Reyes, the rock were going to be in the cocaine of the future, making users want it, crave it and need it like the mighty heroin. Reyes further related that he would sell me 3 ounces of heroin the next time but only when his connection was not around. He related that he was getting newer customers each day.

About a week later, I telephoned Reyes and attempted to arrange for the 3 ounce purchase. Reyes was very evasive on the telephone and feigned that he did not remember me and became cryptic in his conversation. He denied even knowing the CI. I decided to eliminate his amnesia. Under the surveillance of DEA and LAPD, I drove over and met with Reyes undercover. He appeared nervous, denied again of ever meeting me, denied the transaction and related that he had never seen me before in his life. When I inquired about Reyes' neatly dressed friend's conversation on the first deal, he denied that I had ever been I this house. I suspected that someone in Reye's house that had compromised my identity or that the connection was more that what and who Reyes had originally believed him to be.

I went back to the office, telephoned the CI and advised him what had transpired. The CI related that Reyes had been the same toward him. The CI further related that he paid him an unexpected visit, Reyes was selling rock cocaine and that he had learned from the streets that Reyes had expanded his business and his connection was selling rock cocaine to only Blacks. When I asked why only Blacks, the CI related that the word on the streets was that Blacks seemed to have or develop more of a craving for the rocks, that they will commit any crime, even rob their own mother in order to get more rocks. The CI further related that the word on the street is that the rock is the main killer coke, main killer drug on the streets that was going to replace heroin and methadone. The CI added that methadone does not appear to work on "rock addicts" that the "rocks" were devastating abusers beyond their ability to resist. According to the CI, a heroin addict usually cannot work, especially when he is in on the nod.

Once the rock addict smokes a few rocks, he goes crazy. When the high wears off, he will immediately go out and rob or steal to buy more rocks to smoke. Rock houses have been established in many places around the city. Lastly the CI stated "man this rock thing is a most mother, you guys better stay on top of this one."

I decided to get a federal warrant to Reyes and the neatly dressed Hispanic male. I conferred with several AUSAs and all refused to issue a federal warrant, relating that it did not meet the new federal threshold. I referred the case to LAPD.

The same CI telephoned and advised that PCP was flooding the market and that he could introduce an agent undercover for a proposed purchase. My partner Roland Talton and I instructed the CI to order 2 pounds of PCP for his partner (agent Talton) to be delivered at the Holiday Inn Hotel, on Olympic Boulevard and Figueroa. The CI advised that he had ordered the PCP and that the crook had agreed to meet at the Holiday Inn in 2 hours. Roland and I put together a surveillance team and had anticipated buying the 2 pounds of PCP as a prelude to a larger seizure involving identifying the source of supply and other coconspirators. We were advised that there was insufficient purchase of evidence funds available. We then decided to do a take down and flip the defendant back into his connection.

SA Talton and I met with the CI, searched him and found him devoid of any narcotics. He had over $200 in cash, which he was allowed to keep. We then drove in tandem over to Holiday Inn. I conducted surveillance of the UC agent and CI in the lounge and about an hour later saw a neatly dressed male meet with them. After talking for a few minutes, I heard the crook advise that they were going upstairs to a room he had checked into for the deal. Surveillance in the lobby had made his check in and obtained a surveillant room diagonally across the hall and one next door to the crook. I joined the surveillant agents in the adjacent room. After about ten minutes, we heard SA Talton give a prearranged arrest signal (telephoned agent downstairs and told him to bring the money up to room 414). One agent knocked on the door, the crook answered admitting him and the other agent into the room, simultaneously 3 agents and I forced entry from the adjacent room. The crook was immediately placed under arrest and handcuffed. He had delivered 3 pounds of brown rock crystal PCP, hermetically sealed in two plastic bags. A presumptive field test was made of the substance and a positive reaction was noted.

SA Talton and I took the crook down to the office and tried to flip him. The crook went into absolute denial. He denied ever seeing the U/C agent, the delivery, ever being at the Holiday Inn, ever knowing the CI, ever having contact with the UC or arresting agents and as far as he was concerned he was "being humbugged." When asked to describe being humbugged, he went into vivid details relating that when the police needed an arrest they would arrest a Black male. The police would run a record check and if there were no warrants they would then manufacture evidence for a case.

We allowed the crook to make two completed telephone calls and asked if he wanted to talk in privacy. He advised that we could stand by. On each call, the crook advised the other person on the telephone that he had been arrested on a "humbug." On the second call after talking for a while, he handed me the telephone relating that his attorney wanted to talk to me.

"Hello, I am Agent Sutton, may I help you," I asked

"Yeah, Agent Sutton, I'm Attorney Schwartz, what is the citation for federal humbug. My client advises me he's being held on a humbug charge. I am not familiar with this charge, can you enlighten me", he asked.

"Yes, Mr. Schwartz, your client was arrested for violation of 21USC 841(a) (1), sales of PCP, two pounds of PCP, a significant amount of PCP that some judges will view as a very large amount", I advised.

"How much bail are you going to recommend, 2 or 3 thousand dollars?" he asked.

"We will recommend $100,000 for your client. You can probably get the Magistrate to lower it if you think that's too much. We are interested in your client flipping, helping us undo his connection, helping us eliminate the availability of the awful drug, PCP. Mr. Schwartz, could you convey that to him for us. He apparently has a dislike for us at this time", I added.

"Yeah, I'll talk to him and let you know what w decide, okay", he advised. Needless to say we never heard from Attorney Schwartz or his client. We later placed several telephone calls to Schwartz's office and left messages. He never responded.

I finally got my orders for the transfer. I flew to Detroit in early January for my house hunting trip. It was the coldest week I had experienced since my army days in Germany. The ground was covered with snow; a chilling wind blew from the north off the lakes that made it even colder. Each day the sky was gray, cloud laden, windy, cold, chilling and there was no sign that the sun would ever shine; it had gone into hibernation like the animals, gone for what seemed forever. I watched passerby in cars and on foot heavily clad in layers of clothing; some wore jackets referred to a down jackets. When they walked the cold streets for short distances steam shot out of their mouth and nose like a furnace.

Neither the cold, snow, wind, gray skies or threat of more snow kept people off the streets. I drove down Bagley and Cass streets and could see prostitutes snuggled in door wells trying to keep the wind away as Johns cruised the streets peeking and honking horns beckoning for the prostitutes to join them in their car. Homeless men and women dragged broken down grocery carts across the streets, into alleys and nooks and corners of vacant buildings in vain attempt to keep warm. I drove down Cass away from the downtown and saw several late model Cadillac, Lincolns, and a Mercedes Benz. Neatly dressed men and women dashed in and out of cars and buildings, all trying to escape the chilling cold. I turned around and drove back toward Howard Johnson hotel downtown and several blocks in the heart of the Cass corridor gunshots rang out, two men from a building jumped into a late model Cadillac and sped away. I drove gingerly toward Grand River and in a short while I heard the horns and sirens of police cars rolling code -3.

When I arrived at the Howard Johnson, I saw a white male recluse that I had seen several years prior dressed in a burnt orange raincoat blowing a whistle and partially directing traffic at the intersection. I found an apartment at the Southfield Towers on 8 mile and Lahser, across the street from Detroit in Southfield. The week was as sad as my previous trips and the gray skies made it seem even sadder.

I cut the trip short and flew back to California prepared to make the move the first week in February. A week later, the CI in the Reyes case telephone and advised that the rock cocaine had really taken off, spreading like mad all over Los Angeles mainly in the Black community. The "rock" is being called the dope of the future, the death wish, the mighty high, the poor man's high. The CI related that cocaine once snorted in thin white lines and considered the rich man's high is now available in poor areas for $15 and $20 a rock. He believed that once it spread to other cities, crimes would escalate to a worse level than the big heroin epidemic. According to the CI, some heroin addicts were switching over to rock cocaine and that it made them more bizarre now then when in need of a heroin fix. People all over are extremely frightened and scared of their own relatives using rock cocaine.

Several other CIs telephoned almost reiterating verbatim the evil of abusers of rock cocaine. The Los Angeles Times and Los Angeles Herald Examiner newspaper reported the beginning of violent crimes occurring in the Los Angeles area. I knew then that the rock cocaine abuse would eventually also spread into the white, brown, yellow, and red communities around the country bringing with it the attendant violence and increase in crime noted in the black community.

The morning of my transfer flight to Detroit, I sat in a Jacuzzi of the Oakwood apartment building in North Long Beach reading the Los Angeles Times. The temperature of the water as 105 degrees and the jet streams blew strong bubbly, swirling relaxing streams of water all over my body, relaxing every muscle, making them feel very light, feathery and thrilling. I closed my eyes, sat back and imagined that I did not have a single worry in the world. The words, peaceful, calm, nice, pleasant, relaxing, quiet, endemic, paradisiacal, heavenly and blissful flowed in my mind. I sat back and dozed into a short sleep, awoke and continued reading the newspaper. I looked at the temperature section and noted heavy snow in Chicago and Detroit, with a forecast of a high temperature of 9 degrees and a low 6 degrees below zero. Despite the hot Jacuzzi water flowing I felt a cold chill and then remembered the thing they called the wind-chill factor, which was even colder.

The temperature in the area was in the low 60s with a slight overcast. On occasions I stared up at the sky and saw the sun momentarily disappear behind small patches of fleeting clouds. Each time it reappeared it made me a tad happier. I began to think of the sad gray skies of Detroit, how cold, chilling, and even on the faces of people walking how they seemed always sad, gloomy devoid of a real life, devoid of smiles, friendliness, cheer and laughter that I had often seen on many faces in many cities.

At noon I boarded the big jet bound for Detroit with a stop in Chicago. As the plane ascended over the ocean banked left and headed east, I said in my mind goodbye Los Angeles, goodbye California, it is possible I will never live in you again.

John P. Sutton

ISBN 1412025400